THE LIGHT BEING

Ann Carol Ulrich

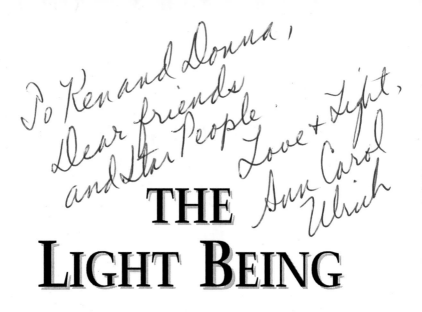

To Ken and Donna,
Dear friends
and Star People.
Love & Light,
Ann Carol
Ulrich

THE
LIGHT BEING

Ann Carol Ulrich

EARTH STAR PUBLICATIONS

Ann Carol Ulrich

THE LIGHT BEING

Ann Carol Ulrich

Earth Star Publications
Paonia, Colorado

FIRST EDITION
First Printing January 2005

Library of Congress Control Number: 2004118248

ISBN 0-944851-23-1

Printed in the United States of America

Cover Art by Emma O'Brian

THE LIGHT BEING

To Ryan, Marty and Scott

Three Blessings in my life

Contents

Acknowledgements

I wish to thank those who inspired me and encouraged me to write this novel, which completes the space trilogy. My husband, Ethan Miller, has been patient, supportive and loving. My son, Marty, who brought the character of Blake more fully into focus. My thanks to Emma O'Brian, for putting up with working under an almost impossible deadline. Also, I acknowledge and warmly thank my friend, Marcy Beckwith (a.k.a. Commander Sanni Ceto), for her invaluable help in accurately depicting the more technological aspects of the story. And it would be discourteous on my part not to mention that I am grateful for the unseen help that came forth from beyond.

Other Books by Ann Carol Ulrich

Intimate Abduction

Return To Terra

Night of the November Moon

Permutation, A True UFO Story
(with Shirlè Klein-Carsh)

Cosmic Cooking, Healing Potions and Other Magic
By Star Beacon Readers
(edited by Ann Ulrich Miller)

1

The Summons

He traveled alone. No planet was his home. The vast reaches of space held no limits, for he was free. Completely free of any encumbrances, free to go where he pleased, to do what pleased him most. Nothing bound him nor restrained him in any way. He had chosen freedom after the Separation, after knowing unification but nothing more.

The Other had chosen challenge. She desired to expose Her beingness to the diverse array of experiences the universe had to offer. She was an explorer. Her desire had been to know what it was to be separated, to be a fragment, to undergo unlimited physical lifetimes in order to understand the purpose of it all.

And in so doing, he had granted Her that desire, and had experienced separation in his own way. Yet he always knew that one day She would return to him. When She grew weary of the game, perhaps, or when the great cosmic clock had come full circle, the waves of time would pull the two drifting soul-halves together.

He didn't know what it was. Perhaps it was his own thought to beckon Her back, for he had waited an eternity. A nagging urgency prompted him to find Her. It was as though something deep within him knew when She was ready to join him again.

A stimulus from an unknown source began to prick at the inner core of his being. "Go home," it prompted.

"Where is home?" he asked. "I have no home. I travel the universes."

"Look within," said the voice.

"Who are you?" he demanded. "And why should I listen to you? I am free."

"Yes, you are free," it said, "but what have you gained?"

He thought for a moment. "Nothing," he admitted. "I have

gained nothing. But I am free!"

"Then if it has fulfilled you, go on as you were," the voice told him. "You are free. It is your choice."

"What are you talking about?" he cried. But the voice had left him. Now he was disturbed. Before, he had been free of any such feelings, but the voice had spoken to him and left him with unanswered questions.

What had it meant when it talked of fulfillment? What was there to gain except a whole lot ofcomplications and trouble? He had observed. He had watched many lives living on many planets in many galaxies. He had seen a whole lot of trouble and had wanted nothing to do with any of it.

He tried over and over to forget the intruding voice. But now there was a growing ache from within. As it grew stronger and his thoughts began to stray, he realized it was Her. He missed Her. He began to remember what it had been like when they had been one, and his thoughts could focus on only one thing: It was time to find Her and go home.

2

Reluctance

B lake Dobbs sat on the end of his bed near the window. A warm spring breeze rippled the maroon curtains as he gazed out into the night. The traffic from downtown was a constant blend of noise and a neighbor's yapping dog made him wonder who was walking the streets. He longed to be out with his buddies, reveling in the cool night air with the delicious freedom of school being out.

Around his room were scattered half a dozen boxes, most of them empty. Frowning, he reached for his guitar and pulled it onto his lap as he sat back against the wall and began to pick out a tune.

Footsteps from the hallway stopped at his bedroom door. Dorothy Dobbs, clad in blue jeans and a sweatshirt, stood with her hands on her hips. Her dark brown hair was gathered up in a pony-tail as her green eyes flashed. "Blake! You're supposed to be packing. The movers will be here first thing in the morning!"

Blake rubbed an eye and sighed. He was tall like his mother, but with light-colored hair that graced his shoulders. He wore a simple gold earring on his left lobe. "Mom, why do we have to move? I don't want to leave my friends."

"We've already discussed why," said his mother. "Now put down that guitar."

Blake groaned in protest, but leaned the guitar up against the window. "Nobody cares what I think anymore," he muttered as he stood up."Just because Dad's friends are all moving, I don't see why we..."

"Blake! Get packing," ordered Dorothy. "I don't have time to argue with you. I have to get Kelly's things together, too." She left and Blake could hear his sister's voice whining from the other end of the house.

"She never has time to argue with me," Blake grumbled to

himself as he started pulling things out from under his bed and tossing them haphazardly into the boxes. "In fact, she never has time to do anything with me anymore." Bitterly he tossed a dirty sock that was encased in a dust clod toward the door.

He didn't want to move to Colorado. He had spent all of his sixteen years in this house — in this city — and now they were moving. Sure, lots of his friends over the years had moved, many of them more than once. But this had been so abrupt. Just last week his father had announced that the time had come and they had to leave DeKalb. It was no longer safe, he had said. He remembered the wild look of ecstasy in his mother's eyes when Dad had divulged that he had been told where to go and that they were moving to a small town on the Western Slope of the Rocky Mountains.

Blake knew it wouldn't have been so bad if Dad had received a work transfer like his friends' fathers did. But Dad didn't work for a company or a government agency that transferred their employees. Dad was a counselor for people who claimed they had been abducted by extraterrestrials. It was difficult enough trying to explain to your friends what your parents did for a living, but it was worse yet when they explained that the space people were telling them to move.

For most his years Blake had never minded being the son of Manley and Dorothy Dobbs of the UFO Contact Center in DeKalb, Illinois. He had grown up with lots of different people around, most of them extremely nice, seemingly intelligent, who didn't seem abnormal or the least bit crazy. They were, for the most part, no different from so-called *normal* folks. Some, of course, had been more memorable than others. The years had been good and Blake had been content, outgoing and friendly. He was popular at school and had discovered early in his life that music was an important part of him.

He recalled the piano that his father cherished. It was stored in a small room by itself and as a small boy Blake had been told many times that to touch it was a "no no." Somehow that sacred instrument that never got used had drawn him with a fascination until he would find opportunities to sneak into the forbidden room to sit at it and run his tiny fingers over the polished wood. Once he was strong enough to open the keyboard cover, he began toying

with the ivory keys. His mother would come rushing in to scold
him. Yet he'd return again and again, and one evening he played a
song that he had picked out of his head. He was surprised to look
up and find both his parents standing behind him, gaping at him
in wonder.

From that time on, Blake had been permitted to not only play
his Aunt Jo's piano, but they sent him to a private music teacher for
lessons. Blake's love for music had mushroomed and he was now
not only first-chair trumpet in the high school band, but a strong
member of the jazz band with his electric guitar, and he even gave
his own private guitar lessons to junior high kids.

Blake had often wondered what had been so special about
Aunt Jo's piano. Aunt Jo had been Dad's younger sister who had
toured as a concert pianist. Dad said he used to go on tour with her,
and that they had been very close until Aunt Jo went away.

"Where did she go?" Blake once asked his parents.

Then Mom and Dad would glance at one another with that
look that said, "Should we tell him?" But they never did. Blake knew
they were keeping the truth from him. It was perfectly clear that
there was some mystery with regard to Aunt Jo's disappearance.

Blake's guess was that poor Aunt Jo was locked away in some
insane asylum somewhere. They had told him that she had
suffered a mental breakdown and had to be committed. But he
didn't understand why his father never visited her, if he cared as
much as he said. Obviously the piano was evidence of the high
regard he held for this beautiful and talented aunt whose photograph was displayed on the piano. Blake often thought of her and
wondered what she had been like.

When he was ten years old, Blake's sister was born. He
remembered that his mother had suffered a lot during the
pregnancy. His parents hadn't been that young when Blake was
born. To have another child ten years later had been unexpected,
and then all the more troubling due to the fact that Kelly had been
born with Downs Syndrome. She was mentally retarded and,
although not severe, she required a whole lot of attention, which
changed things considerably in the Dobbses' household.

It seemed that suddenly all the time his parents had spent on
Blake now went to Kelly. His mother, in particular, became devoted
to the little girl and she stopped helping Manley at the UFO

Contact Center. This meant that his father had to spend more time at the center, and in the last couple of years the increase in people seeking help had grown so that it seemed as if Manley was never home.

At first Blake had been resentful of his baby sister getting all the attention. If it hadn't been for his music, all that anger might have resulted in damaging his self-image. Fortunately, a close friend of his dad's, a psychiatrist friend, had seen that Blake was unhappy and had befriended him. Barbara Wetzel had been a family friend for years and helped Blake through his crisis months, steering him more toward his music and encouraging him to express his feelings.

Eventually he found solace in activities at school and discovered that he was a naturally likable person and enjoyed socializing. This was why the sudden move away from everything he enjoyed was so difficult. He was stable and secure, yet now his parents wanted to uproot him and plant him upon foreign soil. It wasn't fair.

Blake looked out the window into the night as he pushed a box full of guitar magazines toward the corner. Tree branches and city lights prevented him from viewing the starry sky. He often watched the sky, looking for unusual lights. He believed in UFOs, of course. The family used to go on skywatches out in the country at night and sometimes Mom or Dad would point out a strange moving light. Mom told him of the time before she met Dad, when she and a friend had been driving through Nebraska at night and had seen a UFO. She said the aliens on board had stopped her and taken her on their ship. Dad had been present at the hypnotic regression in which she recalled being examined and attended by strange-looking beings with large heads and big slanted eyes.

The story had always intrigued Blake and he had no reason to doubt his mother's story. The fact that there were spaceships from beyond and extraterrestrials among the people on Earth was as natural to him as anything he had been taught in school. Yet there were many who remained in denial. Some of the kids at school tried to make fun of him and his parents' work. Most people he met were fairly open-minded and had experienced a UFO sighting at the very least. But the disbelievers could be cruel and even hostile.

Blake had gotten into some fights over the years, particularly with two brothers who came from a strict religious family and claimed that the ships carried agents of the devil and that anyone who sympathized with ETs was in league with Satan and would go straight to hell. Blake had no reason to think there were evil aliens flying around. If so, why hadn't they taken control of the earth long ago?

Blake longed to have his own encounter with someone from space, yet he'd never tell that to any of his friends. He had his own beliefs, but he kept them to himself. As long as he wasn't considered *too* weird, his friends accepted him. He found that avoiding the topic was in his favor, and yet deep inside he longed to see and experience something as fantastic as his parents. Dad often hinted that he, too, had experienced some extraordinary events, but he never discussed these with Blake. When asked, Manley would dismiss the question with a wink and a change of subject. Even Barbara Wetzel seemed to be in on some wonderful secret she shared with his parents.

"Blake, are you making any progress in there?" It was Dad this time who stood at the doorway. Manley Dobbs was almost completely bald at sixty-one. Despite his age, he was remarkably fit and had lost some pounds, thanks to a change in diet and lifestyle after meeting his wife. He wore dark slacks and a blue sweater as he stood looking around the room.

"I dunno," grumbled Blake.

"Better get those posters off the wall," said Manley.

"I know."

His dad came into the room and sat down on the bed. "I realize you're not happy about this move."

Blake shrugged and continued packing.

"You're sixteen now," continued Manley. "I think it's time for you to know a few things. After all, you're almost a man."

Blake scrunched up his face. "Dad, spare me. I know everything there is to know about the birds and bees."

Manley laughed and slapped his knee. "I don't doubt that," he said. "But I'm not talking about where babies come from. Son, your mother and I have talked, and we've decided the time has come to disclose some things we think you should know."

"What kind of things?" Blake's curiosity piqued.

Manley rubbed his chin. "About our family, for one," he said. Then he stood up to leave. "But not tonight."

"Then... when?"

"Tomorrow, when we're driving to Colorado," Manley said with a sly smile as he walked out of the room.

Blake stared after him, puzzled. Why did he have the feeling that come tomorrow, things were never going to be the same?

3

Night Light

In her dream the wide viewing screen before her was filled with stars streaking past. The black of space was a never-ending backdrop as the ship slid through the mid-section of the galaxy.

Crystal sat before a panel of controls and knew what each of the colored lights at her fingertips was for. At last! Finally she had passed her trials and was permitted to show what she could do in this test flight to Alcyone. She was well aware of the commander's presence behind her, and what an honor to be overseen by Preejhna Chiyuub herself. How proud Father and Grandfather would be.

Then, suddenly, a bright light flashed in front of her face. Crystal could no longer see the stars or the viewing screen. The blinding golden light dissolved the colored light panel, the streaking stars, the helm — *everything* was gone.

With a jolt she awoke as the light vanished. She was lying in her bed and darkness surrounded her.

I'm no longer in space, she thought in dismay. *I was flying the ship, but it was just a dream.* There was no Preejhna Chiyuub looking over her shoulder. No stars. She was home in her bed in the Terran colony beside the River of Determination on Karos. Everything was still. Mother and Father were sleeping in their room. It was the middle of the night.

Crystal rolled onto her side and pulled the cover up to her chin. Where had that bright flash come from? How intrusive it had been. She wished she could return to her dream. More than anything in her young life she wanted to pilot a spaceship, to cruise between the stars and be part of the Estronian fleet. But the light had rudely disrupted everything. What had it meant?

The dwelling was quiet. Crystal decided she must get a drink of water before going back to sleep. She waved her hand over the table beside her bed and immediately a soft pink glow filled her room. It was just enough to see where she'd kicked off her slippers.

She quietly made her way to the bathroom. The door to her parents' bedroom was closed and in the hallway she could see Kameel-37, the family's domestic android unit, recharging in its energy chamber. The robot had no perception of Crystal's presence as she turned on the bathroom light and found a glass and filled it.

She gazed into the mirror over the sink as she drank some water. She was a slender girl of seventeen years, rather tall with blue eyes and shimmering golden hair that flowed down her back. Right now her hair was tousled from sleep. She had delicate features, which included high cheek bones and a slightly turned-up nose. Her doe-like eyes were a little puffy from sleep. She was physically mature for her age, yet at school several of the Estronian girls her age were remarkably adult-like. Other humanoid girls seemed to look up to Crystal and often commented on her beauty. She hadn't had the heart to confess the truth about her physical form and wondered if they would understand.

Crystal finished her glass of water and turned out the light. Just as she started back to her room, she was startled by a bright ball of golden light. A little larger than the size of a grapefruit, the ball of light hung, suspended, in the air about two feet from her face. It seemed to be radiating energy of some sort.

Instinctively Crystal drew back. It was all she could do to keep from shrieking, which would have alarmed her parents. Her heart plunged into a series of pounding as she shielded her sleepy eyes from the penetrating brightness. She was frightened and didn't know what the light was. Ordinarily her reaction would be to get away from it, if it was any kind of threat, but the ball of light was hovering between Crystal and her bedroom. She could have run to her parents' room, but something was happening in her mind. Some calming sensation had taken hold of her and was reassuring her that the light meant no harm. An intuitive feeling told her she was safe.

Crystal had no clue how long she stood in the bathroom doorway with the light staring her in the face. It could have been ten or twelve minutes, but it seemed as if time stood still. Her fascination held her in a pose that seemed to control her and prevent her from taking any kind of action. A flood of thoughts rushed at her brain in such a sweep that she was overcome and confused.

Through the swarm of perplexity there emerged a sudden strong impression of familiarity — even intimacy — with the energy form in front of her. It had come and interrupted her dream about the spacecraft. It had come for a purpose. But that's all she could ascertain from its presence.

In the next instant the light vanished. Crystal stood for a moment, bewildered. Where had the light gone? Then she quickly returned to her room with the red-glowing night light and her warm bed. She was suddenly very sleepy. She could hardly keep her eyelids open as she reached her hand out to wave the light off. The room was dark then and she fell instantly asleep. No dreams, no disturbances.

Crystal didn't remember anything more until she awoke to her mother's voice calling her and she opened her eyes to a bright new day.

4

Defiance

Piano music flooded the stone cottage as Johanna practiced her latest composition. She hoped to have it perfected in time for the grand opening of the concert hall. She had titled the piece *Cosmic Journey*, which was part of a more complex creation, aptly named *The Karosian Suite*, which had taken years to develop and was, more or less, a masterpiece for her.

Serassan, her Estronian mate, walked into the room and stood over her as her fingers worked confidently over the ivory keys. He touched her shoulder with affection and she glanced up at him and smiled, but continued playing. She loved how he became so absorbed in her music, but then his love and his light were what inspired her.

Finishing the piece, she turned to Serassan and he embraced her. "What do you think?" she asked with a twinkle in her brown eyes. At 53, Johanna's dark brown hair was tinged with gentle streaks of silver, but she had held onto her beauty and did not show the few extra pounds she had gained after giving birth to their daughter. A glow of contentment radiated from her face.

"Absolutely stunning," replied Serassan.

"Do you think it is an appropriate selection for the opening?" she asked.

"Johanna, my love, you couldn't have chosen a more suitable piece of music."

"Are you on your way to the center?" Johanna stood up from the piano.

Serassan took her hands in his. "Yes. There is a lot to be done yet before the visit of the High Council. I have some projects to oversee."

"Will you be long?"

He hesitated, then said, "I have an idea. Why don't you bring Crystal and we'll enjoy lunch in the new café."

"You mean it's open?"

"Well, not officially... but I'll get Justine and Sam to fix us something. It will please them. Besides, the help have to eat, don't they?"

Just then Crystal emerged from her bedroom, dressed in a neon-blue colored robe. Her golden hair had been brushed and there was color in her cheeks. "Good morning, Father." She smiled at Serassan, then turned to Johanna. "And you, too, Mother." She fell into a chair and put her bare feet up on a hassock.

"You slept rather late this morning," remarked Johanna. It wasn't meant as a criticism, yet she detected annoyance in the girl.

Serassan kissed Johanna, then his daughter, and headed up the stone stairway toward the entrance to the cottage. "I'll see you two later," he called.

"Yes, my love," Johanna replied. Turning to her daughter, she sighed. "Well, what have you got planned for your first day of school vacation?"

Crystal examined her toes. "I was hoping to go visit Grandfather and Granna Soolàn."

"And take the shuttle, of course." Johanna nodded knowingly.

Crystal eyed her hopefully. "May I?"

Johanna stacked her music and shook her head. "Now, Crystal, you know you need to pass your trials before you can leave the planet."

"But, Mother, I've flown to the Planetoid twice already."

"That was with your father along," Johanna said, "and I can't let you go alone."

"Come with me," begged the girl.

Johanna's brown eyes widened. "Crystal, I can't pilot one of those things. What if you lost control? What if something went wrong?"

Crystal frowned. "Oh, Mother."

"Besides," continued Johanna, "your father plans to have us meet him for lunch at the arts center."

Kameel-37 glided into the room and hovered between Johanna and Crystal. The robot unit was small and white, cat-like in appearance, encased in metal with ear-like projections on top and two glowing silver eyes. "Good morning, Crystal Dobbs," it said in a cheerful, high-pitched voice. "What may I prepare for your breakfast today?"

"I don't eat breakfast," Crystal pouted.

Johanna stared at her daughter. "What do you mean you don't eat breakfast?" she exclaimed. "Is that what they encourage on board the starships? Of course you'll have breakfast, young lady, even if it's simply a piece of toast and some Mupani tea!"

With a grimace Crystal waved to the robot unit. "Toast... no butter. But I'll pass on the Mupani tea. Bring me juice."

"I will prepare it," said Kameel-37 and returned to the kitchen.

"Crystal," Johanna said, "since you're on break between semesters and will be here for the big grand opening, your father and I were hoping that perhaps you might want to sing for the opening concert." Johanna saw her daughter's mouth twitch. "Before you say no, you might consider the fact that a lot of people have put a lot of time and effort into making the arts center on Karos a reality. Your father has been instrumental in getting cooperation from the planet Estron, and your grandfather has worked very hard to persuade the High Council to provide support from throughout the galaxy. And as for myself..."

"Mother, save it," Crystal interrupted. "If it's that important to you, I'll sing." Then she sighed, tossing her blond hair behind her. "But you might as well know. I have plans for joining the fleet."

Johanna tried not to show her alarm. "And what makes you think you'll be accepted into the fleet?" she asked. "Who has been talking to you?"

"Mother, I know what I want. I want to be in space... all of the time. I want to see all the different forms of life in the universe, and be a part of an exciting command." Crystal's face brightened as she stared ahead, smiling.

"And what about your musical training?" Johanna crossed her arms.

"What about it?"

"Crystal, you have talent," cried Johanna. "You have a future. You are the envy of the Estronian people. Don't you see? You are the first of their kind to be born with such."

Standing up, Crystal wrapped her robe tighter around her. "If it's the hybrid lecture you're starting on, you might as well save your breath. It's *my* life."

Johanna lost control. "Crystal Dobbs, that's no way to speak to an adult! What has got into you, anyway?"

"I'm tired of everyone telling me who and what I am supposed to be," fired the girl. "I'm sick of people looking at me and thinking, 'There she is, that's the hybrid.' "

"For heaven's sake, Crystal, where did you ever get an idea like that?" Johanna retorted.

Kameel-37 entered the room, carrying a plate of toasted bread and juice for Crystal.

"It's true!" insisted Crystal. "I'm a freak! Half Terran, half Estronian."

"It's nothing to be ashamed of!" cried Johanna. "Do the other students on the ship make fun of you? Have they actually said anything?"

"No, but it's in their thoughts," said Crystal. "They don't like me."

"Here is your breakfast, Crystal Dobbs." Kameel-37 extended the plate. "May I be of assistance in this mother-daughter altercation?"

"No, thank you, Kameel," Johanna replied. "There is no altercation. Crystal and I are discussing a school matter."

The robot unit turned to go. "Very well, then I will mind my own business."

Crystal sat down and began eating her toast. "Sometimes I wish I looked more like other Estronian women," she commented. "I stand out with my altered features."

"But Estronians are not the only race at school," Johanna reminded her. "What about the others? There are many that have human features."

"They don't count," said the girl.

Johanna sighed, recalling the newborn infant she had held in her arms seventeen years ago. Crystal had been born with characteristics of both races. Her skin had been whitish-gray and her mouth had no lips. Her misshapen, elongated head had a few strands of human hair and there had been a small nose. Her blue eyes resembled those of her Estronian father. Johanna, who had once looked upon the Estronians as loathsome, had loved her child despite the alien appearance.

When Crystal was a few months old, Plipquum, the Estronian healer, had been summoned to begin the long, arduous process of biochemical alteration used on Estron to change physical appearance. Two decades before, Serassan had undergone the technique, which had taken several weeks, and now retained his human body with the aid of frequent checkups and careful diet. They had decided before their daughter's birth that the biochemical process was best in order for Crystal to live a normal and accepted life on Karos, the Terran colony.

The other colonists were human and some had married and produced human offspring. Due to atmospheric differences, it was not possible for Estronians in their natural form to live on Karos without the biochemical transformation. When Plipquum or one of Serassan's relatives visited the planet colony, they needed a supplement that temporarily adjusted the oxygen level in their blood. The same was true for any Terrans who might visit the sister planet Estron.

Oxygen supplements were offered in the form of bubble devices, which were carried around, or wafers to be taken orally. The bubble devices were small, handheld instruments that, when inserted under an entity's skin, generated an invisible bubble of air that surrounded the being and provided the correct oxygen and gas atmosphere to enable that being to breathe without distress. The devices could be programmed for different atmospheres and different lengths of time and carried in one's pocket. The wafer supplements, although less expensive to use, had to be consumed several times a day to prevent lack of oxygen. Injections were also given and were often the choice for humans who visited Estron or her ships.

Johanna and Serassan had been delighted with the results of Crystal's biochemical transformation. She grew up among the human children of the colony, a beautiful, golden-haired child who was bright and daring and possessed a melodious soprano voice. With her mother's coaching, Crystal learned the piano at an early age and delighted everyone — particularly her father, who adored her — with her musical talent.

"What's going through your mind?" Crystal's voice startled Johanna out of her reminiscence. "You're smiling. What's so funny?" She crunched her toast.

"I was just remembering when you were a little girl," said Johanna, "when you would perform for the neighbors and then sing for them."

Crystal didn't comment. She finished the last of her toast and juice, then started for her bedroom. "I'd better get dressed." She turned to Johanna and said, "But I've made up my mind. I'm going into space, whether you like it or not."

5

Blake's Dream

The last night he would stay in the house he grew up in, Blake had a memorable dream. He called it a dream because of its unusual quality. Reality, as he knew it, had altered when he awoke to find his barren room filled with an unusual golden light. Its source was a human form that gave off a brilliant glow. It could only have been a dream, and yet he wasn't exactly sure.

Sitting up in his bed, Blake stared at the glowing figure. "Who are you?" His own voice sounded real enough.

The phantom continued to stare at him, but it said nothing.

"Hey, are you actual?" Blake blinked his eyes. "Or are you part of my dream?" He was surprised that he had no fear, but then, after all, this was only a dream figure. "I know," he said after a pause, "I'm having what they call one of those lucid dreams. My mom and dad talk about them all the time. Hey, this is pretty cool!" He studied the glowing form before him and could vaguely start to make out a face with eyes, a nose, a mouth. The being had masculine features, but because of its radiance, he could hardly make them out. "So what's your name?"

The ghost appeared to respond with a puzzled expression, but still it did not speak.

Blake sighed. "Where are you from?" Glancing out his window into the night, he said, "Oh, I know, you're from space. Are you one of my father's friends?"

The being slowly shook his head.

Blake climbed out of bed and started walking toward the luminous figure. He was forced to stop as soon as he felt a protective wall of energy that made it impossible for him to approach further. "Wow," said Blake, stepping back, "that's awesome. Hey, don't you speak?"

The being nodded and gestured toward its head. Then Blake heard the words in his own head as the being answered him telepathically, "I communicate, yes."

"Wow!" Blake sat back on his bed. "Do you have a name? Where are you from? What do you want with me?"

"One question at a time, please," the voice in his head pleaded.

"Oh... sorry." Blake was excited. Even if this was just a dream, it was a fantastic one. "My name is Blake Dobbs. What's yours?"

"My... name?" The light being hesitated. "My name... is too long. You would not be able to remember it."

"So what should I call you?" asked Blake.

"What comes to your mind?" the being replied.

"I dunno. You're a... a being of light... an extraterrestrial. I don't want to call you 'E.T.' You don't look a thing like him. Let's see." Blake thought hard. What would be appropriate for this dream character's name? "I've got it," he said, "L.B. I'll call you L.B. It stands for Light Being."

The Light Being said nothing.

Blake frowned. "You don't like it?"

"L.B. is sufficient," said the Light Being. "If that's what you prefer to call me, then do. My like or dislike is not important."

"Then L.B. it is," said Blake. "Now tell me, L.B., what you are doing here in my bedroom. Are you from space? I've always wanted to meet somebody from space."

"I come because I am on a mission," said the Light Being. "And you are correct in your assumption. I live in space, as do you."

"No, wait a minute," said Blake. "I don't live in space. I live on Planet Earth."

"Terra... yes." L.B. nodded his glowing head. "But you want to live in space."

"Well, I don't know about that," replied Blake. "As a matter of fact, I'm happy to be right where I am. I don't want to go anywhere, in fact. But they're making me."

"Making you?"

"My parents. We're moving to Colorado."

"You mean you're moving to space," the Light Being told him.

Now Blake was confused. "I don't think Colorado and space are the same thing."

L.B. smiled. "Believe me, Blake, you are going into space."

"Never mind." Blake didn't want to argue. "What's your mission, anyway?"

"I must go home," L.B. told him.

Blake laughed. "Just like good old E.T. Why don't you build yourself a device like he did and 'phone home'?"

"First I must manifest a body."

"Why? What's wrong with the way you are? I think you're great! I love the way you light up a room."

L.B. intensified his brilliance until Blake had to shield his eyes.

"But let's not overdo it," said Blake. "I don't want to go blind. What do you need with a body?"

"So that I can appear to one who needs me," replied L.B.

"Uh... okay," said Blake, not getting it. "And how do you propose obtaining this body?"

L.B.'s laughter filled Blake's head. "Silly human, you've got the wrong idea. I do not steal bodies. I am *not* after yours!"

Blake sighed in relief. "Well, for a moment there, I admit you had me a little worried. I mean... I guess I've seen too many movies."

L.B. ceased laughing. "There is much I must learn first," he said seriously. "I came to you because I need a mentor. I need assistance on behaving as a human adolescent male. If you are agreeable, the lessons can begin whenever you are ready."

Blake was astonished. "You want me to show you how to act human?"

L.B. smiled. "Think upon it, my friend Blake. You will see me again soon. I promise." And with that, the Light Being began to dematerialize before Blake's eyes.

Blake found himself sitting in his bed in his darkened room. It was half an hour before he was finally able to fall back to sleep. When he awoke the next morning, the dream was still vivid.

He could almost believe that he had actually been visited by a being from another dimension.

"Blake, get dressed," his mother called as she passed his door. "The movers are here."

With a sigh of resignation, Blake got up and looked across his room where, in his dream, the Light Being had stood. Clearly he remembered the words that had been spoken in his head: *"You will see me again soon."*

6

Elucidation

It was approaching mid-afternoon and the traffic had picked up on the interstate as the Dobbs family traveled west through Iowa. Manley sat behind the steering wheel of their late-model Subaru wagon. Blake rode in the passenger seat, secured by the safety belt. He watched the fields of corn as they passed, all in neat rows of green, for what seemed endless miles.

His mother and sister sat in the back seat. Blake could see that Kelly had fallen asleep in her car seat. Even at six years old, she preferred her baby seat to sitting upright inside the car. Dorothy gazed drowsily ahead as the car continued to cruise.

"Will the moving van get there ahead of us?" Blake asked. They had left in the family car before the movers had even finished loading everything from the house.

"Hard to tell, son," said Manley. "The truck will most likely keep going with two drivers. I'm sure it'll beat us."

"How soon before we reach Nebraska?" asked Dorothy. She leaned forward and gripped the front seat.

Manley glanced at her, then reached back and placed his hand over hers. "We're not too far," he replied. "Are you getting concerned?"

Blake turned to his mother and noticed a distant look in her eyes, as if she were in a daydream. Turning to his father, he caught a look of resignation as Manley refocused on the road ahead of them. Blake knew something significant was in his parents' minds. He guessed it had something to do with Nebraska.

"Let's tell him now," said Dorothy abruptly. "Kelly's sleeping."

Manley nodded and turned to Blake. "Yes, the time has come." He ran his hand over his almost bald head. "Blake, we both feel you're old enough to handle the truth. What do *you* think?"

Blake grew excited. "Yeah, sure."

"Okay, then." Manley cleared his throat and then began. "Your mother was abducted many years ago. She's told you a little about it."

"No, Manley, go back," said Dorothy. "Go back to when it started. That's what's important."

"Okay." Manley hesitated, as if a painful memory had seized him. "Back to when it started... yes."

Blake folded his arms and made himself comfortable on the seat. He knew this was going to be a lengthy narrative.

"Years ago," Manley began, "my sister... your aunt... and I went to see the ballet. It was in January of that year. I was working as a used car salesman in Northport. This was when I was married to my first wife. Your Aunt Johanna lived by herself and she loved the ballet. So when this man came by the car lot and left me two tickets for the ballet, I decided to take your aunt to see it."

Dorothy leaned forward. "That man turned out to be a contact," she explained. "He was setting your dad and Aunt Jo up for a meeting that evening."

Manley continued. "While we were at the ballet, that same man came and sat next to my sister. I didn't recognize him that night because he had dressed up, and besides, I didn't think anything about it at the time."

Blake waited for his father to go on.

"While we were at the ballet, the man next to Johanna kept getting up and leaving. During intermission, Johanna visited the lady's room. She ended up being gone for forty-five minutes."

"Where did she go?" asked Blake.

"I didn't know at the time," said Manley. "When she came back to her seat, she didn't realize she'd had... missing time."

"Later we found out that she had been abducted by the man in the next seat," said Dorothy.

"Yes, he turned out to be... an alien," said Manley.

"Wow," breathed Blake. "So then what happened to Aunt Jo?"

"Well," sighed Manley, "everything was fine until the next day. Your Aunt Jo lost her ability to speak English. All she could do was babble idiotically in the alien tongue. We all thought she had gone crazy."

"You didn't know an alien had abducted her," guessed Blake.

"No," said Manley. "We didn't know. She had been implanted with some strange device in her brain that was set to alter her speech. She was so upset and hysterical, all I could think to do was take her to the hospital. So my wife and I took her in and she was taken to the psychiatric ward right away."

"But she *wasn't* crazy," Blake protested. "Was she?"

"At the time we were sure she had suffered some kind of mental breakdown," said Manley. "I mean, she was terrified. Imagine how you would feel if suddenly your whole world was in an altered state and you couldn't communicate."

"So it's true Aunt Jo went to a mental hospital," said Blake sadly. "Is she still there?"

"No, she's not," said Dorothy.

"But you said..."

"I know," his mother interrupted, "but we had to protect her."

"The authorities believed she died in an accident," continued Manley. "Two doctors were driving a van full of patients to a distant research facility. The van was found in the river."

"That's what they told your father," added Dorothy.

"However," said Manley, "the truth is, the two doctors were impostors. They were aliens and they were taking the abductees to meet their mother ship."

Blake was amazed at this disclosure. He eagerly waited for the rest.

"And the one doctor," explained Dorothy, "was the same man from the ballet."

"Serassan," said Manley, "or Doctor Serassan, as Barbara Wetzel remembers him."

"She knows about this, too, doesn't she?" asked Blake.

"Yes, Barb was Johanna's doctor," said Manley. "She and I got to be good friends after Johanna disappeared." He smiled. "A lot of things began to happen to me after Johanna was gone."

"But, Dad, how did you know about the alien doctors? How do you know your sister *didn't* die in the road accident?"

Dorothy smiled now. "Your dad always knew she didn't die. He dreamed that the spaceship came and carried Johanna away."

"But... Dad, a *dream*?" Blake was stumped.

"There's more, son," said Manley. "Much more."

"Several months later," Dorothy began, "I was traveling with a friend from California. I was driving this same interstate at night, in the middle of Nebraska, when we saw a UFO."

"I know," said Blake. "You've told the story many times. You were somewhere near Grand Island when your car died, and the UFO came and your friend wouldn't wake up."

"And I was taken on board the craft," said Dorothy. "They examined me and I was given a set of instructions for the future."

"Your mother was traumatized by her experience," said Manley. "When she got to DeKalb, she called me at the UFO Contact Center. You see, after all that had happened with Johanna, my life changed. I got divorced and moved to DeKalb and set up the center with Barb Wetzel's help. She, too, went through a life change and became a more spiritual and open-minded person."

"We found out during my hypnosis session what had happened to me," said Dorothy. "I couldn't remember until the regression."

Blake sighed. "So... that's what was kept from me all these years. But I still don't understand... how can you be so sure that Aunt Jo wasn't killed in that accident? What makes you so sure aliens came and took her away?"

Manley drove in silence for several moments and then looked at Blake. "Because... she came back. Right at that time when I was first getting to know your mother, Johanna returned."

Dorothy sighed. "And Serassan was with her," she added.

"But how..." Blake looked from one parent to the other. "I mean, did a spaceship land in the yard or something weird like that?"

"Not exactly," said Manley.

"Actually," said Dorothy, "they drove up in a rental car."

"Oh, right." Blake was beginning to wonder about his parents.

"There was an awful lot of confusion happening at that time," Manley tried to explain. "That was the year of the big earthquake that killed about a hundred people in the Chicago area."

"We thought the end of the world had come," said Dorothy with a smile. "I'll never forget how frightening it was when the power went out and those winds began to blow. And Johanna..."

Manley interrupted her. "What I'm about to tell you, son, is going to sound unbelievable."

Blake shrugged. "Shoot," he said.

"I was abducted that day." The words were coming hard, Blake could see. His father continued, "I was having a difficult time. Feeling sorry for myself, you might say." Manley sighed. "Oh, wow... it's hard to admit everything. Blake, I was planning to take my life."

Dorothy reached over and put her hand on her husband's shoulder.

Blake was stunned. He had never imagined his father to be anything but strong, yet here he was confessing that he had once been suicidal.

Manley went on. "I drove to the place where Barb Wetzel and others from our group used to go for skywatches."

"The same place we went?" asked Blake.

Manley nodded. "I got there and I was going to leave the car running with a towel stuck up the exhaust pipe. Then I saw a craft that landed in the field."

Blake jerked up. "I remember those marks in the field! You just told me a UFO may have landed there. I never knew you had actually seen that UFO!"

"That's right, Blake. I was there, and I was taken on board. I don't remember the details too well."

"What did they look like? The aliens, I mean."

"They were Grays, I think. They were acting under instructions from somebody else. I was knocked out and the next thing I remember was waking up in a dark, cold cave near an underground river."

"Dad!" cried Blake. "What did they do to you? Where were you?"

"I was at Dulce, New Mexico, at the alien base you have heard us talk about on occasion."

"Were you a captive?"

"Yes... along with Kapri."

"Who is Kapri?"

Dorothy cut in. "Kapri was a good friend of your father and me. She was another alien."

"Whoa," said Blake.

"Kapri turned out to be an undercover agent for the

Federation," said Manley.

"The Galactic Federation," added Dorothy. "You see, the Dark Forces kidnapped Kapri from my apartment the same night your dad was at the skywatch area. They were both taken to Dulce."

"And that's the reason your Aunt Jo and Serassan came back to Earth," explained Manley. "They, too, were working undercover for the Federation, to discover who was responsible for attempting to bring destruction to the earth."

"A band of power-mongers that were outside the Federation had in their possession some kind of doomsday device that was triggering earthquakes and storms," said Dorothy. "These people... these aliens... whoever they were... wanted to create chaos and panic all over the world so they could take control of it."

Manley said, "Anyway, Serassan found out where Kapri and I had been taken." He turned to Dorothy and smiled. "Thanks to your mother."

Blake was puzzled. "Mom? How did *you* know where Dad was?"

"I was able to channel Kapri's thoughts," replied Dorothy. "Dr. Wetzel hypnotized me and we were able to locate the area."

"So then what happened? How did Dad escape?"

"Well," said Manley, "Serassan summoned a shuttle from one of the mother ships in orbit around our planet. He and Richmond Hayes, a UFO investigator, flew to the Dulce area, then hiked in with the help of an Apache medicine man."

"By the name of White Feather," Dorothy added. "But then Mr. Hayes and your uncle were also captured."

"Wait a minute," said Blake. "My uncle? *Who* is my uncle?"

"Oh, that's something else we wanted to tell you," said Manley. "Serassan is your uncle."

"He's married to Aunt Johanna," said Dorothy. "In fact, poor Johanna was going through a terrible time while all this was happening. She had a miscarriage."

"You mean... she was going to have an alien baby?" Blake's eyes were wide.

"But she didn't," said Manley.

"No, she lost the baby," added Dorothy.

"I'm sure it was for the best," Manley said.

"Well, how did you all escape?" Blake asked. "You were all captured at the underground base. Tell me what happened next."

"The Jicarilla tribe was having a pow-wow," said Manley. "They were a tremendous help in raising the vibration at Dulce. And then Kapri and Serassan used their mental ability to raise the consciousness in Rich and myself. Between the drumming above ground and the almost hypnotic-like trance they induced to keep us from giving in to our fears and the negativity, and the intervention of the mother ship... we were beamed out of that hellhole in the nick of time."

"And the doomsday... or holocaust device," said Dorothy, "was vaporized, thanks to our Space Brothers and Sisters."

"Wow," said Blake. His thoughts played over and over as he rehashed the story in his mind. "Where are Aunt Jo and Serassan now?"

"On Karos," Manley replied.

"Where's that?"

"Somewhere in the galaxy," said Dorothy.

"We don't know where Karos is exactly," Manley told him. "But Johanna described it as a small planet in the same solar system as Estron. Estron was where Serassan and Kapri were from."

"Kapri called it the Blue Planet," remembered Dorothy. "I've often wondered what became of Kapri."

"Yes," sighed Manley. "She was very special."

"So, did Aunt Jo and Serassan go back to Karos?" asked Blake.

"Yes," said Manley.

"Do you ever hear anything about them?"

Manley shook his head sadly. "No, not in all these years."

"We only know that they must still be there," said Dorothy. "Every so often I've meditated on it and I keep getting that both of them are well."

Blake knew his mother was referring to her psychic ability to tune into higher frequencies. How often she used her God-given talent he didn't know, for she didn't often mention it to him.

So, thought Blake as he stared ahead at the long stretch of interstate, *I have an aunt living in space on another planet, and I have an uncle who's an alien.* He felt comforted by the fact that his beautiful aunt, whose portrait from her concert touring days that had been displayed on the piano, was alive. He suddenly felt close to her and wished more than anything that one day he could meet her face to face. He wondered what it was like living on another world. What was it like for her to be married to an alien? He wanted to meet Serassan, too.

"Mom," said Blake.

"What, dear?"

"I had a strange dream last night." Blake turned his head and saw that both his parents seemed to be interested.

"What did you dream?" asked Manley.

"Maybe it wasn't a dream." Blake sighed. "It seemed so real, but... I'm sure it must have been a dream."

"Please tell us," prompted Dorothy.

Blake told them about the Light Being and what he had said. He laughed. "Can you imagine? He wanted me to teach him how to be human!"

Manley nodded his head. "Good dream."

"Look," said Dorothy, pointing ahead. "We're coming into Nebraska."

7

Lunch on Karos

Serassan was waiting inside the newly constructed concert hall when Johanna led Crystal through the door. Johanna wore a pale green tunic and black tights, considered casual attire on Karos. Her dark brown hair was gathered in a bun and revealed her slender neck. Crystal had chosen to wear an aqua-colored frock with tapered sleeves and a rounded neckline. Her lustrous golden hair flowed behind her back and she wore dangling silver bracelets on each of her wrists.

"We're not late, are we?" Johanna leaned over to accept Serassan's kiss.

"Not at all." Serassan grinned when he saw his daughter. "Crystal, you are radiant."

The girl smiled and embraced her father. "Mother says I spend too much time fussing over myself."

"Well, it was certainly worth it." Serassan winked at Johanna, then led both of them down the corridor. Some workers were painting the ceiling as they passed. They turned and greeted Johanna and Serassan, then continued with their task. An android unit resembling a crab with multiple arms emerged from one of the rooms and floated down the hallway toward marble steps that led to the big auditorium. Drilling came from inside, but Serassan led them past into the restaurant area, where several people — mostly workers — were eating at oval tables. A few of them were Estronians who had offered their services on Karos to help complete the much anticipated Galactic Arts Center. Their alien bodies with large white heads and slanted blue eyes contrasted the half dozen or so Terrans.

"Over here." Serassan led them to a corner where two Estronians, a man and a woman, watched them from where they were seated.

Crystal gasped when she saw them. "Grandfather! And Granna Soolàn!" She ran ahead of her parents and embraced Emrox first, who stood up with his arms stretched out, then Soolàn, whose blue wrap-around eyes seemed to sparkle as she smiled at Crystal, then at Johanna.

"Soolàn! Emrox! This is a surprise," cried Johanna. She touched her fingers and palm to Emrox's as a gesture of affection and warmth, then gave Soolàn a hug.

"Sit down," urged Serassan.

"Crystal, you're looking quite grown up," commented Soolàn, "and we wanted to see how the concert hall was coming along."

"Son, it's remarkable," said Emrox.

"Thank you, Father."

Johanna squeezed Serassan's hand. "Serassan has done a tremendous job. I'm proud of him."

"So are we," added Soolàn.

"Well, as you know," said Serassan, "the cafeteria is not yet officially open. The workers use it for their lunch, of course, but I've arranged a special..." He turned around. "Oh, here comes Sam now. Justine and Sam Oliver have prepared us a meal."

A solidly built, red-haired man with a bristly face and mustache brought a tray to their table. "Hello, folks." Grinning, he began placing bowls of fruit before them. "Justine and I have cooked up something quite tasty that I hope you will enjoy."

A small, round woman in her late forties approached, rolling a cart with plates of food and a pitcher of something to drink. She had short brown hair with bangs and pale green eyes. "Hello, Johanna," she said. "Hello, Crystal, welcome home."

"Thank you, Mrs. Oliver."

"Sam and Justine are managing the café," Serassan explained to his parents. "Sam is a wonderful chef, as well as a talented painter."

"And Justine is a singer," said Johanna. "They both were on the mother ship when I came here. They were two of some of the Terrans who volunteered to stay and make Karos their home, as I did."

"Mrs. Oliver gave me voice lessons," said Crystal. She reached for a grape-like fruit and popped it into her mouth.

"Here we go... fresh from the River of Determination." Sam began serving them portions of steaming fish that had a spicy, lemon aroma.

"My best pupil," remarked Justine as she poured fruit juice into their goblets. "I always said Crystal Dobbs had a voice of gold. I do hope you're planning to perform a solo at the grand opening, Crystal."

Johanna watched for her daughter's reaction and was relieved that the girl did not scrunch up her face in protest.

"Oh, Crystal, how lovely," cried Soolàn.

"How soon before the grand opening?" Emrox took a slice of bread from Justine's tray.

"It's just a matter of days before everything is ready," replied Serassan.

After the Olivers finished serving them lunch, Soolàn insisted they all acknowledge gratitude. With elbows on the table, she raised both of her slender white arms with her index fingers extended, and the others did the same until they formed a circle, touching fingertips. Johanna took a deep breath and closed her eyes as she reflected on the many blessings in her life. No one spoke. It was a private, personal ritual and to have words spoken in prayer by any one individual seemed to distract from the deeper communion they felt with the Creator. After several moments, it was over and they began their meal.

Emrox discussed with Serassan some of the political issues facing Estron and the High Council. Soolàn wanted to hear what Crystal had to report about her schooling on the mother ship. Johanna ate, listening alternately to each conversation, but not participating in either. She was still disturbed at what Crystal had told her earlier, about her desire to join the Estronian fleet and spend her life in space. She could see nothing beneficial in that life choice, not when Crystal had such a promising career in music ahead of her. Such a waste of talent! Johanna suspected that her daughter was being influenced by some of her classmates, most probably the Estronian females.

Being half Estronian, Crystal had always been proud of that lineage and wanted to identify herself as such. The Estronian women, Johanna knew, were domineering and overly ambitious. She had learned in her early relationship with Serassan that the females on his home planet were career-oriented and considered themselves superior to the males. Most of them, she discovered, smothered their sexual desires in work and programmed the younger members of their sex to avoid what they considered to be the derogatory path of wifehood. Many females seemed to lack the sex drive entirely. Reproduction on Estron was accomplished in the laboratory in most cases, although it was known that there were a few Estronian women who still held the desire to bear children, or at least raise and nurture the ones who were born.

Serassan's mother was an exceptional Estronian, yet she had been brought up elsewhere and had known a loving set of parents and been schooled in higher spiritual values. She and Emrox considered themselves social outcasts, more or less, although Emrox was still a highly respected member of Estron's High Council. They resided on a small red planetoid between Karos and Estron, all part of the same star system. Johanna loved them both as if they had been her own parents, which seemed quite natural as her birth parents had been killed when she was a young girl. Her brother, Manley, had been most supportive from that time in her life until her abduction. He had devoted much of his life to her and ushered her through her concert career in her twenties.

It was only natural, Johanna supposed, that her daughter should want to identify with her classmates and follow their example. But she knew there were other humanoids besides Estronians with whom Crystal shared her days and nights on the mother ship. A handful of Terran children had been born on the planet colony and there were children of many races, from several star systems in the Federation, in Crystal's peer group.

Johanna started into her dessert — a light, foamy cold substance that resembled ice cream, only it was less dense and tended to dissolve in her mouth. The Estronians called it frupagi, which meant *royal feast*. It provided the same satisfaction as ice cream and was just as delicious, but it contained few calories and wasn't fattening. Johanna had taken to frupagi right away. No matter how often she ate it, it was a delectable treat.

She overheard Emrox say to Serassan, "Terra is due to shift any day now," and her attention was immediately drawn to the men's conversation.

"You mean it's that close?" Serassan replied.

Soolàn and Crystal were still engaged in their own conversation as Johanna leaned closer to her husband. "What's this about a shift?" she asked.

Emrox sipped his cup of Mupani tea. "There is no need for you to be concerned, Johanna."

"No need?" She stared at her father-in-law. "Emrox, Earth is my concern. It was my home."

"The shift has been expected for a long, long time, Johanna," Serassan explained. "The time is very near."

"Well, what are you talking about? I want to know." Johanna put down her spoon. "What kind of shift are you talking about, anyway? A pole shift?"

Emrox cleared his throat. Serassan's look had turned serious. "Your planet has been through pole shifts before. It's nothing new. But this time Earth is going to experience dimensional shift."

"Meaning... what?" prompted Johanna. She immediately considered Manley and all her friends on Earth. What would become of them?

"Perhaps we shouldn't discuss this now," Emrox said to Serassan.

Serassan reached over and placed his warm hand on Johanna's wrist. She immediately felt his powerful and soothing energy begin to flow into her body. She knew he wanted to calm her. "Father, Johanna should not be kept in the dark about her home planet. You confided in her before."

"Yes, but only because she insisted..."

"Well, I insist now, too!" cried Johanna. Soolàn and Crystal stopped talking and turned their attention their way. "If something is about to happen to Earth, I have a right to know."

Emrox sighed. "Perhaps you are both right." He stared into his mug of tea. "My sources say that Terra will enter its new dimension and the Federation is already on full alert to assist in all capacities."

"Grandfather," said Crystal, her blue eyes wide, "when is this to occur?"

"I don't know the precise time of the event," replied the older Estronian, "but it could be a week, it could be a day, or it could be one hour from now."

Johanna stared at Serassan. "Won't you please tell me what

that means? What is going to happen to Earth's inhabitants?"

"That depends," said Serassan.

"Our hope is that enough of them have opened their hearts," Soolàn commented. "If enough Terrans are prepared, the shift will be nothing more than a slight jolt of electricity. This is why it has been so important to bring love and light to the people on your planet."

"Oh, Granna, you're so spiritual," Crystal said fondly. She blinked her eyes. "We've read a little about the phenomenon at school," she added. "I think it could be a very exciting time for Terra. But also it could be a most difficult time."

Johanna was remembering the last time she had been to Earth, when she and Serassan had traveled undercover. There had been earthquakes and storms when the Dark Forces had attempted to implement the holocaust device that would have triggered a premature shift, resulting in death and destruction of the planet. She shuddered as she recalled all that had gone on, and how, in the midst of what was happening, she had gone into premature labor — like Planet Earth — and miscarried her first child.

"Do I have any relatives on Terra?" Crystal asked.

Johanna looked at Serassan. He said, "Yes, Crystal, your mother's brother is on Terra."

"His name is Manley," Johanna whispered.

"Anyone else?"

"As far as we know, your uncle is your only Terran relative," Serassan replied.

Johanna set the empty dish of frupagi down in front of her and picked up her napkin. This news of a shift had dropped an anchor on her heart. If only there was some way she could know for sure that Manley would be all right.

8

Sudden Darkness

After spending the night in a motel in central Nebraska, Blake was eager for his family to reach their destination. Everything they had discussed the day before in the car kept coming back to him. The fact that he had an aunt living on a different planet intrigued him, but that her husband was an extraterrestrial was totally mind-blowing. He couldn't get them out of his thoughts.

Manley was cruising west on the interstate and Dorothy sat in front this time. Blake sat in the back seat with Kelly, who watched out her window from her car seat and was busy babbling to all of them about everything she was seeing. Every time Blake caught his mother staring at him, she smiled and turned away. He guessed she was thinking about all that had been disclosed and he knew she was pleased that he had been able to accept all of it.

His mother had always been intuitive. He knew she was a healer. He remembered how, throughout his childhood, his mother had been closest to him the times he had been ill. He fondly recalled massages she had given him and the soothing touch of her hot hands. She had done wonders with his sister. At least that's what Dr. Barbara Wetzel had said with regard to Kelly's handicap.

Outside his window Blake watched the fields and fences. He had never seen Colorado. He hoped the scenery was better there, like everybody promised. He noticed off to the northwest the sky was rosy. It was a blue-skied morning with some wispy white clouds, just what you'd expect for early June. So why was it getting red around the horizon? He shrugged it off as some kind of strange weather pattern and leaned back and shut his eyes.

A few minutes later he opened them because Dad and Mom were talking excitedly.

"Manley, it's only ten forty-nine," his mother insisted. "Look at the car clock."

"I see," his father replied. "I don't get it."

Blake was surprised to see that it was actually getting dark outside. The redness around the horizon was in every direction and the light outside was growing dimmer.

"Do you suppose it could be a solar eclipse?" Dorothy asked.

Manley craned his neck to gaze at the sun as he drove, since the sun was on his side of the car. "I sure haven't heard about any solar eclipses happening lately," he replied.

Blake leaned forward. "What's going on? Why is it getting so dark?"

"And why is the sky such a strange color?" asked Dorothy.

"Did we experience missing time?" Manley wasn't joking. He appeared to be worried.

"Time fo' bed!" Kelly announced from her car seat.

"No, it's not," Blake reassured his sister. "Maybe we're going through some kind of a fog."

"Manley, let's turn on the radio." Dorothy reached over and pushed the power button.

"Good idea," he said. "Maybe we'll get some kind of explanation."

Static came from the radio. Outside the daylight was giving in to dusk and a dark red band of sky seemed to hang over the horizon.

"Manley, I think we should stop," Dorothy advised. She turned the dial in an attempt to find a station that they could listen to. "I really think we should turn off at the next exit. This is too weird!"

Blake didn't understand what was happening. It was growing darker and cars turned on their headlights. Some of the traffic had stopped along the side of the interstate, but Manley kept driving.

"I'll get off at the next exit," he said.

A staticky voice came through the radio just then. An announcer said, "The governor has issued a statement for everyone to stay in their homes. Martial law is in effect. I repeat, martial law is in effect. If you are listening to this broadcast, I urge you to stay where you are. If there is..." The static took over.

Dorothy fumbled with the dial to find another station.

"What in God's name is going on?" cried Manley. Ahead of

him the traffic had slowed and both lanes were clogged with vehicles.

"Mom, what do they mean about martial law?" Blake felt a lump in his throat. Fear was beginning to take hold of him.

People in other cars on the interstate appeared agitated. The flow of traffic moved slowly. Passing wasn't possible with both lanes practically bumper to bumper. Dorothy continued to try to find a radio station, but all they received was static.

"Dad, what are we gonna do?" asked Blake.

"There's not much we *can* do," said Manley. "Just keep driving."

Kelly began to cry. She seemed to understand that something unusual was happening and it frightened her. Dorothy turned her attention toward the six-year-old. Outside the window Blake watched people in other cars. They all seemed to be scared. Behind them a sports car was approaching on the shoulder, weaving its way past several vehicles. Cars began honking as if in protest, but soon others were following suit.

"Somebody's going to get themselves killed!" Manley rolled down his window.

It was almost completely dark out now. The sky was black except for that mysterious red glow around the horizon. It was now fading as well.

"I think the exit is just ahead," Manley said. "That's why all the traffic is backed up."

"Everyone wants to get off at the exit," said Blake. His body felt tense and his heart was racing.

Kelly was still crying. Dorothy fussed over her, but couldn't get the little girl to stop. The wailing was getting on their nerves.

"Manley, get us out of this nightmare," cried Dorothy. "Can't you do something?"

"I'm trying, I'm trying!"

"This can't be happening!" Dorothy suddenly burst into tears, which made Kelly scream even harder.

Blake leaned forward to touch his mother's shoulder. "Mom, calm down," he said. "It's going to be all right."

"How do you know?" Dorothy sobbed. "I think it's a pole shift! Oh Manley, drive faster!"

"I can't!"

"Mom, don't panic," said Blake. "It'll just make things worse."

"I know it's a pole shift," gasped Dorothy. "It's been predicted for years! Oh, we're all going to die!"

"*Mom...*" Blake pleaded.

Manley's voice rose. "You're losing it, Dorothy! We're not having a pole shift! How can it be a pole shift, for God's sake?"

"Then what happened to the sun?" Dorothy continued to sob. "We'll all die without the sun! Oh no, what if China exploded an atomic bomb? Maybe we're experiencing a nuclear winter!"

Her words chilled Blake's heart, but something inside of him urged him to speak. "Mom, stop it," he said. "You're getting worked up and for no reason. Believe me, we're not having a pole shift and there is no nuclear winter!"

To his surprise, she turned around and pulled him close, hugging him tight. "Thank you, Blake," she whispered as her sniffing subsided. "Of course you are both right." She let go and found a tissue in her purse. "There has to be some logical explanation."

Kelly's crying dwindled to a whimper as Manley reached the exit and they began to work their way down the exit lane. They hadn't gotten very far when suddenly the car died and the dash lights went out. Around them everything was pitch black. The other vehicles on the road had quit running and all their lights had gone out as well.

"Oh, God!" Dorothy began to whine.

"Shh," said Manley, "don't start."

Strangely enough, Kelly was silent for a minute. For a few seconds there was no sound. Blake was frightened now and couldn't speak. Then he heard the faint cries from people outside. Terror began to set in and it was contagious.

"Manley..." Dorothy's voice wavered.

"Let's all just remain calm," said Manley. "Blake, can you see anything?"

"It's too dark," said Blake.

"What happened to the lights?" asked Dorothy. She was fighting to control her fear.

"I don't know." Manley tried starting the car, but it wouldn't turn over.

"Dad, there's a flashlight in the glove compartment, isn't there?" Blake heard his mother fumbling around in the dark, trying to open the compartment.

"I've got it," she said. She clicked the flashlight several times. "It doesn't work! The battery must be dead."

"No, I just put new batteries in before we left Illinois," said Manley. "It can't be dead."

"Well, it's not working," said Dorothy.

"Mama..." Kelly began to cry again. "Scared... Mama!"

Blake put his arm around his sister. "It's okay, Kelly Belly."

"Dark," the little girl sobbed. "Dark!"

"I know."

Manley opened the car door.

"Where are you going?" Dorothy cried.

"The light doesn't even come on when I open the door," said Manley. From outside came cries from the people whose vehicles had stopped near theirs. Hysterical voices rose in the pitch black around them.

"Who's got a light?" a man called out.

"Flashlights don't work!" someone else shouted.

"Manley," Dorothy called nervously, "maybe you'd better stay in the car."

Blake remembered the lighter he carried in his pocket. He reached into his jeans and pulled out the disposable bit of plastic. After a couple of clicks he had a small flame lit that illuminated his face, Kelly's and their mother's.

Manley climbed back into the car. "Good idea, Blake."

The light went out. "I can't hold it open too long," said Blake and clicked it again.

"If only we had a candle," said Dorothy.

"Or a lantern," added Manley.

"Dad, are we carrying any flares?" asked Blake.

"Excellent." Manley got out of the car and groped his way to the back door to open the hatch. They began to notice little specks of light here and there as people found matches and lighters to quell the total blackness.

"It's starting to get cold," Dorothy said.

"The temperature must be dropping," said Blake.

"All we brought were sweaters," said Dorothy. "I hope it

doesn't get *too* cold."

Manley scrambled around in the back of the car and then returned to the driver's seat with the flare sticks. "Blake, let me see that lighter." Stepping outside, Manley lit a flare and the immediate area was filled with the blaze. He set the flare on the road beside their car and almost immediately other people began to gather, like moths drawn to a flame.

"You were certainly prepared," a woman remarked, wrapping a blanket around herself. Two small boys stood beside her, shivering in jackets.

"Somebody ought to start a bonfire," a man suggested.

"Hey, you got any more of those things?" A husky figure of a man moved into the fringe of the light. He wore coveralls and had a black, frizzy beard.

"Only three," said Manley.

"Give 'em here," the man said gruffly.

"I don't think that's a very good idea," Manley replied. "I'm sure it's not wise to burn more than one at a time. We have no idea how long..."

"I said give 'em here!" The husky man lurched toward Manley, who held the three remaining sticks behind his back.

Blake got out of the car and instinctively grabbed the flares away from his father. Then he moved away from the men.

"Hey, kid, give me those flares!" the man commanded.

"Now let's be reasonable about this," Manley began. "Blake, get back in the car." Keeping his voice calm, Manley closed the car door on the driver's side.

Without hesitation Blake swung around the front of the car and hopped into the back seat with the flares.

"No, you don't! Give me those sticks!" The husky man with the beard pushed Manley against the car and tried to open Kelly's door, but it was locked.

"Manley!" Dorothy cried in terror.

"Mom, lock the door!" shouted Blake.

Kelly began screaming.

"What about your father?"

"Just do it!" Blake locked his own door.

The man moved quickly and managed to get Manley's door open before Dorothy could lock it. Then Manley grabbed the big man and pulled him away from the car. The man swung at Manley, who anticipated the reaction and ducked as the man's fist punched through the car window, causing chunks of broken glass to fall inward.

Dorothy screamed and Blake jumped into action. He dove into the front seat and crawled out the driver's side, where the husky man slammed his fists into his father, who slumped to the ground and was covering his face. People in the small crowd were backing away from the scene. Blake leaped onto the man's back and tightened his hands around the man's neck.

"Stop hurting my dad!" he yelled.

"Blake! No! Somebody help us!" he heard his mother yell from inside the car.

Blake was tall and strong for his age, but soon discovered he was no match for this heavy brute. The man grabbed Blake's fingers and pried them painfully off himself, then hurled Blake onto the hard ground beside his writhing father. The next thing Blake knew, he was being kicked by the man. Sharp blows erupted on his hips and sides. Then he felt something rock hard hit him in the jaw, and everything went dark and cold.

9

Separated

In the minutes that followed the attack on her husband and her son, Dorothy Dobbs would remember two vivid things: a flash of blue light, and then the cluster of amber lights approaching from the distance.

She stood outside the motionless cars after the husky man in coveralls took off with the extra flares. In the dim light of the still-burning flares, on the pavement in front of her, lay her unconscious son. People from the other cars huddled around in the light of Manley's flare, some shouting, others milling about, visibly in a panic.

"Blake!" Dorothy crouched beside the boy as tears gushed from her eyes. He groaned a little as she placed her hand on his blond head. Thank God, he was coming around, she thought. Looking around the small crowd, she grew alarmed once again. "Manley!" she cried. "Manley, where are you?"

Just then the flash of blue light appeared directly above her. Dorothy stood up and noticed the bright blue luminous object that hovered above the car. The people around her gasped and began to back away.

The next thing she knew, a group of amber lights appeared—perhaps eight or nine of them—and as they grew larger in size, the roar of helicopters filled the air. The choppers were approaching.

"Manley!" Dorothy called. She started searching the crowd for him. The stranded motorists cheered when they saw the aerial display.

"The military will help us," someone called out.

"I think it's the National Guard," called out someone else.

"Hallelujah!" cried an elderly woman.

Amid the relieved chatter and excitement, Dorothy returned

to the spot next to her car and was startled to find Blake no longer lying on the roadway. She frantically called out for him. How could he have picked himself up so quickly after being knocked out cold? Where was he?

"Blake?" Dorothy cried. "Blake!"

Turning back to the car, she let out a shriek. Kelly's car seat was empty! The little girl, who had been strapped in moments ago, was no longer there.

Dorothy's heart pounded. She searched everywhere she could. She even looked under the car. Then she began pushing her way through the crowd that was focused only upon the amber helicopter lights that circled above them. In the din she could hear her own voice as she screamed out the names of her family members.

A uniformed man in a dark suit and helmet grabbed her. Dorothy was frantic. "Let me go!" she cried out.

"Move along," the soldier snapped as he led her along with some others toward a waiting helicopter.

"Where are you taking me?" cried Dorothy. "I can't go! My family is missing! My little girl needs me."

No one paid any attention to her. She was pushed onto the ship and forced to sit in a packed row of alarmed people. When she tried to get off, she was rudely shoved back down. Then, before she could do anything further, the craft was airborne and she and the others were being transported in the darkness to some unknown destination.

When Manley had recovered from the blow which had thrown him to the ground, he watched as the brutal man in coveralls struck Blake in the jaw, knocking the boy to the pavement. Then the man had grabbed up the extra flares and taken off. Enraged, Manley had run after the man, even though he could hear Dorothy screaming and calling after him. Adrenalin surged through his body and he felt a fury he had never experienced before. All he could think to do was stop that piece of scum any way he could.

The man had quickly vanished in the total darkness. All around him Manley heard voices and had to slow down as he bumped into stalled cars and ran into obstacles, some of them human as people stood outside their vehicles. It was useless. He couldn't see.

Turning, Manley strained his eyes to determine from which direction he had come. How was he going to find his way, in this cursed blackness, back to Dorothy and the kids? There were more than a few flares lit now, and it was hard to know which one was his. People shouted and moved around him, confusing him more.

Manley saw the blue flash of light and turned his head in that direction. He gazed in awe at a bright blue disc about the size of a Volkswagen, giving off a beautiful glow and suspended about fifteen feet in the air. It hovered for maybe eight or ten seconds, and then, suddenly, its light went out. It had vanished.

"What was it?" asked a teenage boy nearby.

"The hell if I know," an older man replied. "The hell if I know what's going on here."

Manley thought he'd grope his way toward the spot where he'd seen the blue flying object. But just then he caught sight of lights coming from another part of the sky. Helicopters were zooming in, their amber lights illuminating the ground over which they flew.

A new panic rose in Manley. He didn't understand why, but he felt compelled to get away from those choppers. Martial law had been declared. In his mind he envisioned rough men in camouflage, holding guns and ordering people around. He feared being herded like an animal and thrown into some managed care unit set aside for people like him who were involved with extraterrestrials.

As the helicopters began to land around them, Manley watched the frightened people gathering in the circling lights. Some expressed relief and gratitude, but not Manley. He needed a place to hide. Turning, he began to run away. He knew his best chance of escape would be to stay on the highway and weave his way in and out between the cars that were unable to move. He knew if he took off through a cornfield, choppers with their lights might find him.

When a helicopter flew near and the people began to cluster together, Manley dropped to the ground and rolled beneath a semi. He waited there on the gritty concrete, his body cold and aching, the smell of diesel and oil flooding his nostrils. There he lay, not daring to come out, while lights from the choppers revealed people being led away, some of them onto the roaring crafts that eventually lifted from the ground and flew off.

Probably half an hour passed before all grew quiet once more and there were no more lights. The drone of choppers faded in the distance. The wind blew and Manley crept slowly out of hiding, groping his way until he no longer felt the truck's chassis. He was out from beneath the semi now. The wind whipped his face and clothes. Total darkness was everywhere. Not a soul appeared to be around.

For the first time in his life, Manley was so scared, he wet himself.

10

Rescued

Blake stirred and opened his eyes. A soft humming sound vibrated all around him and he was propped on a recliner that was soft and comfortable. A blue, dim light filled the area he was in. As his eyes grew accustomed, he began to focus on his surroundings and saw walls that were rounded. He was in a small, dome-like room.

Familiar laughter erupted behind him. His sister, Kelly, was cackling in delight. Blake turned his head to look, but felt pain on his left jaw. He touched the tender spot on his face and remembered someone had hit him there. Kelly sat in a similar seat close to him, laughing and clapping her hands together.

Suddenly Blake saw the brilliant, phantom-like form of the Light Being from his dream. The figure was glowing like before — a male human form sitting and interacting with the six-year-old girl. Blake could only stare in astonishment.

"Blake! Look!" Kelly's eyes danced with excitement. "Look! It's a lightning man!"

The Light Being turned to Blake. Like before, it was difficult to make out any facial features. Blake detected a warm smile, however. He had the feeling that he and Kelly were safe and no harm would come to them. "Hello, Blake, my Terran friend," the Light Being said. Like before, his voice seemed to be more in Blake's head than coming from the figure's mouth.

"It's... it's you," Blake breathed.

"I'm getting acquainted with your small sister," he said. "What a beautiful soul she has."

Blake looked around. It appeared they were on board a flying saucer. A window revealed total blackness and a panel of controls jutted inward from the curved walls. The lights from the instrument panel changed colors and flickered off and on. The ship seemed to be flying itself. "Where are we?" Blake sat up straighter.

The Light Being had somehow caused a box of lights to appear in Kelly's hands. The toy displayed streaks of different colored lights and sounds that changed whenever she touched it. Kelly squealed with excitement as the luminous being turned to Blake. "You and your sister are on board my shuttle."

"You mean... we're flying?"

The Light Being nodded. "I told you that you were going into space. Do you remember?"

Blake rubbed his sore jaw. "Tell me how we got here," he said. "I must have gotten socked pretty hard." He then recalled the scene in which his father and the husky man were fighting over the flares. "What happened to the sky? Why did everything suddenly go dark?"

"One question at a time, my friend," said the Light Being. "Let's begin with how you got here. I picked you up, along with your sister."

"But what about..."

"I wasn't very far away," continued the Light Being. "In fact, I was following your vehicle."

"Yes, but... but what happened?" asked Blake. "The earth... the sun... *where the hell is the sun?* And how come there aren't any stars out that window?"

"Blake, do not be afraid. Terra has entered the Null Zone. It is temporary. Your star has gone nowhere. In three days there will be light — and such a light as you have never seen."

"The Null Zone? What's that?"

The Light Being smiled. "That's not what is important right now. What is important is that you are safe."

"What about my parents?" Blake grew worried.

"Ah yes, your parents." The Light Being seemed to sigh. "I had planned to rescue them as well. Unfortunately, troopers came and there wasn't time. I had to get out of the quadrant."

Kelly played with the light box and laughed. Blake was still trying to put things together in his mind. "L.B.," he said, recalling the name he had given the entity, "are my parents going to be okay?"

"That is a question I cannot answer," said the Light Being.

"Well, can't we go back and find them? I don't want to leave them on that exit... in total darkness. What will happen to them?"

The Light Being approached the shuttle's window and seemed to command the ship by his very thoughts. The saucer appeared to be swerving, but Blake felt only a trace of motion, and the black curtain of space did not change. "I must take you and your sister to safety now," L.B. explained. "That is my priority."

"And what about my mom and dad? Mom's probably worried out of her mind!"

"There is no immediate cause for concern," said L.B. "I will go back for them."

"Now?" Blake asked anxiously.

L.B. glanced at him, then back toward the window. "First I must procure a body. Then I will look for your parents."

"When will that be?" asked Blake.

"After I have taken human form, I can be of aid. Until that time, there is little I can do."

Blake did not understand. How could this entity have successfully picked up himself and Kelly, yet been unable to take his parents? What had he meant about *troopers*?

"There is danger," L.B. told Blake, as if he had read his thoughts. "Troopers were already on alert and had use of photon energy to light and power their crafts." He hesitated, then added, "You call them helicopters. But I assure you, my Terran friend, they were made to resemble helicopters to fool your people."

"I'm afraid you've lost me," Blake admitted. "Are you saying that the earth is under some sort of attack?"

"Your planet has been held hostage for quite some time," the Light Being explained. "Now that Terra has entered the Photon Belt, those that would exploit you Terrans have found a perfect opportunity. They are in control now."

Blake recalled what he knew about the Photon Belt. "I've heard about the Photon Belt," he said. "Mr. Lewis, our science teacher, used to talk about it. He said it was discovered by astronomers in 1961 and was a band of light particles — sort of like a huge doughnut in space — and he said someday it would reach our solar system."

The Light Being appeared to be busy concentrating on his navigation. Kelly was still captivated by her newfound toy. Blake settled back and let his thoughts unravel.

"So that's what this is all about," he murmured. "The sun entered the Photon Belt first, before the earth did, and so everything got suddenly dark. And all electrical devices quit working. That's why the cars all stopped running and the flashlight didn't work, even though Dad just put fresh batteries in it." He also remembered mention at some time by somebody that there would follow three days of darkness. He was quite sure it was in the *Bible*. The Light Being had called it the "Null Zone."

Blake sat up straight. "Hey, L.B., why did you rescue me and my sister? Where are you taking us?"

The Light Being finished his task at the controls and turned to Blake. "You will demonstrate to me how to be human," he said. "I've already learned a great deal from observing you."

"But... why me?" asked Blake. "There must be millions of guys like me you could have picked."

"You have the right connections," the Light Being replied.

Blake was puzzled. "What does that mean? What connections do I have?"

"You wanted to meet somebody from space, didn't you?"

Blake remembered that many times he had wished just that very thing.

"Be careful what you wish for," the Light Being continued. "You could have been contacted by those from the dark side. They have abducted thousands of you Terrans. They have used many of you for their ulterior motives and have created a great imbalance."

Blake sighed. He was tired all of a sudden and closed his eyes. His jaw throbbed and his mind was in a whirl from all that had happened. Somehow he would have to sort it all out.

11

Pillow Talk

It was one of those enchanting summer nights on Karos, when the stars felt close and shone brightly in the moonless black sky. The air was cool and crisp after a hot, arid day.

"Something has been on your mind." Serassan cradled Johanna's head against his shoulder as the two of them lay side by side in bed. The room was dark except for the long narrow window near the ceiling that let in starlight from outside their stone cottage.

Johanna sighed, content to be in Serassan's arms. She learned long ago that she could never keep anything from him. "You're right, something has been worrying me," she admitted.

"You are thinking about Terra," he guessed. "What Emrox said this afternoon has upset you greatly."

"Well, yes, that, too." Johanna sighed again. "Naturally, I'm concerned about Earth and about Manley. With the shift happening, I can't help but worry. Will my brother survive?" After a short silence, in which Serassan did not reply, she added, "But actually, Serassan, it's Crystal who's been on my mind today."

"Ah... Crystal. And what has our daughter done now?"

"Serassan, I think you should know. She plans to join the Estronian fleet."

Now it was Serassan's turn to release a sigh. "And when did she make this decision?" he asked.

"She told me this morning."

"I see." He gently unwrapped his arm from around her and pulled himself up into a sitting position.

Johanna sat up, too. "Serassan, we must stop her."

He reached for the light. "It would be a mistake for her to make space her career," agreed Serassan. "After all her training and hard work, it would be sorrowful indeed." The soft glow from the bedside lamp just barely illuminated their faces.

"She is being influenced," said Johanna.

"And perhaps she is acting a trifle rebelliously," added Serassan. "Isn't that a common trait in Terran adolescents?"

Johanna twisted around to face him. "Well, her Estronian half is what I'm worried about. I'm afraid she's turning into one of those competitive women on your planet."

She expected him to squirm, but instead he grinned. "My dear Johanna..." Serassan reached for her and drew her head against his chest. "No one warned us how hard it would be to raise a daughter who is half Terran and half Estronian."

"Oh, she hasn't been that bad." Johanna pouted. "If you could have seen what my brother had to put up with..."

He laughed. "I must remind Soolàn to fill you in on some of the tales when I was a boy."

"She already has." Johanna chuckled. "But at least you had the benefit of loving parents as well as being able to experience what your peers had to endure on Estron — in those concentration camps you call schools."

"Oh, my love, you do exaggerate." Serassan paused as he thought back through his younger years. "Our system of education on Estron is vastly different from what you experienced, yes. But there were far more advantages than you have imagined."

"From what you've told me," said Johanna, "you were lucky the authorities even allowed you to visit your parents on their planetoid."

"Emrox and Soolàn were outcasts, but not outlaws," Serassan replied. "They are both still highly respected."

"Maybe so, but hardly the examples your planet wanted for its citizens."

"Definite outcasts," said Serassan, "daring to marry and live a life together loving each other. Then to conceive a child!"

Johanna recalled that Soolàn, although Estronian by birth, had been raised on a planet where love and family had been held in high esteem. Her values were different from most women's on Estron, where competition and the work ethic mattered more than nurturing or caring for progeny. Marriages on Estron were practically unheard of, and reproduction was a process taken care of in laboratories because women were too involved in their careers to procreate. In many of them the sex drive had been eliminated through sheer willpower and chemical adjustments in their bodies.

"But I hear more women on Estron are wanting that kind of life now," said Johanna. "Things are starting to change."

"I'm afraid too slowly," added Serassan.

Johanna pondered a moment, then glanced at her husband's face, which hadn't seemed to age in the last nineteen years she had known him. "Serassan..."

"Yes, my love?"

"Are you happy that you married me and we settled here on Karos?"

He looked at her, his deep blue eyes full of love and light. "Johanna, what kind of question is that?"

"You could have gone on to be a high authority on your planet," she said. "You would have gone far and been respected and honored. Instead, you chose to live here with me and struggle through harsh conditions."

Serassan gently pulled her close and looked into her eyes. "Johanna, my life is what I've made it. I am happy here with you. Nothing else matters but that." He kissed her then, a deep and passionate embrace that melted all her doubts.

When he pulled away, Johanna asked, "Now... about Crystal... Serassan, what are we going to do?"

Serassan leaned back against the pillow. "Ah yes... Crystal."

"Can you talk to her? If not, perhaps Emrox can."

Serassan squeezed her hand. "I think Crystal needs to find herself. Our daughter thinks she has all the answers right now. Let her find out what her true destiny is."

"Are you saying we should allow her to go into space?" Johanna grew worried at the thought. "She has no idea what she's getting into or what lies ahead."

"As much as I, too, am against it, we must let her decide what her life is to be," he said.

Johanna was heartsick. "But all the years of music lessons and training. How can she throw all of that away?"

"It is a risk we must take," said Serassan.

"But, she'll listen to you. Talk to her."

"What makes you think Crystal will listen to me?"

"Because she adores her father." Johanna shrugged. "She can't stand her mother."

"Stop that, Johanna. That's a falsehood."

Johanna bit her lip. A tear formed in the corner of her eye. "I'm sorry, it's just that... sometimes I feel like she... well, she talks back to me a lot." She blinked her eyes. "It was you who she always went to when something was wrong. Not me."

Serassan shook his head. "I don't want to start a quarrel, my love, but wasn't it you who made her this way?"

"Me?" Johanna tensed up. "Serassan, you spoil her rotten!"

"But you've always disciplined her so hard," said Serassan. "Long hours of practice and strict rules. No wonder she resents it."

"Well, someone had to keep her in line." Johanna felt a lump in her throat as hot tears pushed under her eyelids. "Music requires great discipline. Talent is developed from hours and hours and years and years of hard work. I should know!"

"You should know, of course," he said gently and put his hand on her face to wipe away the tears. "Crystal couldn't have a more perfect mother. And one day... one day, Johanna, she will wake up and realize it." He reached for the light and dimmed the glow back to darkness. "And now, my love, we must sleep. We have a big day ahead of us with the grand opening. I'm sorry if I upset you."

Johanna snuggled down against him and sniffled. "You're right, Serassan... as always. We must let Crystal choose her own path. Good night."

"I love you, Johanna, my Special One."

She closed her eyes and murmured softly, "My love is yours... always."

12

Incarcerated

Dorothy awoke from a fitful sleep. It was dark and cold. Others were around her because she could hear their moans, breathing noises and occasional coughing. The smell of body odors surrounded her as well. She was lying on something firm and a coarse blanket kept her body warm. As her consciousness cleared, she struggled to remember what had happened and why she was here.

Slowly her memory started bringing back the pieces. She remembered being in the car with her family, and then it had gotten suddenly dark while it was still mid-morning. She then remembered the panic she'd felt and how Blake had tried to pacify her. The car had stopped on the interstate exit and then Manley had gotten into a fight with that man who stole the flares. In a flash she recalled Blake being knocked unconscious, Kelly screaming, the blue light, and then the helicopters.

She didn't recall anything after being pushed onto one of the huge helicopters with a bunch of other people. As it had lifted off the ground, a strange dizziness had seized her. Whatever happened next was not coming back to her.

Dorothy attempted to sit up in the darkness. She was weary from sleep, but aware of hunger, thirst and the need to relieve herself. A flicker of light, as if from a fire, came from the distance and allowed her eyes to barely make out her surroundings. She was in some kind of structure, almost like a warehouse, and others were lying on mats with blankets all around her. As she struggled out of the blanket, she hit something heavy with her foot and gasped when it moved. It was the person lying next to her.

"Oh God," Dorothy cried, "what is this? What am I doing here?"

"Sppsst." Someone on the other side of her hissed. "What's your name?" It was the voice of an older woman right next to her.

"I'm... I'm Dorothy... Dorothy Dobbs."

"Well, I'm Louise," said the woman. "Did you come on the chopper?"

"I... I think so. I really don't remember," said Dorothy.

"They gassed you," said Louise. "They did it to some of us, not all."

"Who? Who are they?" Dorothy asked.

"The ones in charge here," said Louise. "The military, perhaps? The National Guard? Who knows?" She moved closer to Dorothy. "From what I can determine, we're all women here."

"Women?" Dorothy was confused.

"In this particular camp," said Louise. "We're all in a camp of some kind. They took the men elsewhere. I don't know where my husband is."

Dorothy saw that the light in the distance appeared to be some kind of campfire. "I don't know where any of my family is," she said. "I've got to find them."

"If the helicopters came, rest assured they've been taken to similar camps. But why they had to separate families is beyond me."

Dorothy tried to stand. She was quite wobbly. "I've got to go," she said.

"It's outside," directed Louise. "Be careful. There are sleepers all over the floor. Here, let me come with you. I know the way."

Dorothy was grateful to have a companion to help her toward the outside. A couple of times she nearly stumbled over resting bodies on the floor in front of her.

Finally, they came to an opening in the wall which led outside. A large fire pit provided heat and some light. People stood around it, huddled together with blankets wrapped around their heads and bodies. Dorothy saw Louise's face in the firelight. The older woman was tall and wiry with gray curly hair and bright eyes. She pointed toward some structures which appeared to be outhouses.

Dorothy hurried over and found the first one occupied. The next one was available. After she was through, she stumbled out into the cold and looked around. Louise was no longer standing in the same place.

"Move on to the mess tent," a voice commanded.

Dorothy turned and saw a hefty woman in a camouflaged uniform and jacket. The woman's voice was stern as she pointed Dorothy in the direction of a tent set up behind the campfire. Dorothy did what she was told and soon found herself inside where kerosene lamps provided light and women shuffled alongside a serving table. Others were seated at long tables with benches, eating out of metal plates and mugs.

Someone handed Dorothy a bowl, spoon and mug and she got in line. The conversation around her was low and guarded. Everyone's main preoccupation seemed to be getting some food and drink and finding a place to sit.

Still groggy from sleep, Dorothy welcomed the smell of oatmeal and toast. She spooned some of the gruel onto her plate and filled her mug with coffee from a huge urn. Unbuttered toast was stacked on a plate and Dorothy took two pieces. She looked around and found an empty place at a table near the doorway. She sat down, shivering from cold, and drank long hot sips of the coffee, using both her hands around the mug in an effort to warm her fingers. She was still too much in shock to think straight.

"Bad dream," muttered a woman across the table, who stared, glassy-eyed, at Dorothy. "That's all this is, you know... a bad, bad dream."

Dorothy didn't reply. She looked around at the other women, some as numb and confused as she was, others too busy eating to care about anyone else.

"Oh Dorothy, there you are." Louise approached the table with a bowl and mug and took the seat next to her. "I brought your blanket. Here, wrap it around yourself and you won't be so cold."

Dorothy took the wool blanket Louise handed her. "Thank you." She stood up to drape it around her shoulders, then took her seat.

"Are you all right, hon?" Louise was gentle and Dorothy welcomed her soothing voice.

"I don't know." Dorothy managed a smile. She felt as if she were going to burst into tears and quickly sipped more of the coffee. "I'd sure like to know what is going on... why we're here... why it's dark and cold."

"Shh, don't ask too many questions," cautioned Louise. Her eyes darted right and left. "There are ears everywhere."

Dorothy wondered what that meant. She followed Louise's example and the two of them ate their oatmeal in silence, aware of camouflaged military women passing by now and then. Dorothy felt like asking one of these soldier ladies what was happening, but Louise kept giving her warning looks. Once Dorothy heard two of the soldiers in conversation. One said, "I think most are awake now. Maybe we should notify headquarters." The other one responded, "Not yet, Sergeant. We're expecting one more load of refugees."

When Dorothy had finished her meal, she got up to get another cup of coffee, then returned to the table with Louise. "I can't stay here," she said. "I've got to find my little girl and my son."

"Where will you look?" asked Louise. "You are miles from where you were. And you can't see in the darkness."

"But it will be daylight soon," insisted Dorothy.

"No, it won't," said Louise.

Dorothy was confused. "But... of course it will."

"No, there is no night and day. Your best bet is to stay here. We're at least safe for the moment."

"Louise, you're talking in riddles!"

Louise pulled her closer. "Calm down, dear. I wasn't gassed like you. I didn't resist, you see. That's why I know more than you do. I've been able to pick up information here and there over the last two days."

"What are you talking about?" asked Dorothy.

"Most of you have been asleep for the last two days," Louise explained in a low voice. "You see, they didn't want you to panic. So many people would have, you know. That's why they gassed you. Are you feeling better now?"

Dorothy felt much better after eating, but she was still cold and uncomfortable. Nothing was clear to her yet. She clung to Louise, though. Somehow this woman seemed to understand and was a comfort in her confusion.

"Yes, I'm okay," she said.

"Good. We'll talk more in a while."

Dorothy wanted to find out what was happening in the world

before deciding what to do next. She desperately needed to find her family, but for now she let Louise reach out and pull her close. It felt good just to have a warm body to rest against, even a stranger's.

13

Desolation

Manley had at first been completely disoriented. He was alone in total blackness with cold wind whipping his bare face, his head and hands. No one was around. All the people had been collected by the helicopters and he didn't know where to turn. Fear gripped him, but he refused to let panic overtake his common sense. Manley had enough wisdom to know that he was never totally alone. And so he did the one thing he knew to do in such a situation. He began to talk to the Creator.

"I know there is a reason for everything," he began as he rubbed his hands together for warmth. "But I am scared, God. I mean, *really* scared. This is so out of reality, I don't know what to make of it. So please, please help me now. Help me at least to understand what is going on and how I can make the best of this unfortunate predicament."

His teeth began to chatter. He would not allow his mind to think the worst. "There has to be some shelter somewhere," he reasoned. "We got off on the exit. Somewhere there's going to be a gas station, or a convenience store... something. I just have to find it. Then I can at least be warm."

Manley knew that shelter was his prime concern at the moment. He steered his thoughts away from trying to rationalize what catastrophic event might have happened to the earth and the sun, and began walking with his hands out in front of him. He knew there would be obstacles that he couldn't see. He would have to keep his faith and feel his way to safety.

"Loving Spirit," he continued, "if I am to continue, then please show me the way. But if it is my time to leave this world, then so be it." His voice cracked as he staggered forward in the dark. He stopped when doubts began to form in his mind. What if he was heading in the wrong direction? What if he wandered away from civilization and froze to death?

"God, forgive me," Manley muttered. "I know You in Your infinite wisdom will help those who help themselves." He brought his clenched fists together and blew his warm breath onto his stiff fingers. Then he closed his eyes and began taking deep breaths. "Point me in the right direction, Spirit," he murmured.

The deep breathing was a calming technique he had learned. By relaxing his mind and pushing out the negative thoughts, he would be able to reach that deep center within himself where the answers could be found.

In a flash he saw in his mind's eye Dorothy's stricken face, crying out to him while he had struggled with the man in coveralls. He quickly dismissed it and whispered, "Everything is okay, Dorothy." Then he saw his son jumping on the attacker's back. "Blake, no..." He drove that image from his mind as well and began a mantrum. "Be the love," he chanted into his fists. "Be the love... be the love... be the love..."

Several minutes passed and finally Manley felt calm, even though he was still cold and the blackness surrounded him. He continued thinking in his mind, "Be the love..." and finally he opened his eyes and waited. "Thank you, God," he whispered.

Even before he finished saying the words, a distant flicker of light appeared in front of him. It was extremely dim, but it was at least something. Manley started toward the light and felt renewed hope and joy. It was far away—miles, perhaps, but God had given him a beacon and he would follow it.

Along the way he encountered several solid objects and often stumbled and had to pick himself up. But he kept moving. He had no other choice. The light continued to flicker faintly what seemed to be a long distance away. Manley followed it, keeping the mantrum in his mind so as to keep panic at bay. He soon lost his awareness of time and place. All that mattered was getting to the light. He knew that the light was his only hope.

Blake didn't remember when he had drifted off to sleep, or for how long he had slept. He only knew it had been a restful sleep and he was relaxed and warm. He opened his eyes and saw that he was still on the Light Being's small ship. L.B. stood at the controls, his opaque form almost shimmering in its brightness. He was not a tall being, maybe five feet at the most, and his back was to Blake. The lights were a mixture of colors that reminded Blake of swarming electrons or a lot of noise on a television screen in between channels.

Kelly was sleeping in the recliner chair behind him. The little girl looked angelic and Blake sighed, relieved that his sister was safe. Her little mouth was shaped like an O and her round cheeks tinged with pink. Kelly's mongoloid features were not as severe as some children's with Downs Syndrome. She had light brown hair below her ears with bangs above her thick eyebrows.

Then Blake noticed the window. There were now stars visible. He touched his sore jaw and nursed it gently with a fingertip.

L.B. turned to him. "We are approaching the mother ship," he said, the words again forming only in Blake's mind. "There you will find what you need to sustain yourselves."

Blake rubbed an eye. "You mean food?"

"Nourishment for your bodies," said L.B., "as well as others who will assist you."

"Others? Who?" asked Blake.

"Others," L.B. replied.

Blake watched as the shuttle drew toward a huge vessel in space that appeared outside the window. The craft was long and cylindrical, glowing in a soft silver light of its own. There were many levels of lights which Blake perceived to be windows on different decks. He was startled to see a small flying saucer glide across the screen on its way to dock with the huge ship.

"Wow!" Blake was excited about getting to see what was inside that mother ship. It was hard to believe that he was not dreaming. He sat, glued to the window, as they flew past the side of the huge silver ship that was like a horizontal skyscraper in space. Finally, they slowed and entered through a huge opening in the ship. Blake saw lots of smaller spacecraft of various sizes and shapes, and was reminded of a large hangar. The shuttle kept moving until the Light Being pulled them into a docking area of their own.

Kelly awoke and began squirming in her heat. Blake turned to comfort her. "It's okay, Kelly."

"Mama," Kelly said.

"She's not here," said Blake, "but you're all right. Don't cry."

Dress rehearsal for opening night at the new Galactic Center for the Performing Arts was a bit chaotic. Crystal had withdrawn to the dressing room to keep from being embarrassed on account of her mother. Johanna was having quite a time getting everything organized. Since Crystal had always thought of her mother as structured and disciplined, it bothered her to see her in disarray.

She wouldn't be needed for some time yet, so Crystal sat in front of the mirror and studied herself.

Her long golden curls cascaded over her bare shoulders, and her slender figure emphasized her maturing bosom in the glittery silver strapless gown that sparkled with tiny gems. She realized just then how grown up she looked and what a pretty face she had, in Terran terms. Her Estronian features, like her father's, had been altered so that her resemblance to her paternal side was hidden. This had been necessary, she knew, in order for her to survive physically on Karos with her parents and other humans.

The sparkles of light reflecting on her dress suddenly brought to her mind the memory of the other night, when she had experienced that strange golden light hovering over her. She remembered clearly its small round presence, a dazzling yellow light that burned in mid-air just above her face, and how it had seemed to be alive. What was it? What did it want with her? Why hadn't she thought much about it until just now? Why, she had practically forgotten about it the next morning. It had been like some vague memory that stirs at the least prompting, like a forgotten dream image that returns for a brief second only to dissipate.

Somehow the idea came to her that the bright object had something to do with space and possibly her future. Crystal's main objective was to have a space career, to be a scientific astronaut and travel vast distances to study the stars and expand her horizons as in her dreams. It would be a challenge, there was no doubt about that. She found the other girls at school hard to compete with, especially the girls who had been raised on Estron. They were geared to outdo their peers, where human girls their age were more interested in social games and the excitement of their quickly maturing bodies.

Crystal had human friends, but she thought they were often ridiculous and overly concerned with things such as clothes, hair, and particularly males. She preferred the no-nonsense mindset of the Estronian girls, who enjoyed ridiculing their male peers and who put themselves above the rest. They were dignified and she couldn't help but look up to them.

A noise started Crystal. She spun around and saw an Estronian man watching her from outside the dressing room. He was not as tall as her father and had a solid build. He stared at her with slanted blue eyes that wrapped around the sides of his bulbous, grayish-white head with no hair. His mouth slit was rather crooked and he had a sly appearance that put her immediately on guard. He was dressed casually in a black tunic with silver trim.

"Please excuse me," he said. He spoke the Estronian language, which she was fluent in as well as her mother's English. "I was passing by and couldn't help but notice you."

"Who are you?" Crystal rose to her feet and her gown made a gentle tinkling sound. She wasn't used to having visitors enter her dressing room. There was just a hint of something sinister about this alien man that triggered caution in her.

"Allow me to introduce myself, madam."

"I am *not* a madam." Crystal frowned in annoyance.

"Do pardon me," he said quickly. "My name is Thorden. I am from the Planet Estron. I am an old friend of your father's." His eyes dropped lustily over her womanly figure and he smiled with his mouth slit tight and taunting. "What a lovely specimen you turned out to be..."

"Specimen!" Crystal wrinkled up her nose in disgust. "Please go away, Mr. Thorden. Patrons are not supposed to be backstage, you know."

Thorden thrust his hands out in protest. "I'm not making a very good impression. I can see that. I just wanted to sneak a quick peek is all. I have always been fond of... *talented* women."

Crystal did not like the way he talked, much less the leer he bestowed upon her. A shiver of loathing shot through her.

Footsteps sounded and suddenly Johanna appeared in the doorway to Crystal's dressing room. "Crystal..." She stopped and her brown eyes grew huge as she regarded the Estronian man standing between herself and her daughter. "Oh!" she exclaimed.

"Johanna..." Thorden reached for her hand and bent his head forward to touch his mouth slit to the back of her wrist.

"Thorden?" Johanna pulled her hand away. Crystal could see her mother had been startled by the man's appearance, possibly even afraid.

"Yes, it is I, Johanna, lovely Johanna. You are as beautiful as ever, my dear." Thorden glanced at Crystal. "And your lovely daughter is splendid indeed... just splendid!"

Crystal stepped closer to her mother, who seemed to recover

her manners after a few seconds and offered a somewhat cordial smile. "Thorden, what a surprise. What are you doing on Karos?"

"I heard about the opening," he said. "I heard that you and Serassan were instrumental in making the galactic performing arts center a reality. I have come to congratulate you and pay my respects."

Johanna put her hand on Crystal's shoulder and began to lead her away. "That is wonderful, Thorden. But Crystal is needed on stage. This is our final rehearsal before the grand opening. Come along, Crystal."

For once Crystal didn't protest at her mother's bidding. The man, Thorden, made her feel uncomfortable, as if his eyes could see what she looked like underneath her sparkly gown. She followed Johanna through the corridor.

"Who is Thorden, Mother?" she asked.

"It's a long story, Crystal. I'll tell you later."

"But, Mother..."

"He was on the mother ship that I was on when your father brought me to Karos."

"How come you and Father never mentioned him?"

Johanna waved her hand as if to dismiss the subject. "Let's not discuss it now. You're about to go on." Then, with an apologetic smile, Johanna added, "Don't give a second thought to Thorden."

14

Blue Jay

The spacecraft had docked and L.B. instructed Blake on how to disembark. Blake took his sister's hand after helping her out of her chair. Together they walked through the portal that opened automatically for them, revealing a short ramp that led onto the hangar. L.B. remained on the ship, but Blake knew without being told that he would see his unusual friend again.

L.B. had said he was to go to the entrance marked for visitors. Blake saw a sign in lights that had many different languages, some that resembled hieroglyphic symbols. The words "Welcome Visitors" was in English, and he led Kelly toward that archway.

No one seemed to be in the hangar, but there were many space vehicles, smaller and larger shuttlecraft than L.B.'s ship. Outside huge windows Blake could see stars and the blackness of space. Kelly didn't seem to be afraid of any of this as long as she was clutching Blake's hand. The little girl made no protest as they walked into the wide corridor inside the mother ship.

Blake saw people in this corridor. They were walking in both directions, and their sizes and shapes varied. He was startled by a couple of small grayish humanoids with large bald heads and black wrap-around eyes. He had seen such beings on covers of his Dad's UFO books. Some of the humanoids looked just like ordinary people, while others were extremely tall or remarkably short. Most of them looked at him as he led his sister down the corridor.

Some humanoids watched from doorways as Blake led Kelly down the corridor. His heart was beating quickly. He didn't know where he was supposed to go, and the strangely dressed observers with their unusual features unnerved him a little. He was glad the aliens did not seem to frighten Kelly.

"Ah, children," a female voice called out.

Blake turned his head and saw a woman approach from behind. She was human with long blond hair, narrow gray eyes and a straight nose. Smiling, she appeared to be in her mid-twenties. She wore a long blue skirt and a tight T-shirt made of a glittery gold material.

"Welcome, my young Terrans." Her voice was warm and musical. Blake immediately liked her without understanding why. She caught up with them and put her hand on Kelly's head. "Hello. I am Greta. I will escort you."

"My name's Blake. Blake Dobbs. And this is my sister, Kelly." Blake almost added, "She's mentally retarded," but he thought better of it.

"Aren't you a brave girl?" Greta bent over at the waist and took Kelly's cheeks in her hands. "Do you know where you are, Kelly?"

The little girl shook her head slowly.

"Well..." Greta laughed and stood up straight. "You're on a big spaceship. But it's a very nice place, and there are lots of friendly and helpful people who are going to take good care of you."

Blake sighed, looking around. Some of the humanoids in the passageway had moved on while a few others lingered out of curiosity.

"Follow me, Blake Dobbs. You look like you could use some freshening up, and I quite imagine you are hungry."

Blake felt his sore jaw and could just imagine how disheveled he must look. He was starved and was sure his sister was hungry as well. He let Greta walk them down another hallway, where they continued through another corridor on the ship.

"I am from Earth, too," Greta disclosed.

Blake looked up in surprise. "You are?"

"But yes, of course. Oh, it's a long story. You'd be surprised, really, how many of us here came from Terra. And I love what I do — greeting people who arrive on the ship." She laughed again.

"What were you... *abducted* or something?" Blake asked.

Greta twittered. "Now why would you think that? Oh, but of course... TV... and movies! No, I am not an abductee. This way, please." She motioned them toward an escalator that was sloped, without any steps. It started moving them to a higher level on the ship.

"I just wondered," said Blake, "how you got here."

"I come and go often," replied Greta. "A shuttle takes me to Earth now and then. But I'm sure you want to know how I came to be here in the first place."

"Yes, that's what I meant."

"I'll tell you then. I used to dream of being in space. I prayed for it. I wished for it more than anything else since I was a little girl," she said, the dreamy smile still stretched across her face. "And then, one night, they brought me here."

"Who did?" asked Blake.

"My friends. They were Sirians."

Blake saw that they were approaching the next level. Still holding Kelly's hand, he stepped off the ramp.

"I volunteered for this," Greta told him, "and because I wanted it so much, the space people came and brought me here."

They began to walk toward a large circular room. It appeared to be some kind of lounge, with lots of chairs and corners where people could sit, with tables and plants and water fountains. The room was dimly lit with a maroon color. Blake could make out mellow jazz tones coming from somewhere. He noticed some beings sitting around conversing. He felt strangely at ease.

Greta led them to a counter behind which a man stood up to greet them. He was black-skinned with short curly hair and a pleasant face.

"Blue Jay, what have you got for a couple of hungry children?" Greta asked him.

The black man smiled broadly. "Hello. Welcome to space." He bent down to greet Kelly. "How are you, young lady?"

Kelly suddenly began to cry. Blake realized his sister was overwhelmed by this strange new environment and was no doubt missing their parents.

Greta wrapped her arms around the little girl. "Maybe I'd better just take her to the infirmary," she said as Kelly cried harder. Turning to Blake, she said, "Why don't you stay here and let Blue Jay fix you something to eat?"

It was with some reluctance that Blake agreed to let the blond-haired woman take his sister away. But he was feeling too wiped out to object. The young black man stood with him as he watched Greta leave with the sobbing Kelly.

"It's okay, man, she's in good hands," said Blue Jay. He wiped his hands with a towel. "Hey, sit down over there and rest. I'll bring you out some grub. Anything you want..."

Blake thought a moment. "You got any pizza?"

Blue Jay grinned, revealing straight white teeth that seemed to sparkle in contrast to his face. "Only the best in the galaxy. Go sit down. I'll bring it right out."

Blake found a small table nearby and sat down. The music soothed him, and he was really getting into the rhythm of it. Before he knew it, Blue Jay set a round pan down at the table and lifted the cover to reveal a steaming cheese-covered pizza with tomato sauce, vegetables and different nuggets of meat. Blake had never seen a more scrumptious pizza, and the aroma was heavenly. His mouth began to water.

"Thanks," he said.

"No problem." Blue Jay lingered, then asked, "Hey, do you mind if I join you a minute?"

"Please do." Blake reached for a napkin. "Here, have some of this. I'm sure I can't eat the whole thing."

Blue Jay laughed. "I would, but I just ate. Man, you look like you've kicked some ass."

Blake rubbed his jaw. "Is it bruised?"

"Not too bad," said Blue Jay. "I seen worse... a lot worse."

Blake tasted the pizza, which was even better than it smelled. He began to eat heartily.

"Let me get you something to wash that down." Blue Jay left and returned in a flash with a glass vessel.

"Will my sister get to eat?" asked Blake.

"Oh sure," said Blue Jay. "She's in good hands." Then he added, "You two are a lot luckier than the rest of the folks on your planet right now."

Blake continued to eat and drink. A fruity carbonated juice was in the glass vessel. "Yeah, what happened down there?" he managed to ask. "I mean, one minute it was mid-morning, and the next thing I knew, it was night!"

"Yes, I know," said Blue Jay, "sort of like a time warp thing."

"Is that what it was?" asked Blake.

"What do you remember?" asked Blue Jay.

"The last thing I remember is that dork hitting me," said Blake. "He attacked my dad and I sort of went crazy myself." He chewed awhile, then said, "Next thing I knew, I was in some kind of spaceship with my dream pal, L.B."

"Dream pal?"

"Yeah," said Blake. "He was in my dream the other night. At least... I *thought* it was a dream. It was so *real*. Now I'm not sure what it was, because I'm either in a dream now or I'm hallucinating."

Blue Jay chuckled. "You think this pizza is part of your dream?"

Blake shook his head. "No way. I've never tasted pizza this good before. This cheese is out of this world." He caught the look in the black man's eye and reached for his drink. "Do you know L.B.?"

"Who?" asked Blue Jay. "Oh, you mean the pilot?"

Blake nodded.

Blue Jay shook his head slowly. "No. There were some early rescues took place. You were one of the lucky ones that got picked up."

"What is happening on Earth?" Blake wanted to know.

The young black man stuck a toothpick between his lips and sighed. "Earth's in the Null Zone," said Blue Jay. "But it's only temporary. The darkness lasts three days."

"We read about the Photon Belt in school," said Blake, "but everyone thought it was just science fiction."

Blue Jay laughed. He was easy to be around, so calm and laid back. Blake liked him.

"Why are you called Blue Jay?"

The black man stretched one of his arms across the backrest where some plants separated the table from another booth. "I came here pretty much the same as Greta," he said. "Same as a lotta folks. Been here five years now. Been preparing for this time so's I can help folks like you."

"Well, where did you come from?" asked Blake.

"Chicago."

"Hey, that's not far from my hometown," said Blake. "I grew up in DeKalb."

"No kidding?" Blue Jay's eyes brightened.

"Yeah, but we were moving to Colorado when this

happened."

"Where in Colorado?"

"I don't know. Somewhere in the mountains, my dad said." Then he added, "He got the message."

"Oh." Blue Jay didn't comment further. "What's your name?"

"Blake."

"You in school?"

"Just got out. I'll graduate from high school in one more year."

"Got more education here than I could'a ever had on Earth," Blue Jay remarked. "I'm workin' on my second college degree."

"That's cool," said Blake. "Hey, what kind of name is Blue Jay, anyway?"

"Name was Jay Harris on Earth, but somewhere along the way I became *Blue* Jay Harris." He laughed. "Since I dig the blues... that's why I work in this lounge."

Blake wiped his mouth with his napkin. "I'm a musician. I play the blues."

"Guitar player?"

"How'd you guess?"

Blake picked up one of Blake's wrists and turned it over. "Your calluses, man."

"What instrument do *you* play?" asked Blake.

Blue Jay pulled a harmonica out of his back pocket and immediately played a scale.

"Hey," said Blake, "we could jam... only... I don't have my guitar."

"No problem," said Blue Jay. "We got plenty of those on the ship. Hey, you ready for me to show you your cabin? You really oughta get some rest. We can get together later."

That sounded perfect to Blake. He was tired and let Blue Jay lead him to the section of the ship where there were guest quarters. He was shown a small cabin that contained a bunk bed and a small bathroom with a shower. A port hole in the wall revealed the blackness of space and the stars. Blue Jay showed him where to call for assistance, should he need any, using a small intercom device built into the wall near the doorway. Then he told him someone would come around in an hour or so to check on him.

"Don't worry about anything," Blue Jay said before he left. "You and your sister are in the best hands."

Blake had no choice but to trust his new friend. After Blue Jay left, he sat on the bed and just tried to absorb all that had happened to him since that morning. It had been an amazing day. He had to assume that his parents had been rescued by a similar shuttle and were perhaps aboard this very spacecraft. Tomorrow they would find each other and all would be well. But for now, he just wanted to take off his clothes and climb beneath the sheets of his beckoning bed.

15
Campfire chat

Manley was numb with cold as he stumbled in the dark through the last section of a cornfield toward the flickering firelight. A campfire burned next to a roadside, where two male figures crouched and appeared to be cooking something over the fire. They both stood as he came into earshot. Both men were young — in their twenties — and dressed in sweat pants and warm shirts. The tall, thin one had dark, shoulder-length hair and a trimmed beard and wore glasses. His companion was of medium height, husky, and blond-headed.

Manley was exhausted and cold, but also thirsty. He had trekked blindly for hours and had no concept of time, since the blackness was constant. He nearly fell on his face as he reached the campfire, his breathing irregular and labored.

"Steady, man," called out the dark-haired guy with the beard. "Here, let me help you." He reached out an arm and kept Manley from losing his balance.

"Sit down and rest," invited the blond guy. "Would you like some coffee?" He handed Manley a white Styrofoam cup that steamed in the frigid air.

Manley welcomed their hospitality and sat on the ground between the two men. The warmth of the fire soothed his aching muscles and he pressed the fragile cup to his trembling lips, then closed his eyes as he sipped the hot drink. It wasn't the best tasting java he'd come across after crossing a cornfield in the dark, but it was hot and wet and he thanked the Creator.

"What's your name?" asked the blond guy.

When he could control his breath again, Manley said, "Dobbs. Manley Dobbs."

"I'm Joe," said the dark-haired guy, "and this is Kevin."

"I saw your fire," puffed Manley, "miles away. I've been walking... a long time."

Joe knelt over the fire and turned his stick, which held a lump of meat of some kind. "Anyone else with you?" he asked.

"No," said Manley. "The choppers came. They took my wife and kids."

"And not you?" asked Kevin. He was stirring some kind of vegetable in a small stainless steel pot.

"I managed to run." Manley swallowed half the coffee. "Maybe I should have stayed. I just... panicked. I don't really know why." His shoulders began to heave as emotions overcame him. He felt as though he had deserted his family. How would he ever find them?

"We hid from the rescuers, too," said Joe.

Kevin picked up the camp coffeepot and poured more of the drink into Manley's cup. "We're biking across the Plains," he explained. "At least we were until this happened."

"You're very lucky you have survival equipment with you," noted Manley.

"Yeah," agreed Joe. "When we saw what was happening, we took cover fast. Figured the feds would nab us like everyone else."

"The feds?" asked Manley.

"The National Guard then," corrected Kevin.

"How come you didn't want them to find you?" Manley knew he was being bold asking such a question.

"Why didn't *you*?" Joe retaliated.

Manley sighed. "Like I said, I panicked."

"Instinct," said Kevin. "That's what it was. I'm the independent sort. I don't appreciate being told where to go in a national disaster."

Joe smirked. "You don't appreciate being told where to go *any* time," he added.

"I guess I've been told where to go more often than I want to admit," said Kevin, and the two of them laughed.

After a short pause, Manley said, "I take it you guys have some kind of clue as to what has taken place." He continued to sip at his coffee.

"Not really," said Joe. "Do you?"

Both men were looking at him for an answer. Manley

wondered how he was going to put it into words, when he wasn't even sure himself what had happened. "Well," he said, "most people didn't believe in it." He looked at his companions. "But we were warned."

He was met with expectant silence.

"Sorry. I don't mean to sound so esoteric," he continued. "You guys probably never heard of the Photon Belt."

Joe retrieved his meat and checked it over to see how done it was. "You see, Kevin, I told you there was a good explanation." He wasn't laughing as he turned to face Manley. "You see, Kevin was scared shitless. He thought a nuclear winter had occurred."

Kevin's eyes were wide now. "Well, what was I supposed to think?"

"What's the Photon Belt?" asked Joe.

Manley huddled closer to the fire. "Okay, I'll tell you what I know," he said, "if you can spare a few bites of whatever that is... it sure smells delicious."

"Of course." Joe dug for a tin plate in his pack and pulled out his knife and began cutting the chunk of meat.

While his supper was being prepared, Manley began to tell the two young men about the Photon Belt. "Back in the early '60s, some scientists discovered out in space a band of energy," he said. "They decided this band of energy was composed of light particles — photons, if you will — and the band of energy was actually this humongous doughnut-shaped belt.

"They also noticed the energy was approaching... or, to put it more accurately... our solar system was moving toward the belt."

Kevin handed Manley a fork while Joe heaped a slab of meat on his tin plate.

Manley continued. "Back just before the end of the century, a man by the name of Sheldan Nidle began lecturing about what was going to happen when we started entering the Photon Belt. He predicted that Earth would enter it the end of 1996. But it didn't happen the way he said—or rather, the way the Sirians told him it would."

Joe interrupted. "Wait a minute... Syrians... from the Middle East? Do you mean to say this Nidle guy listened to a bunch of camel jockeys?"

"I'm not talking about Syria," said Manley. "I'm talking about

Sirius."

Kevin turned to his companion. "You know, the dog star, Sirius... up in the sky."

Joe drew in a breath. "Are you... serious?"

"Very funny," chuckled Kevin. "Go on, tell us some more."

Manley went on. "Well, this guy Nidle had all kinds of people believing that spaceships were coming to land and prepare us for some unbelievable changes in nature and technology."

"So why didn't it happen back in '96?" asked Joe.

"Nidle obviously wasn't getting accurate information," said Manley. He took a bite of the meat and chewed. It tasted sweet and hot, though it was a bit tough. But he was hungry and appreciated the food. "However, the Photon Belt theory was not a joke. The energies began hitting the Earth just a few years ago, and they have been affecting people in different ways. For the most part, the rays have been subtle."

"Well, how come this wasn't in the news?' asked Kevin. "Certainly a discovery such as this would have been broadcast. People have a right to know."

"It was played down as a hoax," explained Manley. "Nidle was considered on the fringe. You see, unless people can see and touch a phenomenon, they won't believe in it. Since the light particles are invisible, there was no proof."

"Well, if the particles are invisible," said Joe, "why did they block out the sun?"

"The Bible talks about the three days of darkness in Revelations," said Manley. "The predictions given by the space people talked about what would happen if our sun entered the Photon Belt before the earth. If the sun entered first, we'd experience three full days of darkness. We are in what is called the Null Zone... at least that's my guess."

The campfire crackled as the three of them sat in silence for a few moments. Manley ate his meat, then said, "When we are in the Null Zone, all electricity is disabled. That is why there is no power. Not even flashlight batteries will work."

"Okay," said Joe, "so what happens *after* the three days? Do the lights come back on and things continue as before?"

Manley let Kevin place a ladle full of cooked vegetables on his plate. "Thanks," he muttered. "From what I've read, after the three days of darkness, we enter a new phase of existence — one that lasts for 2,000 years. You see, the Photon Belt follows a cycle of roughly 26,000 years. Earth has been in its 12,500 years of darkness and is now about to enter 2,000 years of light."

"What do you mean 2,000 years of light?" asked Joe. "Does that mean there won't be any more night?"

"Well, that remains to be seen, obviously," said Manley. "I don't have all the answers."

"You've got a heck of a lot more than we do," remarked Kevin. "Shit, I don't know if I'd like living in world without any night time."

"What I'd like to know," said Joe, "is how those helicopters knew this was going to happen, and how *they* managed to have lights."

"Yes, that is intriguing," Manley agreed. "Somehow somebody knew in advance, and they were able to prepare for it." He thought a moment while he ate. The rescuers were obviously using photon energy to run their crafts and light them. If the government knew all this was going to happen, they must have had a plan and the necessary technology in effect for some time — perhaps months, or even years.

The two young cyclists ate their supper in silence. They seemed to be pondering the information Manley had shared with them. Manley was tired and sat with his cup in one hand, his eyes closed. "I've got to find my wife and kids," he muttered out loud.

"How are you gonna do that?" asked Joe.

Manley shook his head. "I don't know."

"Well, there must be a shelter where they were taken," said Kevin. "Somewhere close by, where they could be looked after."

"Yes, I imagine a lot of stranded motorists are all hanging out together in some church basement," surmised Joe.

"Most likely in a camp," added Kevin.

The word startled Manley. "You mean like a concentration camp?"

"Probably," said Kevin. "The government has dozens of them. I think we came across one not far from here."

"In what direction?" asked Manley.

"West of here," said Joe. "Maybe fifty miles west."

"But you're not going to find it in this darkness," said Kevin.

"And chances are slim your family was taken there, to begin with," added Joe.

Manley sighed. "I'm not going anywhere right this moment. If you two don't mind, I'm just going to curl up beside this fire and sleep awhile."

"That's exactly what we had in mind," said Kevin, unrolling his sleeping bag. He invited Manley to use it.

"I can't take your bed from you," Manley protested.

"Go ahead," urged Kevin. "Joe and I'll share. Good God, man, you don't even have warm clothing on!"

Manley accepted the offer and was soon snuggled inside Kevin's sleeping bag. He welcomed the warmth and curled up inside the cocoon while the two younger men talked in low voices beside the campfire. Sparks snapped and rose in the frigid air before the embers disintegrated. It was only a couple of minutes before Manley fell sound asleep.

16

Louise

Dorothy learned from her matronly friend, Louise, that they were confined to a concentration camp in the middle of Nebraska. Women and men, boys and girls had been divided up and taken to separate installations.

"I feel like we're cattle being penned up," said Dorothy after she had sat and listened to Louise explain a few things. "How long do you think we're going to be in here?"

"Well," said Louise, "I've overheard some of the guards talking. I find ways to listen in to their conversations when I can. I know there is some kind of protocol, but I think it's going to depend on what happens after we pass through the Null Zone."

Dorothy was familiar with the Null Zone, having heard about the Photon Belt theory from Manley and their clients over the past few years. "We should be on the third and last day of darkness by now," she guessed. "I wonder what will happen."

"That's what they are waiting to find out, I'm sure," commented Louise.

Not far from them, a woman began wailing. This led to others joining in. Fear and panic had hit some members of the encampment. Right away the ones dressed in military garb took charge and escorted the troublemakers off somewhere. Outbursts such as these were common, Louise had explained, and had been occurring sporadically since she had arrived and watched everything going on.

"Some of them just can't handle the reality," Louise said. She sipped hot tea from a Styrofoam cup. "Many are traumatized from being separated from their men and children."

Dorothy could easily relate to that. She wondered where

Manley was, and the kids... poor Kelly, who wasn't used to not having her mother around. She knew Blake could take care of himself, at least. She felt so hopeless. There just wasn't anything she could do. As far as she could tell, there was no way out of this camp. And even if there was, how was she going to know where to go? Total darkness was outside the camp. Darkness and cold.

"Do you think they're taking good care of my little girl?" Dorothy asked Louise.

The older woman sighed. "From what I can see, this event was anticipated. FEMA had the camps supplied and in place well in advance. I don't understand why mothers and children had to be separated, but one must assume the little ones are in good hands."

"But Kelly is special... with special needs."

"I know, dear. We've just got to trust."

After a short silence, Dorothy asked, "Louise, tell me about your family... your husband."

"Well, all right, dear. Maybe it will take your mind off your worries." Louise then began to tell Dorothy a little about herself. She was a school cafeteria cook from Lincoln. She and her husband, Roy, had been returning from a visit in Scotts Bluff when the darkness had put everything at a standstill. "We were visiting my sister, who has been a little upset lately with her son and daughter-in-law. That's my nephew, Bobby. Anyway, Roy's retired from an engineering firm, but I decided to keep working. I enjoy the kids and the job. Roy does a lot of fishing and I've always enjoyed my garden club friends. We have a good life..."

Dorothy only half-listened to the rest as Louise rambled on about her home life. She was wondering how she could get information on other camps. Maybe if she asked the military women, they might tell her. Louise seemed to think any communication with the soldier women was risky. They were not friendly with the refugees and, in fact, would take people away for the slightest disruption. Where they took them, Dorothy had no idea. She was tempted to try and find out.

"Uh, where are you going?" asked Louise when Dorothy stood up and headed for one of the guards.

Dorothy did not answer. She was already halfway to the gate.

17

Lotus

When Blake awoke, there was a faint light coming from the door that led into the bathroom of his quarters. He felt well rested and roused himself to discover the source of the light, which suddenly pulsated brighter. Then the Light Being emerged from the bathroom in his familiar brilliant translucent form.

"L.B.," said Blake. "You came back."

The Light Being hovered in the doorway. "Yes, I returned to the mother ship. How are you, my Terran friend? Did you rest well?"

Blake rubbed an eye. "I must have. I feel like I've had a really good night's sleep."

"It must have been needed," said L.B. "And now you will want to take some nourishment."

Blake recalled the scrumptious pizza he'd eaten last night — well, it seemed like night, though he realized it could have been morning or afternoon on Earth. Anyway, he was hungry and could have enjoyed more of that pizza.

"Someone will bring food," the Light Being explained. "But before that, I have a favor to ask of you."

"Wait. Did you find my parents?" Blake suddenly became concerned as the previous day's events rushed back at him.

"Negative," said L.B. "I realized after I left you and your sister in the hangar that I couldn't attempt that kind of rescue without a physical body. That is the favor I am asking."

"Favor? What favor?"

"I need to acquire a male body."

"You want to use *my* body?" Blake grew alarmed at the prospect.

"No, my friend. It is not anything like that."

Blake sighed with relief.

L.B. continued. "I must undergo a very risky operation on the ship. I need a body right away and cannot wait for the usual transformation process. I am asking to borrow some of your DNA."

"What!" Blake got out of bed and began dressing in his clothes from yesterday.

"The process we must use involves cloning a body," L.B. explained. "By contributing some of your blood, the scientists will be able to quickly clone a physical vessel in which I will be able to sustain myself and interact more effectively with your people."

"You're going to *clone* me?" Blake cried out in disbelief. He shook his head. "I don't think so, man."

The wall of Blake's cabin opened to one side and a young woman with a cart of food came into the room. She was dressed in a uniform that resembled white tights and a matching tunic with long sleeves. She was human-looking except for the color of her skin, which was blue, and her shoulder-length hair was white and fine, parted down the middle of her head. She appeared young and had beautiful blue eyes. She smiled at Blake, revealing perfect teeth that had a blueish tinge to them. As she wheeled the cart into the room, the wall closed up again.

"Your breakfast is here," she said in a pleasant young girl's voice. Blake couldn't help but notice the shapely young feminine curves beneath her white tunic. She wore white slippers. The girl did not seem to be alarmed at the presence of the Light Being.

"That's for me?" Blake asked incredulously. The cart contained serving trays of eggs, bacon, pancakes, fruit slices and toasted muffins and sweet rolls. Underneath the top shelf were a coffee thermos and various juices, cups, plates, bowls and silverware.

"Eat what you like." The girl giggled in a strange but pleasant way. "Eat small or eat large."

Blake looked at the Light Being, who nodded at him. "Please replenish yourself," he said. "And while you are enjoying your repast, I will explain how the procedure works."

The blue girl with white hair made no attempt to leave the room. She stood with her hands folded in front of her while Blake took a plate and began filling it.

"Won't you sit down?" he invited.

The girl sat on Blake's bed.

"What's your name?" he asked as he dished up scrambled eggs mixed with bacon bits.

"Lotus," she told him. "And yours?"

"Blake." It made her giggle, so he added, "Blake Dobbs."

Lotus smiled and watched him eat.

"Who is she?" Blake asked L.B. "Why is she staring at me while I'm eating?"

L.B. explained that it was simply Lotus' job to serve new arrivals on the ship. "Now I want to explain everything to you in detail," he said. "In order for me to function on your level, I must borrow some of your DNA."

"How?" Blake asked.

"They will draw a little blood."

"Ow!" Blake cringed at the thought.

"It is nothing. You won't even feel it," said L.B. "Then they will begin the process of providing me with a temporary physical form."

"What's wrong with your present form?" Blake bit into a slice of rye toast. "I rather dig the way you light up a room."

"Being an energy form has its drawbacks, my friend. How can I truly relate to you and your people when I have none of your senses?"

"But you're communicating with *me*," said Blake.

"True, but the energy level I must sustain in order to accomplish this communication takes a great deal of effort. I normally vibrate at a much higher level than this. I have had to lower my vibration in order to interact with you and rescue you and your sister."

Blake bit into a muffin and was surprised when Lotus got up from the bed and began pouring him a glass of orange juice. He had just been thinking that he wanted the juice. Could she read his mind? As if in answer to his thought, Lotus smiled, handing him the glass, and she winked one of her bright blue eyes.

"L.B., do you think my parents got rescued, like Kelly and me? Is it possible they're on this ship?"

L.B.'s form began to flicker. "No, Blake. I know that your parents were not rescued. I am sorry."

"Well, do you know where they are?"

"I do not." The flickering continued. After a moment, L.B.

said, "I am growing fatigued now. I must withdraw. But before I leave, do you give permission to use your DNA?"

Blake sighed. L.B.'s light was dimming and he was starting to disappear. "Well, if I say yes, will you do everything you can to help me find my parents?" he asked.

"I cannot promise anything," L.B. said. "I can only try."

"Do you even *know* who my parents are?" Blake asked.

"Manley and Dorothy Dobbs," L.B. replied. "Blake, please... give your permission... I must now withdraw."

Lotus looked a bit worried as L.B.'s light flickered rapidly. She stared at Blake with a pleading face.

"Okay, L.B. Go ahead, man. Tell them to use my blood." Blake took a drink of the orange juice as his Light Being friend suddenly vanished in a flash of light.

Lotus turned to Blake, bright-eyed and concerned. "Giving him what he asks is a great favor," she said. "You are a brave human."

Blake continued eating. "Yeah? How do you figure?"

Lotus smiled, folding her hands as she sat on the bed. "For a light being to request use of one's body, it takes great faith and trust on one's part."

She wasn't making a lot of sense to Blake. It was as though the blue girl had trouble with his language.

"What planet are you from?" Blake asked.

Lotus flashed her eyelids almost coyly at him. "I come from Andromeda."

"That's not a planet, it's a galaxy," said Blake, trying not to be critical.

"I come from the planet Torphu," she added.

"I never heard of it," remarked Blake, "but I'm sure I have never heard of a lot of things in space."

"You want to learn things about my world?" Lotus asked eagerly.

"Sure," said Blake. "But I have to do some other things first. I've got to find my parents."

The door in the wall of the cabin opened again. This time Greta stood there with Blue Jay beside her.

"Hello, Blake," said Greta, smiling broadly at him. "How did you sleep?"

"Great," said Blake.

"Mind if we come in?" asked Blue Jay.

Blake looked around at the small quarters of the cabin, then shrugged. "Sure. Come on in."

Lotus began packing up the cart. He realized his breakfast was over. Greta and Blue Jay entered the cabin and Blue Jay helped himself to a chocolate doughnut before Lotus left with the cart.

"I'll see you later, won't I, Lotus?" Blake called out to her.

The blue girl with the long white hair smiled at him. "If you desire." Then she left and the wall closed after her.

"We thought we'd show you around the ship," said Greta. "Did you enjoy your breakfast?"

"Oh yeah," said Blake. "The food on this ship is really good."

"So glad you approve, man," said Blue Jay.

"Hey, can I see my sister?" asked Blake.

"Of course," said Greta.

"I want to make sure she's all right."

"She's adjusting quite well," said Greta. "I think she understands what has happened and is progressing rapidly."

"I thought I'd tag along," added Blue Jay. He took a bite of his doughnut. "I have a few hours off. Thought we might visit one of the music studios on the ship, after the tour... that is, if you don't mind."

Blake was more than happy for the companionship of his new musician friend. So far he really liked the people he'd met on the ship and he was fascinated with life in space and wanted to discover all he could about it.

"That's fine," said Greta, "but before that, we need to take Blake to the infirmary for a blood draw. I have a special request from the lab."

The door in the wall opened as Greta walked toward it, and then all three headed down a wide corridor of the ship. Blake felt excited and a little apprehensive at the same time. He wondered what was in store for him.

18

Opening Night

"Shuttles have been flying in all afternoon," Johanna told the performers backstage in an excited voice. Her brown eyes twinkled as she passed out programs and peeked out the edge of the curtain. "The auditorium is full."

"That is so wonderful," exclaimed Justine Oliver, the voice instructor and café manager. She was dressed in a long black gown and dangling earrings. "Johanna, this is a dream come true for so many of us. You must be so proud to have a full house on opening night."

"Well, you've all worked so hard for this night," Johanna replied. "Crystal, how are you doing?"

Crystal sighed, rolling her eyes. "Just fine, Mother."

"Crystal, you are dressed to kill." Justine chuckled. "Are you nervous?"

Crystal shook her head. She didn't have a nervous bone in her body. Why were Mrs. Oliver and her mother making such a fuss? Oh sure, she knew her mother had worked for a long time to have the performing arts center built. She knew her parents were instrumental in establishing the center and that it had taken lots of effort and planning, especially on their part. But so what? This was her mother's big night, not hers. She was going into the fleet, after all.

"Time to take your places, everyone," Johanna told the performers. "It's almost curtain time."

Crystal was second on the program. After Serassan's introductory speech, welcoming the patrons to the grand opening, Johanna would sit down at the grand piano and play the composition she had prepared for this night. Then Crystal would fulfill her obligation and sing the song she had rehearsed, *Rainbow Love*. She had no reason to be nervous or scared. Everything had gone smoothly at dress rehearsal that afternoon. She had been encouraged by the sound of her own echo across the gigantic auditorium.

Soon the house lights blinked a couple of times, and then they dimmed and the audience grew quiet. Soon a spotlight came on and the curtains parted. From the wings, Crystal watched her father, Serassan, walk to the center of the stage as the light focused on his tall form. She swelled with pride as she realized how handsome her father was, especially dressed in his white tux, not looking a day over 40. She suddenly wanted more than anything for her father to be proud of her.

"Welcome, everyone, to the opening night of the long-awaited Galactic Center for the Performing Arts." Serassan's deep voice penetrated every corner of the auditorium, which seemed to be packed with individuals of diverse races and species, but mostly inhabitants from the planet Estron.

"I am pleased to be your Master of Ceremonies for this momentous occasion," Serassan continued. "Tonight's grand opening features talent to span the galaxies. We on Karos have built a dream that began nearly twenty years ago, when several Estronian astronauts made the journey to a unique little planet named Terra. There we discovered a world brimming with artists of all kinds. On Estron such individuals are rare. Our plan at that time was to bring some of those talented beings to this planet, Karos, and start a new race of the best musicians, the best performers and the best visual artists in the galaxy. We hoped that through genetics we could infuse their talent into our own race, which lacks the gifts but has come to greatly admire what has come to be a passion for us.

"Now I see that the majority of you here tonight are citizens of Estron and her colonies. Your planet — which was once my home as well — has been most generous in helping us here on Karos bring into fruition this event and this majestic facility. Engineers have used the highest technology to accommodate the comfort levels of all. For, as you well know, Karos is a Class M planet, conducive to the survival and comfort level of Terrans. Unaltered Estronians must use oxygen supplements to remain on Karos for any length of time. Atmospheric bubble generators can be purchased in the hotel and gift shop. You will also find oxygen wafers at your disposal in the pockets of all seats, as well as in all lounges, restrooms and the café. It is our wish that you relax, sit back, and enjoy tonight's performances, commencing with my beautiful wife, Johanna, who could have returned to Terra when the Earth-Star mission failed, but instead chose to remain with me and devote her life to our dream of making this facility a reality. And now... please welcome... lovely Johanna..."

The auditorium resounded with thunderous applause and Serassan turned and beckoned to Johanna, who walked toward him on stage. Crystal clapped, too, actually quite impressed with the grace of her mother's walk. Johanna wore a long gown of pale lime green with sequins that caught the light and sparkled. Her dark hair was styled in a thick coil on top of her head, with a thin strand that hung loosely over her shoulder in a spiral. She bowed to the audience, and then strolled over to the grand piano, where she sat.

The hall grew quiet as Johanna positioned herself on the cushioned seat. The spotlight focused upon her slender form and her posture was straight, her features relaxed, yet poised. Crystal had watched her mother perform for small gatherings, but had never seen her play to a big audience. She couldn't help but admire the confidence her mother exuded. If Johanna was nervous, she didn't show it. She thought back to the times her mother used to tell about the concerts she had given in her younger years. She wondered if Johanna was recalling those times from her youth.

Suddenly Johanna plunged right into her music. *The Cosmic Journey* from *The Karosian Suite* was a composition she had worked up specifically for this evening's performance, and Crystal was familiar with many of its strains. Her mother practiced different segments whenever Crystal was home from school. She knew the entire piece by heart.

The acoustics of the building enhanced the splendor of the piano music as it filled every corner of the auditorium. Colored lights played a visual accompaniment and Crystal saw her father standing off stage, watching her mother perform, and she knew Serassan was off in a different dimension. Her mother's music had always had that effect on him. He was mesmerized by it. She knew that when she sang, her singing had a similar effect on her father.

The music continued through its different levels. Crystal could see the faces of the audience from her small break in the curtain, and all eyes were focused in wonder and awe upon her pianist mother. She felt something stir within her breast as the slower, gentler passages began. A longing she didn't understand caused her to feel sad.

And then during the composition's final and passionate recap, Crystal felt her heart beat faster. She felt uplifted, renewed, and experienced the energy that was vibrating at a higher and higher level. The listeners were involved and so into her mother's music. It was exhilarating and so rewarding to experience. In that moment she felt closer to Johanna, to Serassan, and to every being present, than she had ever felt in her life. She had been swept up in the passion of the music and the higher vibrations it created in that very time and space.

For a second Crystal had a strong flash of emotion in which she remembered something — or someone — so very familiar to her that she suddenly had this desperate longing in her heart to connect with whatever — or whomever — it was.

The auditorium swelled with resounding applause after Johanna's composition ended. It served to shake Crystal out of her momentary reverie. She realized that now it was *her* turn to perform in front of all these people, some of whom had come from other parts of space. Would they find as much enjoyment in her voice as they had in her mother's piano playing?

For the first time, Crystal had doubts about her ability. How could she, a 17-year-old Estronian hybrid, expect to live up to her mother's performance? After all, Johanna had been a professional concert pianist. She had experience and poise and so much talent.

Serassan took to center stage once again as the clapping died down. Johanna was at Crystal's side, all aglow.

"Mother..." Crystal wanted to tell her how beautiful her music had sounded, how impressed she had been. But her mother didn't let her finish.

"Crystal, your turn is next," whispered Johanna as she bent over to straighten Crystal's shoulder straps and fuss with a stray blond hair. "Are you ready?"

"Mother..." It was suddenly as if Crystal had lost her tongue. She saw the stricken look in her mother's eyes.

"Oh my God... stage fright?" Johanna whispered frantically.

"And now... another special treat," Serassan announced as his deep voice echoed through the auditorium.

"No, no, I'm fine," Crystal insisted.

"What, then?" Johanna's brown eyes were wide.

"Nothing."

Serassan continued. "My daughter, who is also Johanna's daughter, the beautiful Crystal Dobbs, has been a blessing to our union, and also a blessing to the Planet Estron, not to mention the pride and joy of her grandparents, Soolàn and Emrox, who are with us tonight."

Crystal was annoyed with her mother's concern, but even more annoyed with herself for not being able to express the emotional reaction she'd just experienced moments ago.

"I can get the dancers to go next, if you're feeling uncertain," Johanna told Crystal.

"Mother, it's okay."

"Are you sure?"

"Mother!" Crystal's voice must have been louder than usual because Serassan's head turned toward them off-stage and he hesitated for a few seconds.

Johanna signaled him that everything was to proceed as planned, then she quickly left to stand near Justine and the other performers. Her arms were crossed in frustration, which caused Crystal only to have further regrets for her own behavior.

Serassan had shared a little anecdote with the audience about Crystal's hard years of music lessons with her mother as teacher. The audience chuckled, and then he stretched his arm out toward her and said, "Please welcome Crystal Dobbs as she sings *Rainbow Love*."

The applause picked up as Crystal walked out onto the stage, the spotlight escorting her. She smiled at Serassan, and then out into the black ocean of faces. Serassan kissed her hand and then he left the stage, leaving her there alone.

The music began and Crystal closed her eyes and felt the confidence flow into her. She started the song right on cue and poured her heart into it. The sound of her own sweet voice coming back to her prompted her on so that she was able to perform the entire piece without flaw. The music flowed throughout her being so that all other thoughts vanished. The song was everything in her life at this moment, and she was pleased with herself and it.

After she was finished, the audience filled the auditorium once again with voluminous applause. Crystal bowed a couple of times, smiled, curtsied, and then blew a kiss meant for Soolàn and Emrox. She was filled with joy and accomplishment and knew she would cherish this moment always.

"Crystal, you were superb!"

"Stupendous performance!"

"Oh, Crystal, you were wonderful!"

The other performers flocked around her backstage. Crystal thanked them all and found her mother prepping the next performers, a pair of dancers.

Johanna glanced at Crystal quickly, a look of relief more than anything else, and Crystal wished she could put her arms around her mother, but Johanna was busy with the dancers.

"I didn't know anybody could sing like that," one of the performers was saying to the group.

"That girl has a future," said someone else.

"Don't think so," Crystal heard another one say. "Haven't you heard? She's joining the fleet."

Crystal noticed the look on her mother's face when those words were said. Johanna's brow wrinkled and she turned away. Crystal blinked, then sighed and walked toward the dressing rooms.

So what if she was going into the fleet? If her mother didn't want to accept it, too bad. Nothing was going to stop her. Space was her future, not the Galactic Center for the Performing Arts.

The music began for the next act as Crystal reached her dressing room. The light came slowly on as she walked in. She had such a rush of different emotions and she needed to sort them out.

"My dear, that was most exquisite." The male voice startled Crystal and she jerked. Turning, she saw the Estronian named Thorden standing outside the door. "You were truly worth coming several million miles to see."

Crystal was caught off guard and not sure how to treat this stranger, who claimed he was a friend of her parents. Instinct told her to be careful, that perhaps he was not to be trusted. But of course those were her mother's words. He obviously had enjoyed her singing.

"I suppose your mother told you not to speak to me."

Thorden smiled slyly.

"Uh... no," said Crystal. "She didn't say I wasn't to speak to you. I just..."

"You appear to be mature enough to choose your own friends," said Thorden. "And I hope you and I will become... friends." He looked around the room. "Would it be all right if I sit down?"

Crystal motioned him into a chair. "Just what did you do, anyway, that makes my mother not trust you?" she asked.

Thorden chuckled and shook his head. "That was a long time ago. We were on the same mission, Serassan and I. We served together as physicians on the planet Terra. The purpose was, of course, to bring people like your most talented mother to Karos for breeding. And I can see the result of that was quite successful."

Crystal didn't know how to respond. She had, of course, heard the story of how the Estronians had managed to abduct a group of artists, which was how her parents met, but they had not gone into a lot of detail. She knew of only the small group of Terran volunteers who had remained behind while the majority of abductees had elected to be returned to Earth.

"You must not become alarmed," said Thorden. "None of this should be of concern to you now. Not someone who has as much beauty and talent as you, dear Crystal."

Crystal smiled very slightly. This being was a flatterer. "Well, I might as well tell you, Mr. Thorden. My plans are *not* to follow in my mother's footsteps. Instead I plan to join the Estronian fleet. I want to be a space explorer."

He perked up. "You don't say! You are inclined to follow in your father's footsteps, then."

Crystal picked up the brush on her dressing table and began pulling it through her long blond curls. "I want to be in space," she declared. "I want to pilot a ship and explore the star systems, not be stuck on some forlorn planet like Karos."

"Well..." Thorden chuckled again. "I think that is delightful. Yes, indeed, delightful. And what a lovely pilot you will make, too." He nodded his oversized head, smiling.

"Do you really think so?" Crystal eyed him curiously.

"Well, of course. You are the loveliest hybrid I've seen yet."

"No, that's not what I meant," said Crystal. "I want to know...

Do you think it is possible I could one day pilot a ship in space?"

"Oh, that," said Thorden. "My dear, anything your heart desires can be yours."

"Really?"

"If you pay the price."

"What price?" asked Crystal. "What are you talking about?"

Thorden sat back in his chair and folded his hands in front of him. "There is always a price to pay for everything you accomplish in life," he said.

"What do you mean?"

Thorden sighed. "For instance, if you want to be a scientist, you must first get educated and invest many years in research. Or, if you want to be an astronaut, you must first serve in the fleet for many years and be trained in all aspects of piloting a vessel."

"I know it can't happen overnight," said Crystal.

"Why can't it?" Thorden leaned forward and stared into her face reflected in the dressing room mirror.

"You said everything has a price," Crystal reminded him.

"My dear, you are absolutely right," said Thorden. "And if you are willing to pay the price, I could get you to the place where you want to be. You could be piloting your own craft by... say... six months to a year."

Crystal winced. "I'm going to get my shuttle license real soon."

"I'm talking about a starship, not a shuttlecraft. What did you think I meant?"

Crystal simply stared at him, uncertain.

Thorden continued. "Crystal, you are going to rise through the ranks in space."

"How can that happen?" Crystal was dubious, thinking of all those competitive Estronian girls at school. It was going to take all she could handle just to keep up with half of them.

"Because I, Thorden, have influence in high places."

"Hmm." Crystal finished brushing her hair and set the brush down. "And how is your influence going to help someone like me?"

"Out of the goodness of my heart, I am willing to offer you the chance of a lifetime. All of your dreams can come true... that is, if you are willing to pay the price."

She was almost afraid to ask. "And what is the price?"

"Come with me. Be my protégé. Let me make your success my next project."

"And why would you want to do this for me, Mr. Thorden?"

He laughed. "Crystal, Crystal... how little you understand. I am drawn to your beauty, to your magical voice."

"But in space I won't need it," she reminded him.

"You will sing for *me*... not others."

For some reason Crystal did not like where this was leading. She wondered if Thorden held ulterior motives. At the same time, she couldn't help feeling excited at the prospect of being able to pilot a ship through space vast distances. Was it really possible? Finally she sighed and said, "I'll have to think about this."

Thorden rose and started to leave. "I understand. Yes, think about it. But don't take too long. This is a chance of a lifetime, and I don't make these offers every day."

She managed a smile. "Okay, I'll give it some thought."

"I will contact you soon," he promised, and then he left.

As soon as he was gone, Crystal stared into the mirror at herself and wasn't quite sure how she felt. She was still overwhelmed by the emotions of both her own performance and the feelings that had caught her by surprise when she heard her mother play.

Now, it seemed, her future was in her hands, and she knew Thorden would be back, expecting her to give him an answer, and it would determine which path of life she was to take. She longed for adventure, for new places, new friends, new challenges. But at the same time a terrible fear was welling up inside her. Thorden had been cordial, but for some reason his presence disturbed her and made her feel strange, almost guilty.

She wanted to discuss this with Serassan, or her mother, but she already knew what their reaction would be. No, this was a decision that Crystal had to make all by herself.

19

The Visitation

"Excuse me. Excuse me!" Dorothy trotted after one of the women in military garb who was walking the fence line. At first the soldier ignored her, but Dorothy caught up and reached for the woman's sleeve. "Please stop! I have a question."

The female in uniform wore a khaki overcoat and her narrow eyes shot rays of annoyance at Dorothy as the two stood facing each other.

"My orders do not include answering questions," the soldier woman fired as clouds of breath billowed in the frigid air.

"But I..."

"Therefore, do not ask any." The soldier turned away and started walking the fence line again.

Dorothy was not to be put off. She quickened her pace to keep up with the woman. "Look, I just want to know if there are any other camps nearby. My husband and my children are..."

"Go back to the tents," the soldier woman commanded. "Now!"

Dorothy kept walking alongside the soldier. "I just need to know if they are all right. Please!"

It seemed as though the troops appeared out of nowhere to surround her. The soldier woman stopped with her rifle raised and three other military women closed in with their guns raised.

"Another troublemaker," one of them snorted.

"Let's move." One behind Dorothy prodded her with the butt of a rifle. "Move!"

Escorted by three of the women soldiers, Dorothy was led a long ways from where she had last had coffee with her friend Louise. It was dark and cold and she couldn't see exactly where they were going. Grass and rocky ground was beneath her feet.

After several minutes they arrived at a shelter of some kind. It was a quonset hut and inside burned Coleman lanterns. There were several people — all of them women — standing around or sitting at desks, dressed in military fatigues.

"Where are we going?" Dorothy dared to ask.

"No questions," snapped one of her escorts, who prodded her butt with the rifle. "Just keep going straight."

As they walked past a kitchen of some sort, Dorothy saw a tall woman dressed in red leggings, a bulky beige sweater and fashionable black boots. This woman stood out from all the others because of her street dress, but it startled Dorothy to see her face and she let out a gasp. It was none other than Ernestine Glenn, former candidate for president of the United States. What was a prominent woman such as Ernestine Glenn doing in a concentration camp in the middle of Nebraska?

Ms. Glenn happened to glance up from a conversation she was having with several officers and noticed Dorothy's stare. For a moment the two women locked eyes, and then Dorothy was shoved down a stairway that led into a jail cell. Although it was dark, she sensed the presence of others in the cell, women like herself who had rudely been rounded up and labeled as "trouble-makers" because they dared to ask questions.

The cell was cold and damp as the door banged shut and was locked behind her. Dorothy felt panic well up inside of her when she realized she was now incarcerated and unable to move about freely. She turned and grabbed the cold steel of the bars and cried after the retreating soldiers, "Wait! Don't lock me up! I haven't done anything! Oh, please!"

Several of the women prisoners moaned. It was then that Dorothy realized they were, for the most part, sedated, some of them huddled in a heap, passed out on the floor. They had obviously been drugged to keep them from disturbing the peace. Dorothy shuddered to think what might happen to her. She immediately quit yelling after the soldiers, for fear they might return and feel the need to drug her as well.

There was a cold hard bench that she sat on. Miraculously she had held onto her blanket and wrapped it around her shoulders in an effort to warm her body. She realized she was shaking, more from fear than the cold.

Glancing up at the stairway from which she had been shoved, Dorothy made out the silhouette of a guard. The light that came from the quonset's main quarters was enough to cast a dim outline of objects around her in the cell basement. Bodies of women filled the cell, most of them unconscious. She did not wish to converse with any of them. She wanted to get out of this horrible place.

Her mind flashed an image of Ernestine Glenn's face as she closed her eyes. What was this outspoken feminist leader doing here? she wondered again. Was it really Ernestine? How could it be? Dorothy had followed the woman's presidential campaign with much hope and enthusiasm over the past few years, up until she was defeated in last fall's election. Ernestine was greatly admired and stood for so much of what Dorothy believed in, particularly women's rights and equality. Ms. Glenn's environmental views were especially appealing and Dorothy had applauded many of the woman's speeches after she and Manley had sat through them in front of the television.

"I just don't trust that woman," Manley would say, shaking his head.

"Oh, Manley, she's brilliant," Dorothy would argue. "Ernestine Glenn is the answer to women's rights, the environment, and all that we believe in." Dorothy really couldn't understand what it was about the woman that disturbed Manley, who was usually very liberal in his thinking. "She's bound to run in the election again in four years. And I'll bet she'll win next time."

"That's what I'm afraid of." Manley sighed in his recliner. "No offense, darling, but I don't think our government is ready for a woman president."

"And why not?" she fired.

"Don't get defensive, Dorothy. I'm just saying I don't think it's the right time."

"What about what you used to say?" Dorothy challenged him. "Remember when you said the only way there will ever be peace on Earth is when the female race takes over?"

"And I still believe that," he replied.

"So why not now? Why isn't now the time? We're overdue, as far as I'm concerned." She could feel her cheeks burning. "Women have been second-class citizens for too many centuries. At last here is a strong individual who isn't afraid to challenge the status quo. We need a change, and now has never been a better time."

Manley would sigh and start flipping through the channels on the remote control, at which time Dorothy would get up from the couch and stalk off toward the kitchen or go check on Kelly.

She opened her eyes now and felt a tear push its way down her left cheek. Where was Manley? Where were her children? Why couldn't they all be together? Just what was going on, anyway? How long would she be kept in this confined hell hole?

Sudden fatigue seized her and she let herself sink back on the bench. Pulling the blanket around her head, Dorothy drew her knees up toward her chest as she rolled sideways, then closed her eyes and let the soft sobs escape as she surrendered to sleep.

Disturbances kept Dorothy from sleeping for any length of time. Moans and cries from her fellow prisoners disrupted dreams that were fragments of people dressed in military fatigues, with the stunning face of Ernestine Glenn fading in and out, always portraying that fiery countenance that reminded Dorothy of fireworks. In her dream, Dorothy watched Ernestine being cheered by vast crowds, her pleased smile and upraised arms drawing it all in.

Then, a bright flash drowned out the vision of the political candidate in the crowd. A ball of golden light was so intense, it hurt Dorothy's eyes, yet she couldn't open them. She felt herself surfacing from the dream state as she once again grew aware of the jail cell in the basement of the quonset. She was awake, and yet she wasn't. She couldn't open her eyelids and the bright light caused her to shield her face.

"Go away," she murmured in a strained voice. She could barely form the words. She expected the soldier guards to shake her rigid body, but instead a strong male voice boomed inside her head, the words echoing through her brain.

"Dorothy," it thundered, "you are aware of my presence?"

Unable to reply, Dorothy grunted. Her eyelids felt bolted to her face. She thought the voice had to be someone in authority standing over her in the dark cell. Perhaps somehow they had drugged her and she couldn't remember, and now they were interrogating her, using that excruciating light.

"Good," the voice continued, "I'm glad you can hear me. I want you to know... your children are safe."

A small cry caught in Dorothy's throat.

"They both are on a spaceship orbiting your planet," the voice explained. "You need not worry about your son. He is strong and advanced for his race. And the young girl is in good hands. She is being well taken care of. I want you to understand that they are all right. Do you understand that?"

Dorothy struggled to speak, but all that came out was a croak. She felt paralyzed by the light, but the reassuring words relaxed her a little.

"You are concerned about your husband, Manley Dobbs," the voice continued. "He is safe, for the moment. What I am about to tell you is important. Do not be frightened. Fear only serves to feed the flames of deception. All that you see and hear around you right now is illusion. Do not absorb it. There are those who would deceive Earth beings. They are in league with others who have the technology to create much destruction. That is what they are trying to do now, and to do it they have created a drama."

Dorothy was mortified. Who was this voice that was telling her all of this? And could it be true? Had the Dark Forces faked the coming of the Photon Belt? How could they? Who could successfully blot out the Sun for three days? The Photon Belt had been anticipated for years by scientists and lightworkers, and she had bought right into it.

"I must leave you now," said the voice as the light began to shine less intensely. "I cannot come for you just yet, but I will return as soon as I am able, and then we will find your husband."

As the power of the light freed up her ability to open her eyes, Dorothy found her vocal cords functional. "Who... who are you?" she asked.

"That is not important now," the voice said. "Did you understand everything that I told you?"

"Yes." Dorothy nodded, then shook her head. "Wait! How do you know the Photon Belt isn't real?"

"I never said the Belt wasn't real," said the voice. "Did I?"

"Well, actually..."

"The Belt exists," the voice told her. "But so does deception. You must discern."

Dorothy sighed. "But how..."

"One more word of advice," the voice thundered in her head. "Beware of the one in whom the majority has put their trust!"

"Who is that?"

The light faded away and Dorothy sat up in the dark cell.

"Wait!" she called out. "Come back! I must know more!"

But it was too late. The visitation was over and Dorothy found herself in the cold, damp cell with the other women prisoners.

Before she could recover and reflect on what had just happened, there was a commotion in the stairwell. She assumed the guards were bringing another person into the jail cell. The door rattled as the guard unlocked it and Dorothy instinctively huddled in her corner with her blanket wrapped around her neck and shoulders.

She was startled when the guard entered the cell and grabbed her arm. "Okay, toots, on your feet." The guard jerked Dorothy to her feet. She was led outside the cell, where the other soldier helped haul her up the concrete steps to the quonset and the lantern light.

Dorothy was pushed along until they came to an enclosed area that served as a private office headquarters. Dorothy was startled to see a pale rosy sky coming from outside the window.

"It's dawn!" She gasped a cry of delight and one of the soldier women indicated that she was to sit in a metal folding chair. The long darkness appeared to be ending. And yet, what lay ahead, Dorothy had no clue. The words of the Light Being kept playing over in her mind. She dared not breathe a word to anyone about her communication in the cell.

A moment later in walked the elegantly dressed woman in red leggings and black boots. Dorothy stared into the face of Ernestine Glenn, presidential candidate of the Purification Party for the United States of America.

20

Ship's Tour

B lake was given a tour of the mother ship. First he was taken to a medical facility, where a technician drew a small amount of his blood. He knew this had been requested for his light being friend, who was procuring a body.

The lovely Greta then took Blake to the section of the ship where Kelly was being cared for. They entered a large room that reminded Blake of a school. There were smaller cubicles that appeared to be classrooms for the very young.

Kelly was playing with colored blocks that emitted light. She was dressed in a one-piece play suit, neon pink in color, and two alien beings stood near her, both of whom were less than five feet tall and had large heads with no hair.

When the little girl glanced up and recognized her brother, she broke into a grin and ran toward him, wrapping her fat arms around his waist. Blake knelt down and embraced his little sister.

"Hi, Kelly Belly," he greeted her with the familiar nickname.

She laughed and said, "Wanna play with me?"

"Wow, Kel." Blake looked around at all the toys and play equipment. "You've got quite a playground here." The two aliens nodded and blinked their slanted dark eyes at him. They were apparently assigned as caregivers or child attendants of some sort. "I'll come back and play sometime soon. I'm on a ship's tour right now."

"This is where you'll find your sister if you wish to visit her," explained Greta. "She sleeps and eats in the nursery down the corridor."

"This is a lot like a day care center," commented Blake.

"It's actually a school," Greta said. "Children begin their education from Day One on the mother ship."

"Are you okay, Kel?" Blake asked his sister.

Kelly nodded, then returned to her block building.

"She's in the best hands," Greta assured him once again. "If you're ready, we'll tour more of the ship."

Blake spent a couple more minutes watching Kelly build a structure. The lights given off by the colored blocks fascinated him. His little sister seemed pleased to have him nearby, but he was surprised she didn't seem to be missing their parents.

"They've blocked her trauma temporarily," explained Greta when Blake asked about it. "She can't remember what happened before she was brought here. She remembers you, of course, and she'll remember the rest once she sees her mother again."

"When do you think that will be?" Blake asked, wondering with concern what had happened to his parents.

"I don't know," Greta replied. She put a hand on Blake's shoulder. "Let's move on now. There are some interesting things on the ship I'd like you to see."

Before leaving, Blake gave Kelly another hug. It was a relief to see his sister so adjusted to the new situation. He had been doing pretty well himself up till now. The reminder that his mom and dad were still on Earth, having to deal with the chaos of the Photon Belt, now weighed heavily on his mind. L.B. had promised to help find them, but there was little he could do without being in physical form, he had said. Blake knew he would have to be patient and keep faith.

Greta showed Blake the recreation facilities. Several levels of the ship were devoted to recreational pursuits, from swimming to racquetball, to bowling to skating, with an indoor track, weight rooms and even park-like areas where people could stroll and experience trees, birds and gardens. He was quite impressed with this exciting vacation land in space. One would never get bored here with so many opportunities to indulge in.

"Blue Jay wanted you to meet him at his music studio." Greta led Blake to another level of the ship, where there were music halls and study areas. He was blown away by everything he saw. Greta showed him where their friend was practicing his harmonica in a soundproof room. When Blue Jay saw them through the window in the door, he flashed a big grin.

"I will leave you," Greta told Blake.

"Thanks for the tour," said Blake.

"There's plenty more to see, believe it or not," exclaimed Blue Jay as he stepped out to join them. "But how's about a jam session first?"

"Sure." Blake let his musician friend lead him down a hallway to a room where various instruments were stored. Blake picked out a twelve-string guitar, not unlike his own back on Earth. He spent a couple of minutes tuning it up to Blue Jay's harmonica, and then they returned to the soundproof studio that was filled with all kinds of recording equipment and lights.

"Want to hear what I worked on so far?" Blue Jay turned to his computer console.

"Sure," said Blake.

A moment later they were surrounded by blues sounds and Blue Jay's harmonica. Before ten bars had gone by, Blake fell in with his guitar and picked up the accompaniment. He could see out the corner of his eye that Blue Jay was pleased. They ended up playing music together for at least an hour. Blake felt refreshed and recharged after the session. It had eased his depression and invigorated him.

"I knew you could kick ass," Blue Jay said as they returned the guitar to its compartment. "We'll have a go at it again soon. Hey, man, let me take you to some parts of the ship Greta didn't show you."

"Okay," said Blake.

"Then it'll be time for me to take my shift at the café," added Blue Jay. "You can come along and get something to eat."

That sounded good to Blake. He followed his guide to areas on the spacecraft that were not often shown to visitors. Blue Jay Harris, Blake soon learned, had many connections with crew members on the mother ship. He knew somebody in just about every department. Their last stop was the monitoring room.

"What do they do in here?" Blake wanted to know.

"This is where crew members watch what goes on," said Blue Jay. "They monitor all sorts of things on Earth. Right now they are extremely busy, what with the shift and all."

Blake could see people of different species, some standing,

some sitting at stations in a large, darkened room. They watched screens and worked controls as they scanned various scenes. Most of the screens he could see were dark. Often more than one observer stood over a screen, and some of the people communicated with each other about what they were seeing or — in this case — what they were *not* seeing.

Blue Jay strolled in with Blake at his heels. They approached a small alien woman with grayish-white skin and a large bald head. She was dressed in a one-piece white uniform with gold braid trim. As she turned to look at them, she smiled, and Blake noticed large, wrap-around eyes that were a deep color of blue. He immediately perceived that Blue Jay found her somewhat attractive.

"Hello, Blue Jay," she spoke in a pleasant feminine voice. It surprised Blake to hear perfect English and through her mouth rather than through telepathy. The alien woman's gaze focused curiously upon Blake.

"How's it goin'?" Blue Jay grinned. "Hey, I want you to meet a new friend of mine, Blake Dobbs."

"Greetings." The alien smiled warmly at him, still studying his face.

"This is my friend, Kapri," explained Blue Jay. "Her job is to help make people aware of life in space."

"Oh," said Blake.

"Actually, that's just one of my jobs." Kapri reached out a thin grayish hand. "How do you do, Blake Dobbs?"

Blake shook her hand and noticed the strength in her grip. The name Kapri suddenly seemed familiar and he wondered where he had heard that name recently.

"Blake... Dobbs..." Kapri's expression changed to momentary excitement. "Of course. I thought you resembled someone I once knew. Now I understand. I can see that you must be related to Manley Dobbs."

"You know my dad?" Blake then recalled that his parents had mentioned the name Kapri just the other day — or was it more than three days ago? He had already lost track of time as he once knew it. When they had told him the remarkable story about his aunt, they had mentioned someone named Kapri.

"Your father is Manley Dobbs," the alien woman reflected. "Yes, I knew him very well for a short time while I was on your planet. He is a good man."

Blue Jay watched, amused that there was a connection already between his two friends.

"You must know my mother, too," said Blake.

"Oh, you mean Dorothy," said Kapri. "Of course. She and I were roommates for a few days. Without your mother's psychic ability, we might not have been able to escape Dulce."

"I just recently heard all about that time," said Blake, "and about my aunt and my... uncle." Blake still found it strange to think he had a space alien for a relative.

"You speak of Serassan," said Kapri, "and his mate, Johanna."

"Yes, she's my aunt," said Blake. "And all these years I thought she was locked away in a mental asylum. I'd give anything to meet her."

"Where's your aunt now?" Blue Jay wanted to know.

Blake shrugged, but Kapri held up her hand. "Serassan and Johanna live on the planet Karos," she revealed.

"Karos? Where's that?" asked Blake.

"It's near Estron, my home world and Serassan's."

Again Blake was startled. "You mean..." His eyes quickly scanned Kapri's humanoid form. "My uncle is from your world... does he... does he look... like you?"

Kapri couldn't help but be amused. "Serassan is Estronian, yes. On Estron our features differ from you Terrans."

"Whoa!" Blake then caught himself. "I mean... I'm sorry... I don't mean to sound rude. It's just that I can't believe that my aunt would... well, you know..."

Kapri put a hand on Blake's shoulder. "Come with me, young human," she said, then turned to Blue Jay, who was still watching the two of them in awe. "Do you mind if I borrow your friend for a while?"

Blue Jay shrugged. "Go ahead. I've gotta get down to the café. My shift's gonna start soon." Grinning at Blake, he said, "Come on down when you get hungry. Think you can find your way?"

"I'll see that he does," said Kapri. She began leading Blake out of the monitoring laboratory and Blue Jay took off in the other direction.

"I have something to show you in my quarters," Kapri said as she led Blake down the corridor. They wound through a series of hallways and up a level or two until they reached what Blake guessed were crew quarters.

Kapri stopped at her cabin and opened the doorway by placing her hand over a signal in the wall that allowed the cubicle to open. She then beckoned him inside. The quarters were clean and lavish, much larger and more elegant than the little bunk room he had been given. She had a small living room and he saw a door that he presumed led into a bedroom. Another doorway led into a bath. There was furniture to sit on that appeared ultra modern and functional, although alien. She told him to sit and then disappeared through the bedroom door.

Blake couldn't believe he was in an alien woman's quarters on board a mother ship. He had certainly taken in a lot of new experiences in the last couple of days.

Kapri stepped out of the bedroom, carrying a small book, which she handed to Blake. He opened it to find photographs of several beings. He recognized Kapri's face and moved through the pages until he saw a holographic picture of his aunt standing with a tall, dark-haired man whose hand was around her slender shoulders. The man had the same deep blue eyes that matched the color of Kapri's.

"That is Johanna and Serassan," Kapri said with pride, "my dear friends on Karos." The background in the photograph showed a barren landscape of rocks and hills. There was a blue sky and some plant growth that reminded Blake of a desert.

"I thought you said my uncle came from the same world as you," said Blake.

"He does. Serassan and I are of the same race. But he is in human form right now, just as I was while my mission took me to Terra. I changed back to my true form afterwards. Serassan has maintained his diguise."

"What did you look like when you were on your mission?" Blake asked.

Kapri took the book from him and flipped through the pages, then showed him the picture of an attractive young woman in her twenties with pale skin and long black hair.

"Wow," breathed Blake. "How did you do that?"

Kapri laughed. "The process of physical transformation is not an easy one. The process is complex and takes anywhere from three of your months to a year. We are not shapeshifters that change form in a moment's notice."

"Why didn't you stay in human form?" asked Blake.

"There was no reason to keep that form." Kapri let Blake page through the rest of the book. "There is discomfort maintaining a form other than our own. Serassan does not have an easy time remaining as he is. He must undergo regular checkups by one of our Estronian physicians. Yet it was necessary for him in order to continue his life with your aunt on a Class M planet."

"Class M? By that you mean a planet conducive to oxygen-breathing life and temperatures adequate for human life."

Kapri's eyes danced with delight. "You are acquainted with galactic concepts."

"I just watch a lot of *Star Trek* reruns," he admitted, to which Kapri nodded.

"Our Federation implanted much knowledge into the minds of those science fiction writers. You'll find that much of what you consider make-believe is based on fact."

Blake thought of something. "Well, if Serassan has to have a human form to live with my aunt, then does that mean your world isn't Class M?"

Kapri patted his arm. "Such a bright boy you are, Blake Dobbs. The oxygen level on Estron is not exactly compatible with Karos, which is similar to Terra. Although the levels do not vary that much, it is enough that your uncle could survive on Karos using oxygen supplements, but his being in human form works better for the long term."

"Well, wait a minute," said Blake. "Why are you able to breathe the same as me on this ship?"

"Very good," she praised, amazed at his intelligence. "While on the ship, I must either have regular injections to balance the oxygen levels in my blood, or wear this device."

She reached under her left sleeve with her right hand and its long, thin, gray fingers, and pulled out a compact metal case with programmable buttons that reminded Blake of a pocket calculator. A wire thread ran underneath from the device up into Kapri's sleeve.

"What's that?" Blake asked.

"For the sake of simplicity, it is an atmospheric bubble generator," explained Kapri. "Around my head right now is an invisible bubble of air containing the right oxygen and gas levels so that I can interact aboard this ship. I have the device programmed for Estron's atmosphere."

"Wow," breathed Blake.

"It would be the same for you if you were to board an Estronian craft. You would need oxygen injections of the opposite effect."

Blake turned the page in Kapri's photo album and was startled to see a beautiful little girl with long blond hair and the same color of blue eyes. "Who is this?"

Kapri looked, then said, "That is Serassan and Johanna's child, Crystal."

Blake felt his heart begin to pound. "Their... child?"

"She is their daughter," added Kapri.

"Then she'd... she'd be my first cousin!" Blake cried.

"That photograph is several years old," said Kapri.

"How old would she be now?" asked Blake.

"I believe Crystal is seventeen," said Kapri.

"Whoa!" Then he murmured, "A year older than me. What is she like?"

"I have never met the young hybrid," Kapri said, "but she is reportedly very talented."

"In what way?" asked Blake.

"She is musical," said Kapri. "Apparently she is the first of Estronian blood who possesses true musical ability."

"Is that right?" He sighed. "She's a knockout." He looked up, suddenly embarrassed. "I mean... she's not bad looking... for my cousin."

"Blake, would you like to meet your aunt and uncle?" Kapri took the book from him and placed it on a shelf.

"Meet them? Where?"

Kapri rubbed her pointy chin as she thought a moment. "I think it could be arranged for you to travel to that part of the galaxy. Would you want to go?"

Travel across the galaxy? Blake was ecstatic. "How long would that take?" he asked.

Before she could respond, a signal of some sort sounded in

the cabin and Kapri gently pushed him toward the door. "I must return to my post," she told him. "We will discuss this later. Come with me and I'll show you the direction to the café."

Blake followed the alien woman, his thoughts in a whirl. He had been blown away to learn he had an alien uncle. Now to discover he had a *cousin* who was an alien hybrid!

21

Expectations

When Manley awoke, the campfire was blazing and Kevin was feeding sticks to the flames. Off in the distance they heard a cow bellow. The other young man, Joe, was curled up in his sleeping bag. Manley sat up. He had slept fitfully on the hard ground, but for the most part he had stayed warm inside Kevin's sleeping bag.

"Want some coffee?" asked Kevin. "There's some left over in the pot."

"Thanks." Manley scratched his head and looked around at the blackness. "Nothing's changed."

"Nope," said Kevin.

"Did you sleep?" Manley asked.

"Yup. Joe and I took turns."

Manley found the styrofoam cup he'd used before and crawled over to the pot beside the fire. His stomach growled from hunger. He didn't know how much food the two boys were carrying with them, so he didn't ask about breakfast. If they offered him something, fine, but he felt he had already imposed enough on their hospitality.

"You boys have jobs?" asked Manley as he poured the coffee. "Or do you ride around the country on your bikes all year long?"

"We both have jobs," Kevin disclosed. "We're teachers. And what is it that you do?"

Manley settled himself closer to the fire. "I'm a type of counselor, I suppose."

"You mean an attorney?"

Manley smiled. "No, nothing like that. I counsel people and try to help them."

"Oh, you're a shrink then."

"No, not exactly," said Manley. "I run a UFO Contact Center."

"A what?" Kevin was startled.

"A place where people can deal with their UFO experiences," explained Manley. "I've been running the center for almost eighteen years."

"No kidding." Kevin sighed. "Is it profitable?"

Manley laughed. "Absolutely not. It's nonprofit."

"Well, how do you keep it going? How do you get paid at a job like that?" asked Kevin.

Manley explained briefly about the grants he had obtained and how he had inherited his sister's estate, which had helped carry him through the years. "The center doesn't make any money in itself," he said, "and it's certainly not government funded. But we get by."

"I thought maybe you were some kind of professor," said Kevin. "You knew all about this photon thing. Any idea what's going to happen next?"

Manley sipped some of the warm coffee. The cow bellowed again in the distance. "The Null Zone is supposed to last three to five days," he recalled. "Then... it's really anybody's guess." He paused, then asked, "What would you like to have happen?"

Kevin smirked. "What would *I* like to see?"

"That's what I asked."

The young man laughed nervously. "I don't see where that is going to make any difference."

"Answer the question."

Kevin thought a moment. "Ask me again."

Manley took another sip of the coffee. "After the darkness ends, what is it you'd like to have happen?"

"You mean, if it was up to *me*?"

"It *is* up to you."

"Oh, come on. When we hit daylight again, it's going to be utter chaos. Troops are going to be everywhere, dealing with freaked-out people, and how are we going to hide from them?"

Manley put up his hand. "Stop. Is that the scenario you really want to see?"

"Well... no... not really."

"Do you really *want* to live in a messed-up world? People

scared... fighting... running?"

"Why, no."

"If you expect something like that to happen, *you will create it.*"

"What are you saying?" asked Kevin.

"I'm saying, your thoughts are very powerful," said Manley. "They've always been powerful in that you've created exactly what your thoughts have conjured. But now, after the photon effect, you're going to be even *more* powerful, and your wishes are going to manifest instantaneously."

"I think that's a bunch of new-age baloney," scoffed Kevin.

"It's not," said Manley. "Our thoughts manifest, and... depending on what we think and put out to the universe, that's what we will get."

"Well, if that were true," mused Kevin, "then the things we desire... why don't we have them?"

"What do you desire?" asked Manley.

Kevin thought for a minute. "Probably what most people want... a high-paying job... a nice home... a gorgeous wife... lots of money."

"Uh-huh." Manley sipped more coffee. "A high-paying job? Does it matter what you do, or is it only important to bring in those big bucks?"

"Well, I suppose *what* I do matters somewhat. I'd like to be able to keep on teaching."

"And the wife... she's gorgeous, okay, but what if she can't stand you?"

"That's no good," said Kevin.

"And lots of money? Are you sure you want to deal with the kind of responsibility and headaches that come with having lots of money?"

Kevin sighed. "Well, now that you put it that way."

"With the photon effect in full force, things are going to happen more quickly with our desires. We need to be very specific about what it is we want to bring into our life experience," explained Manley. "Believe it or not, the universe gives us exactly what we ask for."

"I really don't believe that," said Kevin. "I mean, look around us. We didn't ask for all this darkness and cold."

"Didn't we?" Manley hugged the sleeping bag tighter around himself. "You see, Kevin, we are not always aware of what we ask for. In a collective way, perhaps all of humanity was crying out for a change — a major shift on this planet — that would once and for all force us all into changing our lifestyles and acting more cooperatively rather than continuing on the destructive path we have been on."

They were silent for a while and Kevin seemed to be pondering these ideas. Joe stirred and then sat up and moved himself and the sleeping bag closer to the fire. "Got any of that coffee left?" he asked.

"Sure man, right here." Kevin got up and brought the simmering pot over to his friend. "Manley and I were just having an interesting discussion."

"Yeah, I know," said Joe, holding out his cup. "I was listening."

Manley sipped the drink that was now turning cold. He was about to say something, but his eyes had caught the faintest glimmer of gray color in the distant darkness. "Hey, is it my imagination, or is the sky getting lighter?"

Both Joe and Kevin cheered. "Dawn is breaking!" cried Kevin. "It's definitely happening."

"Praise God," murmured Joe.

"Remember," Manley said as he sipped the last of the coffee in his cup, "it's up to you."

22
Early Morning Walk

Sunshine from the high window streamed into Crystal's underground bedroom. It softly caressed her face. She stirred, then awoke to a refreshing breeze that swept off the nearby mountains and filtered through the opening in the tiny window above. She realized she had slept better last night than she had in months. Her dreams had been full of music and applause, with flashes of memory from the previous evening's performance.

Crystal smiled and stared up at her little window, basking in the magical feeling of ecstasy that was so new to her. She had given all of herself to the performance. Her voice had responded beautifully and the audience had adored her.

Something special had happened to her last night. For perhaps the first time in her life — or at least since she could recall — Crystal had seen her mother, Johanna, in a different light, and had shared a sense of equality with her. For the first time, she had truly admired Johanna and had been actually proud of her.

A sudden urge prompted Crystal to get up and find her parents and share this revelation with them. She pulled on her robe and dove into her slippers, then headed into the stone hallway. There she met Kameel-37, the robot servant, waiting for the day's first orders.

"Oh, Kameel, I'll have breakfast later," said Crystal. "Are Mom and Dad up yet?"

The cat-like unit with glowing silver eyes hovered in the same spot. "Johanna Dobbs and Serassan left orders not to be disturbed this morning," responded the mechanical, high-pitched voice. The blue voice light flickered in the throat area of the unit when it spoke. "They arrived home late following last night's celebration. They are sleeping in."

Crystal noticed the closed bedroom door and sighed with

disappointment. Her happy mood tumbled a few notches as she shuffled toward the bathroom.

"However, if it is important, Crystal Dobbs, I can awaken them," Kameel added.

"No, it's nothing important," Crystal grumbled as she closed the door on Kameel. After she had washed up and dried her face, she decided to get dressed and take a walk in the fresh morning air. The sunshine on her skin would feel good. Besides, she had all this energy and excitement to burn off from last night. She pulled on a sweater and told Kameel-37 she was going out for a little exercise and would return shortly.

The mountains practically sparkled against the blue-green sky of Karos and new green leaves were budding on the forest trees across the River of Determination. Crystal set a pace toward the clearing and away from the cluster of stone residences that had been erected nearly nineteen years ago, when the volunteer Terrans had settled on this colony planet. Crystal had been told that Karos resembled Earth in many ways. That was the reason her father's people had chosen it and used their technology to transform its terrain and atmosphere to make it habitable for the humans they had brought from Earth.

Karos was the only home Crystal had known. She had been off planet several times since her childhood, mostly to visit her grandparents, Soolàn and Emrox, who lived in solitude on a small planetoid near Estron. There the landscape was dry and barren, red and hilly, with little, if any, vegetation. Visiting Granna and Grandfather had been highlights of her youth, even if she hadn't much appreciated the regular injections to balance her oxygen level required during her stay with them.

Her father's home world, Estron, was close by, yet her parents had taken her there only twice in her lifetime. Estron was a busy world with a lot of activity and hovercraft buzzing around towers of crystalline structures. Crystal hadn't cared for it, even though she fantasized quite a bit about what big city life might be like. She had read about cities on Terra and been captivated by the stories her mother had shared. Even though Estron was the planet of her father's people, she had never desired to reside there. And Karos, peaceful and pretty as it was, seemed too confined for a girl who had great ambitions and dreamed of cruising the galaxy and discovering all the different worlds and their races.

She thought of Thorden, the Estronian man who had visited her dressing room the evening before. He had offered her an opportunity to live that dream. Although Crystal didn't care for the alien man upon first meeting him, and it was obvious that her mother found him disturbing, she couldn't help musing over his tempting offer. What would it be like, she wondered, to be on board a starship and to be part of a crew that traversed the universe?

Crystal feared it would take many years before she could even hope to be considered for a menial position on an Estronian space cruiser. It required many years of hard study and training, and it meant stiff competition with her female Estronian peers, whose minds were geared toward getting to the top and not wasting any time.

It was only a short while ago — yesterday, as a matter of fact — when Crystal would have considered nothing other than making a career of exploring space. But the grand opening had prompted new feelings and caused her to view her life from a different perspective. All these years she had resisted, to the point where it even hurt, the idea of a musical career. Her mother had tried to drum the idea into her that this was the reason she had been conceived. Crystal had resented that and had retaliated every way she could. She almost went so far as to deny her own talent, yet something deep inside of her always surfaced when the singing began and the music started to possess her very soul.

Something mystical and uniquely Estronian hungered in the deepest way for the beauty of music and art. She understood why it was her father, Serassan, was often entranced by the music Johanna played on her piano. Serassan couldn't help it, no more than Crystal's stubborn resistance could fend off the powerful force of beauty and how the music nurtured her.

"But I *want* to go into space," Crystal said out loud, kicking at some weeds as she wandered into the clearing. She startled a Karosian grouse, which darted frantically away from her. She watched the tan, speckled bird until it found refuge in some brush, and then she proceeded. "Space has always been my dream. I can't give it up. Anyway, what would I do here on this lonely planet?"

She wished she had someone to talk to, to discuss things with.

How she longed for a friend her age to confide in. Long ago she'd had such a friend, a girl her age who had been born to Terran parents on Karos. Curly, dark-haired Amanda had been Crystal's best friend in the early years. They had played together and shared secrets and giggled most of the time. But then Amanda's mother had suffered post traumatic stress syndrome from the abduction. The family departed from Karos to reside on an orbiting space ship. At least that's what Crystal had been told. It had been years ago, and she still missed the companionship and the fun she'd had as a girl with Amanda. Crystal recalled Amanda's round face and green eyes that appeared to flash mischievously when she got excited about a game they were playing or some scheme for trouble that the two of them would cook up when they were together.

After Amanda and her parents left Karos, life had become more challenging for Crystal. There had been no other children her age whom she had associated with. Shortly after that, Johanna and Serassan had made arrangements for her to attend school on one of the educational space vessels that orbited Estron. In the last three years, Crystal had made friends with Estronian girls and had occasional contact with a few Terran teens whose parents served in space aboard the starships. The craft she had been on was a boarding school of sorts. She would be there three or four weeks at a time and then would get shuttled to Karos for a home visit that would last four to seven days.

The school ship only whetted Crystal's appetite to be in space. Field trips to distant planets, though far and few between, had been thrilling in many ways, and she envisioned herself as a crew member on the bridge of one of those light ships.

Estronian girls her age often engaged in debates about cosmic theory and time travel. Their intellectual exchanges, though often above Crystal's head, always intrigued her and she would sit in on the discussions, rarely participating, but always stimulated and enthused by the atmosphere of the higher mind levels.

Terran girls, on the other hand, tended to bore Crystal. There were a few younger Terrans on the school ship. Only a handful were from the Terran colony on Karos. The rest came from orbiting ships of the Federation. Their parents served on various ships, many of whom had been born in space and whose ancestry could be traced to early Terran abductions.

In addition to the girls, there were members of the male gender on the spaceship school, although they were usually schooled on a different level of the ship. She had enrolled in a few courses where Estronian males shared the classroom. Crystal had had very little contact with any young males, particularly of the Estronian race. She had grown up with a few younger Terran boys, but had not made friends with any of them.

She did notice how silly and flirtatious the younger Terran girls acted around the boys. She didn't understand their behavior. To her it was ridiculous and entirely frivolous, especially after listening to how the Estronian girls laughed over it and put the Terran girls down.

Estronian boys interested Crystal only in the way that she found them curious. Aside from their bald-headed, slanted-eyed appearance, the Estronian boys were always staring at her and probing her thoughts. She usually managed to shut off her mind from them, but once in a great while one would catch her off guard. They often sent suggestive, sexual images into her mind when she let herself drift off. She would bolt upright in her desk and turn to find the young chap leering at her. In anger she'd toss her head with the long blond curls and force herself to concentrate on the subject matter being taught to her in the front of the classroom.

"Crystal's face turned crimson again," one of the Estronian girls would mention to the others that night in the dining hall. They would all twitter with laughter.

"Tell us, Crystal. What causes one's face to do that?" another would ask.

Crystal would turn away, embarrassed.

"Look, she's doing it now," they'd marvel.

"Red corpuscles in Terran blood," one would begin to analyze. "The cause: feelings of inadequacy, inferiority, or a flush of anger. Or, in some cases among Terrans, *sexual arousal*."

"Oooh… *disgusting*," one would moan.

Humiliated, Crystal would excuse herself and leave the room.

The girls weren't really mean to her. They didn't taunt her the way Terran children had taunted her, at least. The Estronians picked on her because she was different, but they meant no harm by it. They were intellectual by nature and analyzed everything to pieces, whether it was complimentary or critical. Crystal preferred that to how her Terran peers treated her.

Terran girls seemed to move in clusters. Three, four or five in a group always managed to stick together as if being alone was a dangerous thing. They huddled together and giggled and squealed, and it made Crystal uncomfortable being around them when the noise would suddenly halt and all eyes followed her every move. Then they'd whisper and start giggling again once she'd passed.

For years she had endured the label "hybrid." Kids and adults had called her that, and sometimes she had been given the impression that being a hybrid was an unfitting characteristic. Her parents had brought her up to respect others, even those who appeared different in any way. She simply did not understand why anyone should treat her as a freak. Her attempts to be friendly and pleasant were often met by coldness or disrespect. Even those who had the common courtesy to reply amicably gave off a vibe of false pretense that Crystal picked up on and which told her it was useless to try to advance the friendship. So she chose to hang out with the highly intellectual, obsessively ambitious Estronians, and began to daydream about her future life in space.

She craved a life in which she would be respected, where her lineage was of little importance to her rank, and where she could search the stars for her place among them. Something in the stars called to her whenever she sat in the Stellar Alcove and had the view of space all around her. The Stellar Alcove was a quiet, café-like section on the school ship where one could relax and watch stars in the dark. Crystal spent a lot of time there when she was on the school ship. She would watch the stars, think thoughts about those worlds so far away, and wonder if she would ever get to see any of them.

Something out there beckoned to her as if she belonged to it. But what it was she did not know. The feeling filled her with such longing that she sometimes wanted to weep.

As she stepped out of the woods Crystal found herself in view of the Galactic Center for the Arts. Its huge marble structure was impressive today against the Karosian sky, which was filled with wisps of puffy white clouds between patches of blue-green. Several shuttles were parked around the huge center. Many guests had stayed overnight in the new hotel.

Crystal wondered if Thorden, the Estronian, was staying at the hotel. She really wanted to speak with him about what he had proposed the evening before. Her stomach rumbled a bit and she realized she was hungry. Certainly the café would be open for breakfast this morning.

She walked to the main entrance and found the doors were open. A few beings leisurely roamed the hallway as Crystal made her way to the café. Several patrons were already seated in the restaurant, sipping from cups or eating breakfast. Jasmine greeted her warmly.

"Good morning, Mrs. Oliver," replied Crystal.

"What a spectacular performance you gave us last night, my dear." Jasmine grinned broadly at Crystal as she led her to a small corner table. "Will your parents be joining you this morning?"

Crystal sat and accepted a menu. "They were still asleep when I left the house," she explained.

"Well, of course. No wonder!" Jasmine touched Crystal's shoulder. "I'll bet they are so proud of you. Would you like me to bring you some citrus juice?"

"Sure." Crystal smiled politely at her old voice teacher.

Jasmine left, still bubbling about "our little star."

Crystal was startled to suddenly catch sight of Thorden standing at the door of the café. He noticed her and strolled over. The short Estronian man was dressed in a gray tunic and matching leggings. He appeared smaller and a bit older than Crystal remembered from last evening. She invited him to join her at her corner table.

"Good morning, good morning, lovely Crystal Dobbs." Thorden bowed, then took his seat across from her. "What a glorious surprise to find you here this morning."

Crystal sighed, a little embarrassed by all the admiration. Some heads were turning their way. "I was hoping to see you this morning," she admitted. "I wanted to speak with you further about... about space."

Thorden's smile broadened. "Ahhh... yes." He glanced around nervously and bent forward. "Perhaps we should keep our voices down a bit."

"Why?" she asked.

He put a long thin grayish finger to his narrow mouth slit and smiled nervously. "There are many ears, my dear. Many ears."

Crystal didn't know why this had to be a secret, but she nodded her head. "Okay. But I wanted…"

"Have you ordered your meal?" he asked.

"No, not yet."

"Do Serassan and Johanna know you are here?"

Crystal hesitated. Then she said, "No."

Thorden folded his hands and seemed to ponder something. Then he looked at her with a gleam in his blue slanted eyes. "And do you *really* want to go into space and pilot a starship?"

"More than anything," she said.

"More than… anything?" He cocked his head.

"Yes," she insisted. "Oh, yes. It's all I've dreamed of." As she spoke the words a flash of last night's applause popped into her head, but she drove the thought away. "For years I've wanted a space career," she told him. "It means more to me than anything."

Thorden snatched the menu from her hands and gently laid it on the table. "Then we must go… now."

Crystal's mouth opened in surprised. "Now? You mean *right now*?"

"Precisely."

Crystal gazed around. None of the other patrons seemed to be paying any attention. Jasmine was in the kitchen, out of sight. "But," said Crystal, "I need to get some things at home first. And what about my mother and father? I can't just go without saying I'm leaving. They…"

Thorden peered into her face with stern alien eyes. "Crystal, if you want this opportunity, then you must seize it. There is no time for saying goodbyes. My shuttle leaves in ten minutes. I have made arrangements to dock with the mother ship. It's now or… not at all!"

Crystal's heart was pounding. Leave *now*? She wasn't ready to go with Thorden at a moment's notice. This was too sudden. She wanted to explain to her parents about her decision. They would be devastated, to say the least. Besides, she was still a little confused by the emotions from last night and this morning. Her musical career would be interrupted, if not yanked away from her altogether. She had wanted some time to sift through her feelings and sort out her thoughts about pursuing the kind of life she had been trained for.

But at the same time there was this yearning, this driving force in her head that made Thorden's offer irresistible. Now or... never?

"Crystal, make up your mind," prompted Thorden.

Crystal swallowed the lump in her throat and ran her fingers through her hair. Then she looked at Thorden without smiling and said, "All right, then. I'll go with you."

"Come, then. Quickly." Thorden pushed back his chair and stood up. "The shuttle awaits."

Crystal rose and let the Estronian lead her out of the café. She did not see Jasmine standing at the kitchen door, staring after her with a glass of orange juice in her hand.

23

Alarming News

Johanna stirred and then awoke to find Serassan sitting on the side of the bed next to her. He was staring into her face and the deep blue color of his eyes still left her in awe each time she looked into them. His smile was gentle, filled with love. "Good morning, Johanna, my love," he said in a soft deep voice.

"Oh, it's late," she replied, noticing the brightness of their room. "How long have you been up?"

Serassan leaned over to kiss her. "Long enough to order breakfast in bed for my beautiful wife."

Into the room glided Kameel-37 carrying a tray with coffee cups, juice and muffins.

Johanna sat up in bed. "What did I do to deserve this?" she asked.

"You need to ask?" Serassan seemed surprised. He motioned the android over to the side of the bed. "After last night's opening... your performance and production of the entire evening was absolutely magnificent. I thought I'd let you sleep. You were, after all, exhausted after last night's party."

Kameel held the tray and they each reached for the coffee cups.

"I didn't do it all alone," Johanna reminded him. "You were a large part of all the planning. Without you, Serassan..."

He held up a hand in resistance. "We pulled it off," he said and sipped his coffee. "And from all I can tell, the Galactic Center for the Arts on Karos is going to be a tremendous success."

"Yes..." Johanna smiled and rested against her pillow. "It was a splendid evening. I truly enjoyed myself, even if it was exhausting." She turned to Kameel. "Is Crystal up yet?"

"I believe she's been up for hours," said Serassan.

Kameel spoke in her metallic, high-pitched voice. "Crystal

Dobbs went for a walk earlier today. She did not say when she would return."

"Hmm." Johanna took one of the freshly baked orange muffins. "Crystal was high class," she said. "I was very impressed."

"She practically stole the show," Serassan remarked.

"I'm anxious to speak with her," said Johanna. "Kameel, how long has Crystal been out?"

Without hesitation the unit said, "Three hours, fifty-two minutes and forty-four seconds."

"Wow, she did get up at the crack of dawn." Johanna bit into her muffin. "She should have been home by now."

Serassan shrugged. "Maybe she stopped off somewhere to visit someone."

Johanna frowned. "I don't think Crystal has many close friends in the colony anymore." After a minute of silence Johanna looked at Serassan. "You don't think she's mad at us, do you?"

Serassan pouted. "Over what, my love?"

Johanna sighed. "I had a funny feeling yesterday that she was not happy with me. We had a disagreement about her plans for going into space."

"Nonsense. Things were well between the two of you last night at the performance," said Serassan.

However, Johanna did not feel comfortable. Perhaps it was only a mother's tendency to worry about her child, but she had a disturbing feeling that told her Crystal might be up to something not to her liking.

After breakfast Johanna got dressed and she and Serassan waited for Crystal's return. As the noon hour began to approach, Johanna was too nervous to wait any longer.

"Serassan, we've got to go look for her."

The tall Estronian rubbed his chin and looked at the steps that climbed to the doorway to their underground stone dwelling. "Indeed, it has been five hours since she left."

They told Kameel-37 to inform them immediately should their daughter return to the stone cottage. Then Johanna and Serassan left the house and began to walk toward the main part of the Terran village. Their own dwelling was remote, set apart from the cluster of other homes also built of native stone and wood. In the nineteen years they had resided on Karos, thirty dwellings had been erected and were home to a Terran population of nearly seventy-two. Some occupants had immigrated to Karos after the original colony had been set up following the failure of the Earth-Star mission that Serassan had helped lead. The immigrant Terrans had lived on orbiting mother ships and had heard of the new colony and its plans for establishing a galactic center for performing arts. Many were artists themselves who wanted to settle down on a planet after many decades in space.

Johanna and Serassan stopped at several homes to inquire if Crystal had been by. No one had seen her that morning, but all whom they talked with congratulated them on last night's tremendous success of a grand opening and remarked on how much they had enjoyed Johanna's playing and Crystal's singing.

Finally, in frustration, Johanna and Serassan reached the Galactic Arts Center with the parked shuttles and the diversity of beings roaming the grounds. Johanna felt Serassan squeeze her hand. She looked up at him and he smiled down at her. "This is what we worked so hard to accomplish," he said with admiration.

Johanna smiled, but the worry was still strong within her. "Let's go inside," she said. "Maybe someone has seen Crystal."

Many heads looked in their direction. Some waved and smiled or closed their fingertips together in diamond fashion, bowing to show their respect and gratitude.

"The café," Johanna said and led her husband inside, where Jasmine and Sam were now busy with the lunch crowd.

A teen-age Terran girl from the colony tried to seat them, but Johanna shook her head. "We just had breakfast."

At that moment Jasmine caught sight of Johanna and Serassan and hurried over, holding an armful of dirty plates. "Johanna, Serassan, hello! Are you here for lunch?"

"No," said Johanna.

"It looks like business is booming," said Serassan. "Where's Sam?"

"In the kitchen." Jasmine's eyes darted right and left. "Are you looking for Crystal?"

Johanna nodded. "How did you know?"

"Johanna, you've got that worried mother look."

Serassan asked, "Have you seen her?"

Jasmine's lower lip trembled. "Yes, she came in this morning and ordered breakfast. But... actually, she didn't get around to ordering breakfast. She... she left before I could bring out her juice."

"Where did she go?" Johanna demanded.

Jasmine shrugged. "I don't know. But she was with someone."

"Who?" pressed Johanna.

"Well, I don't know who. But it was... he was... an Estronian." Jasmine's eyes focused on Serassan. "He was wearing a gray tunic and was rather short."

Johanna's eyes grew wide with fear. She turned to face her husband. "Oh, Serassan, it was Thorden!"

"Thorden?" Serassan was surprised.

"Yes, I told you he was at the opening last night. I walked into Crystal's dressing room and he was there with her."

A deep concern spread over Serassan's face and he put his arms around Johanna and led her out of the busy café.

"Our daughter's left with Thorden!" cried Johanna. "Oh, no! I'm so frightened, Serassan."

"We don't know anything for sure," he told her. "We really don't know if it was him. Let's check at the hotel desk to see if he has checked out."

A few minutes later the desk clerk told them Thorden had checked out of the hotel earlier that morning. That's all he knew. Next, Serassan consulted the shuttle parking attendant and learned that Thorden's space shuttle had departed.

"Do you know if he left alone?" asked Johanna.

The attendant was an elderly man who was one of the Terran immigrants who had come to Karos to be involved with the galactic arts center. He nodded his head. "The young lady who sang like a bird left, too," he disclosed. "Your daughter? My, what talent she has. You must be very proud, the two of you."

Johanna and Serassan thanked the man, then walked back toward the center. Both of them were stunned. Before they reached the entrance, Johanna stopped and Serassan did the same. She grabbed his arm. "Serassan, why would Crystal leave with Thorden? Last night she appeared to be afraid of him."

Serassan's forehead was creased and his eyes had that look of deep concern that Johanna knew from time to time. "Let's not overreact," he advised. "It's possible he just promised our daughter a ride. Maybe she asked if she could pilot his shuttle. You know how she is always begging for a chance to go somewhere so she can fly."

Johanna sighed. "Is there any way we can find out? Can we contact Thorden? Oh, how could Crystal *do* this?" Tears exploded from Johanna's brown eyes and she fell against Serassan's strong chest.

He held her and let her weep, then said, "I will do my best, Johanna. I am sure we can find out where Thorden has taken Crystal."

"How could he *do* this?" she continued to sob. "I want my daughter back! My poor little girl... in the clutches or that horrid man!"

People were beginning to stop and stare at them, so Serassan began leading Johanna home. Just as they got within sight of their stone cottage at the far end of the colony, a shuttle lowered itself to the ground in front of their dwelling.

Johanna cried out in joy. "It's Crystal! She's back!" She started to run toward the ship, but Serassan caught up with her and held her back.

"It's Crystal! I know it," cried Johanna. "She was just out on a joy ride."

"No, Johanna," said Serassan. "It's Emrox."

Just then they saw the door open and the ramp unfold. The older Estronian who was Serassan's father emerged from the shuttle and held up his hand in greeting.

Johanna's disappointment was prominent, but she composed herself as they walked over to greet Emrox, who was alone.

"Father," said Serassan, "I greet you."

"And greetings to you, my son." Emrox turned to Johanna. "How are you, Johanna?"

She sniffled and wiped tears from her cheeks. She couldn't answer him.

"Forgive us, please, Father," said Serassan. "Johanna has had a bit of a shock, I'm afraid."

"Oh?" Emrox turned to her. "Then you have already heard the news. There is no sense in sparing you, then."

Johanna looked up in surprise. "What news?"

"About Earth," said Emrox.

Serassan put his arm around Johanna's shoulders. "Let's go inside and talk," he suggested. They headed for the cottage.

Johanna shuddered nervously with fear as they went through the door and stepped down the long stairway into the living room. She let her husband lead her to the couch, where he sat beside her. Emrox took the seat across from them.

Immediately Kameel-37 entered to offer the elder Estronian a mug of Mupani tea.

"Thank you, but I must decline," said Emrox. "This is not a social call. Serassan, Earth's shift has begun."

"How long ago?" asked Serassan.

"Three days ago," Emrox replied.

Johanna covered her mouth with her hand. "Oh... my... God..."

"Survivors?" asked Serassan.

"Unknown," said Emrox.

"How bad?"

"We do not yet know."

"Natural... or induced?" asked Serassan.

"Unknown."

There was a short silence, and then Johanna burst into tears once more. Not only had her only daughter run off with a man of ill character who couldn't be trusted. Now she had to bear the news of her home planet undergoing the dreaded and predicted disaster in which most of its population would be wiped out. She couldn't bear it.

Serassan called to Kameel-37. "Please bring Johanna some Mupani tea," he instructed. He held her as she sobbed. "Father, that is upsetting news."

"I'm sorry," said Emrox. "I thought you already knew."

"Crystal has disappeared," Serassan explained.

The elder Estronian cocked his head. "Oh?"

"We have reason to believe that Thorden of Estron has persuaded her to go with him."

"Your old friend Thorden?"

"Thorden was a fellow guide on the Earth-Star mission. I wouldn't call him exactly a friend. He had... ulterior motives."

"I see." Emrox nodded his head.

"He craved beautiful, talented Terran women."

At that Johanna's sobs began again.

Emrox, obviously disturbed at the emotional outburst, waved his hands and shook his gray bald head. "Let's not upset Johanna any more, son."

"Thorden..." Johanna blurted out between sobs, "he... he... he once tried to... rape me!" She continued to sob, then managed to say, "He took advantage of the young ballerina, Radya... he... he... he'll do the same to Crystal."

Serassan tried to calm her, but his special touch was not working. He, too, was upset at both the news of Crystal's disappearance and Earth's shift.

It wasn't long before Kameel-37 brought in a tray of the desired Mupani tea. All three of them took the tea and within minutes had calmed down enough that Johanna quit crying and they could think more rationally.

A deep desire to sleep came over Johanna then, and Serassan helped her to the bedroom, where he left her and pulled the blinds, then returned to the living room in the stone cottage. He then began to discuss with one of Estron's high advisors what to do about Earth.

24

Recruited

Dorothy stared up in awe at the composed, handsome face of Ernestine Glenn. She was a striking woman with sharp features and fiery green eyes. Her shoulder-length, reddish-brown hair was styled in curls. Her cheekbones were prominent, made more so by the makeup she wore, along with dark red lipstick. She stood over Dorothy with her hands on her hips, looking a bit top heavy with the bulky beige sweater in contrast to the tight red leggings and shiny black boots.

"Dorothy Dobbs," Ernestine said without changing the expression on her face.

After swallowing from nervousness, Dorothy said, "Yes. And you... you are Ernestine Glenn."

"That is correct," said Ms. Glenn.

"How did you know my name?" asked Dorothy.

The presidential candidate's face remained stern as her eyes seemed to shine. "I have an excellent memory for names and faces. I suppose that is one reason I came so far as to be nominated for president."

Ernestine drew a chair up next to Dorothy, then continued. "All of those letters of support and donations you made to my campaign. Do not believe for a moment that they went unnoticed." Her face softened just a bit.

Dorothy sighed and smiled, her first smile in days, it seemed.

Ernestine reached out a thin hand with nails polished in red to match her lips and her tights. "I have chosen you, Dorothy, to work with me now. The country is in crisis, and there is much for us to do. I would like you to assist me."

Dorothy was dumbfounded. It still mystified her that Ernestine Glenn knew her name. Her mind kept trying to piece together the puzzle. She had submitted guest editorials during the months of last year's campaign and one newspaper, at least, had requested her photo. She had given her permission for syndication, and perhaps Ms. Glenn had received one of the articles and it had caught her attention.

"I'll be glad to help," said Dorothy, "but can you explain to me first what has been happening?"

Ernestine kept the same stern face. "It was necessary for us to declare martial law," she explained. "The world is in chaos. When we learned that Washington had fled, the Purification Party stepped in."

"Fled? Where did it flee to? Who fled?" Dorothy cried in alarm.

Ernestine let go of Dorothy's hand and her face grew serious. "Obviously those in power had prior knowledge of this devastating event," she said. "They arranged for departure long ago."

"What? Where did they go?"

"All VIPs were removed to some secret base. My sources tell me that this evacuation was well planned."

"And who is left to run the country?" asked Dorothy in amazement. "How could they do this?"

"Precisely." Ernestine's teeth glittered when she grinned. "The Purification Party has taken control and now we must all work together in order to bring about a new world order... the kind of world we deserve to inhabit. No longer will the men whose greed and lusty ways that have brought about so much destruction be allowed to continue on their path of pollution and economic downfall."

Dorothy nodded her head in agreement, her green eyes wide. She was familiar with Ernestine Glenn's campaign speeches and literature condemning the male establishment. How she admired this brave and beautiful woman who she had hoped would lead the country into a New Age of Enlightenment and Progress.

"Well, Dorothy? Are you with me?" Ernestine peered expectantly into the dark-haired woman's face.

"Of course I am," said Dorothy without hesitation. "There's no question. I've been behind you since I first learned about you, Ms. Glenn."

Ernestine folded her hands together with the red-tipped

fingernails straight out. "Good. Then let's get started." She rose from the chair. "The first order of business will be getting you cleaned up. Follow me. You will need a shower."

Dorothy stood up, feeling a little stiff. She knew her face was dirty and her mouth felt like she hadn't brushed her teeth in days — which was true, she hadn't.

She stared in awe out the windows of the quonset at the breaking daylight as she followed Ernestine Glenn toward a passageway. She wondered where Manley was. She remembered the voice of the Light Being, telling her that her children were safe. When would she be allowed to see them? And what about Manley? How would he find her?

Outside one of the windows she caught a glimpse of a crowd of women, their arms waving as they shouted in the distance on the other side of a large barbed wire fence. Female military guards with rifles patrolled them. Dorothy didn't like what she saw, but continued to follow Ernestine Glenn down the passageway until they came to a door that led into a private bathroom.

"Here you go," said Ernestine. "You'll find everything you need. I'll send the major in to get you in about twenty minutes. Then we'll have breakfast and discuss my plans for you."

Dorothy turned to her. "How can I thank you?" she said with tears welling in her eyes.

"Don't mention it." Ernestine spun around and walked back down the hallway.

Dorothy wasted no time stripping her old clothing off. The elegant bathroom had an ample supply of towels, soap, shampoo, toothbrushes in wrappers, and a rack of clean clothes that reminded her of some kind of uniform. She soon had hot water splashing over her tired, stressed-out body, and its soothing heat and wetness penetrated her aching muscles. She closed her eyes and breathed a prayer of gratitude, letting the steam caress her face. Then she found the new bar of soap and began scrubbing arms, breasts, legs and hips, drinking in the perfume of the lavender soap and thinking this had to be the most welcome shower she'd ever taken in her life. She hummed to herself and felt very, very fortunate. She was on her way to becoming Ernestine Glenn's right-hand assistant, and Ernestine Glenn had assumed the role of leader of the country... that is, if what she had said had been true, about the government vacating Washington, and leaving the citizens to fend for themselves.

"I wonder what Ms. Glenn has in mind for me to do," Dorothy murmured to herself after she had gotten out of the shower and dried off. With a green towel wrapped turban fashion around her head, she chose one of the uniforms on the rack that appeared to be her size, then found clean underpants and a bra in a box under the rack. Soon she was dressed and brushed out her long dark hair. There was makeup on the vanity, but Dorothy didn't touch it.

She was still brushing out her hair when a knock came on the door. A second later, a stocky woman with short blond hair and pudgy cheeks stepped into the room. "If you are ready," she said without smiling, "you are to follow me."

Dorothy straightened her dress and immediately followed the major out the door.

25

Embodied

It was late and Blake strolled along the crystalline walkway in the Crystal Fountain quarters of the mother ship. Lotus, the blue girl from Andromeda, strolled alongside him. To Blake it felt like late evening, even though he knew there really was no day or night on the ship because it was in space. He marveled at the magical beauty of the colorful water fountains surrounding them. Huge jutting crystal terminals with gentle rivulets of water gushing down their sides captivated him with their shimmering green and blue lights, and the trickling sound of the flowing water soothed him. There were brilliantly colored crystal sculptures and fountains surrounding him.

"I thought you would enjoy this," Lotus told him in a soft voice. "When one is stressed or troubled in any way, the Crystal Gardens are pleasing and help one to relax and sort out one's thoughts."

"It's awesome," said Blake. He turned to the alien girl who smiled at him so invitingly. "Thanks for spending time with me tonight. I enjoyed hearing about Torphu, and it helped me forget my own problems — at least for now."

"My pleasure always." Lotus reached for his hand and squeezed it. She continued to hold onto him for longer than he felt comfortable.

"Uh..." Blake pulled his hand away, embarrassed.

Lotus continued to stare at him. "You are hesitant?" she asked. Her smile faded.

Blake wasn't quite sure what she meant.

Lotus twittered with laughter. "Oh, I see now! You believe I am trying to... put the makeup on you."

Blake laughed out loud. "That's put the *make* on me," he

corrected, "not makeup."

Lotus flushed a tinge of pale blue and smiled. "I always did have trouble with Terran terminology," she confessed. "I really like you, Blake. I was just offering... in case you wanted to..."

Blake stared at his feet and scratched his blond head. "Well, I like you, too, Lotus." He dared to look up at her. "But I hardly know you."

"Well, part of the fun is learning... getting to know one another," she said.

"Tell me something," said Blake. "How old are you?" Just as soon as he said it, he felt foolish. What if she was offended?

But if Lotus was disturbed by his question, she didn't show it. "I'm eighty-seven of your Terran years," she stated.

"What? But... you're... just a girl," Blake protested.

Lotus nodded. "Perhaps, but I actually reached maturity at seventy."

Before he could comment, Blake heard footsteps hurrying toward them.

"There he is," a male voice called out.

Blake turned in the direction of the voice and saw Blue Jay coming toward him with Kapri right behind him. The Estronian crew woman wore a dark brown shiny robe with sparkling tiny gemstones dotted throughout the fabric.

"Blake Dobbs," Kapri called out. There was a twinkle in her slanted blue eyes. "I have news for you."

Blake immediately perked up. "You've found out something about my mom and dad?" He felt his heart quicken its beat. Blue Jay stroked his chin and glanced at Kapri, who blinked.

"No news of either of them yet, Blake," she said.

"Sorry, dude," said Blue Jay, then grinned. "But wait'll you hear the good news."

"What?" asked Blake.

"You will be traveling on a ship to Estron," announced Kapri.

"I... what?"

Blue Jay nodded excitedly, his white teeth a contrast to his dark skin.

"What is on Estron for Blake?" Lotus wanted to know.

"Actually," said Kapri, "the ship Blake is taking is en route to Estron, my home world, but Blake will be going directly to Karos."

"Oh, delightful!" Lotus' face lit up. She turned to Blake. "Karos has built a wonderful performing arts center. The whole galaxy is talking about it."

"I'm going there to meet my aunt and uncle." Blake turned to Kapri. "Right?"

Kapri smiled proudly. "I've arranged for you to have passage on the *Resilience*, but it will take four days, according to your time, before you arrive. Do you still wish to go?"

This, Blake knew, was the chance of a lifetime. He hesitated, thinking of his parents still on Earth. He felt he should stick around, at least until there was word of them. He explained his concern to Kapri.

"Of course, it is your choice," stated Kapri. "However, if your parents are found, you will be notified just as quickly aboard the cruiser to Estron as on this mother ship."

Blake sighed. "And what about my sister?"

"Kelly is in the best of hands," said Lotus.

"Come on, you have nothing to worry about, Bro," insisted Blue Jay. "Think about it, man! It's the opportunity of a lifetime."

Blake really wanted to go to Karos. He wanted very much to meet his aunt and his Estronian uncle and hybrid girl cousin. But... four days to get there?

"It's a lot faster than it used to be only a few years ago," said Lotus, obviously picking up his thoughts. "And besides, you could always return here if you're needed."

Kapri was quick to explain. "There are hundreds of ships that intercept the space cruisers. If you don't wish to continue your voyage to Karos, you can always catch one of them."

The idea began to appeal to Blake even more.

"Say yes," encouraged Blue Jay.

"You mean... you're that eager to get rid of me?" Blake joked.

"Say what? I'm going with you!" cried out Blue Jay.

"You are?"

"Absolutely!" Blue Jay seemed more excited than Blake. "I've got vacation hours coming. I'll be accompanying you."

Blake turned to Kapri. "When do we depart?" he asked.

"There is a shuttle that leaves in approximately twelve hours," the Estronian scientist told him. "It will take you to meet the cruiser en route to Estron."

Lotus squeezed Blake's hand and smiled at him. "I will see you when you return."

Blue Jay beckoned for Blake to follow him. "Let's go, man. We've gotta pack."

Blake let his musician friend lead him away. "But... I don't have anything to pack." He turned to the women. "Thank you, Kapri. And... bye, Lotus."

A moment later he and Blue Jay had slipped out of the hall of crystal fountains toward the crew quarters.

The transformation was complete. The Light Being's consciousness surfaced to full wakefulness as he grew aware of his own breathing. Slowly he opened his eyes and found himself lying on his back in a dimly lit room. A couple of humanoid beings stood over him, but his vision was still unfocused and he could not make out faces, only their forms in fuzzy white attire.

"Vital signs appear strong," one of them said. It was a male voice. The other touched his forehead ever so gently, and a woman's voice said, "He is reaching awareness."

"Master... can you hear me?" asked the male.

The Light Being blinked his eyes and the fuzziness began to fade. He made the effort to speak using his new vocal cords. "Y... e... es," he croaked, surprised at the strange sound that reached his ears. The vibration of his throat was strange, too. "I... hear," he added. "My... throat... dry..."

The female removed her soothing hand and went to get something for him to drink. He read her thoughts just as clearly as before he had taken this body. The male in the white coat leaned nearer to his face. The Light Being was starting to make out a human countenance with brown eyes and light, wavy hair. A smile formed on the man's lips. "Welcome to 3D," he said.

The Light Being squeezed his left hand and felt the muscle tighten in his elbow. He stretched a foot and then turned his cheek and felt his neck and shoulders. Everything felt strange, but nothing hurt except for the dryness of his throat and a feeling of chill over his chest and shoulders, which were exposed above the white sheet that covered him from the waist down.

Now he could see the female, a woman in white coming toward him, carrying a clear vessel containing liquid. She smiled as she offered it to him. The man helped him sit up in the bed. "How do you feel?" asked the man.

The Light Being sipped the water. How delicious it tasted and how soothing the trickle of its coolness on his parched throat. He knew better than to take it any faster. "Good," he managed to say. "I feel... good."

The woman took the glass when he was through, but continued to stand over him, watching and smiling encouragingly.

"Master, the cloning was a success," the man told him. "What do you remember?"

The Light Being lifted his fingers to his face. His cheek was smooth and warm. "The last thing I recall is being told to go to sleep. I didn't know if it was possible. Your names... I don't quite recall who you are."

"That's understandable," said the man. "I am Doctor Volnov and this is Doctor Kito. We were not in your attendance until after you started the procedure."

"You are... Sirian?" asked the Light Being.

"Very perceptive," Doctor Kito said and set the empty glass down on a nearby tray. She picked up a hand mirror and handed it to him.

The Light Being peered into the reflective glass and was momentarily startled by the familiar young face he wore. The resemblance was uncanny. Staring up at him in the mirror was the likeness of Blake Dobbs — only about five or six years older than Blake.

"Satisfied?" asked Doctor Volnov.

The Light Being nodded his approval and handed the mirror back to Doctor Kito. He started to get up from the bed, but Doctor Volnov restrained him.

"Where are you going in such a hurry?"

"I must," said the Light Being. "I am needed."

"Oh, but first you need rest," insisted Doctor Volnov. "The new body is not conditioned to stressful activity."

"Affirmative," said Doctor Kito. "Master, you must stay in bed for at least another twelve hours and regain your strength. The shock of embodiment could unbalance you."

The Light Being understood, but he also felt the urgency of those right now who needed him, who were counting on him, and as his mind began to clear more, he was suddenly seized with a terrified projection of thought from Her. He shot to his feet and the white sheet fell away, revealing his full nakedness.

Both doctors stepped back in alarm. "What's wrong?" asked Doctor Kito.

The Light Being quickly recovered himself and allowed them to help him back into bed. Doctor Kito picked up the sheet and draped it over him. "It is urgent that I leave here as soon as it is possible," he said. The effort of standing so quickly had tired him. Now he felt impossibly fatigued and his eyelids closed against his will. "Right now, though... I must... I must... rest..."

Doctor Volnov turned to his colleague. "See to it he is sedated."

Doctor Kito nodded and reached for a hypodermic needle.

Crystal sat on the stiff, narrow bed in her cramped quarters aboard the Estronian ship that orbited the planet. It was dark and dingy in the windowless cubicle and she felt depressed and somewhat scared. Hours had passed since she had been escorted on board following the short shuttle ride with Thorden.

The Estronian pilot had whisked her away from Karos so quickly that morning, she hadn't had time to think about what she was doing. He had treated her kindly enough, so far, even permitted her to fly his craft a short time, to prove to him that she could fly it.

For the moment she had forgotten the spontaneity of her decision to go with Thorden and had let go of the guilt feeling of not informing her parents. She had once again grown excited about piloting the shuttle until the Estronian cruiser came into sight and her host made her relinquish the controls to him.

On board the cruiser she had been booked into special quarters on a remote part of the ship. Oxygen injections were administered periodially by androids. Although Crystal was half Estronian, her physique was Terran and she needed the equivalent of the Karosian atmosphere to survive while on board an Estronian ship.

While she had been schooled aboard the Estronian educational vessel, she and the other Terran children from the colony had been given regular oxygen injections which were administered twice daily. Their nights were spent in Terran quarters away from their Estronian peers, yet the furnishings on the school ship had far exceeded these stark accommodations in which she now found herself. The poor lighting made the room appear dim and smaller than it was. She felt uncomfortable, anxious and bored, and she missed her parents very much.

They had given her something to eat and drink before Thorden had left her alone. He had summoned a meal to be delivered to her by one of the ship's many robot units. But Thorden hadn't stayed. He told her he had the arrangements to make for her so that her future in space would be secured.

"Oh, what have I done?" Crystal moaned as she turned to gaze at the bare walls that seemed only to be closing in on her. "And what will he ask from me in return?"

Thorden had seemed to take control of her from the start. He made her uncomfortable the way he watched her. His voice was sharp and sinister and it sent a chill up her spine whenever he spoke. What frightened her most was how he had commented before leaving her quarters. "And now... you are *mine... all mine.*"

A sob escaped her throat as a dread feeling crept into her mind. "Mother... Father... I'm so sorry... I didn't even tell you goodbye." She sank onto the hard bed as tears spilled down her cheeks.

26

A Promise

It was late in the afternoon and the sun cast long shadows. Manley trudged westward along the lonely road that stretched in front of him. He had been traveling since that morning, after Joe and Kevin had mounted their bikes and headed east. They had left him a water bottle and a small pack containing matches, some dehydrated food packets and a wadded-up space blanket. Manley had thanked them and started out until he found the county road upon which he now trod.

His mind wandered to everything that had happened in the last few days. He had one purpose in mind — to find Dorothy and the kids. He assumed they had been whisked off by one of the helicopters that had come upon the scene just after the sudden darkness had blanketed the earth. Most likely they had been carried away to a concentration camp. Joe and Kevin had mentioned how they had seen one not far from them.

What a relief it was to have daylight once again and the warmth of the sun. But the atmosphere seemed to have an entirely different hue to it. There was a tinge of red that hung like a haze in the air. Manley had no idea what it meant. It was also strange to him that nobody was around. No cars, trucks or vehicles traveled on the road. There were just the few abandoned vehicles that had stalled. He wasn't able to get any of them started, although he had stopped and tried several times. Of those in which the keys had been left, when he tried the ignition there was only a "click."

On both sides of this county route there were fields of corn and alfalfa and a few farmhouses along the way. No one was in the houses either. Manley had stopped, in case someone was still around. But, like the vehicles on the road, the homes had been abandoned as well.

So where is everybody? Manley wondered. Certainly there had to be others, like himself, who had managed to escape the authorities. He figured eventually he would find somebody who was hiding out.

"Could the Photon Belt have caused all this?" Manley asked himself. It didn't make sense to him that the vehicles had all lost power, and there was no electricity, and yet the choppers were able to have lights and fly. It didn't make a lick of sense to him, after all he had read about the bizarre phenomenon. "Nobody thought it was real," he muttered to himself. "Nobody expected it to really happen, especially after Sheldan Nidle's false prediction last decade."

As the reddish sun began to lower in the Nebraska sky, Manley saw another farmhouse ahead. He made up his mind that he was not going to spend another night on the cold, hard ground. He sighed, pulled his pack tighter around his shoulder, and forced his tired feet to keep going. It looked like only a quarter of a mile or so. He'd be able to find some food and drink in the house, although he knew he had to be cautious about spoilage. He didn't want to make himself sick.

A buzzing noise caused Manley to look up in the direction of the north. Two black dots appeared in the distant sky. Choppers! And they were heading in his direction. Manley grew frightened and immediately looked around for cover. He couldn't let them see him. There wasn't much in the way of trees or brush, but he ducked down into the ditch along the side of the road and burrowed his way into the corn that was not very tall yet. He crawled in about fifteen feet and then lay flat on the ground, praying he hadn't or wouldn't be seen.

The buzzing became a droning sound, and then the clap of the choppers seemed right overhead. Manley could feel his heart banging against the ground and he didn't dare look up. Within a minute or so the worst was over. The helicopters had passed and their roar diminished. Not until the noise was almost completely done did he dare to move.

He slowly pushed himself up and knelt for a few seconds. He saw that the two black dots were just about out of sight and he released a big sigh of relief. Then he stood up and brushed himself off. The light was starting to grow dimmer now as he made his way back onto the pavement and hurried toward the farmhouse. It was just about dark when he reached it and found the back door unlocked.

Before stepping inside, Manley knocked and called out, "Hello. Anybody home?" When there was no sound, he walked in and found himself in a fairly large kitchen that was dark, but he was still able to make out the shapes of a table and chairs, sink and counter, stove and refrigerator. He thought of his matches in the small pack Joe and Kevin had given him and set the pack down on the counter as he unzipped it to retrieve the matches.

When he had a little flicker of light, he made his way to some drawers and began searching for candles. He found one propped upon the window, near the kitchen sink. It looked as though someone had burned it down quite a ways just recently, but it would work.

Manley lit the candle, which gave off better light than the single match. He began searching for more, but then a thought occurred to him. If he had a bunch of candles lit, it might attract attention from the outside — if there were more helicopters patrolling the area. So he used the one candle and went about checking out the food situation in this house.

He was delighted to find food in the refrigerator, but everything felt warm from the power being off. He didn't dare eat any of the roast beef that had been saved and wrapped in plastic, or the souring milk or the wilting vegetables. He did choose some fruit and an unopened package of cheddar cheese. In one of the cupboards there were sesame crackers, a half-empty jar of peanut butter, and an assortment of cereals and snack foods. Manley gathered them all up, carried them to the table, and then sat down to begin his solitary picnic.

When Johanna arrived at the auditorium, she was already an hour late and rehearsal was in progress. She apologized to everyone and set about with the preparations for that night's performance. She had slept most of the afternoon and Serassan had suggested she skip the rehearsal, but Johanna wouldn't hear of it.

"Are you sure?" he had asked with deep concern.

"Yes, Serassan," she had replied while donning a fresh set of clothes. "We've worked too long and hard for the arts center. I cannot let people down on account of Crystal."

"But you were also upset about the news Emrox brought," he reminded her.

"That's true, Serassan, but there's little either of us can do about Earth now." She fought to keep the tears back as she remembered her brother Manley's face the last time she had seen him — eighteen years earlier. She didn't want to think about the possibility of him being a casualty on Earth. But she knew, as well as Serassan, that the odds were not in Manley's favor. It weighed heavily on her heart.

Johanna was grateful to have the assistance of the stage managers, because she simply was finding it difficult to concentrate on the business at hand. In the back of her mind, she kept thinking of Crystal and how proud she had been of her daughter's singing last night. Just what had that scoundrel, Thorden, promised her in order to entice her into leaving Karos with him? Johanna could well imagine. And what would become of Crystal once she discovered Thorden was manipulating her in order to take advantage of her? The more Johanna's thoughts wandered in this direction, the more she fretted.

Johanna was appalled when she made several mistakes during rehearsal. She hadn't realized Serassan had come into the auditorium and was watching her. He stopped the rehearsal and consulted with the stage managers. The other performers murmured among themselves and Johanna sighed, frustrated and anxious.

Serassan called to her and she got up from the piano and faced him. "You don't need to say it," Johanna announced. "I'm unable to perform tonight. I'm... I'm so sorry..." She quickly ran out of the auditorium as tears streamed down her cheeks.

B lake had slept about six hours. Now he was up and dressed, knowing that in just a short time someone would come to his cabin to escort him to the shuttle dock. Then he and his friend, Blue Jay, would embark on their journey to Karos.

A knock on the door caused him to jump up from his bed, where he had been sitting. He pressed his fingers over the eye in the wall that caused the door to slide open, expecting to greet Lotus with his breakfast tray. Instead he received a shock that made him quickly draw in his breath. Nothing could have prepared him for the sight that met his eyes.

"Hello, Blake."

Speechless, Blake stepped backward, his eyes wide. The man standing at his door was exactly his height, with exactly the same head and features. The only difference was that this man appeared a few years older than Blake, and he was wearing the white, one-piece uniform that Blake had noticed on several of the ship's crew members.

"Mind if I come in?" asked the man at the door.

Blake blinked, then finally composed himself and found his voice. "Uh... sure." He still couldn't tear his gaze away from that face.

The Light Being understood Blake's reaction and smiled patiently. "I can see that you are unprepared for how I look."

"L.B.?" Blake swallowed. "Is it... really you?"

The Light Being nodded. "It is I. But I resemble *you*... in the future, at least."

"How... how did you... how did they..."

"I was cloned," said L.B., "and rather quickly, even by their standards."

"W... will you... how... how long will you stay this way?" Blake was baffled.

The Light Being walked over to the small mirror on the wall beside the sink next to Blake's bathroom. He looked at his image and glided a hand through his blond, wavy hair. "This body is only temporary. It cannot sustain my energy indefinitely."

"But... but how long... I mean, how long will it last?"

"That is unknown." The Light Being turned to face him. He had such a mature, intelligent look in his eyes. It blew Blake's mind. "In most cases a cloned body will last a few years."

Blake was hesitant to ask the next question. "Then... what... what will happen to you?" he asked. "Will you... will you... die?"

"I could, yes," said L.B. "I am embodied now and just as mortal as you or any other humanoid."

"And before?" asked Blake.

"I was an energy form."

"And you were... immortal?"

"Yes. But, Blake, we are all immortal. These bodies we wear are temporary encasements... housing for the spirit, if you will. I do not fear death as you know it." He stepped closer, then sat on the bed as Blake continued to study him in total fascination. "I now have many limitations. The body is dense and cumbersome. It requires fuel, oxygen and rest. But I will adapt to these restraints. I must. For, you see, I am on a mission." He smiled then and placed his hand on Blake's arm. "But first, I wanted to thank you for permitting me to use your DNA. I am leaving for Terra now. I will find your parents as I promised."

Blake managed a smile. "Thanks again for rescuing me and my sister."

"I know you are going on a journey," said L.B., ignoring Blake's gratitude. "Didn't I tell you that you'd be going into space?"

Blake recalled the first night, back in Illinois, when he'd met the Light Being and had been told that very thing.

"I have a favor to ask of you," L.B. disclosed and his face suddenly grew serious.

Blake sat next to him on the bed. "Anything," he said.

L.B. looked down at his hands and let out a sigh. "There is someone you are going to meet on your journey. Someone very important to me."

"Oh? Who is it?" asked Blake.

L.B. looked up and seemed to be staring into space. "Look after her for me. She is unhappy. I sense it strongly."

"But... who are you talking about?" Blake asked.

L.B. sighed again. "Her." Then he added, "My... Special One."

Blake chuckled. "L.B., don't tell me you have a girlfriend out there in space! Is she an energy form, too?"

"We all were at one time," he replied distantly. "No, she is embodied and she is... your cousin." He turned and stared directly at Blake. "Please look after her... until I come for her."

"Oh, you mean you're going to meet us on Karos?"

"Yes, but first I must fulfill my promise to help your parents." L.B. squeezed Blake's arm. "Promise me, Blake, that you will do all you can to help her."

Blake was puzzled and just a little frightened by the urgency in the Light Being's eyes. "Well... sure, L.B. I'll do what I can. I don't know what that is yet, but... you can count on me."

At this the Light Being relaxed and once again smiled at him.

Then he rose from the bed and sauntered toward the door. Turning, he said, "I knew I could count on you, my Terran friend. Thank you, Blake."

"Don't mention it. And... L.B.... good luck."

With a quick nod of understanding, L.B. turned and headed out the door.

Blake sat back on his bed for several minutes, completely shaken by the experience he had just had. How strange it had been to come face to face with himself, only several years older. He felt a sudden kinship with the Light Being and feared for his safety and well being, knowing intuitively that the space being who had taken on his body had a difficult scenario ahead of him.

27

Resistance

Soolán stretched her long tapered gray fingers out in front of her and gazed through the window of the stone dwelling she shared with Emrox. She could hear him moving about in the back room. He had been asleep but was now awake. She watched the red landscape and sky, but her mind was troubled. Emrox had brought home the news of Crystal's disappearance. Soolán could feel Serassan's and Johanna's grief and concern.

"You stirred most of the night." Emrox entered the main room of their modest home and stood behind her. "I barely slept myself."

Soolán turned to her mate with pleading eyes. "Emrox, we must do something."

He sighed and watched out the window with her. "What can we do? Crystal is her own person. She is practically an adult."

Soolán moaned softly. "She is a child. She is vulnerable. Someone must go after her."

"We don't even know for certain where she has gone," Emrox reminded her. "It is only assumed that Crystal has left Karos with Thorden."

"Why hasn't Serassan gone after her?" Soolán demanded.

"You must remember, Johanna and Serassan are in charge of the arts center. They can't just leave. Years of preparation have gone into ..."

"*Plug* all their preparations!" Soolán stormed. "*Plug* the galactic arts center! Our granddaughter's happiness is at stake."

Emrox drew back at Soolán's outburst. She was usually soft spoken and never one to lose control over a situation. But he could see that she was gravely worried. He knew that Soolán sensed things that he often did not. Her intuitive gifts had always earned his respect.

"Soolán, is Crystal in some kind of danger?"

She stared at him with concern in her large, slanted blue eyes. "She is frightened, Emrox. And yes, I feel strongly that she is in some sort of danger."

"From Thorden?" he asked.

"Yes, but not just from him." Soolán wrung her hands. "I sense there is something more. It has to do with... Terra somehow."

Emrox stepped closer to her. "Would he dare take her there?"

"Of that I cannot be certain," she said. "But something connected with Terra keeps drifting through my mind."

"The shift?" he prompted.

Soolán shook her head. "No, it is not that, Emrox." She gazed at him, puzzled. "I'm not convinced that Earth has actually gone through its shift."

"What makes you say that?" he asked.

"Something tells me it was contrived. The Dark Forces have been at work again." She held her head with one of her gray, long-tipped fingers. "Oh, Emrox, I can't be sure. I just know that things are not right on Terra."

"Things have not been right there for quite some time, Soolàn."

"The shift is overdue," Soolán continued, "but the time was not yet. Someone forced this upon the planet. Someone who wanted control."

"And what has any of this got to do with our granddaughter?" Emrox asked patiently.

"She is half Terran," Soolán answered. "I suppose I have come to care much about her mother's home world since Serassan..." She sighed. "It's just a feeling I can't explain, Emrox. There is a connection, and I don't know what it means, but it fills me with uncertainty and with... yes, with fear... for Crystal... because I don't know how she will react when she comes face to face with whatever it is I am picking up on."

"Then, if your feelings are this strong about Crystal's situation, we must go to Estron," declared Emrox. "We will search for her there."

"I do not feel Crystal is on Estron," Soolán told her mate. "She is in space."

"We will start with Estron." Emrox turned toward the door. "I will begin the arrangements."

"Emrox..." Soolán watched as he hesitated, then turned to look at her. "I am grateful." She smiled slightly, then left to brew their morning tea.

Crystal had slept fitfully in her oppressive cabin. She had feared the return of Thorden and worried about how she would elude him should he attempt to harm her in any way. Oh, why hadn't she listened to her mother and used better judgment? Obviously Johnanna had experienced some kind of distasteful encounter with Thorden in the past. At least she hadn't wanted to talk about it.

When breakfast arrived, Crystal breathed a sigh of relief and ate halfheartedly. She needed to think of a way to get herself out of the situation she was in, without causing Thorden to become angry and vengeful.

"I'll just tell him I've changed my mind and I want to go back to Karos," Crystal told herself as she poked at an omelet with her fork. But then she remembered the stirring deep inside of her, the longing she couldn't describe, that beckoned her into space. It had been the reason she had been so easily talked into leaving Karos. Some vague feeling tugged at her heart, but, try as she might, she just could not put her finger on it. What was this strong pull she felt to venture into the unknown? What, or *who*, was calling to her?

Unexpectedly the door to her cabin slid open and there stood Thorden in a maroon robe and tan-colored cape. His sharp alien features momentarily startled Crystal and she choked a bit on some toast. She reached for her vessel of juice and quickly composed herself.

"My dear." Thorden walked into the cubicle and, even though he was less than five feet tall, his presence seemed to take up much of the space in the small cabin. The door behind him slid shut. "It is good to see you looking well rested," Thorden continued. His slanted blue eyes examined her closely. "I presume you slept well."

Crystal cleared her throat and set her juice glass down, aware that her hand trembled. "I slept fitfully," she admitted, then dared to look pleadingly at him. "And I have a request to make."

Thorden didn't move. He waited for her to ask.

"I want to return to Karos," she said, surprised at her composure, despite the fact that her heart was hammering.

Thorden let out a slow breath and began to pace the floor in front of her, his white thin hands folded behind him. Finally, he said in a derisive tone, "Dear girl, *why* would you want to return to that forsaken planetoid *now*? After I have offered you the chance to be part of something so grand?" His eyes appeared to shoot sparks as he peered at her. "You insult my generous hospitality."

Crystal drew a breath and let it out. "I appreciate your offer, Thorden," she said. "However, I wasn't thinking. I... I didn't even say goodbye to my mother and father."

"Obviously, you are not as mature as you made me believe." Thorden's words grew sharp and he continued to pace back and forth. "I don't think you understand. I have taken painstaking measures to assure your success, and I have already invested heavily in your future."

"What... what are you saying?" Crystal asked in a timid voice. The Estronian appeared menacing and she wasn't sure how far his impatience with her would go.

"I will not allow you to return to Karos," Thorden vowed. "You said you wanted a career in space. Isn't that what you told me?" His face pressed close to hers. "Isn't it?" he hissed.

Crystal drew back at the foul wave of odor from his person. It was unlike human body odor, more like a stench from a swamp. "Yes," she had to admit in a small voice. She swallowed. "Space has been my... my dream." Then she added reluctantly, "It *still* is."

"And just how do you think you will ever be able to rise to the top ranks?" Thorden demanded. "You know as well as I that the competition is fierce among Estronian females. Just what chance do *you* have, daughter of an Earth woman?"

Crystal shrank from his words. A lump in her throat made it hard to keep back tears. He had said it as though it were a curse to have Terran blood. She had put up with that kind of racism her entire life, until she had finally given in and agreed with her peers that her Estronian genes were the only ones that mattered. In the past, she had been ashamed of her mother's race, but now she felt insulted and it aroused her defenses.

Crystal's blue eyes widened and her chin quivered. "I want to go home," she told Thorden in a trembling voice. "I've changed my mind about space. I want to go back to Karos."

Thorden's laughter mocked her and he placed both hands upon her food tray and leaned toward her in a threatening manner. His eyes burned with a wild indignation. "Well, my pretty little singer, it is too late for that. The arrangements have been made and you are to be my protégé, whether you like it or not!"

Crystal leaned back as far as she could, but he had her trapped. "I will not be your... your protégé," she insisted, her voice almost a croak. "I... I don't want anything to do with you!" His smell was nauseating her.

"We'll see how you feel about that after you've spent some time at Level One Tasking."

Crystal had no idea what that was. She turned her face to avoid him. Finally, disgusted with her refusal to cooperate, Thorden backed off.

"Be ready promptly," ordered Thorden as he headed for the door to her cabin. "The Task Master will not tolerate tardiness. A unit will be sent to bring you."

Crystal's blue eyes filled with blinding tears as the sinister Estronian left her quarters. Alone once again, she buried her face in her hands and cried. "Mother... Father..." she sobbed. "Will you ever forgive me?" Her crying spell lasted several minutes. She pushed her food tray aside and sauntered into the tiny cubicle of a bathroom to wash her wet face.

Just as she was running warm water over her face as she bent close to the automatic faucet, she was startled to hear a deep voice above her. "Crystal Dobbs, put aside your fear," the voice said.

Crystal jerked her head up and looked around. She saw nothing out of the ordinary. "Who's there?" she asked.

"It is I," the voice replied at once. "I shall be there soon."

Frightened, Crystal backed against the wall. "Who... where...?"

"But there is something I must do first," the voice said. "After that is accomplished, I shall find you."

There was something comforting and strangely familiar about the voice. She realized that it must be coming from inside her head. "Oh no," Crystal murmured as she placed her hands over her cheeks and stared into the tear-stained image in the bathroom mirror. "I'm going insane. I'm hearing voices in my head!"

The male voice, so calm and gentle, spoke to her again. "No, Crystal, you are not out of your mind. You cannot see me, but I am sending you a telepathic telegram, just to let you know, my Special One, that I am on my way to you."

Crystal's eyes grew wide with wonder. "Who are you?" She turned around as if searching the empty air for the source of the voice. "Wait!" she pleaded. "Tell me your name, at least."

Silence. The voice did not speak again.

Crystal stood there, confused, staring at her reflection for a long moment. The voice had been real, of that she was certain. It had been masculine and soothing. For a few seconds she experienced a deep sense of tranquility and warmth, as if she were receiving an embrace. Her heart felt a glow and she basked in the peaceful wave of loving energy that encompassed her. It was *His* essence... the voice had belonged to *Him*!

She smiled ever so slightly, a dreamy gaze on her face, and then she caught herself. Who had she been thinking about? She really had no idea who had just spoken to her in her head. Yet the vibration of the presence had awakened something buried deep within her. Crystal sensed she knew the voice from somewhere. There had been something totally familiar and alluring about it. She wanted to remember... but she couldn't. It was just beyond her reach.

Someone entered Crystal's cabin. Poking her head out from the bathroom, she saw that one of the ship's robot units had come in and hovered in front of her.

"Crystal Dobbs," the metallic voice said without any inflection, "you are to follow me." The unit was much newer than her parents' servant, Kameel-37. The units on board this Estronian ship were smaller, more compact and less individualized. The Estronians no longer engineered their labor units after personalities. They preferred automatons that were direct, efficient, and lacking in their older counterparts' ability for sociable communication.

"Where must I go?" asked Crystal.

"Follow me, Crystal Dobbs," ordered the unit. "If you delay, you will be penalized. You must report immediately to Level One for your labor instructions."

Crystal wanted to protest, but she knew too well that the Estronians still used Pacification Chambers when they met with those who resisted their protocol. So, extremely unhappy about the situation she found herself in because she had defied Thorden, Crystal sighed and walked out into the corridor behind the Estronian unit that led her first to a station where another oxygen injection was administered. Not knowing what lay ahead, she rolled up her sleeve and presented her bare skin, then shut her eyes as she always had in the past. The shots were never painful, but there was a slight feeling of pressure.

As her eyes remained closed for a moment, Crystal saw a glimpse of a face. It lasted only a couple of seconds, but the face was that of a young Terran man with blond hair and eyes the color of sand. He had broad shoulders, but was slender and willowy in stature. She knew in an instant he had been the man whose voice she had heard just minutes ago.

"Just to let you know, my Special One, that I am on my way to you..." His words echoed in her brain as the image faded.

Crystal opened her eyes. The unit was prodding her to move on. She lifted her chin and followed. A great wave of hope swept over her. *He* was coming... but when?

28

A New Regime

Blake paid a quick visit to his sister before embarking on the journey to Karos. Kelly was asleep, so he didn't disturb her. He just wanted to be reassured that she was all right. An alien nursemaid was in the adjoining room and told Blake she would watch over the small girl and tell her that he had come to see her.

Kapri met Blake and Blue Jay at the shuttle dock. She had arranged to pilot them to the cruiser herself, and Blue Jay seemed especially pleased at this news. Blake could see how much his dark-complected friend admired the Estronian scientist. Lotus appeared just as they were about to board the shuttle.

"Don't tell me *you*'re coming along, too," Blake said hopefully.

The blue girl smiled. "Oh, I cannot. But I wanted you to have this." She held out her hand and Blake reached over to receive a small box.

Kapri motioned for Blue Jay to climb inside the shuttle, but allowed Blake a moment with Lotus.

"What is it?" Blake asked. He opened the box and found a ring that glowed like one of the blue crystals in the room of fountains. It produced a light all its own.

"Do not be concerned, Blake Dobbs." Lotus laughed. "It does not mean we are engorged."

Blake laughed out loud and doubled over.

Lotus blinked her eyes innocently. "What did I say now?"

"Engaged!" Blake corrected her. "Not... engorged."

"Oh." Lotus giggled. "Of course."

After he had recovered, Blake cleared his throat and studied the sparkling blue gem. "It's... it's awesome, Lotus."

"It is a protection ring, a tradition of my people. Wear it in friendship and safety."

Blake didn't know what to say. Slowly he took the blue ring from its box and started to place it on his right finger. But the ring was too small.

Immediately Lotus touched the ring and it seemed to flare up and sizzle. Then she stood back and watched him. "See if it will fit your finger now."

To Blake's astonishment, the ring slid onto his finger with ease. "Wow... thanks, Lotus."

"Be safe," she told him, her blue eyes dancing with delight at his surprise. "May you cherish the meeting with your aunt, uncle and cousin. Perhaps I will see you when you return."

"Come on, Blake," called Blue Jay from the shuttle doorway. "We have a ride to catch, man."

Blake allowed Lotus to embrace him, then thanked her once again and hopped on board the shuttle with Blue Jay and Kapri. The ship was smaller than the one Blake had last been aboard, when the Light Being had rescued Kelly and himself. The shuttle was only large enough for four individuals. Kapri sat at the front, where she operated the craft from a computer-like console. Blue Jay and Blake took the two seats that faced one another on the sides. The rear seat was empty. Blake noticed a large, wrap-around window that allowed them to see out the entire ship.

"What's that you're wearing?" Blue Jay studied Blake's hand with the glowing blue ring on his finger. "Did Lotus give you that?"

"It's some kind of friendship ring, I guess," Blake replied.

"It will protect you," Kapri said without looking. She was busy on the console and the shuttle had begun to move toward the space port exit.

"Hey, that's special," said Blue Jay. "I'd keep it on at all times."

"I intend to," said Blake. Automatically the lights flashed on inside the shuttle and he stared, fascinated, out the panoramic window as the space portal slowly opened and Kapri guided them off the mother ship and into the boundless depths of space.

Dorothy sat in Ernestine Glenn's makeshift office in the quonset, where she was busy sifting through stacks of papers on a desk. The task she had been given was fairly simple, to arrange in categories the various reports on individuals and families in their jurisdiction. Although Dorothy had no idea what the classifications stood for, she was happy to have been chosen to assist the highly respected presidential candidate. It was a far cry from being confined in that dank prison cell from which she had been released the day before.

Ernestine had been generous, allowing Dorothy to sleep in comfortable quarters after she had showered and been given a military uniform to wear. Later, she had joined the candidate-leader for a meal in Ernestine's private dining area.

"I have so many questions," Dorothy had blurted. "But I want you to know, if you are in charge of everything now, that is a great relief. Just how did all of this..."

Ernestine immediately cut her off. "Let's not get into any of that now. There are more important matters we need to discuss." Her stern look and authoritative voice subdued Dorothy, who realized this was one of the traits that had always made her look up to Ms. Glenn.

"Well, I'm honored," Dorothy said. "I really am. I want you to know that."

"Eat," ordered Ernestine.

Dorothy did as she was instructed and noticed that Ernestine Glenn ate very little on her tray. After Dorothy had gotten through half her meal, she felt she just had to ask again. "Tell me... why did you pick *me*?"

Ernestine's eyes twinkled with amusement. "You are bright, courageous and... devoted."

Dorothy puzzled over this a moment, then took a sip of coffee. "But it's like... you recognized me the other day, when I was brought in by the guards."

Ernestine nodded. "You are also very perceptive, my dear. You have the qualities I need for my right-hand assistant."

Dorothy's green eyes widened in surprise. "Your... right-hand...?"

"How would you like to be instrumental in bringing about a New Order to a dying world?" asked Ernestine.

"What do you mean... dying?" Dorothy set her cup down. "What's happened to our world?"

Ernestine sat back and let out a sigh. "The old regime is over," she declared. "The men who have ruled this planet have lost control. It is now up to us women to run things right. We shall tolerate no more war, no more pollution, and no more of their greed and destruction."

Dorothy had heard a lot of this before in Ernestine Glenn's speeches and commentaries. "That can only be an improvement," she agreed. "You know, I had made up my mind to vote for you and the Purification Party last November. And you can count on me when you run again..."

Ernestine interrupted her. "Fortunately, that is no longer necessary. There are to be no more silly elections. No more petty campaigns, and no more mud slinging."

"No more of those disgusting political ads on TV," Dorothy added.

"That's right," said Ernestine. "There is no choice now but to take charge."

Now, as Dorothy picked up one of the stacks of papers for Category D, she felt proud to be Ernestine Glenn's assistant. She felt confident that everything was going to fall into place and new order and progress would be initiated to enable Earth's people to get back into a functioning society. Only this time there would be true equality and plenty of resources for all. No longer would a small, elite minority squander everything for themselves.

Looking out the quonset window, Dorothy saw the huge barbed-wire fence that contained the hundreds of women in the camp. Guards still patrolled the area with their rifles, and Dorothy wondered how soon it would be before Ernestine gave orders to free those women. Certainly it would be taken care of soon. The conditions in the camp left a lot to be desired, and Dorothy felt for those others who had gone several days without a shower or even a wash basin.

Every time she had tried to ask Ernestine about the state of affairs, the candidate-leader would cut her off. Dorothy wanted to ask about how she could locate Manley and her two children, but

Ernestine was always busy, and constantly being interrupted by the other women officers. There was always some excuse and promise to discuss it later.

None of the other women in the quonset discussed anything with Dorothy. Most of them regarded her jealously because Ernestine had chosen her to be of special service. The few times Dorothy had approached any of the women on the subject of men and children, they clammed up and walked away, or suddenly thought of something more important that had to be attended to. Dorothy was starting to get the feeling that the women had been given strict orders not to talk among themselves.

A commotion outside immediately drew Dorothy to the small window. Two women were screaming and carrying on at the fence. They were too distant to recognize, and Dorothy couldn't hear what they were shouting. But suddenly two guards overtook the women and a skirmish followed in which one of the women was thrown harshly to the ground. The other received a blow to the head from the butt of one of the guard's rifles. Dorothy gasped in horror. How could this be? What had the women said or done to deserve such treatment?

"I must tell Ernestine at once!" she said to herself and looked around as if to decide where she might find the candidate-leader. But then she saw out the window the figure of Ernestine Glenn walking toward the guards and the two women on the ground. Both were squirming and obviously hurt. Dorothy watched as Ernestine spoke to the guards. She was too far away to hear any conversation, but it appeared that Ernestine was upset about the situation as she well should be. Soon the two guards picked up the troublesome women and marched them toward the gate. Dorothy knew they were being led to the basement room and into the cells.

"Certainly they must have posed a threat of some kind," Dorothy said aloud. But it didn't set well with her. Something just did not feel right about the situation. She made a point to ask Ernestine about it later. With a sigh, she turned back to the stacks of paper on the desk.

29
A Startling Appearance

The sun was intense and beads of perspiration erupted on Manley's forehead as he trudged along the back road past more cornfields. He had rested well in the farmhouse and had plenty to eat and drink. He had even been able to wash up with soap and cold water in the morning. But now he was tired and beginning to wonder how he was ever going to find Dorothy and the kids. The heat was wearing him down.

Some horses fenced inside a pasture trotted over to gaze at him as he passed. He watched them, wondering if they were needing water. He wondered about people's livestock and pets. The people had been rounded up and the animals were left behind to fend for themselves.

With a sigh, Manley looked around and saw the gate to the pasture. Even though he was hot and tired, he dropped his backpack and wandered over to the gate as the horses eagerly trotted toward him. Then he unlatched the gate and let it swing wide open. The horses could now leave and perhaps wander off to find a ditch with some water in it.

What a cruel world. But Manley knew he couldn't stop and help every living thing he came across. He had to get to that camp that Joe and Kevin had said they had passed before the three days of darkness. They had indicated that it wasn't that far away. He walked back to where he had dropped his pack and continued on his way.

A flock of birds passed overhead. Manley saw a tree ahead and decided to rest in its shade when he reached it. He had pondered the fact that everything appeared to be fairly normal after the three days of darkness. In all the literature he had read about the Photon Belt, he had expected the world to be completely different afterwards. Photon energy was supposed to replace electricity and become the new resource, the free energy that everyone had full access to, and no one could exploit. In some literature he had read that there would be twenty-four hours of daylight. But the sun had set, as usual, last evening, and had come up again this morning.

So what the hell had gone on? Manley wondered. Why did everything go dark? Were they or were they *not* in the Photon Belt? If Earth was in the Photon Belt, then why weren't things different? That first day after the darkness he had noticed that a strange kind of red mist hung in the atmosphere, but now it had dissipated. Things appeared just as they had before, only the power was still off and all the people had vanished. He had not met a soul since Joe and Kevin had hopped on their bicycles and pedaled east.

Another thing Manley had expected when the Photon Belt reached Earth was to see extraterrestrial spacecraft everywhere. Where was all the assistance that had been promised by those who had channeled information to psychics in the last decade? Hadn't the space beings talked about how they would be arriving visibly in fleets to help humanity stabilize after the shift?

Manley swung the pack off his shoulder and pulled out his plastic bottle of water, which he had filled back at the farmhouse. It was a relief to stretch out in the grass and rest his tired legs. For a man who was 64, he thought he was in pretty decent shape. He was grateful now for the healthy cooking Dorothy had insisted upon, and her prompting to join the athletic club, where he discovered he actually enjoyed lifting weights and walking the treadmill. If it hadn't been for the regular workouts all these years, he wouldn't have been in good enough shape to walk across country like this.

Part of it had been his desire to stay fit and attractive enough for his much younger wife. Dorothy was only 49, a few years younger than his sister, Johanna. Dorothy had been vivacious and passionate when he had met her at 31. He remembered the day she had arrived at the UFO Contact Center in DeKalb, confused and distrusting after her abduction experience the week before. He recalled how Kapri had been there. Manley had been out on an interview with Nicole Getz and her mother-in-law.

Kapri, an extraterrestrial in human disguise, had been an enigma in Manley's life. Appearing as a beautiful girl in her twenties, Kapri unintentionally had captured his heart. She hadn't been able to remember her mission or the fact that the Dark Forces had abducted her and erased her memories. And when her memories had come flooding back to her, Dorothy had been the one in whom Kapri confided. At the time this was going on, Manley had been blind to how beautiful and caring Dorothy Myers had been, or how much she had been attracted to him.

But now she was his wife of eighteen years and they had been blessed with a bright and talented son, Blake, and with Kelly, who may have been born defective, but was a ray of golden light in their lives. Dorothy, his companion, lover, career partner, was the center of his world, and he now longed to set his eyes upon her cheery face with the brown hair, green eyes and high cheek bones, and he remembered the loving smile she gave freely to all. He longed for her soft, low voice and especially for her soothing, healing touch, for she had proved to him time and again that she was a psychic healer. Before Kelly had been born, Dorothy had been instrumental in contributing her talent to his clients at the UFO Contact Center. He wondered if she and the children had been taken by the helicopters to the concentration camp Joe and Kevin had spoken of, and if so, how were they handling it?

They had often talked about the possibility of what could happen if a disaster of some sort occurred and martial law was declared. Because Manley was so outspoken in his field and had discovered on numerous occasions that his phone was tapped, his mail intercepted and his general comings and goings watched, he realized that the authorities might take a disliking to him and find any excuse to immediately incarcerate him. Dorothy had always laughed at the notion and dismissed his concerns as being paranoid. However, she understood that if ever such an event were to happen, she should expect that he would flee to avoid any harm coming to his family.

He wished he understood the whole thing. It was so puzzling to him. Part of him was greatly relieved that his world was back to the familiar cycle of day and night. But another part of him was uneasy, even disappointed at the prospect of business as usual. Yet, it certainly was not business as usual with no people around, starving pets, and black helicopters periodically flying overhead. Plus he felt hopeless. Just what was he going to do when he *did* arrive at the camp?

Manley was so comfortable under the tree that he decided a short nap was in order. Making sure he was not going to be easily spotted in case a chopper flew over, he wedged his pack under his head and stretched out on his back. A summer breeze was blowing and off in the distance he could hear birds chirping and the occasional lowing of a cow.

He must have drifted off, but suddenly he was awake. His eyes opened and he sprang up with a jolt. Someone was standing right in front of him. A cry escaped as Manley's eyes focused on the figure of his son. "Blake!" he yelled.

But the word caught in his throat. Was he imagining it? The young man who stood before him resembled Blake, but he was older, and he was wearing some kind of one-piece white uniform. "Wait... you're not Blake."

The young man took a few steps backward. He stared at Manley as if to study him, but he didn't smile.

Manley scrambled to his feet and brushed off his arms and legs. He continued to meet this stranger's eyes and his mouth dropped open. He looked so much like Blake, it was unreal.

Finally, the young man managed a slight smile. There was such a wise expression in his hazel eyes. Blake had never appeared wise before. "You must be Manley Dobbs," he said.

Again Manley was startled. It was Blake's voice. "How... how... how did you...?"

"I understand your confusion," said the young man. "I know that I resemble your son."

"You look just like him. It's astonishing," Manley muttered. "But you're... you're older."

"Yes."

Manley rubbed his head, which was a little sun-burned, and looked around. "Which way did you come?"

The young man glanced back from where Manley had walked. "I'm parked nearby."

"You drove? I don't see a car."

"Not exactly."

"Then..."

The young man interrupted him with a broader smile. "Forgive me for not introducing myself. And I'm sorry if I startled you. For the sake of simplicity, I am called... L.B."

"Elby?" Manley rubbed his nose. "What is that, some kind of a nickname?"

L.B. nodded, then said, "I am glad I found you."

"How did you know *my* name?" Manley was at once suspicious.

"We must not waste any time," L.B. said, ignoring his question. "I am here to help you and your wife get to safety."

Manley's eyes widened. "You know where Dorothy is?"

"I have a very good idea," said L.B. "Come along." He started in the direction from which they had both come.

Manley grabbed his pack and followed without question. "What about my kids?" he asked. "Are they with my wife?"

"They are not together."

"What do you mean?" Manley grew worried. "Where are the kids?"

"Your son and your daughter are safe," L.B. replied.

"And Dorothy?"

"Your wife is safe, for the moment."

"What does that mean?" Manley demanded. The younger man was walking at a brisk pace that Manley found hard to keep up with. "Where is she? Where are Blake and Kelly?"

L.B. led him toward a dilapidated structure down the road that might once have been a barn. "I was able to rescue Blake and Kelly before they could be captured. They were both taken to the mother ship *New Jerusalem*. If all goes well, your entire family will be reunited." The barn-like structure was open on one side and, as they approached, Manley could see a shiny, silvery object hidden inside. It was a spaceship!

Manley's surprise lasted only a moment. Then he grinned. "I was wondering when I was going to see some extraterrestrials."

L.B. glanced at him curiously. "I am not in my true form."

"I gathered that," Manley quipped. Then he frowned. "Wait... you didn't... you didn't take over Blake's..."

L.B. shook his head emphatically. "Your son is completely intact. He gave his permission for me to use his DNA. I underwent a very quick cloning operation on the ship."

"That is incredible!"

"But I must warn you."

"What?" asked Manley.

L.B. hesitated. It seemed hard for him to admit what he had to say. "I am vulnerable in this form. I'm going to require your assistance and your cooperation. Will you help me?"

"Of course," Manley assured him.

"I am still getting used to the density of this body," admitted L.B. "It feels very awkward to me."

"You must be an ethereal being," Manley guessed.

"The body is new to me," said L.B.

"You're a Light Being," murmured Manley in awe.

"You are correct."

"Phenomenal," breathed Manley.

"Come, we must hurry." L.B. somehow managed to cause the ship to open so that they could climb inside. Manley hadn't noticed any device or motion on the young man's part. He rationalized that the response had been the result of telekinesis. He stepped inside the ship and found a recliner seat. L.B. jumped in and the ship's outer casing closed up and a vibration began to hum around them.

Manley had a flashback of memory to the time, eighteen years ago, when he had been captured by aliens and taken aboard a shuttlecraft the night he had left his house in so much despair. It had been a terrible time for him. He shuddered with the horror of the memory that he had meant to do harm to himself, all because Kapri had made it clear to him that she did not return his affections and, in fact, was leaving his house to go room with Dorothy Myers. He had been so hurt and filled with self-pity that he had actually written a suicide note, addressed to his sister, Johanna, whom he hadn't seen since her abduction many months before.

"Are you feeling ill?"

Manley's thoughts were interrupted by a look of concern from the Light Being.

"No, I'm fine," said Manley. "I was just remembering the last time I flew in something like this..."

L.B. piloted the craft swiftly and easily into the Nebraska blue sky. "Not to worry," he said as he manipulated controls on a panel on the wall. "We are cloaked."

"Then the choppers can't see us." Manley sighed with relief.

"Where are we going?"

"Your wife is staying at the facility near what you call Grand Island," said L.B.

"You mean concentration camp," grumbled Manley. "Why were the people taken there?"

"Unknown," said L.B.

"Well, who had the capability of flying choppers in the Null Zone?" demanded Manley. "I thought nothing was supposed to operate during the three days of darkness. Our cars didn't operate. Even our flashlight batteries went dead. How could the helicopters fly?"

"There is much secrecy on your planet," replied the Light Being. "Even I do not have all of the answers, Manley."

"So... what you're saying is, basically, we are *not* in the Photon Belt."

L.B.'s attention was on his panel of lights. "That is not for me to disclose," he replied.

"Well, why not? You're an E.T. You're supposed to know these things!" Manley was frustrated at L.B.'s vague attitude.

"All I know is that Earth is on the verge of a dimensional shift. It has been for a long time. The vibrational fluctuations occur constantly on your planet. You could have experienced ascension years before this had your planet not regressed into war and conflict. The Lightworkers on your planet have had a most challenging decade."

Manley leaned back in the recliner. "You're telling me," he grumbled.

"Whatever or whoever has staged this worldwide event has succeeded in manipulating millions of your planet's inhabitants. They had their plan in place for a very long time." He turned to Manley with a serious expression on the young face that belonged to Blake. "You are going to have to make a decision, Manley."

Manley swallowed. "What kind of decision?"

"You are going to have to choose between staying on Earth with your wife, or leaving the planet."

His words filled Manley with a sudden fear. "Elby, what are you saying?"

L.B.'s craft came within sight of a vast camp filled with tents and quonset huts, completely encircled with a tall barbed wire fence. Manley could see hundreds of people as the ship stopped and hovered over the area. He saw the female guards in military dress carrying weapons. The thought that his beloved Dorothy was imprisoned there made his blood pressure rise. L.B. glanced at him.

"We can leave right this moment, if you just say the word."

"And go where?" Manley demanded.

"Back to the mother ship," said L.B., "back with your children."

"But what about my wife?"

"She is down below."

"I know that!" Manley was growing impatient. "We must find her. Isn't there some way you can... you can... beam her up?"

L.B.'s voice was gentle. "Manley, I visited your wife while she was being held in one of the holding cells underground."

Manley stared and waited.

L.B. continued, "She was defiant."

"Good!" Manley nodded his head, his eyes blazing. "Let's go get her out of there."

"I'm afraid it's not going to be that easy," L.B. explained. "You see, when I visited her, I was in my ethereal form. Now that I'm embodied, I can no longer just materialize and dematerialize."

Manley sighed. "Well, what *can* you do?"

"We need to find out where she is first," said L.B. "She may still be in the holding cell, but my intuition tells me... No, she is no longer there." He hung his head gravely. "In fact, I am certain of it." He looked at Manley with compassion. "It may be... too late for Dorothy."

"What? What are you saying, Elby? Is she... is she... dead?" He stood up. "Tell me! Is my wife dead?"

The Light Being turned back to his flashing panel lights and sighed deeply. "It is worse than death," he said. "Much worse."

30

The Readings

Manley could not imagine what the Light Being had meant. What could be worse than Dorothy being dead? He sat in the seat on the shuttlecraft, his fingers clenched on the hand rests. "Elby, for God's sake, tell me what you meant by that," Manley demanded. "You told me just a moment ago that my wife is safe."

L.B. blinked as he stared Manley in the face. "She has agreed to help the Dark Forces," he explained without emotion. "In other words, she is lost."

"That's impossible!" thundered Manley. He jumped up and stood beside the pilot. Together they peered down as the people in the concentration camp milled about like ants. "Dorothy would never join the Dark Forces. You're wrong!"

"Then she could be an innocent accomplice," suggested L.B. "She probably believes she is on the side of the Light. In either case she is lost."

"My wife is no moron," Manley insisted. "She knows the difference between the two."

"It is not always easy to tell," said L.B.

"How close can you bring this thing in?" Manley asked, sweeping his hand over the panel. The ship suddenly dipped dangerously toward the ground and he grabbed the curved wall to balance himself.

L.B. acted swiftly. He immediately had the shuttle under control. They hovered just twenty or so feet above the largest quonset building.

"I'm sorry," said Manley as he steadied himself. "I didn't mean to do that."

"My error," said the Light Being. "My thoughts strayed for half a second and I lost control."

"You control this ship by thought?" Manley was intrigued.

"Everything is controlled by thought," was L.B.'s reply.

Manley thought a moment, then smiled mockingly. "Well, then with our thoughts we should be able to get us all out of this mess."

L.B. let out a sigh. "Unfortunately, there are too many conflicting thoughts. Too many chaotic thoughts. That is the trouble with your planet."

Manley gazed down at the quonset. "What's going on here?" he demanded. "Hey, it looks like there are only women at this camp. I don't see any men. And where are the children?"

"There are other camps," said L.B.

"Where is Dorothy?"

"She is inside this structure," said L.B.

"Can we... is there a way we can signal her somehow?"

"Negative."

"Well, then, how are we going to rescue her?"

"Provided she wants to be rescued..." the Light Being began.

Manley's temper rose. "Will you get off this idea about Dorothy defecting?" Then he softened his voice when he saw the Light Being's reaction to his anger. "I'm a little uptight, that's all. Everything that's happened has me pretty upset."

"Understood," said L.B. "I'm going to have to try to re-establish telepathic communication with your wife. Since I'm now in this dense body, I'm going to need to shut out the distractions and go into meditation."

Manley nodded. "All right." A few seconds passed, then he added, "I gather this is going to take a while."

The Light Being didn't answer. He stood with his head bowed and his eyes closed and began to breathe deeply.

Manley sighed and dropped back into the recliner seat. He knew that their only chance of rescuing Dorothy depended upon the skills of this E.T. He decided that some deep breathing and shuteye might be beneficial to him as well and settled back in the seat and slowly began to count his breaths.

When Dorothy got through with the first series of papers, before she tackled the second, she decided to find out what had happened outside by the fence. She walked out of the office and strolled down the corridor, determined to find Ernestine Glenn. Other women were busy in different sectioned-off quarters of the quonset, some of them at desks but most of them moving about, going through boxes and crates, stacking blankets or clothing, examining medical supplies. As she walked by, they stared out at her coldly as if she had a lot of nerve looking in on them. In a large kitchen she could see several women preparing hot food and running dish water in the huge sink. Women guards stood in every corner and Dorothy did not meet their eyes.

She stopped when she entered the main section of the quonset and found a crowd of women in military garb surrounding the two women who had been brought in from the yard. Dorothy was startled to recognize Louise, the older woman who had befriended her the first day in the camp. Louise had been treated roughly and had a bloody gash on her temple. Her clothes and face were smudged with dirt. They had tied her hands behind her.

Dorothy didn't know who the other arrested woman was, but this one was young and feisty with snarly, unbrushed red hair and a dark complexion. Her hands were tied as well and she had a black eye. Ernestine Glenn sat in a folding chair facing the two women.

"We will not cooperate," the red-haired woman fired at Ernestine. "This whole thing is an outrage! You have no right keeping us here any longer. We demand our release!"

Dorothy was astounded at Ernestine's composure. The angry words did not seem to upset her in the least. She calmly smiled at the woman and said, "I assure you, all of this is for your protection. Our efficient and capable government, as you know, has deserted its people. But never fear... we are taking measures to see that everyone is taken care of. As soon as we have confirmation that it is safe... we will release you... all of you."

Louise's lower lip was trembling. She called out in a voice laden with sobs, "What about our husbands? Our children? When will we be reunited with our families?"

"I assure you," said Ernestine, "everything is under control.

Now I want you to go back to your peers and tell them everything is fine. No one need suffer any longer than she has to."

"We need clean water! And food!" fired the red-haired captive. Her eyes flamed. "Those contraptions you call bathrooms are disgusting! There's no spare water to wash with. We haven't had anything to eat but mush for four days now!"

"Open the gates and let us out of here!" cried Louise. "I beg you!"

"Take them to the cells," Ernestine told one of her guards.

Her military protector scrunched up her face. "But downstairs is full," she said. "We're overflowing."

"I don't care!" cried Ernestine.

"Can't they go back to camp?" another guard asked.

Ernestine stared at the guard, then said in a firm voice, "I want them in the cells. I don't want them stirring up more trouble in camp."

"But, ma'am..."

"That's an order!" Ernestine snapped.

The guards led Louise and the red-haired captive through the crowd and past Dorothy. When Louise passed, her eyes met Dorothy's and lit up with recognition.

"Louise..." Dorothy started to say. She was stricken with horror that the older woman was being led into that awful dark cell in the basement. But Louise immediately gave her a look that demanded she say nothing. Picking up on the warning, Dorothy dropped back as the guards passed.

"Ernestine?" Dorothy pushed her way through the crowd to where Ernestine Glenn had stood and was checking over a list an assistant had handed her.

Ernestine smiled up at Dorothy. "Here you are. I was hoping you had finished with those reports."

"Well, I..." Dorothy saw that the captured women had been pushed out of sight.

"Oh, don't worry about that scene," Ernestine told her. She put her arm around Dorothy's shoulder and led her off into a corner where they could speak more privately. "Just a couple of trouble makers getting everyone riled up in the camp."

"Yes, what about the women in the camp?" asked Dorothy, her hands on her hips. "When will they be able to go home?"

Ernestine studied Dorothy's worried face a moment, then sighed. "Reports indicate that transportation and power is still down," she said. "There has been major looting, rape, utter chaos, as you can imagine in a situation like this. Allowing these women to return to their homes in such conditions is unthinkable. I cannot allow it."

"But how can you take care of everyone's needs?" asked Dorothy. "I'd be furious, too, if I was hungry and hadn't had a bath in days."

Ernestine smiled and patted Dorothy's arm. "Of course you would. We all would. But I assure you, things will be better soon. Trust me."

"When?"

"Soon."

Dorothy suddenly felt light-headed and her expression must have changed suddenly, for Ernestine Glenn stared at her oddly.

"What's wrong?" asked Ernestine.

Dorothy felt her temple and steadied herself against a chair. "Nothing, just a dizzy spell."

"Here, please sit down." Ernestine helped her into the chair. "Do you feel all right?"

Dorothy wasn't sure what was going on, but she definitely didn't feel normal. There was a soft humming in her ears. "Yes," she fibbed. "Maybe... I think I'd like a glass of water."

Ernestine snapped her fingers and a guard left and returned a few moments later with a small plastic water bottle, which Ernestine opened and handed to Dorothy. "Drink this."

"Thanks." Dorothy took two sips, then relaxed. "I'm sure it's nothing."

"I want you to go to my quarters right now and lie down for a few minutes," Ernestine directed. "I have an assignment for you later, a most important task. Go and rest awhile. I'll have the lieutenant wake you when I'm ready for you."

Dorothy rose to her feet and sauntered off to the room designated for Ernestine Glenn. Her head buzzed and she was relieved to have the time to herself. Ernestine certainly was understanding and compassionate. She must be under so much stress, Dorothy thought, having to assume leadership and deal with people who are confused and miserable. At least Dorothy wasn't miserable any more, although she had to admit many things still confused her.

She drew a curtain that allowed some privacy and settled down on Ernestine's cot. Outside the window she could hear women's cries and protests. So many of them were wanting their freedom. Was it true what Ernestine had said, that the world was in chaos and turmoil? How could that be any worse than being confined in a concentration camp in the middle of Nebraska in June? In the early hours of afternoon it was already sweltering with heat and humidity. A fly buzzed against the pane of glass above her.

"Dear God," Dorothy began to pray aloud as she lay on Ernestine's cot. "What is happening? Is this the end of civilization as we know it? Are we experiencing Armageddon? If so, dear Lord, please spare my two children, wherever they are... and Manley... oh, Manley..." She began to sob and covered her head with her arm to smother her cries.

The humming in Dorothy's ears grew louder and she quieted her sobs to listen. This was familiar to her. She felt that someone was trying to make contact with her. Being psychic all her life, she had observed this humming in the ears many times before. She forced herself to breathe deeply and relax, to allow the message to come through to her.

Finally, after several minutes, Dorothy moved into a meditative state and heard the words spoken in her head. She wasn't surprised that the voice was the same as the one she had heard while being held prisoner in the basement jail. "Dorothy... I have returned. The ship is cloaked but is overhead. Listen very carefully, Dorothy. I must land in order for you to join me. This camp is not a safe landing place. You must leave the camp and we will track you until it is safe to uncloak."

Dorothy closed her eyes and asked, "Who are you? Please..."

"I am a friend." Then the voice asked, "Are you able to leave the quonset?"

"I haven't tried," Dorothy replied. "But I need to know who you are."

"Dorothy, the longer you stay, the more danger you are in. I cannot hold my position much longer."

Dorothy sighed. "Why can't you land? What are you afraid of?"

The voice was patient. "If I uncloak now, I risk being fired upon. Unfortunately, my shields are not fully charged."

"Are you from space?" asked Dorothy. "Are Serassan and Johanna with you?"

There was a slight hesitation and then the voice continued, "I know of no such ones of whom you speak." Then he said, "There is no time for questions. You must leave the compound and allow us to rescue you."

"Who *are* you?" Dorothy demanded. "How do I know I can trust you?"

"I have your husband with me," said the voice. "Manley Dobbs."

"Manley!" Dorothy's eyes popped open and her emotional reaction broke the communication. She sat up on the cot and looked around. The buzzing in her head ceased and was replaced with a dull ache. Her heart beat wildly and she stood up, wondering what to do. What would happen if she tried to leave the quonset? Was it possible Manley and a spaceship were nearby, waiting to pick her up? It sounded too good to be true.

The lieutenant pushed the curtain aside and stepped into Ernestine's quarters. "Mrs. Dobbs," she said sternly. "Ernestine is ready for you. Come with me now."

Dorothy followed reluctantly, more confused than ever. She was led to the main room, where Ernestine waited with an entourage of about a dozen women who must have come from the camp. Every one of them was dirty, disheveled and wore a frantic look on their faces. They were women of varying ages and races, and they stood huddled together, some holding each other.

"Very good," said Ernestine as Dorothy approached. "Dorothy Dobbs is my Intuitive Specialist. Dorothy, stand over here."

Dorothy was led in front of a black woman of about 35 whose eyes were bloodshot and whose jacket was stained with blood.

"Now, I want you to tell me about this woman," Ernestine said.

Dorothy looked at Ernestine questioningly.

"Go on. I know you can," Ernestine prompted.

Still uncertain, Dorothy asked, "What do you want me to do?"

"You are intuitive," Ernestine reminded her. "I want you to tell me what you see in this woman. I want you to give me a psychic impression of her... you know, do a reading on her."

"But how do you know I..."

"I know more about you, Dorothy Dobbs, than you could ever imagine," said Ernestine. "The reason I wanted you for my right-hand assistant is because of your exceptional talent. Now... what can you tell me about this woman?"

Her heart beating briskly, Dorothy stared at the woman and was immediately overcome by fear. The woman's thoughts seemed to rush out at her and grab her psyche. *Just who the hell do you think you are? You can't read my thoughts!* The words burned in Dorothy's ears and she faltered a little, but Ernestine caught her arm and steadied her.

"Go ahead," coaxed Ernestine.

Dorothy didn't know what else to do, so she closed her eyes and tried to shut out the barrage of profanity the black woman's thoughts were firing at her. Finally, she began to see the woman's aura in her mind, a fiery orange blaze with pinks and reds intertwined. "This woman has been abused in many ways," said Dorothy. "She comes from a large city... I get the feeling... it's... it's... Cincinnati..."

A small gasp escaped from the woman's lips and Dorothy opened her eyes as the fear thoughts that were attacking her began to subside.

"She has been in jail twice... once for prostitution... and again for stealing. She has lived a disturbed life."

"Is she violent?" Ernestine queried.

Dorothy sighed as she concentrated. "She has been violent in the past. Right now she is only scared... she's in survival mode... she has a little boy who she's terribly worried about..."

"Enough!" commanded Ernestine. "Take her downstairs."

The guards pulled the black woman away and then Dorothy found herself facing a young curly-haired blonde in her twenties, with a pudgy face and swollen lips. The woman had a black eye and her shirt was torn. She regarded Dorothy with resentment in her eyes.

"Tell me about this one," said Ernestine.

Dorothy shuddered as she closed her eyes and let her gift flow. "She's single... and pregnant. Her boyfriend left her and she was... was considering... an abortion."

The blond woman began to sob.

"Go on," urged Ernestine.

"She comes from a well-to-do family in Omaha. Quite religious. She has very low self-esteem... she went to college in Lincoln and majored in education."

"Really?"

Dorothy saw the frightened woman nod her head. Ernestine studied her carefully. "How far along are you?" But before the woman could answer, she put up her hand. "No! Dorothy, you tell me."

Dorothy wrinkled her forehead and let the answer come to her mind. "Four and a half months."

"A little late for an abortion, isn't it, dear?" asked Ernestine. "What's your name?"

The blond woman's lip trembled, then she said, "D-D-Debbie."

"And how far along *are* you?" asked Ernestine.

Debbie's eyes rolled toward Dorothy, then back to Ernestine. "Twenty weeks," she murmured.

Ernestine glanced at Dorothy. "Boy or girl?"

Dorothy again closed her eyes, then opened them. "A girl."

Ernestine motioned to the guards and they escorted Debbie off to one side. Apparently she had been saved from the overcrowded dark dungeon below.

"This one next," directed Ernestine as a short Oriental girl, about 18, was nudged forward by the guards. The girl's short black hair was greasy and her cheeks sunken in as she stared ahead, clasping an object in her hands.

"What is that you're holding?" asked Ernestine.

The Oriental girl's fingers tightened in fear, as if the item might be snatched from her.

Dorothy felt a strong wave of power emanating from the girl, and in the brief second that their eyes met she realized this person was an enlightened being. At least there was a strong sense of love exuding from the girl's heart chakra. Dorothy tuned in without waiting any longer.

Don't... don't! the girl's thoughts echoed in Dorothy's mind. *Please don't... don't!*

"Dorothy?" prompted Ernestine. "What can you tell me about her?"

"She's a Reiki master," Dorothy blurted, growing excited. "She is Japanese and a student at the University of Michigan. She was traveling the States for her summer break... just like I did when I... when I... long ago..."

"Dorothy, this isn't about you," Ernestine reprimanded softly. "Tell me what the girl is doing with that object. What is it, anyway?'

Suddenly the girl's face brightened into a smile and she revealed a double-terminated crystal about three inches long and extremely clear, so clear that it seemed to glow as she held it out to show them.

"Oh, it's beautiful!" Dorothy cried out. "I don't think I've ever seen a crystal as clear as that! Where did you..."

Ernestine interrupted her. "Guards! Take her downstairs."

Forcefully, two guards hoisted the Japanese girl away while Dorothy stared, wide-eyed and confused, after her. Then she turned to Ernestine Glenn. "Just what has she done? Ernestine, that girl had the most magnificent aura!"

"Next!" commanded Ernestine, completely ignoring Dorothy's outburst. An older woman with gray matted hair was brought forward. "Now... read her."

Dorothy looked around as the Japanese Reiki healer disappeared toward the stairs. She could see that there were still many more women Ernestine wanted her to psychically examine. She was beginning to see what this was all about. Ernestine Glenn was apparently using Dorothy's intuitive gift to filter out the women in the camp whom she perceived to be some kind of a threat. The young Oriental girl's strong spirit must obviously be a threat, and the black woman's past history of violence...

"Dorothy?" Ernestine interrupted her thoughts.

"I'm... I'm quite fatigued all of a sudden," Dorothy said, feeling her forehead. "I'm not used to doing so many readings, one right after the other. Could we... could I take a little break?"

Ernestine sighed impatiently, then immediately covered it up with a broad smile. "Of course. Please forgive me for not thinking. We don't want to drain you on the first day of your new job. Go and gather yourself, and return here in ten minutes."

Dorothy's head throbbed. "Ten minutes?" she repeated. "But I..."

"We have a lot of women to process," said Ernestine.

"I need some air. May I step outside for a few minutes?" asked Dorothy.

Ernestine sighed. "Very well. But make it snappy."

Without hesitation Dorothy headed for the front entrance to the quonset. She had to squeeze her way between women in military garb and their prisoners. Finally, she stepped outside the door and felt the afternoon's penetrating rays of sunshine on her face and arms. The air was stifling with no wind. Flies buzzed around her as she looked around at her options. Guards were everywhere and there was no place where she could really be alone, but she walked over to a tree and leaned against it, her arms folded, and stared up at the blue sky with wisps of white clouds.

"Oh, where are you, Manley?" she mumbled to herself. Then she shut her eyes and sought the connection she'd had before while resting in Ernestine's room. *Come on,* she called with her thoughts. *Come back! I'm outside, just as you told me. Where are you? Communicate with me, please! Are you there? Is Manley with you?*

31

Space Lesson

A s they traveled through space to meet the cruiser, Blake had the opportunity to learn about various spacecraft. While his friend Blue Jay dozed, Kapri proved to be a knowledgeable and enthusiastic instructor while she piloted the shuttle. He listened wholeheartedly as she explained in language and terms that didn't require a technical engineering degree.

"A mother ship is a large vessel designed for intergalactic travel and transport," Kapri explained. "There are different pressures and oxygen controls that are designed to simulate the worlds to which the beings on them are native. Generally, mother ship crews are from similar planets that are compatible with the air and atmospheric pressure. The exception, of course, is my own race. We who came from Estron chose to serve on the *New Jerusalem*, but must compensate by adjusting our intake of oxygen. Estronians have a choice. We can either undergo a biological transformation, carry around an atmospheric bubble, or we must constantly take oxygen-adjusting supplements."

Blake was fascinated. "And you take the supplements?"

Kapri shook her head. "I invested in the device." She rolled up her sleeve to show him the compact case once again.

"Why didn't you take a human form, like my friend L.B.?"

Kapri's slanted blue eyes smiled at him. "Several of your years ago, I underwent the biological transformation."

"Oh, that's right," Blake suddenly remembered. "You showed me the pictures in your cabin."

"Precisely," she said. "And I believe I told you then it was difficult for me. I had many problems adjusting to the new physical form. I had a lot of migraines."

"It must have been a complex procedure," commented Blake.

"Quite complex. It took several months to complete the transformation. I do not wish to ever go through that experience again."

Blake thought a moment. "And yet L.B. did it in a day..."

"Your friend's cloning was very risky," Kapri said. "For one thing, he is an ethereal being that is taking on a physical body. Such procedures can be disastrous to the organism that is cloned. The DNA and RNA is mutated. Diseases and genetic defects are common in cloned individuals. That is why we do not perform such operations except in an emergency."

Blake pondered this information for a while. The Light Being must have obviously felt this mission was of the utmost importance to have risked such a procedure. He wondered why the Light Being had gone to such an extent to rescue his mom and dad on Earth.

"Let me finish telling you about the mother ships," Kapri resumed.

"Okay." Blake gave her his full attention.

"The *New Jerusalem* is one of four mother ships in Terra's sector. It is the largest ship and is approximately 1,500 of your miles in length and has a diameter of 500 miles from its hull. It has a crew of several thousand."

Blake whistled in astonishment.

"There are twelve hangar decks that hold hundreds of disks and triangle craft," she said.

"What are the triangle craft used for?" Blake interrupted.

"Mostly surveillance," Kapri replied.

"A lot of those triangles have been reported on Earth," Blake recalled.

"Undoubtedly," said Kapri. "Some triangles are drones and are remotely controlled by computers on mother ships."

"The *New Jerusalem*... your ship... does it stay in orbit around Earth?"

"No," said Kapri. "For a long time it has been stationed between Jupiter and Saturn. Only recently were we directed to position ourselves in Terra's orbit."

"Where are the other ships stationed?" asked Blake.

"There's the *Brilliance*, which is mostly a hospital ship," said Kapri. "She is about half the size of the *New Jerusalem*. She is near

Mars. Then there is the *Bethlehem*, which is smaller than the *Brilliance*. The *Bethlehem* is stationed between your planets Mercury and Venus."

"And where's the fourth?" asked Blake.

"That would be *Regel*," said Kapri, "which borders your solar system. The *Regel* is about the same size as the *Brilliance*. It is a surveillance vessel that serves the dual purpose of observation and patrol missions. It is also used as back-up for defense system craft."

"Wow..." Blake was fascinated. "You say they are designed to intergalactic travel. So why are they all hanging out in Earth's solar system?"

"The Federation has them stationed there," said Kapri. "All the craft are cloaked from your people. They will remain as long as they are needed."

Blake understood that the Estronian scientist was referring to all the chaos and trouble happening now on his home planet. "Well, I'm sure glad you're nearby," he sighed. "Tell me some more about the mother ships. How are they powered?"

Kapri seemed delighted by his curiosity. "A mother ship is fueled by reactors and crystal rotors that utilize fuel basketballs of Element 115, which fit into cores in the engine rooms of the vessels."

"Basketballs?" Blake blinked in disbelief.

"On the *New Jerusalem* there are fifteen of these basketball-size reactors that are linked to pipe-like activators — rods that react with a quartz-like substance in conjunction with Element 115 — to split atoms and create a cold fusion type of reaction. These power the ships. On smaller craft they are smaller in size, such as a tennis ball or a marble."

"Oh." Blake was finding it difficult to understand the more technological explanations and changed the subject. "Uh-huh... and how do you get your supplies? Don't you have to stock a bunch of food to feed thousands of crew members for who knows how long? And what about your water?"

"Water and food are recycled over and over," explained Kapri. "Foods are grown in hydroponic conditions. That is, foods are grown in a water-like substance for plant food. Animals are grown in special containment units for food as well."

"You mean, space beings eat meat?" asked Blake.

Kapri was startled by his abrupt question. "Why not? Do not Terrans eat animals?"

Blake sighed. "My vegetarian friends back home would have a fit if they found out about this." He grinned. "But I eat meat once in a while. I like it, actually. I don't think it's wrong to eat animals, do you?"

Kapri relaxed. "Those who choose to not eat animal flesh make that choice," she said. "It is merely a preference. There is no right or wrong about it."

"Well, it's one of those controversial things, you know," said Blake. "People that are supposed to be so highly evolved aren't meat eaters..."

"Blake, eating animal flesh or choosing not to has nothing to do with a being's level of spirituality," said Kapri. "When I was on Terra, visiting your father, I had a Terran body that was giving me a lot of discomfort. I had to be very selective about what foods I placed within it. But I have never condemned anyone for meat eating."

"Do you... eat meat?" asked Blake.

Kapri laughed. "There are times when I crave a good old-fashioned Estronian chipluxqueg burger. Yes, Blake, once in a while I do."

"So, the food I ate on the ship was from plants and animals grown right there in space?"

"That's right. On the ships we can have forests grown this way, without the need of soil. The hydroponic solution is created with every known nutrient needed to sustain them." She described it as a type of thick, gelatin-like substance as clear as water.

Blake found it unceasingly fascinating to hear about the operations on board the ships. He learned that he would be going to Karos on the space cruiser *Resilience*, a large vessel with the main purpose of moving people in space from planet to planet, or to visit other solar systems.

"They are capable of covering vast distances in minimal time," Kapri told him, "through use of space portals or what you call worm holes."

"Yeah, can you explain to me how those actually work?" asked Blake. "I mean, how does a ship enter a worm hole and suddenly come out of it and be light-years ahead?"

"Time is changed — speeded up," she explained. "In a light

portal, which is a type of worm hole, time is frozen as you move forward, and then it speeds up when your craft exits. You can even go back in time when traveling through some portals. Without that technology, we could not travel from solar system to solar system," said Kapri. "Federation vessels are even capable of traversing the galaxies, through warp travel."

As she explained more, her language became complex and technical, until Blake was totally lost. Finally, Kapri seemed to notice his look of confusion and reassured him the lesson on space travel was ended for the day.

Blake settled down beside his sleeping friend, who was starting to snore a little, and let his own heavy eyelids close. As he drifted off to sleep, he murmured a prayer for both his parents and trusted The Light Being would be able to find them.

Emrox and his mate, Soolàn, stepped off their shuttle and found themselves enveloped in a whirlwind of brightness and movement. All around them were dome structures and high rises built from crystal and stone material. Footsteps echoed against the ground and walls all around them. Estronian people dressed in all manner of attire crossed their paths, too busy with their own preoccupations to think about the man and woman in robes who had just landed in their city from one of the neighboring planetoids. Above their heads sky shuttles passed over and on the ground a tramway accommodated those who desired to stand and read or rest their legs while on their commutes to wherever they were headed.

A new dome building was going up near them. The construction sounds were of laser torches cutting and shaping stone, as well as the foremen shouting directions to the laborers. Over the din came occasional chattering voices from the passers-by.

Soolàn touched her husband's sleeve as they looked around at the bustling city, both a little overwhelmed at the acceleration of lifestyle. "Where do we start?" she asked.

Emrox gazed left, then right, and then pulled her closer as if to protect her from being bowled over by one of the anxious local pedestrians. "We must inquire first of Thorden," he told Soolàn. "I suggest we try Mission Central. They keep track of travelers on and off the planet."

"A good idea," Soolàn agreed and let him carefully escort her across a wide walkway of fine stone and crystal. If the two of them were conspicuous as outsiders in their more deliberate and cautious movements, the Estronian city dwellers did not appear to notice. The two managed to cross the busy thoroughfare and walked toward the entrance of the large building that served as planetary headquarters for space missions.

Emrox knew where to go, having served as a member of Estron's High Council for many years. He was well acquainted with the city. Many workers recognized him and greeted him, bowing to show their respect. Emrox and Soolàn climbed a spiral ramp that led to an upper level and Emrox led Soolàn down a corridor directly to the office of Mission Central.

"May I be of assistance?" an older female Estronian asked as they approached the reception area. She was a lofty being with a dignified face and square shoulders, dressed in a gray one-piece uniform. She stole curious glances at Soolàn, but directed her question to Emrox.

"Yes, we are searching for our granddaughter," Emrox revealed.

It was obvious that such a request was not an everyday occurrence on Estron. The receptionist looked startled and eyed Soolàn as if to ask if this man was serious.

"Our granddaughter is missing," Soolàn spoke up. "She is a resident of Karos."

"Of Karos?" The Estronian female's eyes widened and then she smiled. "Oh... Karos. I have heard many interesting things about the new center for performing arts."

Emrox nodded. "Our son is Serassan, who has been instrumental in..."

"But of course," the Estronian female interrupted, growing more excited. "There have been many excursions to Karos in the last few days. Apparently the arts center is gaining a lot of interest. We expect within a very short time it will become the planet's most popular destination..."

"Indeed," said Emrox impatiently. "But right now we are trying to locate a young woman by the name of Crystal... Crystal Dobbs."

"One moment." The receptionist opened up a computer

screen that expanded before their eyes by the touch of a button on her desk panel. After a few seconds she shook her head. "There is no one by that name on the log."

"We believe she is in the company of... a Thorden," said Soolàn. "Do you know where we might locate this Thorden?"

Again the Estronian woman at the desk interacted with the screen in front of her. Then she turned her bulbous white head and looked Soolàn in the eye. "Yes. There is a Thorden in the log."

"Can you tell us where we might find him?" asked Emrox.

The Estronian receptionist studied the screen. "Let's see, he went to Karos..."

"Yes, yes, we already know that," Emrox interrupted impatiently.

Soolàn placed a calming hand on her husband's sleeve. "Do you know where his location is now?" she asked.

"It says here that Thorden is preparing for a space mission and has applied for funds to lead some recruits from the planet's flight schools into space. He plans to take the students to various solar systems in the galaxy in order to offer them experience in space flight."

"Who has given him the authority?" asked Emrox.

"He needs none," was the reply.

"We are aware that Thorden caused problems several years ago on the Earth-Star mission," Soolàn explained.

Again the Estronian receptionist consulted her computer and grimaced. "I see what you are referring to. Apparently there was misbehavior on the part of this Estronian male. He was placed on probation and not allowed to leave the planet." She looked up at the two of them. "But due to good behavior, he has been released from that restriction. He is now being allowed to venture into space without boundaries."

Emrox sighed, then asked, "We have reason to believe our granddaughter, Crystal Dobbs, is with Thorden. How might we find him?"

"You will not find him on Estron," the receptionist said. "Thorden is on the cruiser *Harmony*, which left Estron's orbit two days ago."

Soolàn moaned and held her face.

"Do you know where the *Harmony* is headed?" asked Emrox.

"All I can say is that the *Harmony* is due to rendezvous with the Galactic Federation cruiser *Resilience*, which is on its way to Karos from the Terran solar system."

"Earth?" asked Soolàn and the receptionist nodded.

"And then?" prompted Emrox.

"There is no flight plan noted," the receptionist replied. "Thorden has free control of the *Harmony*'s destiny after the rendezvous — provided, that is, that his funding is secured."

"We must get on board the *Harmony*," Soolàn told her mate.

Emrox squeezed Soolàn's hand, then turned to the receptionist. "Madam, we must intercept the *Harmony*. Do you know of any vessel that may be headed in..."

"The only way you can get to the *Harmony* before its rendezvous with the *Resilience* is to commission a light ship," the receptionist told them.

"A light ship?" grumbled Emrox.

"They are expensive," the receptionist interjected, "and you may find it difficult to find a pilot in such short notice."

"We must try," insisted Soolàn.

"Do you know of any pilots?" asked Emrox.

The Estronian woman behind the desk shook her huge head. "I do not."

"How much time do we have?" asked Soolàn.

"Time?"

"Before the cruisers rendezvous."

"Approximately one solar day," replied the woman.

"We can make it," Soolàn murmured.

"But how are we going to find a light ship pilot in such short time?" asked Emrox.

"We will just have to try." Soolàn grabbed his arm and started leading him away.

Emrox nodded his head in thanks to the receptionist, who saluted in a gesture of good luck, then resumed her duties at the desk. "Soolàn," he said as they glided down the spiral ramp. "Where are we going to find a light ship pilot? Plus we still don't know for sure that Thorden has Crystal in his company."

"There is no question in my mind," Soolàn replied. "Surely there has to be someone... some eager Estronian astronaut... We must not waste a moment, Emrox. We must go out into the city and ask."

"This is going to be a cumbersome task," Emrox replied gruffly.

"Do you have a better suggestion?" she retorted.

Emrox did not answer. They were headed out the door when someone shouted at them from the direction in which they had come. "Visitors! Wait! Visitors, don't go yet!"

Soolàn and Emrox stopped and turned around. The Estronian receptionist they had spoken to waved at them from the spiral ramp.

"I know of a pilot!" she called down to them.

Emrox and Soolàn looked at each other in relief and hurried back to the ramp.

It was late and Crystal was exhausted at the end of the shift as she trudged back to her cubicle of a cabin on board the *Harmony*. For the last ten hours she had been forced to clean the reactor shields and her fingers were black and swollen, her hair damp and tangled from the almost unbearable heat in the engine rooms. She had worked alongside androids, who normally did such work in order to spare humanoids such toil. The Task Master, a tall, cylindrical mechanical unit, had supervised Crystal's every move as she followed his orders, breaking several fingernails to get at the tedious notches and grooves. It had been difficult work scrubbing the casing of the dirty shields. She had broken several of the fine-tipped cleaning instruments used to scour the grills on the shields.

Her back ached from having to manually remove the shields. A couple of times she had nearly slipped on the fuzzy-like byproduct that covered the engine room floor. The substance, which normally was sucked automatically into input valves from the Element 115 reactor cores' propulsion units and discharged outside the vessel, had to be swept up with a common broom.

The worst part had been her fear of making a mistake. Had she carelessly bumped a core in the reactor, she could have risked serious damage to the mother ship as the Element 115 was very unstable. Reinstalling the grids was tedious work and stressful with the Task Master monitoring her every move.

Her throat felt parched. She had not been given enough to drink. Tears of indignity stained her black cheeks. Flecks of fuzzy dust particles had gotten in her eyes and up her nostrils. The Task

Master had no compassion and apparently no understanding of humanoid emotion or suffering. His orders had been to work her to the point of breaking, and now she was spent.

All Crystal wanted to do when she got to her room was collapse upon the bed, but instead she coaxed her tired body into the tiny shower stall in her bathroom and closed her eyes as the jets of warm soapy water gushed over her and gently caressed her head, shoulders, arms and legs. What a blessed relief it was to wash away the dirt and grime and sweat, and feel nothing but the soothing flow of water and drink in the flowery scent of the automatic soap.

After she had cleaned up, gotten into an issued robe and was preparing for bed, Thorden came to see her. She had expected he would show up and gloat over her punishment at defying him. And that is exactly what he did.

"So, you now have a taste of what it is like to work in space." Thorden's sardonic tone chilled Crystal's spine.

She cringed, but was too tired to be afraid of him. "Get out of here, Thorden. I'm tired and want to go to bed."

The Estronian wore a long maroon-colored robe and his eyes burned with vexation. "I had sincerely hoped you might have a change of heart toward me after today's work session," he said in icy tones. "All you need to do is say the word and I will release you from further tasking."

"Send me back to Karos," Crystal begged. "I just want to go home."

"Wrong answer, my little protégé." His voice hardened. "Once you are mine, there will be no more reactor shields to clean. Or... perhaps you will prefer to move on to Level Two tasking... calibrating the instrument panels on all the flight controls. Believe me, if you thought today's tasks were long and arduous, wait until you have to do calibration. It requires utmost perfection and you cannot quit for the day until it is finished."

Crystal sighed and felt the tears about to gush from her tired eyes and throbbing head. "Please... just go away and leave me alone."

"Then there is Level Three tasking," Thorden continued, ignoring her. "Waste management, a task so unpleasant that no organic being can tolerate the stench. A task left to androids and... uncooperative young Terran hybrids." He laughed derisively.

Crystal shuddered and strained to maintain her dignity, even though she wanted to burst into tears. "I'm very tired, Thorden. Go away," she told him in a stronger voice than she believed she possessed.

After a moment he let out a long breath that polluted the air in the small cabin. "Very well then, I shall let you get your rest. We will see how things stand between us after an endless day of calibration." Thorden exited the small cubicle and Crystal wrinkled up her nose at the putrid smell he left behind.

Then she initiated the pull-out of the automatic bed by pushing a button which released the bed from inside a sliding panel on the wall. As soon as it stopped, she tumbled onto it and buried her head into her pillow as great sobs erupted and tears soaked the pillowcase. She was exhausted and afraid, unwilling to face another agonizing day of strenuous labor, yet even more unwilling to give into the lascivious Thorden.

When a meal was delivered to her cabin a little later, Crystal sat up and wiped her eyes, then asked the servobot android if there was someone she could summon to help her.

"I am programmed to fulfill your needs," replied the unit. "How may I assist you?"

"I need to return to my home planet," Crystal said. "I want to go back to Karos."

"This ship is not headed in that direction," came the metallic reply.

"Well, then, who can I speak to about it?"

"Your superior is Thorden," the unit said. "I will summon him."

"No, I don't want Thorden," Crystal protested. "I want to speak to the pilot of this vessel."

"That is not possible," said the unit.

"Why not?"

"The *Harmony* is set on automatic flight."

"Well, who is the captain?" Crystal demanded.

"Thorden has control over this vessel. He alone will decide its course after the rendezvous with the *Resilience*."

Crystal's hopes were crushed at this news, but she perked up at the mention of the *Resilience*. "When will that occur?" she asked.

"The *Resilience* is expected to intercept our course within the next day cycle," same the reply. "There are passengers on the

Harmony that need to transfer to that cruiser as well as cargo to be picked up."

"And do you know where it is headed?" Crystal asked hopefully.

"The *Resilience* is on course back to Estron."

Crystal sighed, her heart hammering as hope once again swelled within her. She asked the android if she could be notified when the rendezvous occurred.

"That is not permitted," the unit told her.

"What do you mean it's not permitted?" Crystal demanded.

"Thorden has given strict orders that you are to be kept isolated during rendezvous."

"He has no right to hold me like this!" Anger crept into Crystal's cheeks and she flushed a deep red. "I am not his property! I want to go home!"

The android said nothing more after arranging her meal tray. It left and Crystal once again burst into tears, her appetite ruined. As more tears gushed forth, she cursed Thorden and she cursed herself for the other morning when she had given her consent to leave Karos with him. What had she been thinking? How could she have let something like this happen to herself?

She knew Thorden would do everything possible to keep her from contacting anyone aboard the *Resilience*. But she must find a way to escape, to somehow get word to someone... anyone... that she was being held against her will and desired to return to her home.

32

Setback

Dorothy's eyes fluttered open. She was on the grassy ground, slumped against a tree as late afternoon shadows stretched across the compound. She was immediately aware of two heavy women guards grabbing her arms and lifting her to her feet.

"What happened?" Dorothy asked. The last thing she remembered was staring up at the blue June sky, frantically calling out in her mind for help from that unseen light and voice in her head. Had there been any response to her summons? None that she could recall. There had been no communication at all. No space ship waiting to pick her up as promised. Instead, she had slipped from consciousness from pure mental exhaustion.

"Let's go, Mrs. Dobbs," one of the guards commanded in a voice that lacked compassion.

"On your feet," commanded the other guard.

Dorothy recovered her dignity and took a few wobbly steps, allowing assistance from the guards. Her head felt foggy and she was troubled still by the sight of the high barbed wire fence and the milling women around the huge canopy shelter, kept at bay by the armed female soldiers. They led her back to the quonset as a dark helicopter flew over and descended behind the building.

"What is wrong?" Ernestine Glenn demanded when Dorothy stood in front of her. The guards released her and she struggled to keep her balance.

"She fainted, ma'am."

Obviously annoyed, Ernestine Glenn shook her head, her red lips pursed and her dark brows furrowed. "Well, you're in no condition to work any more today, are you?"

Dorothy knew Ernestine referred to her psychic readings of the women in the compound. She sighed. "I am drained. You have no idea how fatiguing it is..."

"Never mind," Ernestine interrupted. "Quarters are being prepared for you. Go and get the rest you need."

"Ms. Glenn, the General has arrived," someone called from across the room. Outside the clatter of helicopter blades slowed.

"Very well," the woman leader replied. "Take Dorothy to her quarters. Give her a meal."

"I'm not hungry," Dorothy protested. "Just... very tired."

Ernestine put on a consoling smile and patted Dorothy's shoulder. "You'll feel better in the morning. Then we can resume your important work."

"I apologize..."

"No need." Ernestine dismissed her quickly and turned to follow a lieutenant down the same hallway she had been in earlier. The guard led Dorothy to a cot in a corner which had been closed off with curtains to separate her from others.

Dorothy was too tired to think. She lay down on the cot in relief and almost immediately fell into a deep, exhausted sleep.

M anley watched as the Light Being slumped over the control panel of the shuttlecraft. They had just landed the ship in a woods a few miles from the concentration camp. He had been totally surprised when suddenly the young alien had flown the craft away from the site. There had been no warning. It was almost as if they had been under attack.

"I thought we were going to rescue your m..." Manley caught himself before saying the word *mother*. The Light Being looked too much like Blake. "I mean... weren't we going to pick up my wife?"

L.B. leaned over as if he were in pain.

Manley jumped up and stepped toward him. "Are you okay?" he asked.

The Light Being sucked in a breath and turned slowly to look up at Manley. "I am weak," he managed to mutter. "I need to rest awhile."

"What happened? Are you all right?"

"Uncertain," L.B. murmured. "I think... perhaps..." He reached over to grope the wall. "It may have something... something to do with... my... cloning." He tried to walk, but faltered.

Manley rushed forward and helped the pilot of the craft. "What can I do to help you?" he asked.

L.B. gestured toward the reclining seat in the middle of the craft and Manley led him over to it. He helped the young man into the seat and watched as the seat automatically lowered, allowing its occupant to lie flat.

"Elby," said Manley, "is there anything I can do for you?"

"I must... rest... just... rest..." whispered the Light Being.

"But... how long?" Manley began to worry about Dorothy. And what if somebody saw the craft hidden in the woods?

As if in response to his fretful thoughts, the Light Being opened his eyes ever so slightly and stared at Manley. "The ship is safe... for the time being... not... exposed..."

"You mean it's still cloaked?"

The Light Being didn't answer. He had slipped off into unconsciousness.

Manley looked around, frantic. He had to help Dorothy. The thought of her being in that awful camp made him sick. But he didn't know what he could do without the Light Being's help. The day was passing and soon darkness would envelop the Earth once again. He would wait a couple of hours until sunset. Maybe by then the Light Being would recover. Maybe then they could fly over the camp to rescue her and carry out the alien's plan.

Gazing at the prostrate form of the Light Being, Manley was intrigued. Such a resemblance to his son, Blake. "That's what he'll look like in just a few years," he mused, then wondered where Blake was now. He wondered what Blake thought about all that had happened in the last few days. A lot of changes were in effect. He thought of his son and daughter aboard the mother ship orbiting the planet. At least they were safe — the Light Being had said as much. But would they ever all be together again? Could he, with the help of the Light Being, succeed at getting Dorothy safely out of the concentration camp?

But what if something happened to the Light Being? What if he didn't recover from this lapse of consciousness? He had mentioned something about it being a side effect of cloning... what if...

Manley stood up and paced back and forth in front of the viewport. Outside he could see the surrounding woods and countryside. He knew he had to stop asking "what if" and start putting a plan into action.

Johanna had traveled in space very little since she and Serassan had returned to Terra, then back to their home on Karos, eighteen years ago. There had been only a few short trips back and forth to the planetoid occupied by Serassan's parents. Now Johanna was on board a small vessel headed for the planet Estron, her husband's home world. Serassan had arranged to borrow the small ship from a patron at the performing arts center. He had insisted on taking Johanna to Estron to search for Crystal.

"Are you comfortable, Johanna?" asked Serassan as he put the ship on automatic pilot. He strolled over to the bench where she was resting. They had left Karos only minutes ago.

"I'm fine, Serassan," she replied and attempted a smile. "Thank you for this." She reached out her hand and he took it in his strong, tanned one and stood close beside her, stroking her fingers in his familiar fashion. It always calmed her to have him do that.

"We will reach Estron in just a few hours," said Serassan. "And do not worry, Johanna. We will find Crystal and bring her home with us."

Johanna sighed. "Why did this have to happen? And why now, of all times, when we are in the midst of getting the Galactic Arts Center off the ground?"

He sat beside her and pulled her close to him. "It's a success," he reminded her. "The Galactic Arts Center is a huge success, and it will function well enough on its own until we return. You have done a marvelous job with the others. They will be able to run the show a few days without too much difficulty."

"But, Serassan..."

"I know, I know," he interrupted gently. "It won't be as good without you, my love. Everyone knows that. But I also think everyone understands that crises arise and substitutions are necessary once in a while. Besides, you needed a break. We've both been slaving over the arts center for too long."

Johanna knew he was right. "I just wish our little hiatus could have been under different circumstances," she said. Shifting her weight a little, she withdrew from his embrace and sat back, studying him. "Serassan," she said after a pause, "why haven't we visited your planet before?"

"You mean Estron?"

"Yes, your native world."

He didn't answer right away.

"I know you are considered somewhat of an outcast," she finally said.

Serassan chuckled then. "Maybe at first I was. Not any longer. Not really. You changed that."

"I? How?"

"Yes, my love. By being the beautiful and talented musician that you are... my people are finally beginning to see that the idea of bringing Terrans to Karos was not such a bad idea after all."

"You mean because of the music... and the dance... all the things that Estron lacked."

"That is correct."

Johanna wrinkled her nose. "I never could understand how a planet such as Estron could evolve as it did without music or art of any kind. It's so... unnatural... so... unimaginable."

"We simply lacked talent," said Serassan. "And Terra was full of talented beings. We believed we could integrate some of that talent into our own race through the breeding program."

"Well, if Crystal is any indication..."

"Indeed," said Serassan. "Crystal is a shining example of what my people wanted to accomplish."

"And yet they abandoned the mission," Johanna reminded him.

"Only because it was wrong to abduct Terrans against their will," said Serassan. "I can see how it all should have been approached in a different way."

"And humans proved to be too violent a species... remember?" Johanna smiled.

"Yes, that was the verdict of the Preejhna Chiyuub," Serassan recalled. "She had no choice but to send everyone back to Earth... except the few of you who elected to stay and inhabit Karos."

"And don't forget," added Johanna, "you elected to give up your life on Estron in order to inhabit Karos with me."

He squeezed her hand. "That I did, Johanna." He got up to check an instrument panel. "And now the Estronians are so enamored by the art that you Terrans have brought to Karos. The Galactic Arts Center could not help but be a tremendous success.

Estron realizes that now."

Serassan returned to her side and said, "In answer to your question... why have I not brought you to my planet before now? Aside from the difficulty of the atmosphere and your Terran anatomy being incompatible... Estron only holds disappointing memories for me. The way of life there is so different from what you are used to back on Earth."

"How different can it be?" asked Johanna.

"Men and women, for instance." Serassan grimaced. "I've explained all of this to you before." He stared into his lap nervously.

Johanna couldn't help smiling and blinked at her husband. "Why, darling, I do believe you are embarrassed to be talking about this."

Serassan looked puzzled a moment. "I was different even as a boy growing up on Estron," he disclosed. "My parents believed in marriage and procreation. I suppose others looked upon me as a sort of freak."

"Why? Because you were born in a normal fashion instead of in a laboratory?"

"It was not normal on Estron," Serassan reminded her.

"Yes, I know." Johanna leaned back and rested her head. "But Emrox and Soolàn lived off the planet, didn't they? Didn't you live with them at least part of the time?"

"I resided with them except when I was being educated on Estron," Serassan clarified. "I remember how hard it was having to put up with the ridicule from the other children. Yet I always knew that Soolàn's way was right. I endured endless taunting, yet I always carried my convictions about the love between a man and a woman. And somehow I always knew..." His voice trailed off and he turned to gaze at her with his deep blue eyes. "Johanna, somehow I always knew you were there for me... my Special One... and that one day I would find you. But I had to travel light-years to claim you."

Johanna still felt the prickle of ecstasy and enchantment whenever Serassan gazed upon her in that way. His eyes were such a deep mystical color of blue, and she felt the strong love he held for her, a love that had never wavered nor been challenged in the two decades they had known one another.

"Did I ever tell you about the first time I saw you?" she asked him. "Do you remember? It was the night of the *Swan Lake* ballet in my home town."

"How could I forget that?" Serassan smiled and caressed her hand. "That was the night you were abducted."

"That was when you implanted me with this... this..." She touched a finger to the space between her eyes. "Device," she added.

"You mean the language translator," he said. "It was how we got you to where we wanted you," said Serassan.

"In the mental hospital," Johanna remarked. "Although I've said all along it would have been easier if you had just come along and beamed us up from the very beginning."

"Ah, Johanna..." Serassan smiled at the memory. "I fell in love with you the first time I saw you... long before that night. I attended one of your concerts while you were touring. When I heard you play and saw you... I was mesmerized... I still am... every time I hear you play."

Johanna basked in the memories and snuggled close beside her husband again. They both sat, cherishing the thoughts that ran through their heads, while the black of space outside the window revealed countless stars. She felt happy in that moment, happy to have him close, happy for the daughter they had conceived and who they would find and bring home to Karos. Despite all the petty arguments, the mother-and-daughter quarrels and disappointments over the years, Johanna loved Crystal with all her heart — the product of her own and Serassan's deep love for each other — and she longed to look upon those feminine blue eyes that resembled Serassan's. She longed for one more time to tell Crystal how proud she was of her and that she loved her.

But suddenly another thought crossed Johanna's mind. What if their daughter still wanted to go into space and be with Thorden? What if she had lost Crystal forever?

33

Vameera

"Naturally I have heard of your son. Serassan is known far and wide among the Estronian fleet." The female pilot stepped off the ramp of the shuttlecraft to greet Soolàn and Emrox. She was an Estronian of medium height with grayish skin and a large bald head with huge slanted eyes that were the typical deep blue color of her race. Her uniform was black and shiny as were the small boots on her feet. Silver braid trim on her shoulders told of a high rank among pilots. Her face wore a stern expression as she stood with a hand on each hip, regarding the couple before her. She was direct and did not smile. "I am Vameera. Who sent you?"

Emrox handed the female pilot the small medallion the woman at Mission Central had given them, along with her instructions on finding Vameera.

After studying the object briefly, the pilot beckoned both Emrox and Soolàn into her small vessel. When they were seated comfortably, she asked, "And what is it you wish me to do for you?"

Soolàn explained how they needed to reach the *Harmony* as soon as possible. "Our granddaughter is on that ship," she said, "and we have reason to believe she wants to come home."

"Ah, how interesting," commented Vameera. She leaned back in her seat and her long grayish fingers intertwined. "Your granddaughter must be the Terran hybrid I've heard so much about."

Emrox nodded. "Can you take us to meet the *Harmony*?" He tried not to sound as impatient as he felt. "We were told you have a light ship."

Soolàn put a hand on her mate's knee, as if to restrain him.

"Yes, Crystal Dobbs is half Terran," she said to the pilot. "She is an adolescent and has long carried an ambition about being in space."

"And what makes you think she wants to come home?" asked Vameera.

Soolàn continued, "I'm afraid she has been misled by an Estronian named Thorden. We believe he has enticed our grand-daughter into leaving her parents."

At the mention of the name Thorden, Vameera jolted slightly and her expression grew even more stern. She gripped the arm rests of her seat. "Thorden, you say?" When Soolàn nodded, Vameera stood up and circled the still seated couple. "Thorden... usurper of women... deceitful, conniving, lustful, underhanded... I seem to recall he was also part of the Earth-Star mission and served at Serassan's side."

"So our son has told us," Emxrox said.

"Thorden's reputation is also known," said Vameera. "Unfortunately, I, too, once had an encounter with him." She frowned and turned her face away from them. "Let's just say... it left somewhat of a stain on my otherwise perfect record."

"What did Thorden do?" prompted Soolàn.

Vameera's huge eyes seemed to spark with momentary rage. She seemed about to explode with an answer, but caught herself, perhaps reluctant to disclose too much in front of these strangers. After a couple of deep breaths she composed herself and said, "Never mind. What he did is not all that important. However, it did keep me from fulfilling my dream career... my life's ambition."

Emrox cleared his throat. "A most important aspect of being a female Estronian," he said, and was instantly aware of Soolàn's disapproving look.

If the young pilot found mockery in his tone, she did not acknowledge it. Instead she smiled for the first time, a simple sort of smile that wasn't exactly cordial, but was relaxed. "I would con-sider it an honor to help you," she told the couple.

"Thank you," cried Soolàn and clasped her hands.

"I would find great pleasure in gaining revenge on this... Thorden," Vameera added with a gleam in her eyes.

"What is your fee?" asked Emrox.

"Well... as you already know, it is expensive to operate a light ship," said Vameera. "There are very few of us available, especially for a task such as this one... at such sudden notice."

"How much do you want to take us to our granddaughter?" Emrox demanded.

Before Vameera could reply, Soolàn held up her hand. "Whatever price you desire, we will pay it," she told the pilot. "But we must leave at once. Crystal is in danger."

"I had instruction scheduled for this day," Vameera said. "However, my pupils will wait. The situation that concerns you is more imperative. Can you be ready within an hour's time?"

"We are ready now," said Emrox and Soolàn nodded in agreement.

Vameera started for the hatch. "Wait here. I must change my plans and then we will shuttle to the sky station where my light ship is moored." She was down the ramp before either of them could say another word.

Emrox reached over and gripped Soolàn's wrist. "It will be all right now. We will find Crystal."

A tear glistened from Soolàn's wide eyelid and she smiled at this man whom she had loved and been with for nearly a century. How wonderful it would be to return their granddaughter to Serassan and Johanna. But she was also curious to know what vile act Thorden the Estronian had enacted against the young pilot Vameera. Although most Estronian women felt they were superior to the males of their species, Vameera's reaction to the mention of Thorden's name had been excessively reactive and full of deep resentment.

Vameera stepped back into the shuttle. "You are welcome to rest here till I return," she told the couple. "Or you may wish to replenish yourselves. There is a nutrition station just a short ways from here. Shall I direct you?"

They had been too concerned about their granddaughter to think of eating. Soolàn nudged her mate. "We should take food, Emrox."

"Now that you mention it, I am feeling the need for replenishment." He sighed.

"Yes, thank you." Soolàn nodded at the pilot. "Show us where to go."

B lake wasn't sure how much time had passed. He and Blue Jay had both slept until the time Kapri docked with the *Resilience* and gently called to them to announce their arrival on the cruiser. He remembered how groggy he had felt as he and his black friend had said their farewells to the female Estronian scientist and walked out onto the hangar deck and finally onto the ship that was filled with passengers of various races bound for Estron and then on to its colony world, Karos, where he would meet his father's sister, her alien husband and his hybrid cousin.

Once aboard the *Resilience*, he and Blue Jay were assigned quarters among the crew. He was tired and slept some more. It seemed as though he was asleep for more than a day. Toward the end of his long slumber he began having disturbing dreams about his dad and mom and the strange darkness that had covered the earth the morning they drove through Nebraska. In the dream he saw the bulky man who had stolen their flares and got in a fight with his dad. The man was bigger and much meaner in the dream, and Blake knew he was going to be knocked on the head again by the man, so in the dream he kept trying to escape, but the big thug was stalking him. Blake's dream took him on board the mother ship, where the monster man continued to seek him out, angry and intent on attacking him.

Finally, Blake awoke from the nightmare to find himself in this strange bed. The furnishings were simpler and more compact than his quarters on the mother ship. The room he was in contained four bunks in a cubicle of a room. No one else was present as he roused himself and shook the upsetting dream from his thoughts.

After a minute or two of regaining his bearings, Blake found that the opening led out into a narrow corridor. He needed to find the restroom and shuffled down the curved archway of doors. A being came around the corner just then and startled him. He was a short Gray, probably a Zeta Reticulan, with large black slanted eyes, dressed in some kind of tight blue uniform, with minimalist facial features. The being stopped to watch Blake.

"Hello, Terran." His words sounded inside Blake's head. The voice sounded masculine and was friendly enough, at least. "Are you lost?" But before Blake could respond, the alien pointed down the hallway to a curved door with a lighted border. "Relief is just around the corner, my friend," he said in an almost chuckling fashion.

"Uh... thanks." Blake waited till the small Gray was past, then headed for the restroom. He had noticed that a lot of people he'd met in space seemed to be psychic or could communicate with their minds, some not even bothering to speak with vocal cords.

When he came out of the restroom, he saw his friend Blue Jay conversing with someone in the corridor outside their cabin. His black musician friend grinned as Blake approached. "Hey, dude, glad you got rested."

"Yeah, I'm sort of groggy still," Blake admitted.

Standing beside Blue Jay was a human-looking individual but with some unusual features. He was tall and lean with light-colored hair and almost translucent skin. The blue eyes were bright and filled with intelligence as well as kindness. The forehead protruded ever so slightly and the man's ears were small and close to his head.

"I'd like you to meet one of the *Resilience's* chief officers," said Blue Jay. "Major Luro, this is my new friend from Earth, Blake Dobbs."

Major Luro smiled. "Pleased to make your acquaintance, Blake Dobbs," he said in perfect English. "And welcome aboard the *Resilience*."

"I'm honored," said Blake.

"Your friend tells me you have relatives on Estron," said Major Luro.

"Actually, they're on Karos," he corrected.

"His uncle is from Estron," explained Blue Jay.

"I understand this is your first time traveling in space," Major Luro continued.

Blake nodded, his head still rather fogged up from sleep.

As if reading his mind, Major Luro explained, "Sometimes it's necessary to keep certain passengers dormant while embarking on their first space flight across the galaxy."

"You slept the equivalent of two Earth days," said Blue Jay.

"What?" Blake blinked in surprise. "Two days?"

"That's right, bro." His friend grinned. "But don't worry. You're gonna feel like new soon's we get some grub into ya."

"A good idea," agreed Major Luro. "Take Mr. Dobbs to the galley and replenish him." He smiled once again at Blake. "We will be meeting another ship in a few hours and will take on a few more travelers before we proceed straight to Estron and then continue on to Karos."

Crystal slept fitfully on board the *Harmony* that night cycle. Exhaustion from the day cycle's toil failed to win out over her fear that Thorden might intrude on her. She worried about what he had planned for her next. Tossing and fretting, Crystal whimpered into her pillow, then willed herself to remain calm so that she could come up with a plan. There had to be some way she could escape and reach others who would come to her aid.

She knew there were passengers on board the *Harmony* who would be transferring onto the other cruiser. What was it the android had called it? The *Resonance*? No, the *Resilience*. She had studied about Estronian cruisers at school, learned all their names and what the vessels were used for, where they traveled and the different planets in the Federation that they served.

Fear that Thorden might still come to her cabin and violate her kept her thoughts on edge. She naturally knew about such things and the subject of sex terrified her, for the most part. The Estronian girls at school had talked about the subject as though it was devil worship. They had apparently been programmed from a very young age to regard physical copulation as a disgusting practice, to be exercised only as a release from stress, and only then in a "preferred" manner, which meant — as Crystal discovered — under supervised situations in a clinical setting.

Estronian men, she was told, were not allowed to be involved when women experienced their release. They had their own separate means for dealing with their procreational urges, and laboratories were used for that purpose. The Estronian culture accepted, but did not condone, the special recreational facilities that were frequented by certain males and were operated by deviant females out to make a profit. Some, Crystal was told, even seemed to enjoy this contact with the males, something which most Estronian females could not fathom, due to their conditioning.

Crystal lay in bed, thinking more about what she knew about the taboo subject of sex. Her planet, Karos, was different from

Estron. On Karos the Terrans — men and women — lived together, and they joined physically and produced family units. She was not ignorant of the fact that her own parents, Serassan and Johanna, slept together and probably even enjoyed engaging in sex now and then. After all, hadn't they produced her? Often she had seen them openly showing affection for one another, without shame. They never tried to hide the fact that they loved each other or enjoyed touching each other. Her parents had never tried to make her believe that such a union was wrong or disgusting.

Soolàn and Emrox, her grandparents, were the same way. The two older Estronians had removed themselves from their planet's culture on account of their belief in the male and female being together and sharing intimacy with one another. Crystal knew that her grandmother had been raised in another culture and was unusual in the sense that she had not been conditioned as the typical, ambitious, career-motivated Estronian woman. "Stifled," Granna had said once about her race. "Miserable," Grandfather had added.

Although Crystal overheard the Estronian school girls discussing the subject, she never was that interested in learning about the facilities on Estron that served to relieve females of their hormonal urges. Instinctively she resisted the idea and preferred instead to daydream about her imaginary dream lover. In her mind she had conjured up an intriguing and attractive young man, and in her private meditations she often dwelled on him, how he looked, how he smiled at her with soft brown Terran eyes and a tender gaze. She imagined his hair to be the color of straw, wavy and lustrous as it just brushed his broad shoulders. He had strong facial features, masculine, yet gentle. His voice was deep and soft and when he looked at her there was love in his soul.

She had no name for her dream lover, but she could see him so clearly at times, and she would get chills thinking that perhaps one day she might meet him in space. And so Crystal secretly focused her thoughts on him when the girls discussed the scorned subject. She knew better than to mention her own feelings about the subject because she knew the Estronian girls would torment her and laugh.

The warm glow spread over her now as she thought of her dream lover and envisioned his face. He was so unlike the boys from Estron, those gawking, lusty cads who were constantly shooting rude looks at her and the other girls, or making suggestive comments. Her dream lover was unlike Thorden, whom she feared would eventually force himself on her unless she managed to escape before it was too late.

"Mother! Father!" Crystal sobbed into her damp pillow. "Will you ever forgive me? I didn't mean for this to happen." She cried several minutes more, until exhaustion finally overcame her. Then she dropped off into sleep.

When she awoke a little while later, it was because of a light in her room. Crystal jerked up in bed, afraid that Thorden was there, that he had sneaked in while she was sleeping and was now planning to attack her. But no one was in the cabin. There was a small, bright ball of golden light near the ceiling in the far corner of the room. It brightened in intensity, then dimmed — brightened and dimmed — fluctuating back and forth.

Crystal recognized the ball of light as the same sphere of light she had seen — or rather dreamed of seeing — that night back on Karos after she had come home from school. It had seemed a lot bigger and brighter then, for some reason. Now it was fainter and pulsated slowly.

Strangely unafraid, Crystal stared at the ball of light and then said out loud, "I've seen you before. What do you want? Who are you?"

Nothing happened. The sphere continued to brighten a little, then began to dim. Each time it dimmed now, it seemed to fade a little more, until it appeared it would completely extinguish itself.

She was determined to find out what she could about it. Maybe it was a spy device Thorden had planted. But that wouldn't explain why it had been in the stone cottage on Karos. No, there was something tantalizingly familiar about the light, something that comforted her but at the same time disturbed her. She got out of bed and began to approach the light, but quite suddenly it fizzled out and was gone. The room was dark once more.

Crystal stood, completely transfixed. She felt alone, abandoned, and forsaken.

34

Purification

Twilight blanketed the woods around them as Manley sat inside the shuttle beside the helpless form of the Light Being. The young alien had twitched and gasped, obviously trapped in some kind of seizure, although he was still unconscious. When the spasm had begun several minutes ago, Manley had looked around and found a small tool the size of a comb that was made out of a wood-like material. It had narrow teeth along one side. He had used the small device to insert into Elby's mouth, propped between his tongue and upper jaw, to prevent blockage of the air passage during his fit.

Now the alien had calmed down and his breathing came more slowly. Beads of sweat erupted on his forehead and his eyelids fluttered open as he fully came to.

"Elby?" Manley removed the wooden comb and wiped the damp blond strands to one side with his fingers as he gazed into the face that resembled his son's. "Elby, you're okay. You... you had a seizure... it's... it's over now."

The Light Being focused on Manley's face in the diminishing light. He groaned as his shoulders began to twist to one side, then the other. "Crystal," he murmured. "...in danger."

"What crystal?" asked Manley. He began looking around the small ship. "You want a crystal to hold?" Then, remembering old *Star Trek* TV episodes, he jumped up. "Dilithium crystals?" he asked. "Is that what powers your ship?"

The Light Being sighed and shook his head. "No... Crystal," he repeated. He licked his dry lips and pleaded with Manley. "Crystal... a girl... Crystal Dobbs..."

Manley spun around. "Dobbs? Did you say Dobbs? That's *my* name."

"Yes, I... I know," the Light Being replied weakly. "Crystal is in trouble. I... I tried... to reach her just now... to warn her..."

Convinced his alien friend was in some kind of delirium, Manley went to his pack over on the ship's floor and found a cloth to use to mop Elby's neck and face. "Here," he said as he returned to his side. "Just rest now. Everything will be all right." He just wished he could believe his own words. This was not getting them anywhere. Elby was ill and how were they going to rescue Dorothy?

"Crystal..." the Light Being mumbled as his eyes closed once again. He seemed to be drifting off again. "Crystal... be... careful..."

Manley sighed in futility as the young alien slipped off into blackness. He knew he had to leave the ship before it got any darker and sneak into the women's concentration camp. He had to find Dorothy and get her out of there, and with the barbed wire fence and all those guards carrying rifles, it wasn't going to be a simple task. Especially now, without the assistance of the extra-terrestrial. And there was no telling when Elby would come around again. He had slept for hours before the seizure. Manley feared what might happen if the alien lapsed into another fit without him around to keep him from choking. But it was a chance he had to take. He had to get to the camp, if he could, undetected, and at least find out what was going on.

Certainly now that the Null Zone period had passed, the authorities should have permitted everyone to go about their business. Why were the people being held in camps? Why weren't they being released? And just who in authority was in control of the population?

Before total darkness closed in on him, Manley triggered the hatch that allowed him to exit the shuttlecraft. The door slid to one side and the ramp projected outward toward the ground. With a sigh Manley turned to the Light Being and said before he stepped down the ramp, "I'll be back, pal. Don't go anywhere. Just rest." Silence followed him into the dark woods.

"I don't care about the consequences, General. We simply must hold everyone another week... at the very least." Ernestine Glenn's commanding voice reached Dorothy's ears as she awoke and focused in on the conversation across the room. How long she had been asleep, she didn't know, but it was obviously night time. Candles burned somewhere in their part of the quonset and most of the personnel had cleared out. She rested in her cot with a wool blanket over her and watched the flicker of dim light dance over the hanging curtain from the direction of Ernestine's voice.

"The citizens are not weak, Ms. Glenn," came the deep Southern drawl of a man Dorothy presumed must be the military general who had flown in earlier that evening in a helicopter. "They have been deprived of food, rest and adequate drinking water, and yet they have not succumbed to be the submissive population you hoped. You've rounded them up, separated loved ones, removed children from parents, husbands from wives, and crammed them into these managed care units, and still they resist you."

"I disagree, General." Ernestine's voice was argumentative. "Oh sure, we've had several disruptions in this camp alone. I have eighty-nine rebellious women downstairs in the cooler. The guards have reported fights, hysteria, and one heart attack."

"Just what do you hope to gain by retaining the entire population another week?" asked the General.

"Time," was Ernestine's prompt reply. "I need time to put the purification process into motion."

Purification process? Dorothy thought to herself. *What is she talking about?*

"We have records," Ernestine continued. "Records on everyone. We've been gathering data for well over a decade, and we know who is going to be a productive member of society and who isn't. We know which ones are going to cause trouble and which ones will not... based on our research and surveillance over the years."

"Yes, I read your proposal before the Plan went into action," said the General. "But I must admit, I have... qualms. Ms. Glenn, forgive me for putting this bluntly, but... it's not as easy as you think. There will be resistance... and I mean *genuine resistance.*"

"Naturally there will be resistance." Ernestine's voice rose in irritation. "We expect resistance. But we know who those ones are who will rise up. And we will silence them before they can interfere. General, it is simple. It has always been very simple. The problem is, men in charge have always made things complicated."

The General laughed, but Dorothy detected it as a nervous laugh.

"Men screwed up this world," Ernestine went on. "And women are going to have to repair the damage. We cannot go on the way we have any longer."

She's fanatical, Dorothy told herself.

"Wars must stop," cried Ernestine. "Hunger and disease must cease. There will be no more pollution! The world is changing as of this week. A woman is in charge! I am that woman!"

Good God, Dorothy thought to herself.

"Well..." The General cleared his throat. "I can see there is no way I'm going to change your mind. I just thought it fair to warn you..."

"Don't even think of interfering with my plan, General," Ernestine commanded. "The troops are behind me one hundred percent. There is no way the old regime is going to take control of this country again, or this planet, for that matter. Those who resist me will need to be eliminated. And mark my words, General... I will not hesitate to erase anyone who gets in my way. Purification means just that... and if it means wiping out three-fourths of the population on Earth, then so be it!"

Dorothy gulped and her eyes widened in fear. Her heart began to pound and she was suddenly terrified of the female presidential candidate whom she had long admired. *Ernestine Glenn is insane*, Dorothy thought to herself. Drawing the blanket around herself on the cot, she curled onto her side and began to think about how she could get out of the compound without being caught. She no longer wanted any part of Ernestine's devilry. She knew now, without a doubt, that the leader was using Dorothy's psychic ability to weed out possible resisters or trouble makers. Those women who were any kind of threat to Ms. Glenn had been dragged off to the dungeon below. What was going to happen to those women? Dorothy wondered. Certainly Ernestine Glenn had no intention of releasing them. And from what she had overheard between Ernestine and the General, Dorothy realized no one was going to be set free until the female Gestapo determined who was fit to be released and who was not.

It occurred to Dorothy that Ms. Glenn intended to execute the resisters. That meant that if Ernestine suspected Dorothy's change of heart, things could end up quite badly — quite badly indeed. She knew she had to act and soon. She had to get away and warn as many people as she could. How was she going to accomplish it?

If only Manley knew about this. He'd help her. She recalled how her husband had never trusted Ernestine Glenn and her campaign. Somehow Manley had seen through Ms. Glenn's facade, but his suspicions had been ignored because Dorothy believed too strongly in the things Ms. Glenn had advocated. She had been all for a healthy environment, for peace, for women's rights and equality. Never had she dreamed that Ernestine Glenn's idea of "purification" was eliminating those who didn't agree with her tactics.

Dorothy knew she couldn't just rise up and stroll out of the quonset. There would be questions. Guards would stop her. Ernestine would demand an explanation. She just wished she had not hallucinated that voice in her head earlier that day. She had been convinced that the voice had been someone trying to help her. It had been the same voice in her head when she had lain in the dungeon and the entity had reassured her and given her hope. But after she had followed his instructions and gone outside, nothing had happened. She longed to connect with the voice again. Nothing happened. No one responded. There was no one there.

With a sigh, Dorothy closed her eyes and waited. Ernestine and the General had moved away now, probably gone to the galley area for some refreshment. She knew she was on her own. She couldn't rely on Manley or any space being. She had to get out of this scrape by herself.

35

Rendezvous

Johanna had dozed off, but awoke as Serassan brought the shuttle into Estron's atmosphere. She could see wispy white cloud layers against a blue-green sky as they drifted toward a major land mass. Serassan skillfully steered the craft into the planet's grid system and zeroed in on a large metropolitan area. She was relaxed and confident in her husband's piloting ability and watched in fascination out the portholes as the building structures and landmarks came into view. The city was massive and filled with shapes of all kinds, mostly geodesic and round, domed buildings of crystal, with some made of shiny blue and green metals.

The shuttle was now low enough to hover and cruise. Johanna noticed other shuttlecraft in the air on lower or higher altitudes. "Serassan, this is remarkable," cried Johanna. "Is this the city you lived in?"

"No, my love." He glanced at her, then returned his attention to the sky in front of him. "What I call my home of origin is in another metropolitan area. But I have spent considerable time in this one. It is called Smaheelgum-Rud, which translates as 'City of Domes.' "

"Well, it's certainly a city of domes." Johanna marveled at the rounded tops of the structures as they passed over them. "But like so many cities on Earth, the buildings are too close together."

"Estronian technology makes use of efficient working environments," Serassan explained as he steered the shuttle in the direction of their destination. "Unlike many Terran cities, these are engineered with skill and purpose for every sector."

They swerved suddenly and their craft tilted slightly, sending Johanna's heart up into her throat. She gripped the arm rests on her seat and cried out in alarm. "Serassan!"

"That was a close one," commented Serassan.

"What?" gasped Johanna.

"A near collision," said her husband. His voice was relaxed as they soared over a residential section.

"Serassan!" Johanna put her hand over her heart as if to calm herself. "We might have been in a crash. How can you be so casual about it?"

Serassan turned to gaze at her, his blue eyes full of surprise. Then he chuckled. "I'm sorry, dear Johanna, if it scared you. There are many unskilled pilots in our skies."

"You mean... Estron has those, too?"

"Yes, but there's no reason for alarm. You see, we couldn't collide with another shuttle, even if we wanted to."

"How can that be?" Johanna demanded.

"It's because of the force-field around the shuttle," Serassan explained. "You see, the technology we use prevents such things as air collisions from happening. If somebody happens to make a mistake, the force-field will detect an impending crash and take the necessary maneuvers to prevent such."

"Really?" Johanna's eyes grew wide.

"It's a byproduct of the drive unit's propulsion system," he added.

"That sounds like something we need on Earth. Imagine the lives that could be saved on Earth..." Her voice trailed off as she recalled the news Emrox had brought to them just recently, about how her home planet had experienced a shift. She wondered how bad the devastation was, and whether Manley and Dorothy were safe. The dark thought descended over her like an ominous storm cloud.

"Up ahead is Mission Central," Serassan announced. "They should be able to provide us with some information about Thorden."

Johanna blinked away her worrisome thoughts about Earth to concentrate on the fears that revolved around their missing daughter. When Serassan reached over to touch her hand in comfort, she clasped his fingers and gave a squeeze.

Emrox and Soolàn had said little after boarding Vameera's light ship. Several hours had passed since their journey from the space station that orbited Estron. Vameera was not a conversational-ist and seemed to be focused on her own deep thoughts. Soolàn picked up that those disturbing thoughts festering in the pilot's mind involved Thorden and a long ago incident that had never been forgiven. Soolàn, though curious, did not want to intrude on the other woman's emotions, and had decided that the pilot's agreement to take the assignment had much to do with getting revenge against the deceptive Thorden, who had — for all intents and purposes — kidnapped their granddaughter.

She and Emrox stared out at the stars as the light ship sped through space to intercept the *Harmony*, which was due to rendezvous with the cruiser *Resilience* shortly. Soolàn could feel Crystal's anxiety and remorse. It grew stronger the closer they got. Emrox dozed on and off beside her. This excursion was going to absorb a large percentage of their resources, but she loved him all the more for it, because she knew he loved his granddaughter as much as she did.

Crystal was such a light in their lives. They had taken advantage of every opportunity to have her with them, despite all the inconveniences of adjusting to different atmospheric conditions. It had never seemed much of a problem to the little blond-haired Terran girl who had visited their planetoid and laughed and played among the red rocks and streams. Crystal had always been delighted to see her grandparents and had delighted them further with her splendid singing voice.

A series of tones interrupted Soolàn's thoughts and she turned her attention to Vameera, who touched a panel and held a speaker-clip to her aural opening. A moment later she swung in her swivel seat to face Soolàn and Emrox. Emrox stirred and opened his eyes.

"A message from Estron," Vameera said. "It is from your son, Serassan."

Soolàn nodded, prompting the pilot to continue.

"He says he and his mate have arrived on Estron to search for their daughter. They were told of your excursion to meet the *Harmony* and they send their good wishes."

Emrox cleared his throat and bent forward. "Tell him we will send word as soon as we arrive. Tell him not to worry."

"Very well." Vameera turned around to relay the message

into a microphone.

"And one more thing," Soolàn added.

Vameera turned and stared at her.

"Send him our love and light."

Vameera appeared startled for just a second, but then Soolàn was almost positive she noticed a flicker of a smile as the pilot turned back to her microphone.

B lake and his traveling companion wrapped up their final set. They had held a music jam in the commons area aboard the *Resilience* for the crew members and passengers. Blake saw Major Luro enter from the corridor. He raised his voice to announce that they were just now docking with the *Harmony*.

At this news the small audience broke up. Some had tasks they had to perform. They were a diverse group of space travelers in different shapes, colors and heights. Several clasped their hands and nodded in gratitude to the two young musicians from Earth. Blue Jay put away his harmonica and Blake returned the borrowed guitar from the ship's stores to the Arcturian steward who had brought it to him the day before.

"What now?" Blake asked his black friend.

"The ship has docked with another cruiser," Blue Jay explained. "I think you'll find this interesting. Come on." He then led Blake through the rounded corridor to an observation deck where they, along with others, were gathering to watch the passengers enter through a gate that brought them out of a connecting passageway to the other ship.

A tall blond-haired woman in a one-piece, skin-tight green suit greeted each arrival, while another tall blond, a man with shoulder-length hair and dressed in a blue skin-tight suit held a tray of small packages that reminded Blake from this distance of cigarette packs. But they certainly weren't cigarettes.

A couple of female, grayish-white aliens stepped through the gate. Both were about five feet tall with large bald heads and massive slanted eyes, dark blue and almost liquid looking. Their small mouth slits curved slightly upwards as they displayed smiles. Each of the women wore a robe that covered slender long arms and flowed to their ankles. One had a robe that was black with a pattern of stars, and the other's shimmered in iridescent red tones.

"Hey," said Blake to his friend. "They remind me of... of... Kapri."

"Very good, bro." Blue Jay patted him on the back. "They *are* Kapri's people. They're from the planet Estron."

The women stopped to take a package from the man with long blond hair.

"Those blond people," said Blake. "Where are they from?"

"They are Pleiadian," explained Blue Jay. "Nordics."

"What is he giving them?" asked Blake. He watched as both women immediately opened their packages, took something out and popped them into their mouths. Then they sauntered off to the right toward the stairway.

"It's their supplement," Blue Jay replied.

Blake watched an Estronian man step through the gate next. He was shorter than the two women and wore a black tunic over brown leggings. He stopped to accept his greeting and his package, bowing at the two blond people.

"You see, they have to take their supplement as they come on board our ships," Blue Jay explained. "The wafers contain an ingredient that temporarily changes the way their blood uses oxygen. From what I understand from talking with Kapri, these Estronians live in a different atmosphere than most of us. If they were to walk among us and not take the supplement, they'd soon smother."

"Really?"

"That's right, bro. And if you were to go to their planet, they'd inject you so that you could exist in their world, since the excessive oxygen concentration would eventually cause you to pass out."

"That's far out," said Blake. He watched a different type of alien emerge from the passageway. This one was a small Gray, dressed in a shiny blue uniform of some sort. "What's he?"

"Zeta Reticulan," said Blue Jay.

"Yeah, I've heard of them," said Blake. "Their pictures are on everything back on Earth... key rings, coffee cups, pizza commercials, books... you name it."

"He won't need a wafer," remarked Blue Jay.

"Why not?"

"He's adaptable, though he probably had injections during his stay aboard the *Harmony*."

Blake watched another group of Estronians move through the gate. He wondered how many were transferring from the other ship.

"Come on, let's talk with one of them." Blue Jay led Blake toward the stairway that led up into the corridor. The Estronian man with the black tunic and brown leggings stopped when he saw them approach him.

"Will he be able to understand us?" Blake asked.

"He will speak telepathically to you," Blue Jay said.

"You mean, in my head?"

"Precisely." He grinned at the alien. "Yo!"

"Greetings, Terrans." Blake heard the voice in his head as the short, grayish-white figure with the huge eyes peered into his face.

"How's the trip been?" asked Blue Jay.

"Pleasant, thank you," the voice in Blake's head echoed.

"My friend here is new in space," Blue Jay explained, indicating Blake. "This is his first journey to the stars."

"My name is Krizamju," the Estronian said. "I am on my way back to Estron."

"Blue Jay's my name," the black youth told Krizamju. "This here is Blake Dobbs."

"Blake... Dobbs..." repeated the Estronian. He smiled. "I am pleased to meet you, Blake... Dobbs." Then he asked, "What brings you into space, friend?"

"I'm... I'm... hoping to visit my aunt and uncle on Karos," Blake explained.

"Karos?" The Estronian appeared surprised. "Why, I've just heard that they have the new Galactic Center for the Arts on Karos. A colleague of mine was fortunate to be there on Opening Night. There is a colony of Terrans living there..."

"Perhaps Blake here will sing and play his guitar on Karos," Blue Jay chuckled.

"What? You are... musical?" asked the Estronian, staring at Blake.

"He's good," said Blue Jay. "In fact, we just finished a show, of sorts."

"How very splendid!" exclaimed Krizamju. "I have craved music for a long, long time. I can't seem to get enough of it. You can count on one thing. I will be making a trip soon to Karos to hear the

Terran woman and her daughter." He spread his long gray fingers over his chin as he studied the two of them a moment, then said, "As a matter of fact, I believe they have the same name as you... Dobbs..."

"Aunt Jo," Blake murmured. He turned to Blue Jay. "Isn't that what Kapri was telling us?"

"They say that the Terran girl sings like a goddess," Krizamju continued. "The remarkable thing is, she is half Estronian!" He appeared to beam with pride.

Blake's eyes were wide with interest. "That's who I'm traveling to meet," he explained. "I can't believe it. I've met someone who knows about my Aunt Jo and my... my cousin."

Krizamju turned and signaled toward the two women who had preceded him through the gate. "Ladies!" He motioned them to come over. "Step over here. I want you to meet this young Terran. He is related to Serassan's wife and daughter on Karos."

"Oh!" one of them exclaimed. "Oh, really?"

Blake nodded at the one wearing the black robe with stars. "Pleased to meet you," he said.

"Blake Dobbs," introduced Krizamju. "And he is musical as well."

"Extraordinary!" cried the other woman, the one with the iridescent robe. She seemed about to make a comment when a skirmish at the entrance distracted them.

A juvenile Estronian came through the gate with an adult female who was practically dragging the little one. The child was visibly upset and the alien woman impatient and annoyed. The young one had the same large head and slanted eyes and was babbling in a wailing voice words that Blake could not understand. Its mother, or whoever the adult alien was to the child, answered in the same gibberish, only her tone was clearly one of scolding. Everyone watched the scene that had immediately transformed the serene energy in the corridor to disruption. Blake was reminded suddenly of his younger sister, Kelly, and a deep and sudden sadness seized him as he thought of her all by herself back on the *New Jerusalem.*

"What seems to be the trouble?" Blue Jay asked Krizamju in a conversational tone.

The two Estronian women drew close to the other female

with the disruptive child and appeared to be discussing the situation in their native tongue. Blake noticed Krizamju glance over at the whimpering child, then turn back to his new Terran friends.

"I am sure whatever has upset the child will soon be under control." He grimaced. "Children ought to be more disciplined. Why that one is being swept around the galaxy rather than in a classroom is beyond my comprehension."

The alien child was now throwing some kind of temper tantrum. Blake could see the little gray hands with the extra long fingers waving and shaking as the head shook back and forth and a scream ripped from the little one's throat.

The blond Pleiadian woman pressed her way through the small crowd that was beginning to gather around the disturbance. She bent over to speak to the woman and child. Her calm voice and gestures had no effect.

"Maybe it's some kind of reaction to the atmosphere," guessed Blake.

"Don't know," said Blue Jay, "but whatever it is... she... or he... is sure mad."

One of the Estronian women explained to them, "That little one has left her favorite pet on board the *Harmony*. Her nurse refuses to go back for it, because they've already taken their wafers."

"Pet?" Blake was surprised. "What kind of a pet? An animal?"

"Probably an android," said Blue Jay.

"You mean a robot... for a pet?" asked Blake.

"Yeah, alien kids grow quite attached to them sometimes."

"Why doesn't someone go get it, then?" asked Blake.

Blue Jay merely shrugged.

Again, Blake felt that tug of longing for his sister and suddenly made up his mind. "Shoot... I'll go myself." He moved toward the shrieking Estronian child and knelt in front of her. The startled large blue eyes focused on him and the nurse beside her tensed up as the shrieking ceased immediately.

"I will bring back what you want," he told the child. "Tell me where it is." Blake was reminded so much of his sister Kelly and how attached she had once been to a stuffed Eeyore donkey. He took hold of the child's hands and the little form suddenly began hiccupping after her crying spell as she continued to stare into this strange human face.

The nurse regained her composure and began protesting in the Estronian language that Blake did not understand. The other two Estronian women argued with her and there was a babble of their excited voices as Blake leaned closer to the child and asked, "What is your name?"

"Tulàt," a soft feminine voice echoed in his head. The alien child apparently knew telepathic communication. "What's your name, funny man?"

Surprised, Blake stifled a laugh and said, "I'm Blake Dobbs."

"Where did you come from?" asked the child, blinking now as the hiccups slowed.

"I come from a planet known as Earth."

Suddenly Blake heard the nurse's scolding voice in his head as she turned from shooting gibberish at the other women to telepathic communication with him. "Young man, Tulàt is much too selfish. Do not concern yourself. She shall receive punishment for this intolerable behavior."

The child began at once to protest and cry, having understood the nurse's response.

Blake sighed. "But... all she wants is to have her... her pet robot."

"Android," Blue Jay piped in beside him.

The two Estronian women twittered with laughter, but the nurse's face remained stern. "That ridiculous android belongs on that ship. It does not belong to Tulàt. Come along, child." She began yanking on the small alien's arm to pull her away.

Krizamju spoke up then so that Blake could understand. "Slacken, Sheetul! You are much too harsh toward the girl."

"And what do you know about the situation, Krizamju?" the nurse retorted.

"I have observed your interactions in the last day or two, since we've been aboard the *Harmony*," the Estronian man said. "Why don't you make life easier for all of us and let the Terran retrieve the child's toy?"

The Estronian nurse trembled with indignation, but then, just as suddenly, she gave in with a sigh. "Very well." She gave Blake a piercing look and said tersely, "The thing is in Cabin Four on the first deck."

The alien child quit crying and jumped up and down in excitement, her hand still clasped tightly in the nurse's hand. Then she whispered in Blake's mind, "Thank you, funny man."

"Come on," Blake said, leading Blue Jay toward the gate where the two Pleiadians were just finishing their duty with the tray of wafers.

"Where do you think you are going?" asked the tall blond man as they reached the gate.

"We need to go on board the other cruiser for just a few minutes," explained Blue Jay.

"But why?"

Blake pointed to the child being led away by her nurse. "They left something of importance in their cabin. I said I'd go on board and get it for them."

"What about the atmosphere?" the Pleiadian woman asked with concern. "You can't be on board the *Harmony* more than three or four minutes or you will pass out."

"How long will it take to get to their cabin and back?" Blake asked his black friend.

Blue Jay shrugged. "Probably more than that."

"Can you give us something?" Blake asked the Pleiadians.

"These wafers will not help," explained the woman. "You need an injection. No one is prepared to inject you on the *Harmony*. All passengers have disembarked."

"Who's on that ship?" asked Blake.

Both Pleiadians shrugged. They didn't know.

Major Luro called to them and both Blake and Blue Jay turned to watch him signaling to them from the entryway to the *Resilience*. "The ship is leaving in ten minutes, my friends. There can be no tours of the *Harmony* on this trip. The pilot on board is anxious to leave us."

"We're not going on any tour!" Blue Jay called back to Major Luro. "One of the passengers left an important item on board and we're going back for it."

"I would advise against that," warned Major Luro, stepping toward them. "You haven't been injected. It is dangerous to go on board the *Harmony*."

"We won't be that long," Blake insisted with a glance back at the nurse and the alien child, who had begun to whimper once again.

"I must ask you to reconsider," Major Luro called to them.

Blue Jay hung back. "Hey, man, maybe we better listen to him," he told Blake. "It's not worth having something happen..."

The thought reached little Tulàt that perhaps the Terrans were not going to bring her pet to her after all. She began to scream and carry on once again, and the nurse reprimanded her.

"Come on," said Blake, pulling Blue Jay through the gate. "We'll run!"

Before anyone could stop them, Blake and his companion dashed into the dark tunnel that led from the entryway into the *Harmony*. There was a dim blue light at the end of the tunnel and no one was at the gate when they reached it. They found themselves in a small alcove and steps led to a hatchway, which they quickly climbed.

"Okay, let's find their cabin," said Blake as they started down a dark, curved hallway. The lights had been lowered just enough to make it difficult for them to see where they were going.

"What number was it again?" Blue Jay puffed.

"Number four," Blake replied. But he didn't see any numbers on any of the doors. Instead there were strange squiggles he didn't understand. He slowed to a stop, starting to get slightly dizzy. "Oh, great. Everything's in Estronian."

"We'll never find it, man." Blue Jay was starting to weave a bit. "Come on, we'd better go back... back... before the... the air..."

Blake, too, found that he had to steady himself by grabbing onto a door handle. He knew they had to get back to the *Resilience*. This had been a waste of their time and energy.

"This way," Blue Jay directed, pointing to a curved passageway ahead. Blake was on his heels as they rushed into an opening of a large room that housed control panels, computer consoles and a huge viewing screen that took up one side of the walls. Out the screen they could see part of the hull from the *Resilience* and the backdrop of black space dotted with stars. "We're on the bridge," Blue Jay croaked.

Before they could turn to leave, Blake noticed a figure in a black tunic rise from the central chair. He wore a black cape that swirled from the motion as he spun around to face them. His huge bald head told them he was Estronian, and his dark eyes seemed to flash as his mind spoke in their heads. "What are you doing here? Who gave you authority to enter my ship?"

Blake drew back, equally startled. This alien was repulsive and exuded a hostile aura that caused him to shudder. He steadied himself as his head began to swim.

"Leave at once!" the alien pilot commanded.

"We... we're leaving..." Blue Jay stammered as they both moved backward toward the passageway. "We... we came to retrieve a little girl's toy... b-but..."

An android suddenly appeared and announced in a metallic voice, "Master Thorden, all passengers have disembarked." Then the unit noticed the new arrivals. "What are these humanoids doing on board the *Harmony*?"

"Get them back to the *Resilience* at once!" Thorden's voice thundered in Blake's head. "I have no time for lost pets!"

"Come on, man," Blue Jay said as they started to leave. "We'd better get back before the abundance of oxygen in here does us in."

"We didn't get Tulàt's pet."

"I know, I know, man..."

Just as they rounded the corner, they almost ran into two small android units practically dragging a golden-haired human girl with tear-stained cheeks and eyes red and swollen from crying. Her blue eyes widened in surprise at the sight of them and she tried to wrench herself free from the grasp of the androids. "Let me go!" she shrieked. Turning to Blake and Blue Jay, she pleaded, "Oh please... help me!"

Startled, Blake stared into her face, then at his friend. "She speaks English."

Blue Jay seemed mystified. "I wonder what she's doing on this ship..."

Just then Thorden stepped out of the bridge and called to them. "Pay no attention to the girl! You two must leave this ship at once!"

"No!" the girl cried. She began struggling more and crying at the sight of the pilot. "Don't leave! Please... I need your help!"

"Stay back," Thorden ordered. "She is extremely dangerous... a demented, shape-shifting murderess whom I am escorting to a penal colony on Drofos IV. She's using the oldest trick in the book, and if you listen to her, you will die. Now get back to your ship!"

"He's lying!" the girl wailed. "I'm being held against my will!"

"Go! Go!" Thorden yelled.

A crackle of static came from the bridge just then and they could hear Major Luro's voice coming over the speaker. "This is Major Luro of the *Resilience*. Are there two Terran boys aboard your ship? Please acknowledge."

"Terran?" The girl stared at Blake, pleading. "You're from Earth! I'm half Terran!"

"Let's go, man." Blue Jay was pulling Blake toward the docking area. "We don't... have much... time left..."

"Come back!" the girl cried. "Oh please... help me!" She began to cry as the androids carried her into the bridge area with Thorden, who had already gone inside to deal with Major Luro's communication.

Blake knew something wasn't right with this picture, but all he could think about for the moment was getting off the *Harmony* and being able to clear his fuzzy head. He felt as though he would pass out any second as they both made a beeline for the airlock. They stumbled and groped with lights flashing around them and warning sirens that went off.

"Danger! Docking area is restricted in preparation for ship separation," a mechanical computer voice broadcasted. "All passengers must vacate this passageway." Then the message was repeated in another language.

"What's going on?" Blake managed to ask as they climbed into the airlock and the door to the *Harmony* closed behind them.

"The ship's about to leave," puffed Blue Jay.

Suddenly the gate opened and they found themselves once again inside the docking area of the *Resilience*. To their surprise, everyone had left except the Estronian man, Krizamju, who had waited for them and had a concerned look on his face.

"My friends," he said in relief. "You have returned. I was worried."

Blue Jay coughed and spluttered and Blake took deep breaths to keep from hyperventilating.

"There's... there's a Terran girl on board," Blake began to explain. "She's... she's in trouble."

"I don't understand," said Krizamju.

"We saw her," he explained to the alien. "A blond-haired girl who said she was being held against her will. We've... we've got to go back for her."

"What?" Krizamju was alarmed. "I don't understand what you are saying. There were no Terrans on board the *Harmony*."

Blue Jay bent forward, bracing himself with his knees while he fought to balance his oxygen level. "We... didn't get the little girl's android... sorry."

"I don't know why you attempted it," Krizamju replied, shaking his huge head. "Who is this Terran girl Blake Dobbs speaks of? I saw no such one on board the whole time I was there."

"The pilot..." Blake coughed, then straightened himself. "That man... said she was his prisoner. That he's taking her to some colony... for punishment..."

Krizamju was puzzled and shook his head. "Thorden is on a mission," he explained, "but no one knew what it was. I only know that he was agitated when we reached the rendezvous point. He seemed in a terrible hurry to get us all off the ship."

"Well, she's being held hostage," Blake said. He began looking around. "I've got to go back on board. How can I get myself... injected... or whatever... so I can go back?"

Krizamju turned to a nearby cabinet in the wall and began searching shelves. "You will need injections to survive."

"There's no time to go back there," Blue Jay protested, slowly rising to his feet.

"We've got to," insisted Blake.

"But why, man?"

"Because I recognized that girl!" Blake blurted out. In his memory he saw the photo album in Kapri's cabin on board the mother ship, with the picture of his aunt, his uncle and the little blond-haired girl... *his cousin!*

Blue Jay began to laugh at the absurdity, but Blake started for the gate. "I'm going... with you or without you!"

"Wait! Your injection!" Krizamju stepped forward and held out a hypodermic syringe.

"But Major Luro..."

"Tell him to wait." Blake offered his left arm and rolled his sleeve up as far as he could.

"He won't wait for you. The ship is on a schedule, Blake!"

Blue Jay insisted.

Krizamju pointed the syringe and Blake felt a slight pressure, but no sting of pain. "It will last a few hours, but that is all," the alien told him. "I will see if Major Luro will wait."

"He won't wait!" Blue Jay protested. Blake started through the doorway and Blue Jay called out, "Hey, I'm comin', too." He hesitated for his injection from Krizamju, and then followed Blake through the gate.

The lights flashed and the sirens were whining. Blake glanced back and smiled at Krizamju, who merely nodded and waved them on as the hatch to the airlock closed behind them.

36

Captured

Manley reached the outskirts of the compound by the time it was fully dark. The frogs were serenading from a nearby marshland. The moon was visible as a curved sliver of silver-white light. The stars were plentiful and bright, so much more in focus than at any other time that he could remember. There had been many years of star watches back in Illinois, but city lights had always interfered, drowning out the intimacy and clarity of those distant solar systems.

As he walked along the edge of a woods, he thought over all those times he had gazed up at the night sky, often with Dorothy and the kids along, and wondered when and if his sister, Johanna, and Serassan would ever return in a ship from those stars. Eighteen long years had passed since their remarkable visit before the turn of the century. Where was Johanna now? And was she raising a family of alien babies on the colony they called Karos? Manley sighed. What he'd give to see his beloved sister again.

Up ahead there were flickers of firelight coming from the quonset, perhaps from oil lamps or lanterns. That meant there still was no electricity. He could make out a helicopter shape parked near the large quonset hut, and he was aware of guard activity around the perimeter of the fenced-in area. He could hear subdued voices, some crying and moaning, from the building and tents where so many women were being held. Why? What could this all mean? The crisis was over now, so why hadn't these women been set free? And where were the men?

Manley was close enough now to be spotted, so he carefully moved from tree to bush and watched the movement in the concentration camp. He knew if he was to find Dorothy, he'd have to check out every possibility. Was she in the camp with all those women? The Light Being had made reference to his wife being inside the main headquarters, so that is where he headed. It appeared to be heavily guarded.

Two female guards stood at what appeared to be a large gate. One spoke and the other ambled over and pulled out a lighter. They both lit cigarettes, the tiny orange glows swelling as they took the first puffs. Manley took advantage of their distraction to scurry across the yard and hide behind a cluster of mailboxes. He knelt down and waited, breathless, until he was certain no one had seen him. Then he sat on the ground and looked around, trying to figure out his next move.

His stomach gurgled. He was feeling hungry and tired, not having had anything except a few sips of water since he'd met up with Elby that afternoon. He made himself comfortable in his hiding place as he knew he had to bide his time until these sentries moved out of range and he could risk getting a little closer to the quonset. He could sure use a tasty roast beef sandwich right about now. It would be on dill rye with a coating of Dijon mustard and some alfalfa sprouts, and perhaps even a slab of cheddar cheese. His mouth began to water at the image he'd conjured in his mind.

The cool evening air blew gently across his face and he stroked his whiskers and found he had quite a beard growth after almost a week of neglect. He began to wonder when he'd ever get to shave again, or brush his teeth for that matter.

A woman's screaming in the distance caused him to perk up. Someone was in some kind of crisis over in the tents. The two women guards extinguished their cigarettes and murmured to one another, and then one of them sauntered off in that direction while the other continued to patrol along the fence line.

Manley waited until they were far enough away and then slowly got to his feet. His right foot had started to go to asleep. No time to wait for it. Staggering slightly, he stole over to the fence, knowing he was a visible target but taking the chance. He gazed in frustration at the tall barbed wire. How was he going to get in? This was simply an impossible task. There was no way he could climb it and he sure as hell didn't have wire nippers in his back pocket.

"Halt!" a sharp female voice yelled at him. "Put your hands up. Don't you move!"

Manley froze and felt his hands automatically respond to

orders as he slowly turned his head and saw a shadowy figure emerge from the woods carrying a semi-automatic rifle. She must have been planted outside the compound. Why she hadn't seen him sooner was a mystery, but she might have been dozing or off taking a leak.

"Yo, corporal! What you got there?" called the guard next to the gate. She headed back in Manley's direction, pointing her rifle.

"An intruder," the first guard replied and stepped up close to ram the butt of her rifle into Manley's chest. "Turn around!" she ordered.

Obediently Manley did as he was told. The gate guard switched on a narrow but strong flashlight beam and aimed it at Manley's face. "All right, frisk him."

By now the other sentry had returned. The woods guard set her weapon against the fence and began to shake him down, padding his sides, his hips, his legs with the palms of her hands. She felt his pockets, reached around his ankles and circled his waist with her groping hands. "He's clean," she reported.

"State your business," demanded the gate guard.

"I... I was just out for a... a w-walk," Manley said.

"Why aren't you in camp?"

"Camp? What camp?"

"I think we have an escapee from Wilton," the gate guard told the other two. "We'd better inform Ms. Glenn."

"What the hell are you talking about?" asked Manley. "What's Wilton?"

"The men's facility an hour from here," the woods guard explained. "Ms. Glenn will be interested to know how you escaped."

"I didn't escape!" protested Manley. "I told you... I was out for a..."

"Save it!" ordered the gate guard and prodded him with her gun. She turned to her colleagues. "Open up," she said. "Let's take him to the pit."

Manley knew it would just be trouble for him to resist. He had allowed himself to be caught because basically he figured it was the only way he was going to get into the concentration camp and find Dorothy. But he made up his mind to play dumb. He was not about to explain his situation with these Nazi girls poking at him with their loaded guns. He heard the clanking of locks and then the wide gate swung open and they shoved him through. He had no idea what was about to happen to him. All he cared about was that he was finally inside the encampment and eventually he would find his wife.

"What's all the ruckus out in the yard?" Ernestine Glenn's voice rose in pitch as Dorothy roused herself in her cot to listen.

"A fugitive from Wilton," one of the women said.

"A man?"

"He was found outside the gate," someone else said.

"Anyone with him?" asked Ernestine.

"Negative, Ms. Glenn."

"I want them to search the area," Ernestine ordered. "Wilton is twenty-nine miles away. How could somebody have come that far under these conditions? Summon the General."

"General Rivers asked that nobody disturb him until morning," came the reply.

Ernestine sighed with impatience. "Where did they take the runaway?"

"To the pit, Ms. Glenn."

"Good. We'll see how our intruder likes his night-time accommodations. Now I'm going to bed. But if there are further disruptions, I want to be alerted."

"Yes, ma'am."

Dorothy raised herself up on the cot and looked around in the darkened sleeping area. Around her women were mumbling or snoring and she heard Ernestine Glenn's footsteps clicking across the room to a distant corner. Lights from lanterns and candles dimmed. As she settled back onto her cot, she wondered who had been captured now.

Back on board the *Harmony*, Blake and Blue Jay had no difficulty adjusting to the ship's atmosphere now that Krizmanju had injected them on board the *Resilience*. The two scrambled through the curved hallway that led away from the airlock with its wailing sirens and flashing lights, warning of the ship's plan for departure.

"What are you planning to do?" puffed Blue Jay at Blake's

heels.

"I think that girl is my cousin," said Blake. "But what she's doing here... with that rogue of a pilot... well, I intend to find out!"

"But the *Resilience* won't wait for us. You know that, don't you, bro?"

Blake glanced back at his musician friend. "If you want to go back, Blue Jay, go! Nothing says you have to stay with me."

"The injections don't last more than a few hours," Blue Jay reminded him. "Eventually we'll die."

The dire thought struck fear in Blake, but this compulsion to help the Terran girl was much stronger. He didn't know exactly why he felt so compelled to risk his life to save her, but something kept prodding him. It was almost as if someone else was taking control. "I'm willing to take that chance," said Blake. He saw the bridge opening ahead and headed toward it. Blue Jay stayed with him.

They stopped at the entrance and saw Thorden at the controls. The Terran girl was strapped in the next seat, her hands bound to the arm rests of her chair. She twitched her tousled blond head and saw the boys standing there, but shot a warning look with her eyes. Thorden had not yet noticed their presence, and the androids were busy at the controls.

Blake saw motion on the big viewing screen. The ship was easing its way from the port and the vast darkness of space with the stars in the background dominated the screen. They were leaving the *Resilience* behind. Thorden spoke in gibberish. He was still facing ahead and didn't see Blake sneaking up behind the Terran girl's seat as Blue Jay edged his way to get behind the alien pilot. Just as Blake placed his hands on the girl's shackled wrists, the alien turned his large bald head and his slanted eyes widened in surprise.

"So! You have stolen on board my ship once again!" the angry words exploded in Blake's head. "You shall be sorry you defied me, young Terran fool!" He then turned, having noticed Blue Jay sneaking toward him. "Stop! Come no closer," he reprimanded, fire in his eyes. At once Thorden was on his feet and began to slowly encircle the two boys, whose eyes darted back and forth as they calculated their next move.

"Thorden, don't hurt them! Let them go!" wailed the girl. She struggled to free herself, but the straps bound her tight.

"Are these friends of yours, Crystal?" Thorden demanded. "I do not recall giving you permission to invite any friends to our private little party."

"I've never seen them before in my life," Crystal pleaded. "And... and they haven't done anything, Thorden. Please... please don't hurt them." She began to cry.

"You've taken injections, haven't you? What are you doing on my ship?" Thorden demanded of Blake.

"We... we..." Blake stammered.

Blue Jay held up his hands and stepped forward. "Uh... wait a minute. Let me introduce myself. I'm Blue Jay Harris... musician at your service." He gave a little bow, then pulled his harmonica out of his back jeans pocket. "I understand someone called for some musical entertainment." He ran the instrument across his lips and rippled a scale.

The alien pilot appeared momentarily confused, then amused as a wicked smile spread across his grayish-white face. "Musicians," he mimicked. In his language the alien pilot summoned one of the androids over. "Take these intruders and lock them up."

Blake managed to dodge the android's approach. Blue Jay circled around to the front of the bridge. But the other android had now turned its attention to the ruckus and began to pursue him. Blake continued to avert the approaches of the android as he worked his way around the room, all the while keeping his eye on Thorden.

"Let the girl go," Blake cried.

"She's dangerous, I told you," said Thorden. "She's a shape shifter!"

Crystal shrieked. "What?"

"Do you expect us to believe that?" Blue Jay cried out as he stumbled against a panel.

"You are interfering with Federation business. You will be punished for interfering," Thorden threatened. "Capture them!" he commanded the androids.

"She doesn't look like any prisoner to me," said Blake. "I... I know who she is."

Thorden roared with laughter. "Our little singer's fame spreads rapidly throughout the galaxy. Well, the galaxy cannot have Crystal Dobbs. She is *mine... all mine!*" He turned to the boys, who were doing their best to avert capture by the robot units. "And as for you two... your injections will wear off soon enough. Once you slip from consciousness, I will dispose of your bodies along with the ship's refuse... in the dead of space." Spiteful laughter erupted and a foul smell filled the bridge from Thorden's rotten breath.

"No!" Crystal screamed, struggling with all her might. "I want to go home! Take me home! No wonder Mother thought you were a monster!"

"Your mother is too kind," Thorden sneered. "Johanna was a fool to stay on Karos, and Serassan a bigger fool for staying there with her... keeping his Terran body which has been a curse to him all these years!" He snickered. "It is extraordinary what a man will put up with in order to satisfy his lust." He inched closer to the sobbing girl. "I'll show you just a sample of what's in store for *you*, my sweet little songstress. And your friends can have the pleasure of watching... before you watch them *die!*"

Crystal screamed and in the next second the alien smacked her across the face.

Blake was filled with rage at this insufferable being, this ugly and terrible alien man who had hurt his cousin and had insulted his Aunt Jo. He charged at the Estronian, his teeth gritting, yelling in full force, "Ahhhhhh!!" The impact was like ramming himself into a brick wall, but he felt the wall give way as he pushed Thorden backwards, causing the alien to lose his balance and fall to the floor. He was surprised at the amount of force he had delivered — almost as though someone had helped him.

Blue Jay screamed at him, and Crystal was shrieking. Then as he recovered, Blake felt cold steel against his chest. One of the androids had grabbed him and locked him in a breath-squeezing hold from which he couldn't move. The arms of the android pressed tighter so that he could hardly get a breath. Blake happened to notice out of the corner of his eye that the ring he wore was giving off a bright blue light. He remembered Lotus' explanation that it was a protection ring, and a new calm settled over him. He relinquished resistance as the sinister Thorden staggered up off the floor. Blake saw that the other android had captured his black friend across the room.

"You won't get away with this," Crystal shrieked. "You know these two passengers will be missed on their ship. It's only a matter of time before they come after you."

"I always get away with everything," Thorden taunted. "I always have and I always will." He reached over and flipped a switch that released the straps binding Crystal's wrists. The girl immediately raised her hands to her face, then sprang from the chair in an attempt to escape.

But not quickly enough. Thorden was there in the next instant, and clutched her as she struggled against him, her pounding fists useless against his towering frame as he leaned over her. A thin, forked black snake of a tongue lashed out of his open mouth slit and began pricking Crystal's tear-stained cheeks as she tossed her head side to side, sobbing and protesting.

Blake felt completely helpless. But rage and desperation surged within his chest. He couldn't let this tormentor go a step further. Across the room Blue Jay was yelling at the android to let him go. Thorden managed to tear the front of Crystal's uniform and plunged his long gray fingers into her bosom as she shrieked for mercy. Blake knew he had to do something, but what could he do? This steel robot had him locked so tight he was sure he would soon pass out from not getting enough air. Pain crushed his ribs as he struggled in futility. The blue ring continued to glow.

"*Push the breaker,*" a voice in his head spoke. It was so near, yet with all the noise on the bridge he could hardly make the words out. "*On the android... push the breaker,*" the voice spoke calmly to him. It was familiar, yet he was too upset to remember...

"Where?" Blake demanded out loud. "Tell me... help us... please!"

Thorden's huge gray bald head covered Crystal's face now as the flicking tongue continued to dance over her fair skin. The alien was slowly forcing her down to the floor and her cries were muffled and panicked.

"*Feel with your fingers...*" the voice directed. "*Your left hand... it is close to the breaker. The switch that will dismantle the android. You must try... to reach it.*"

"Where?" Blake began to stretch the fingers in his left hand. Although the android's steel arms held him tight so that his arms couldn't move, he had some flexibility in his fingers. He began to stretch them, to explore.

"*Up... farther... if you can,*" instructed the voice.

Blake felt. The android gripped him tighter and Blake's eyes began to water from the pain. "I can't!" he gasped. "I... can't... I have to... to... breathe!"

Thorden's derisive laughter filled the bridge and Crystal's muffled screams came from the two of them crumpled in a heap on the floor as the alien's tunic loosened and fell away. Blake suddenly felt a knob, a raised button on the casing of the android's neck.

"*That's it,*" the voice instructed calmly. "*Now push it. As hard as you can. Push it until the unit is disabled.*"

Some kind of instinctive reaction caused the android to tighten his grip. Blake thought he was going to pass out. But he kept his finger on the knob and he tried with all the strength in him to keep from losing his position on that switch. He pressed with all his might. The android began to turn, to move in a circle. A whining sound hurt Blake's ears as black spots appeared before his vision and a terrible dizziness overcame him. In the next moment, however, he felt the grip give way and he dropped forward onto the bridge floor as the robot holding him prisoner crashed to the floor with a thunderous clap of heavy metal and rolled a bit before coming to a dead halt.

For the first few seconds Blake had trouble regaining his senses. It was probably due to the fact that Thorden was so involved in attempting to rape his victim, the alien hadn't noticed what had happened. But the other android was alert to the fact that its partner had been disabled and began to send out an alarm. It still gripped the struggling Blue Jay, whose wide eyes resembled white saucers against his dark-skinned face as he tossed his head of black curls from side to side.

Thorden immediately lifted himself and looked from one to the other. Crystal cowered underneath her seat, her clothes half torn off. Sobbing, she buried her face in her hands as the Estronian pilot jumped to his feet and swung at Blake. Thorden was in a rage and fire almost seemed to discharge from those huge slanted eyes. He momentarily caught Blake off guard and knocked him across a panel of instruments, where he hit the side of his head and was seized with stabbing shots of pain in his temple and jaw.

Next, Thorden had Blake in a death grip and dragged him over to the android holding Blue Jay. "Dispose of these trouble makers," Thorden commanded, out of breath.

"As you wish, commander," came the metallic voice in Blake's head. "But before I take them away, I wish to inform you that there is an approaching vessel."

Blake was able to turn his head enough in Thorden's clutches to see on the overhead screen a distant moving light in space that was growing larger and brighter as it approached the *Harmony*.

"Is it the *Resilience?*" Thorden demanded.

"Negative."

"Well, *who is it?*" Thorden shrieked in annoyance.

As if in answer to his question, a voice spoke in the Estronian language over the speaker on the bridge. It was a female voice with a strong, authoritative tone.

"It's a light ship," Crystal managed to say. She sat up, her blond hair ruffled and bloody scratches on her cheeks. She staggered to her feet, but before she could make another move, Thorden grabbed the girl and held both Blake and Crystal in a tight grip.

"A light ship?" Blue Jay managed to utter, still held fast by the android.

"It's Estronian," Crystal explained.

Thorden spoke in answer to the flagging ship, but Blake couldn't understand what was being said. He turned questioningly to the girl who was his cousin.

"It's Captain Vameera," Crystal explained in between gasps. "She's demanding that the *Harmony* allow her ship to dock with us."

Thorden appeared so enraged and so desperate, Blake could feel the surge of venom that exuded from the trembling pilot who continued to grip the two humans. The alien's breathing was labored and he looked around, from the android holding Blue Jay, to the door, to the controls. He finally turned to the other android and said, "I will not give up! We must leave here at once. Dispose of that Terran and then activate this fallen unit!"

"There is no way you can outrun a light ship!" Crystal cried. "I've studied enough about space and navigation to know that!"

"Dispose of the know-it-all girl, too!" Thorden's belligerent voice thundered. He shoved Crystal across the room toward the android, who reached out to grab her as she fell.

The android began to drag both Blue Jay and Crystal toward the door. Blake's head throbbed, but again the voice came through, echoing clearly in his head. *"You must stop Thorden,"* the voice implored. *"All of your lives depend on it."*

But how? How was he going to stop this insane monster? The android was outside the bridge area now, no doubt headed for the airlock with his musician friend and squealing cousin. Blake struggled in Thorden's hold, but couldn't free himself. He was amazed at the alien's strength. He had succeeded at accelerating Thorden's fury, however. With Estronian curses gushing from his mouth slit, the enraged Estronian struck Blake once more and sent him sprawling on the bridge floor as flashing white light exploded in his head and then he knew no more.

37

Desperation

C rystal was terrified, but mostly she was humiliated beyond fear from what the repulsive Estronian pilot had done to her. Her cheeks burned with the pain of his stinging black tongue, and she gagged from the foul taste of his breath and rancid stench of his clammy gray skin.

But as much as her stomach was revolting from his cold touch, and her muscles were bruised and aching from battling against his brute strength, she knew she had to keep fighting... for her life and for the lives of these two brave Terran boys who had abandoned their ship to save her. The android was moving rapidly toward the airlock and she knew it meant to follow Thorden's orders and throw herself and this dark-skinned young man off the ship, into the vacuum of cold space.

"Can't we shut this machine down?" Blue Jay gasped, unable to move in the android's grip as his feet dragged on the floor.

"There's a breaker switch... on... on the neck..." Crystal tried to explain. But she knew she couldn't reach it, and Blue Jay was not in a position to help. She knew that was how the blond-haired boy had deactivated the other android. But how had he known? Had he touched the switch by accident?

Suddenly the ship rocked as an explosion sounded. The android unit slipped back a few feet as they tilted slightly. Crystal was able to glance back enough to see that the light ship was in full view and was close to their ship. She didn't think Captain Vameera would fire at the *Harmony*, but they must have done something to at least let Thorden know they meant business.

The shift in balance and weight gave Crystal the advantage of moving her arm so that her hand was in the vicinity of the android's breaker switch. Immediately its warning sensor came on, sending a whining sound that hurt their ears. Crystal gritted her teeth and felt for the switch as the unit spun the two humanoids around in a circle, attempting to distract the one that was too close to its deactivating button.

"What's going on?" shrieked Blue Jay. "Stop!"

"Hold on!" Crystal begged. "I've... I've almost... I've... *got* it!"

In the next instant she had pushed the switch and was holding it down as hard and as long as her trembling fingers could stand. At last the android's power cut off and she and Blue Jay both dropped from the steel grip as the metallic robot crashed to the floor between them.

Crystal rolled to her side and then looked up in a daze. Blue Jay was astonished, but didn't waste a second. He reached for her hand and helped her up, and then the two of them moved swiftly back toward the bridge, where Thorden was at the controls and the light ship hovered in front of the *Harmony*, as if to block it.

Blake's unconscious body lay in a crumpled heap on the floor. Crystal's heart jumped to her throat. Oh no, he couldn't be...

Thorden turned and saw the two of them standing there. He lifted a short weapon of some sort and aimed directly at them. Crystal had never seen anyone with so much hatred and spite in his eyes, and a wicked grin played across his evil face. "So this is how it ends," he hissed. "Well, my lovely songstress... you had your chance... I could have given you all that your little heart ever desired!"

Panic surged and Crystal's mouth was so dry, she couldn't speak. She knew that in the next few moments someone... maybe all of them... were going to die. She had a dreadful feeling already that the boy on the floor who had been so brave was already dead.

"Thorden of Estron!" Vameera's voice boomed from the intercom. "Turn yourself over. I demand your surrender!"

"I have done nothing to turn myself over to anyone," Thorden screamed back. "I was given license to commission this space journey. Now energize your engines and go annoy some other vessel in the galaxy!"

"We know that Crystal Dobbs is on board the *Harmony* with you," said Vameera.

"And what if she is?" barked Thorden. "She agreed to accompany me..."

"No!" Crystal screamed. "No! I want to go home!" Sobs erupted.

"Crystal!" a familiar voice called from the intercom. "Crystal! Are you there? Are you all right?" It was Soolàn's worried voice. Granna was on the light ship with Captain Vameera.

"Say one more word and it will be your last," Thorden spat at her.

"Granna! He wants to kill us!" Crystal yelled, paralyzed with fear.

In the next moment Blue Jay lunged at Thorden, who discharged his weapon, aiming for Crystal, and the young man's body intercepted the deadly ray of energy. He jerked and then dropped to the floor between them. Crystal screamed and fell to her knees next to the young man, whose neck was burned from front to back. His large white eyes stared lifelessly up at her.

"Thorden, don't harm our granddaughter!" This time the voice came from Emrox over the intercom. He was pleading with the *Harmony's* pilot. "We'll back off... but please... *please* don't hurt her!"

"Granna! Grandfather!" Crystal gushed, beside herself with horror.

"Two are dead!" Thorden fired back in anger. "And unless you want to be responsible for the third, I order you to leave... *now!*"

"No! I'd rather die than go with you!" Crystal glowered through her tears.

"Very well, my dear..."

"Crystal, *no!*" Soolàn's voice was sobbing.

A brilliant glow suddenly lit up the bridge. A golden light emerged around the unconscious boy on the floor. And then Crystal watched as he stirred. As the aura of bright golden light began to grow brighter, she saw his head rise up and then his arm moved and he pushed his body up off the floor. He wasn't dead after all! But what was this unusual golden aura that was filling the room? She felt a dizzying vibration of static energy.

Thorden jumped aside and aimed his weapon at the boy. But as the young man staggered to his feet, his gaze fixed on the alien, he held up the palms of both hands. Thorden at once tried to block it by raising an arm and he stumbled backward, the weapon dangling loosely in his other hand. A cry escaped from his raspy throat.

"What is it? What is happening?" demanded Captain Vameera.

Then Thorden began to wail as if in pain. The boy with his hands still outstretched moved ever closer to him, driving him back. Energy seemed to be shooting from his hands, but all Crystal could see was the light, and the strength of his will. Who *was* this person? He couldn't be a mere Terran from Earth. Not with this kind of ability.

"I can't hold him off much longer," the strained voice spoke from the boy. "I need your help. Get his weapon."

Startled because the voice coming from the boy was not quite the same as before, Crystal regained her composure and darted to Thorden's side as the distressed alien writhed in pain, staring pleadingly at her and unable to speak. She fumbled for the weapon that still loosely dangled in his grip, and quickly dropped back behind the young man and the bright aura of golden light that now was flickering.

"Good... Now... Crystal, you must do exactly as I say," he said in that distorted voice.

"Yes," she agreed. "I'm... I'm listening."

"Go to the control panel and remove the force-field that is shielding the ship and keeping Vameera from docking with us."

Crystal stepped over Blue Jay's lifeless body and searched the control panel with its array of flashing colored lights. "Which... which one is it?" she asked, still wondering how this boy from the planet Terra could possibly know about force-fields and which buttons to push.

"First, hand me the weapon."

Crystal gave him the laser device and in the next few seconds the fluctuating golden light glowed, then dimmed, glowed again, then slowly dimmed. Crystal saw Thorden attempting to pick himself off the floor. But the boy pointed the laser gun at him, to keep him at bay.

"That one there... on the left, above the dial."

Crystal fidgeted, afraid for a moment she would push the wrong button, but then she saw the one he was referring to and activated it.

"We are coming in," came Vameera's voice over the intercom.

"Crystal, are you all right?" Granna's voice demanded.

"Yes, Granna! I'm okay! Thorden is under control... thanks to... I don't know his name!" She suddenly broke down and turned to the boy, who caught the look on her face and backed up toward her, his weapon still fixed on Thorden.

"You are going to be safe now." He reached his arm out to her and pulled her close against him. Crystal allowed him to embrace her, all the while aware that he kept that laser gun pointed at Thorden. She sobbed hard into his shoulder and felt his free hand caressing her back. His touch was the most comforting, warm surge of energy she had ever felt in her life. Being against him like this was not just a shoulder to cry on but something deeper that she sensed from the core of her being.

When she dared to look up at his scratched face, his hazel-colored eyes peered into her own and she saw something there — something that made her draw her breath, because it was familiar and it filled her with a peace she had never before experienced. She had meant to ask him his name, so that she could thank him for saving her life. But in that rare moment of recognition, she forgot.

Crystal didn't know how many minutes had passed, but she roused herself from the cushion of his shoulder when she heard footsteps and then three people rushed into the bridge from the corridor. Emrox was the first one she saw, followed by an Estronian female in uniform, and behind them a very frightened Soolàn. "Grandfather!" she cried out.

Emrox grinned with relief when he saw his granddaughter and quickly embraced her. The Estronian pilot from the light ship took the laser gun from the Terran's hand and stood over Thorden, her legs spread apart as she gloated over the kidnapper turned rapist. "Lights out for you, Thorden of Estron... you slime-covered bag of maggots!" She glanced at the gun and then fired right at him. As the beam of light struck his chest, the Estronian man lay immobilized, his huge slanted eyes staring up at nothing.

Soolàn came over and Crystal fell into her arms as Emrox squatted beside Thorden, then looked at up Vameera. "He's not..."

"No, I didn't kill him," sighed Vameera. "That would have been too good for this waste of gray flesh. The laser was set on stun. He'll be out long enough for us to put him in a cell and transport him back to Estron."

Suddenly the Terran boy moaned, then leaned forward and his head began to drop. He lost his balance and crumpled to the floor. Vameera caught him before he could hit his head and she supported him as the others stared in surprise.

"We must get him some help," said Soolàn.

"Who is he?" asked Emrox.

Crystal sobbed. "I don't know, Grandfather, but he saved my life."

"He is... Terran?" asked Vameera.

"He and his friend... they came from the *Resilience*."

Emrox knelt beside the still Blue Jay and gently rolled him to one side. "I'm afraid we can't help this one," he said sadly.

"We've got to get this Terran to a facility," said Vameera. "Emrox, can you and Soolàn take him aboard the light ship? I will see to this heap of space dung. Someone ought to send a message to the *Resilience*... we will need someone to fly this cruiser back to Estron or the nearest space port."

38

Liberation

The first hint of the morning glow was on the eastern horizon when the Light Being opened his eyes. He was flat on his back on the reclining seat of his shuttle. He stared up at the domed ceiling, blinking to focus as he perceived coldness and his body began to shiver. Moving his right hand, he noticed he was covered with a blanket. He found that he could move his legs, and even though there was a tingle in his lower left arm, he had flexibility throughout his body which was so new to him.

Immediately the memories rushed at him as he slowly lifted his head and sat up. He saw himself in the middle of a desperate scene on board a ship in space. While he held a weapon on the criminal pilot, the demented Estronian who had attempted to harm his divine counterpart, She had clung to his side. He recalled Her warmth as Her head had nestled against his neck and shoulder, Her arms wrapped around his waist and Her breaths short and rapid in Her fear.

He recalled the others rushing into the room — three Estronians — including the angry light ship pilot, who had taken charge just as his eyes grew blurry and he felt himself separating from the boy's living vessel. In a whirl the Light Being had flung himself out of that dimension — that uncomfortable denseness — and had traveled in a flash back into his own container, this cloned body on Earth, aboard his carefully hidden shuttle.

A sudden longing for Her overwhelmed him and a gasp escaped his parched throat. He felt a weight, a heavy pain from inside the middle of his chest, that caused an eruption of moisture that emerged from his eyelids. He had been with Her, felt Her, and held Her to him, but it only served to torment him with this agonizing loneliness.

Yet he knew, had he stayed there a moment longer, it would have meant certain death to the boy, Blake. He couldn't sacrifice another being's life just to be with Crystal. He had connected with her through Blake, whose DNA he now shared, and soon he would make his way back into space to be with Her again... that is, if this body lasted long enough.

Right now, he knew he had a task to perform that was vitally important. He must accomplish this mission before it was too late. He now had the strength and vigor he had borrowed from Blake's very life force. He prayed the boy would be strong enough to hold on until it could be restored. For the time being, there was no choice but to follow through with his plan. He didn't know exactly how much time he had before the life force would flicker again, but he knew he had to try. He understood the bond that tied Blake to his parents and little sister. Just as Blake had felt the Light Being's desperation to save Crystal, the Light Being now felt Blake's need.

He stood and watched the rosy glow of Earth's Star reflecting the sky. There was no time to waste. He began the procedure for preparing his shuttle for flight, and then he checked the storage banks for armament.

Dorothy hadn't slept worth a wink. She had dozed off and on, but her dreams had been filled with disturbing images of hooded black figures carrying scepters with blades, and of a huge tiger that chased her in a Nebraska cornfield. Now her mouth was dry and she had to use the bathroom. It was barely daylight when she rose from her cot and started down the aisle to the same bathroom where she had been allowed to shower and change clothes after Ernestine Glenn had recruited her.

After relieving herself, Dorothy stepped out and saw Ernestine Glenn seated in the main room of the quonset with an elderly man in a military jacket. Ernestine poured the man a cup of coffee and gave it to him, then noticed Dorothy standing there.

"Oh, Dorothy, good, you're up." Ernestine didn't smile. "General, this is the lady I was telling you about." Then Ernestine's mouth twitched as she remembered formalities. "General Rivers, this is Dorothy Dobbs."

The General rose to his feet, then quickly sat down, more interested in checking to see if his coffee was cool enough to drink.

"Pleased to meet you, General," Dorothy murmured.

"This is an important day," announced Ernestine. "Dorothy, help yourself to some coffee. Then we have some important business to conduct outside."

Without hesitation, Dorothy found a chipped cup among the clean dishes drying by the sink and poured herself a cup of black coffee from an old-fashioned metal coffee pot that had finished perking on a two-burner propane stove.

"Your sergeant told me you brought in a fugitive last night," the General said to Ms. Glenn.

"That's right. A man was found wandering out by the gate," Ernestine explained. "We believe he escaped from Wilton."

"The neighboring camp," muttered the General.

Dorothy's ears were perked as she poked around for a clean spoon and some powdered creamer.

"What are you planning to do with him?" the General asked a moment later.

Ernestine sat down across from the General. "I intend to make an example out of him," she disclosed.

"Oh? May I ask... how?"

"Dorothy has been most useful in assisting me to pull out possible traitors," Ernestine Glenn told the General. She was smiling now and beckoned to Dorothy to sit beside her in one of the folding chairs. "Tell the General about your gift, Dorothy."

"I... I don't understand," Dorothy stammered.

"Oh, don't be so modest," Ernestine chided. "General, Dorothy Dobbs is one helluva psychic."

Dorothy was too embarrassed to say anything and stared into her coffee cup.

The General broke into derisive laughter as he swirled the cooling coffee in his mug. "Now, Ms. Glenn, don't tell me that you, of all people, believe in that kind of hocus-pocus."

At once Ernestine's green eyes inflamed and her lips puckered in annoyance. "Do not patronize me, General," she warned.

Clearing his throat, General Rivers said, "You haven't told me what you intend to do about the man who paid you a visit last night."

"That's right, I didn't." Ernestine sipped from her mug, then smiled once again. "I understand he was not very cooperative when he was questioned. Sergeant Yocum couldn't get any information out of him about how he escaped from one of our Purification camps."

"Oh? Then how..."

"We have reason to believe..." Ernestine was interrupted as one of the female guards came in to summon her.

"We are ready," the guard announced.

"You have collected the prisoners?" Ernestine rose and set her coffee cup down.

The guard nodded. Dorothy wondered who the prisoners were. Weren't all of the women in the camp being held against their will?

"Come along, General." Ernestine started for the door, then stopped and turned to face Dorothy. "You, too, Dorothy," she ordered.

The outside air felt cool and moist from dew in the early daylight. Dorothy followed the General, Ms. Glenn and the armed guard toward the big gate where the majority of the women were kept. Many of them were already assembled along the barbed wire fence, watching in curiosity. Dorothy's heart went out to them as she saw the fear and the suffering on their faces. These were citizens of the United States of America, everyday people who had rudely been tricked and then brought to this facility, separated from husbands and children. And what for? Was Ernestine Glenn planning to let them go now? Was that her plan — to finally release these poor women after several days of neglect?

Suddenly her attention was drawn to a line of about twenty women who had their hands cuffed as they were being marched, single file, from the back door of the main quonset. Dorothy recognized them as the women she had been forced to read psychically for Ernestine. Her friend Louise, looking disheveled and beaten, stood, bent over a little, at the end of the line. They had ended up in the dungeon below the quonset, where she had spent the last hours of the Three Days of Darkness. Guards with rifles brought up the rear and directed the women to line up in front of the General and Ms. Glenn.

"Today is a new beginning," Ernestine shouted so that all could hear her. Dorothy wasn't sure how many behind the barbed wire enclosure could hear. "Yes," Ernestine continued, "the beginning of a new way of life here in our nation and everywhere on Planet Earth."

Dorothy waited to hear what else this maniac of a woman had to say. She wondered exactly just how powerful a figure Ernestine Glenn was in the eyes of the world.

"For centuries... no, for millennia... womankind has been subservient to Man," Ernestine continued. "Men have been responsible for the woes of our world. Men have conducted wars, destroyed the environment because of their greed and lust! But I say... no more! No longer will we, as wives, mothers, daughters and sisters of Men, tolerate the kind of abuse and irresponsibility these miserable ones have brought upon us. I have accepted this position of leader, in order to set things straight — once and for all!"

"When can we go home?" a voice wailed from behind the barbed wire.

"Where are our children?" another shouted.

"We want our husbands!" cried another.

Ignoring their outbursts, Ernestine proclaimed, "The Purification Party is in control. Together we will clean up the earth! Yes, we will clean up whatever defiles society. It is the only way we are ever going to save the human race."

"Not *all* men are to blame," a hand-cuffed woman called from the line in front of them.

"Yeah, how can you be so judgmental?" another yelled.

Almost at once, wails and pleas arose among the camp women. Dorothy saw Ernestine's face darken in anger.

"My little boy — he's only eight months old — he's innocent!" cried a woman.

Ernestine's chest began to heave in exasperation. The General leaned toward her and whispered something.

"I will not!" the leader retorted, her eyes flashing. She signaled to one of the guards near the quonset and a moment later two women guards brought out a stocky, balding man, whose hands were tied as well. He had a blindfold over his eyes.

When Dorothy saw him, she let out a huge gasp and covered her mouth with her hands. It was Manley! He was pushed over to the line of women and almost stumbled in his blindness.

Ernestine spun around to face Dorothy. "Follow me," she

commanded.

At first Dorothy couldn't move. She was too shocked. It really was her husband. What was Ernestine planning to do? Why the blindfold? Her instincts filled her with horror as she plainly saw what the insane woman leader had in mind.

"Today we perform the first step in changing our world for the better!" Ernestine shouted to the masses. "We have chosen this male swine as a symbol of our vengeance. With his death, we will make a statement to all members of his sex... that they are no longer in charge! *I* am!"

"No!" Dorothy shouted before she could think to stop herself. "You can't!"

Protests and screams began to erupt in the camp. Dorothy saw out of the corner of her eye that now the General was looking a little worried. But Ernestine Glenn was unstoppable.

"These women are traitors to the cause," she announced. "They, too, must die!"

More shouts and pleas filled the morning air. Manley and the hand-cuffed women began to shuffle and fidget, but the armed guards poked their rifles into their faces to stop them.

"Dorothy," called Ernestine. "I want you to tell me what this man knows. Read him!"

Her heart hammering, Dorothy stepped in front of her husband. "I... I... I can't," she whined.

"And *why not*?" demanded the madwoman.

"D-Dorothy?" Manley's voice croaked.

"Shh," she warned, hoping Ms. Glenn had not heard him. "Be still," she whispered.

"What is that?" shouted Ernestine.

Dorothy was frightened for all their lives. "Oh my God," she murmured, then dropped her eyes and held her forehead as if concentrating.

"Tell me what I want to know," Ernestine commanded. "Before we begin the executions, I must know what is in his thoughts."

A moment passed in which Dorothy merely shook with fear.

"Well? Are you getting anything?" Ernestine's impatience was rising.

"I'm... I'm trying." A sob escaped her throat.

"She's obviously a fake," the General scolded. "I told you... nobody can read minds."

Dorothy snapped her head up and glared at General Rivers. "I can read *yours*, General," she declared in defiance. "You're scared shitless, just like the rest of us. Why are you siding with this woman? She's insane! You're scared to death you're going to be next! Aren't you?"

The General's eyes nearly popped out of his head. But before he could say anything in protest, Ms. Glenn interrupted.

"I think that is quite enough," she told Dorothy. "I will give you one more chance to tell me what I want to know. And, if you don't, you will join that line-up of women and be executed along with the rest!"

"Don't do it!" Manley warned.

"Shut up!" Ernestine screamed at him.

"He's... he's..." Dorothy again closed her eyes and held her forehead. She began sobbing, then said, "He's... he's from that men's camp down the road. He's... he's... he escaped somehow! That's... that's all I know."

Ernestine stepped right up to Dorothy and slapped her on the cheek. "Foolish girl! How dare you try and deceive me? I won't have liars in my employ. My guards already know this man is not an escapee from Wilton or anywhere else. He is a spy!"

"He's not a spy!" Dorothy gasped, touching the stinging welt beneath her cheekbone. "He doesn't deserve to die. None of these women do either!"

"Dorothy... stop..." Manley pleaded.

"This man knows you!" Ernestine accused. "Who is he?"

Dorothy leaned forward and peered into Ernestine Glenn's eyes, completely overwhelmed with the fury she felt toward this woman. "He is my husband!" she seethed. "And you... I can't believe I campaigned for you! I can't believe that I ever got sucked in to your warped way of thinking... your psychotic philosophy!"

Turning, Dorothy wrapped her arms around Manley, whose hands were still tied. "Oh, poor darling," she sobbed, "I was afraid I'd never see you again."

"What kind of display is this?" demanded General Rivers, quite amused.

"It's obvious," replied Ernestine. "They are both traitors.

They shall be the first to die!"

By now the uproar in the camp was deafening. More women had come out of the tents within the barbed wire enclosure and the guards were swarming, finding it difficult to control the squirming women. Dorothy could see guards hitting women with the butts of their weapons, and the scene was beginning to look like an impending riot.

Gunfire erupted and screams followed. Dorothy seized the opportunity to tear off Manley's blindfold. He blinked and gazed around at the desperate situation they were in.

"This is getting out of control!" The General called over the din. "Can't you do something?"

Ernestine Glenn was beside herself. "Kill them! Kill them all!" she commanded, and more gun shots exploded. Louise and a few of the women in the line-up crumpled to the ground.

Dorothy wrapped her arms tightly around Manley and squeezed. At any moment she expected bullets to rip through her body and Manley's. She sobbed, clinging to him, as the faces of Blake and Kelly filled her mind. "My children," she prayed. "My lovely children..."

Just at that moment a piercing sound blotted out the chaotic screams of the camp, the gunfire and the harsh voices of Ernestine Glenn and General Rivers shouting at one another. It was a deafening, shrill tone and Dorothy instinctively tried to plug her ears with her fingers. In the next moment a blinding white light wiped out all else.

Dorothy still clung to Manley, and in a few more seconds the sound dissipated and the brightness subsided. When Dorothy blinked away her momentary blindness, she could see a blueish-white beam of light surrounding Ernestine Glenn. The woman was paralyzed within the beam, her face a complete spectacle of shock and fear.

Glancing skyward, Dorothy and Manley both saw a rounded disk, thirty or so feet in diameter. It hovered at treetop level over them. The round bottom of the object was golden in color and was the source of the light beam that encased Ernestine Glenn.

"Elby!" cried Manley and began to laugh. "It's Elby! He must have recovered."

"Who?" asked Dorothy. She stared at the transfixed General

and guards who could only stand and stare at the ship that had flown into camp and now had their leader trapped in its energy. Within moments the beam disappeared and Ernestine Glenn's body dropped to the grass.

No one dared move. The camp had fallen silent, for the most part, and some of the guards were backing away from the scene, obviously terrified.

"It's... it's a spaceship," Dorothy whispered to Manley.

"Yes." Manley smiled. "He didn't let us down."

"Who?"

"Elby."

The General dropped to his knees. He was shaking from head to toe. Looking around him, he called out to the women guards, "Isn't anybody going to shoot? What's the matter with you people, goddammit! Seize the target!"

One of the nearby guards raised her rifle and aimed at the hovering ship. She fired, but a force-field reaction caused a ripple of blue lightning to spark the protected hull, and a sudden streak of energy zapped back at the guard and sent her sprawling on the ground. The weapon flew out of her hands and disintegrated, leaving a small charred pile of smoldering black metal.

At once all of the guards in the camp began to drop their weapons. The spaceship moved slowly toward the direction of the barbed wire enclosure and as it drew near, another narrow light beam shot downward and caused the barbed wire gates to melt. Smoke rose as the wires fell away and created an opening for the imprisoned women to escape.

Manley and Dorothy watched in awe. Screams and shouts of joy could be heard throughout the camp as women began to pour out, free at last from their interment. Then they watched as the ship moved toward the other gates in the compound and repeated the task. Soon all the gates were burned open and hundreds of women swarmed the grounds. The women guards were helpless to act.

"Untie me," Manley said, turning his back. His wrists were bound together with twine. Apparently the compound had run out of handcuffs, she thought as she frantically worked at the knots.

They watched as the panicking women bustled around them. The quaking General, who kneeled close to the still-paralyzed Ernestine Glenn, made no effort to move, probably fearful that he'd be knocked over by the wild crowd. For a second Dorothy's eyes met the General's and he glared with such hatred it made her shudder.

"Are you getting it?" Manley prompted.

"I'm trying," she panted. "I need a knife... or something sharp."

"Come on, let's get out of here while we can." His wrists still bound, Manley led Dorothy through the crazed crowd toward the quonset. Many of the women had already raided the buildings and were coming out, their arms loaded with food, blankets and supplies. Several had even begun to bicker and fight over their booty.

"Manley, look!" Dorothy pointed to the parking area, where the golden space shuttle was landing beside the General's helicopter.

"Let's go!" Manley wasted no time leading her toward the ship. By the time they reached it, the Light Being stepped down the small ramp and stared at them. A curious crowd of women were starting to gather and gawk.

"His hands!" Dorothy called to the pilot of the craft. Then she stopped in her tracks and nearly fainted.

Manley managed to lean against her to keep her from keeling over. "Are you all right?" he asked.

Dorothy's face was pale. "It's Blake. Manley, it's... it's *Blake*!"

"Yes, I know," he said, beckoning her toward the being who so much resembled their son. "He isn't Blake. He just looks like him."

"What do you mean?" Dorothy gasped as she got closer. The young man reached out his hand. She could see that even though he looked just like her blond-headed son, this man was older, maybe in his early twenties. Still, the likeness frightened her.

"Elby! Thank God!" cried Manley.

The Light Being stepped up to him and in five seconds had his hands free. Dorothy watched in awe as the twine dropped to the grass.

"Thanks, Elby," said Manley, rubbing his sore wrists.

"Please get inside," said the Light Being. "We must leave at once."

With a quick glance Manley looked back at the camp women and the chaos. "Oh?"

"Time is of the essence," insisted the Light Being. He led them inside the shuttle and the door closed behind them. He then indicated where he wanted them to sit as he took control and lifted the shuttle up off the ground and eased it over the roofs of the quonsets.

"That was quite a performance, Elby," Manley said. "I never in my life saw anything like it. It was superb! But... I thought you were ill... in some kind of coma. I stayed with you as long as I dared, but I had to find my wife. I..."

"You did exactly what you had to do," said the Light Being. "It might have *appeared* that I was ill. But it was necessary. I had work of my own to perform. That's why I had to vacate the body for several hours. I apologize for worrying you."

Dorothy was puzzled by their exchange. "What's he talking about?" she asked.

Manley reached over and grasped her hand. It was a silent promise that he would explain it all to her later on. "Elby," he said, "where are we headed now?"

"We are in danger the longer we stay in Earth's atmosphere," the Light Being disclosed. "Soon I will have expended my shields using the beam weapon. That will leave us vulnerable to attack. But before we return to the mother ship, I want to assist a little more." He glanced over at the two of them. "It is vital we return to space as soon as possible, but I want to make sure the Terrans have a fair chance."

They zipped through the morning sky and the Light Being took them to another camp and hovered closely over it as Manley and Dorothy watched in fascination through the small viewing screen. Beams of light zapped each gate, erupting chaos as they witnessed hordes of people below freeing themselves from the confinement.

"That must be the men's camp they were talking about," muttered Dorothy.

The Light Being soared once again and freed eight more concentration camps in the next half hour. Finally, he set his course for the heavens.

"You mean, that's all you're going to save?" asked Dorothy in alarm.

"My shields are depleted. But there are enough freed now to create a stir," replied the Light Being. "And with the leader incapacitated, they have a chance to free all the others. Without leadership, Glenn's followers will have no choice but to give up."

"Well, what if somebody else decides to take her place?" asked Dorothy.

"That's always a possibility," the Light Being said sadly.

"Who are we talking about here?" demanded Manley.

Dorothy turned to him and sighed. "Ernestine Glenn."

"You mean, the presidential candidate?"

"One and the same."

"I never trusted that woman," Manley grumbled.

"What about Earth?" Dorothy asked their pilot. "What will happen to this planet?"

"Only time will tell," replied the Light Being.

"And the Photon Belt?" asked Manley. "Did that actually occur?"

"No," said Dorothy. "Somehow Ernestine and her corps of technologists faked the whole thing!"

"That is not exactly true," said the Light Being. "The shift is under way. There is no stopping it. Look." He widened the outside viewing screen so that they could see the curvature of the earth and the film layer of atmosphere against the blackness of space. Tiny objects appeared like shiny dots here and there, traveling toward the planet's surface.

"What are those?" Dorothy inquired.

"Those," said the Light Being, "are members of the Federation. Apparently they have decided to move in and evacuate those they deem are enlightened enough to leave the planet. Your Earth will be in a chaotic state for many years to come. There will be much hardship for those who remain behind and must learn to live as primitives."

Fearful thoughts seized Dorothy. "What about my children?" Her frantic tone startled both Manley and their pilot.

The Light Being turned to her. "Just as I had told you... they are safe."

Dorothy leaned back in her seat as the realization struck her. "So... it was *you*. You were the one I saw when I was in that dungeon. You were the voice in my head."

"Rest now," urged the Light Being. "In a short while we will be on the *New Jerusalem*, and you will be reunited with your daughter."

Tears seeped from Dorothy's eyes. She felt Manley squeezing her hand. Then she grew apprehensive. "What about Blake?"

"Yes, where is Blake?" Manley asked.

The Light Being released a sigh, then turned to them with a serious expression. "Your son is in space. He had the opportunity to take a journey across the galaxy. He is safe... for the moment."

"What do you mean *for the moment*?" Dorothy sensed grave concern emanating from the pilot.

"How do you know all this?" asked Manley.

"I know," said the Light Being. "I know, because I was there with him." He sighed again. "Just as soon as we retrieve your small daughter, we must journey to Estron to save your son."

39

Starbound

The medical facility in the City of Domes buzzed with Estronian health workers. The bright lights and activity reminded Johanna of hospitals on Earth. As she sat outside the examining room where they had taken Crystal, she recalled that hospital experience nineteen years ago, when her brother Manley had brought her into the emergency room and her nightmare had begun. She had ended up there, in the psychiatric ward, for a couple of months, just as upset and mystified as the doctors and nurses had been because of her inability to communicate.

She remembered fondly how the evening before she had sat next to Serassan at the Russian ballet. Only she didn't know him then. He had been a mysterious and handsome stranger who kept getting up from his seat, only to return, then leave again. Little had she known that January night how big a part he would play in her life, and how being taken to that hospital would alter her destiny.

It had been practically a sleepless night Johanna and Serassan had spent in their lodging facility, waiting word from Emrox and Soolàn in their pursuit of Thorden's ship. The communication had come in the early dawn hours after Johanna had finally dozed a little. Serassan had gently wakened her with the news that Vameera's light ship had succeeded at intercepting the *Harmony*, and that Crystal was on her way to Estron with her grandparents.

In the joy of hearing the news, Johanna had not thought about the possible harm Thorden had inflicted on their daughter. And so, when the light ship landed in the City of Domes, it had been some-what of a shock to see Crystal's stricken face, ripped clothing and bruises. The girl had been immediately taken to the examining room to be treated, with no chance for a warm reunion with her concerned parents. Serassan had to remind her that it was not the

Estronian way. Johanna remembered, with a tug at her heart, the longing look Crystal had given her as the health workers had whisked her away. A half-smile had flickered across the girl's dirty face, which told Johanna enough — that her daughter was happy to see her.

No one had said anything either about the unconscious Terran boy they had transported on a stretcher into their equivalent of Intensive Care in the Estronian healing center. Johanna had not gotten that good a look at the boy, but she remembered light hair and something about his features had prompted a feeling of familiarity in her.

Emrox and Soolàn, exhausted from their excursion into space, had not had the opportunity to explain what had happened when Vameera's light ship had overtaken Thorden. Serassan had insisted his parents go to a resting area and get some sleep. He sternly led them back to their lodging facility, telling Johanna he'd join her as soon as he had taken care of his parents' needs. She understood his concern. Emrox, especially, hadn't looked well. Soolàn was assisting her mate with her own life force and was looking drained.

"You may come in now, Johanna," the soft female voice said, interrupting her thoughts.

Johanna glanced up and saw a tall Estronian female in a white uniform. The woman with the huge bald head and slanted blue eyes smiled at her as Johanna recognized the familiar gentleness and soft creases around the alien's cheekbones. "Plipquum?" she gasped.

"Yes. It is I. How are you?"

Johanna stood up and reached her hand out to the healer, who clasped it. "It is wonderful to see you again, Plipquum." Then, suddenly, she bit her lip. "Oh, how is Crystal?"

Plipquum led Johanna into the examining room. "Your daughter is going to be fine. She is waiting to see you."

Crystal was sitting with her bare feet and legs dangling over the edge of the table. She wore a loose lavender garment and managed a tearful smile when she saw her mother. An android unit was at Crystal's side, holding a small electrical device to her neck, taking some kind of reading.

"Crystal! Oh, Crystal..." A sob escaped as Johanna rushed over to embrace her daughter.

The girl clung to her mother as tears gushed from her blue eyes. "Mother..."

Johanna just let the girl cry. She could feel Crystal's tears spilling onto her neck and shoulder. The android moved away, and Johanna closed her eyes, welcoming the hug. She realized that this was the first time since Crystal had been a small child that there had been the need to cling to her mother. Serassan had always been the parent of choice when things went awry in the girl's life. How good it felt now to be needed and possibly even missed by her only child. How close she had come to losing this love-child of mixed species who meant everything to her.

"Mother," Crystal gasped as she finally was able to withdraw and get a grip on herself.

Johanna pulled a tissue from a triangular container that Plipquum held out. She handed it to Crystal to wipe her nose. "There, there, darling. Here, blow your nose."

Crystal blew, then blinked and looked at Johanna. "Mother, I'm so sorry. I didn't mean to go off into space like I did without saying anything to you and Father. I thought... I thought... Thorden..." At the mention of the evil one's name, Crystal began crying again.

"That horrid man," Johanna chided. "I can't believe he kidnapped you."

Crystal sniffed as she fought to control her released emotions. "He didn't exactly kidnap me, Mother. I went willingly... at first. But then he wouldn't let me come home. All I wanted to do was come home to you and Father."

"I know, I know that, dear." Johanna comforted her. "But you're safe now on your father's planet. You're going to be just fine."

Crystal looked around. "Where is Father?"

"He took Granna and your grandfather to our hotel."

Plipquum scrunched up her face at the word.

"That's a sleeping place," Johanna quickly explained. "On Earth that's where travelers stay overnight." Then she asked Plipquum, "Was she molested?"

Crystal interrupted. "He forced himself on me, Mother. It was the most frightening experience I've ever had." Then she added, "But... I'm okay... really."

"Except for the bruises and scratches, the child is in good shape," explained Plipquum. "We checked her over thoroughly. She is a strong being."

"What about... oh, I don't even know his name." Crystal shook her head.

Plipquum nodded. "The Terran?"

Johanna remembered the unconscious blond boy. "Yes, who was he? What part did he play in all of this?"

"He saved my life," Crystal insisted. "If it hadn't been for him..."

"The Terran has not been identified," explained Plipquum.

"Oh... and poor Blue Jay... ohhhh." Crystal buried her face and sobbed some more.

Now Johanna was puzzled. "Blue Jay? What is she talking about?"

Plipquum had obviously not heard of such a creature. "We took the Terran to Advanced Diagnostics," she told Johanna. "It's still too early to report on his condition. My first concern was for this child."

"Thank you, Plipquum." Johanna smiled in gratitude. "I'm so glad you were here today."

"Blue Jay... is dead..." Crystal continued to cry.

Johanna put her arm around the girl to comfort her. She knew Crystal would explain when she again had control of herself. All of this was a mystery to her. What was the Terran boy doing on Thorden's ship, and why was her daughter crying over a dead bird?

Serassan stepped into the examining room. His worried look turned to relief as he saw Crystal sitting on the bed. The minute she saw him, the girl ceased crying and reached her arms out to her father. Serassan embraced her for a long moment, then gently pulled away to face Johanna and Plipquum.

"Thorden is in custody," he said. "Vameera, the light ship's pilot, has taken control of the situation and is drawing up the report. I don't think Thorden is going to get off easy this time. He has a long line of females eager to sign complaints against him."

"When can Crystal go home?" asked Johanna.

"We'd like to keep her another night, just for observation," said Plipquum. "You can both make yourselves comfortable here at the facility. We have accommodations."

"That sounds good." Serassan looked relieved.

"Yes... a hotel." Plipquum's eyes lit up as she smiled at Johanna. "Excuse me, I must go and check on the Earthling."

Serassan squinted at Johanna. "What was that about?" he asked after the healer left the room.

"Father," Crystal interrupted, "you won't leave me, will you?" She glanced anxiously at Johanna. "And Mother? I need you both."

Johanna said, "Don't worry, darling. We'll stay here with you, as long as it takes."

"And what about the arts center?" Crystal asked.

The question startled Johanna. "Why, I hadn't even given it a thought..."

"The arts center will still be there when we return to Karos... as a family," Serassan said.

"That is... if you really want to come home." Johanna smiled at their daughter. "The decision is up to you. You still have the option of being an astronaut."

"Your mother and I have talked about it," said Serassan. "We will respect your decision."

The girl sighed wearily. "I think I've seen enough of space, at least for the time being," Crystal admitted. "I want to go home... to Karos."

Johanna sat down on the foot of the bed and folded her hands. "Now what was all that about a blue jay?" she asked.

Serassan looked puzzled.

"A blue jay is a bird on Earth," Johanna explained.

Crystal's face fell and she stared at the floor. "There was a second Terran boy on the ship," she explained to her parents. "I believe he said his name was Blue Jay Harris. He was a musician." Looking up once again, tears had formed in her blue eyes. "Thorden... killed him." Her lip trembled at the awful memory.

Johanna gasped, not knowing what to say.

Crystal sniffled, then wiped her eyes. "The other one... he didn't say his name... but he was very brave." Her voice was filled with awe and her eyes grew wider. "Mother, he may have been Terran. But he glowed. He actually glowed!"

"What?" Serassan's eyebrows lifted.

"He... he lit up the room," she explained. "His energy was so powerful." She gazed thoughtfully across the room.

"What happened to him?" asked Serassan. "What did he do?"

"You said he saved your life," said Johanna.

"It was when he lit up that Thorden left me alone," Crystal explained. "I think it must have harmed him. And the energy he gave off was so incredible."

"Did they fight?" asked her father.

"I don't remember. But as soon as Vameera showed up with Granna and Grandfather... he... he... just collapsed."

"Oh, dear," breathed Johanna.

"Please... may I see him?" Crystal implored.

"Well, that I don't know," said Serassan. "Plipquum said he is in a coma. He needs special care."

"I must see him," said Crystal. "Please. I need to tell him how brave he was."

Johanna looked at her husband and nodded at him. Silently Serassan left the room to find Plipquum. When she turned back to Crystal, she found the girl staring across the room like before. She wondered what was going through the girl's mind.

"I imagine you'll want to clean up," she suggested. "You know, take a shower."

"Oh yes, of course." Crystal looked around. "Then I'll probably feel like sleeping."

"Have you been given anything to eat?"

"I'm not hungry," Crystal replied.

An android unit entered the room with a hygiene kit. "It is time for your bath, Miss Dobbs," the metallic voice proclaimed.

Serassan returned then. "Plipquum is busy with the Terran patient," he explained. "Crystal, she asks that you wait until he is out of danger."

Crystal's chest heaved in alarm. "Out of danger? Oh no!"

Johanna placed a restraining hand on Crystal's knee. "I'm sure they are doing everything possible for him. Go ahead and get cleaned up. Maybe then you'll be allowed to see him."

It took some convincing on both their parts, but finally Crystal accompanied the robot orderly down the corridor to the shower facility. Johanna and Serassan retreated to the waiting area, where Johanna said to her husband, "I wonder what is so special about that boy."

"Yes, there is definitely something out of the ordinary going on," he agreed.

"Serassan, I saw the boy's face when they brought him in. He reminded me..." She stopped and sighed.

"What is it, my love?"

"Oh, never mind. Let's find out where Crystal is going to stay tonight." She decided it was best not to say anything more about the Terran's remarkable resemblance.

B oth Dorothy and Manley slept during the shuttle's return to the mother ship. When they arrived, the Light Being had already docked and parked his ship in the hangar next to similar shuttles.

"Manley, wake up, we're here." Dorothy nudged her husband in the next chair.

"Wh-what?" He blinked, a little disoriented.

"We're on the *New Jerusalem*," she told him. She glanced at their pilot, who was resting for a minute. His eyes were closed and once again she was astounded at how much he looked like their son Blake.

"Elby, are you all right?" Manley called to him.

"Affirmative," the pilot answered, then slowly raised his eyelids. "If you're ready, I'll escort you on board the mother ship."

"What were you doing, meditating?" asked Dorothy.

"In a way," he said, then rose from his seat. "It is important to conserve as much of my life energy as I can right now."

Puzzled, Dorothy stood up and followed Manley and the Light Being off the shuttle when its door opened and the ramp extended outward. They found themselves in a huge hangar area with spacious portholes. The large, square-shaped view panels looked out into the blackness of space and multitudes of stars.

"Will you look at that?" Manley was in awe.

"Follow this way," prompted the Light Being. He led them through an arched doorway into a long wide corridor that was populated with various entities who were on their way to different destinations, all of whom appeared friendly as they passed.

Dorothy squeezed Manley's hand. "Would you ever have dreamed..." she started to say.

Manley scratched his whiskers. "Actually... I have." He

chuckled as the Light Being led them on.

They eventually arrived at a welcoming parlor where a hefty human woman grinned as they approached. She was large, middle-aged, with reddish-brown hair and a knee-length blue and green frock with ruffles around the collar and sleeves. Her blue eyes twinkled at them. "Welcome!"

The Light Being stopped and presented them to her. "Please see to their needs," he instructed. Turning to Dorothy and Manley, he said, "I have some business to take care of. I will come for you in a short time and then you will see your daughter." Without waiting for a reply, he continued down the corridor.

The red-haired woman reached out her hand. "My name is Rosie. By the looks on your faces, I'd guess this is your first trip to the *New Jerusalem*."

"It... it is..." Dorothy gazed around at the comfortably furnished room with its exquisite sofas, soft lighting and framed paintings.

Rosie laughed good-naturedly. "Come in and have a seat. What are your names?"

"I'm Dorothy Dobbs, and this is my husband Manley."

"Terrans?"

"Y-yes..."

"Don't worry, this won't take very long," promised Rosie as she led them over to a couch. "We are expecting many more of you in the next several hours and days. I just need to get a little information, and then I'll direct you to your quarters." Her eyes took in their appearance. "I'm sure you'll want to freshen up a bit... and when was the last time you had a decent meal?"

"You're... you're not an al..." Manley stopped himself.

Rosie shook with a belly laugh, her hands on her hips. "No, I'm not one of those funny-looking people," she declared. "I'm from Earth, like you! Now... I just need a few facts..."

Within ten minutes Dorothy and Manley were being shown to another level of the ship by a short amphibian-like creature dressed in an olive-green uniform. He spoke to them using telepathy and explained he was showing them to their room. "I'm an Aquadahn," he said in reply to Manley's unspoken question.

When they arrived at their cubicle, the Aquadahn opened the door for them and then bowed before he left. Dorothy and Manley walked into a lighted area with a double bed, a bathroom and kitchenette. It was simply furnished with white walls, white bedding and plain furniture, but it was adequate. Fresh clothing had been laid across the bed, and in the bathroom Dorothy found shampoo and towels. There was a razor for Manley, as well as a comb and brush.

"You shower first," Manley told his wife.

"No," she protested. "You're the ripe one." Playfully she pinched her nostrils.

Manley made a face, then sniffed an underarm. "You're right," he grumbled and headed for the shower.

Twenty minutes later Dorothy came out of the shower with a towel draped over her dark hair. She found Manley sitting and drinking a cup of coffee at the kitchenette dining table. "Where did you get that?" she asked.

"I manifested it," he replied.

"You what?"

"Here, I'll show you." He pointed to a device next to the wall that was about the size of a microwave on Earth. But before he could proceed, a knock on the door interrupted him.

Dorothy didn't know how to open the door. There was no handle. But a moment later the door slid into the side of the wall and there stood the Light Being in fresh clothes, with his hair combed. It took her breath away once again to see him.

"I'm sorry if I'm interrupting," he said to Dorothy, then turned to Manley. "Have you replenished yourselves yet?"

"You mean... had supper?" asked Manley.

"No," said Dorothy, feeling her wet hair.

"I see you have quickly picked up on how to order refreshment," the Light Being said, indicating the device in the wall. "Please... eat something... I will be back in a short while, and then I will take you to see your daughter."

Dorothy sensed an urgency in the Light Being. "Elby, what's wrong?"

The Light Being glanced at her nervously. "Nothing is wrong. I am simply anxious to go to Estron. We must... get there... soon." He faltered a little.

"Why?" asked Manley.

"I apologize," said the Light Being. "I am not yet used to your concept of time. But the fact is, we are running out of time. In all honesty, I do not know how long this body will hold up."

Manley stood up from the table. "Good God, Elby. Come over here and sit down."

The Light Being took a deep breath which seemed to stabilize him. He attempted a smile. "There is someone I must see, and then I will return for you... shortly."

Before they could protest, he had slipped out into the hallway and the door to their quarters slid shut.

"Kelly!" Dorothy's eyes filled with tears as she recognized her six-year-old across the room. Two grayish-white beings were helping the little girl tie her shoes as she sat on the floor.

Immediately the little round mongoloid face looked up and saw her mother. A big grin stretched across her face and she jumped up and ran over to collide with Dorothy's outstretched arms. "Mama!" the little girl cried joyfully.

Manley bent down to rub the little girl's short brown hair. "Hey there, princess, how have you been?"

"Daddy!" Kelly's upturned face beamed at him.

Dorothy turned her attention to the two alien women in the room. They slowly approached, smiles on their faces.

"You have a precious child, Mrs. Dobbs," one spoke using telepathy.

"She is a jewel," the other spoke in Dorothy's mind. "Caring for her has been a pleasure."

"Mama, look what I can do!" Kelly pulled away and sat down and finished tying the one shoe.

Dorothy gasped and looked at her husband. "I don't believe it."

"I can do lots more, too!" insisted the little girl. "Wanna see?"

Manley's mouth dropped open. "She never talked this much before."

"It's a miracle," breathed Dorothy.

The two gray women looked knowingly at one another, then back at the Dobbses.

"Kelly, do you want to go for a ride?" Dorothy asked.

"A ride?" The little girl glanced at her father. "Where?"

"Like the one you took to get here," Manley explained. "Do you remember?"

Kelly slowly shook her head from side to side.

"She has little memory of what transpired before she arrived here," one of the Grays explained. "It was best to delete some of that from her mind."

"We're going on a trip far, far away," explained Manley. He stroked her hair. "Doesn't that sound like fun?"

Kelly raised both hands up into the air and grinned. "Yes! Yes! I wanna go, too!"

"Thank you," Dorothy told the aliens. "How can I ever repay you for taking care of our little girl?"

"Come now." The Light Being, who had been standing behind them all this time, urged them to follow him. "There is nothing you must bring. Everything will be provided for you."

"Goodbye!" Kelly called to the alien women as she allowed her father to pick her up and carry her out into the corridor. "Goodbye, nice ladies!"

Both aliens waved their thin long hands and smiled. Dorothy again sensed the urgency in the Light Being's voice and followed the rest through the ship to the hangar deck. She had a feeling Elby wasn't telling them everything, and her maternal instinct, combined with her sharpened intuitive gift, warned her that Blake was in grave danger.

40

Infatuation

Emrox and Soolàn joined their son and his wife in the lounge at the medical facility a couple of days after their daring rescue of their granddaughter. Johanna was relieved to find the two older Estronians looking more rested. All four sat in couches facing each other near a bay window that overlooked colorful fountains in the City of Domes.

"Johanna, how are you holding up?" Soolàn reached out to touch the Earth woman in a gesture of deep caring.

"I'm doing my best," she replied.

"You're remembering to get your injections?"

Serassan put his arm around Johanna. "I make sure of that, Mother."

"And you, son. Are you eating?"

Johanna couldn't help chuckling. "Mothers... they're the same on every world."

Emrox cleared his throat. "That depends," he said. "We are on Estron, remember."

"And Estron is not the most maternal planet in the galaxy," Serassan commented.

"Which is why we appreciate Soolàn," added Johanna, and smiled affectionately at her alien mother-in-law.

"How is Crystal?" Emrox asked.

"Yes, we heard there was a setback," said Soolàn, looking concerned.

"It's nothing serious," Serassan reassured them.

"She just isn't ready yet to leave the hospital," said Johanna. "Well, what would you expect after all she has been through?"

"Crystal is seeing a therapist," Serassan added. "She had an emotional breakdown her first night in the facility."

"Oh? Poor, poor child," crooned Soolàn.

"Did anything in particular trigger it?" asked Emrox.

Serassan sighed. "She insisted on seeing the young Terran."

"That disturbed her?" asked Soolàn.

"The young man is still in a coma," said Johanna. "Crystal seems to have developed some kind of attachment to him."

"Attachment?" echoed Emrox.

"More of an obsession, I'd say," said Serassan. "I think the girl is infatuated." He leaned closer to his parents. "What can you tell us about what happened on the *Harmony*?"

"We know very little," Soolàn told him. "As you know, Thorden had a force-field around the ship, making it impossible for us to come close at first."

"And he took the life of the dark-colored Terran," Emrox disclosed. "The boy was shot, already dead by the time Vameera led us on board."

"That was the boy Crystal called Blue Jay," Johanna surmised. "What happened to his remains?"

"The *Resilience* was called back into that sector to recover the ship and return the body of the young Terran to his home," said Emrox.

"We waited only long enough for Major Luro's ship to dock with the *Harmony*. We had to get Crystal and her friend to Estron for medical attention," added Soolàn.

"And Thorden? He wasn't with you on the light ship," Serassan recalled.

"He was taken into custody aboard the *Resilience*," explained Soolàn.

"I hear he has been removed to a penal planetoid," added Emrox.

"Yes, I believe that is correct," said Serassan. "And he won't be leaving there anytime soon."

"It's a wonder Captain Vameera didn't incinerate him on the spot," said Soolàn.

"Apparently there has been some past history between the captain and our friend Thorden," Serassan explained to Johanna.

"Let's get back to Crystal," suggested Emrox. "Is there anything we can do to help?"

"You both have done so much already," said Johanna.

"Yes, I think we need to just be patient with her," said Serassan.

"We must pray for the boy's recovery," urged Johanna.

"What do you make of this story about him glowing?" Serassan asked his parents.

"We did not observe that," admitted Emrox, and Soolàn shook her head.

"Crystal insists he saved her life," said Johanna.

"The boy will have the answer," Soolàn said with an encouraging smile. "You are right, Johanna, we must lift our prayers to the Prime Source and bring healing light to this boy."

"Whoever he is," added Serassan.

That night, Johanna stood at the door as she and Plipquum watched Crystal, dressed in a rose-colored robe and thongs, sitting beside the bed of the unconscious Terran boy. Crystal's long golden hair was curled and styled on top of her head. She looked more grown up than Johanna had ever seen her, with the exception of opening night at the Galactic Arts Center on Karos.

"You must come back," the girl was saying softly to the boy in a coma. "I have waited for you a long, long time. Don't leave me now. You came when I needed you most. I knew you would. I can't bear to lose you. Please... please wake up."

Johanna puzzled over her daughter's words. She wanted to ask Crystal what she meant, but the therapist had cautioned her and Serassan not to make an issue out of the infatuation.

Suddenly the boy's eyelids fluttered open a little bit. It was apparently the first sign of consciousness in days. Plipquum had noticed it and rushed to the bedside.

"He's waking up," Crystal cried excitedly. She turned to her mother. "Look, Mother, he's..."

Plipquum placed her long gray fingers against the boy's forehead as he struggled to regain consciousness. Then, after a few seconds, he lapsed back into his deep slumber.

"Is he going to come out of it?" asked Crystal.

"These episodes are not uncommon," Plipquum explained. "He may do this now and then, but it doesn't mean he is regaining full consciousness." She checked the vital sign readings beside the boy's bed. "It appears that his vital signs jumped up a bit. They are once again what they were."

"But there is hope?" Crystal asked.

"He could wake up tomorrow, or he could stay in this coma for months," Plipquum said gently.

Crystal began to whimper and Johanna came over to put her arm around the girl. "Come on, dear, it's time for you to get some sleep," she said.

"Can't I stay with him just a little longer?"

Plipquum spoke gently but firmly. "Go with your mother now. It is important that you, too, get the rest you badly need."

"Dorothy! Dorothy, come quick!" called Manley from the next room.

Dorothy had been reading a children's story to Kelly in the small library next to the recreation room on board the cruiser they had been traveling on for four days now. She abruptly set the book down and eased the sleepy six-year-old off her lap, then went over to see what her husband wanted.

"What's up?" asked Dorothy.

"It's Elby," Manley said. "He kind of... passed out or something."

"Oh, my God." Dorothy leaped toward the table where the Light Being had slumped over and was just now pulling himself up. His eyes were half-closed and he was panting slightly.

"Elby, what happened?" demanded Dorothy. Behind her Kelly stood in the doorway wearing her nightgown.

"I am well," said the Light Being. "For a moment I was... I was on Estron."

"You were?" Manley gathered up the deck of playing cards they had been preoccupied with before the sudden episode had seized his alien friend.

The Light Being sighed. "It is only a matter of hours before our arrival," he told them. "This kind of thing might occur again. If it does, it is most important that you keep me from losing consciousness again. It could... it could mean the difference between life and death." He looked up at the two of them, then added, "I'm talking about the life of your son."

"Blake?" Dorothy grabbed Manley to steady herself.

"Yes," said the Light Being.

"That man looks like Blake," Kelly cried out from the doorway. She pointed a stubby finger at the Light Being.

"That's right, Kelly," said Manley.

"He's *not* Blake," the little girl insisted.

"No, you're right, he's not." Dorothy smiled.

"Where *is* Blake?" asked Kelly.

"We're on our way to see him," Manley explained.

"When?"

"Tomorrow morning, after you wake up and we arrive on Estron, you will get to see your brother," Dorothy explained.

"I miss him," Kelly said sadly.

"We miss him, too." Dorothy suddenly had to fight to keep from bursting into tears.

"Come on, princess, I'll tuck you in." Manley scooped up the little girl and headed out into the corridor toward their sleeping quarters.

Dorothy turned to gaze at the Light Being. Sudden emotion choked her. "What have you done to put my son in danger?" she demanded.

The Light Being folded his hands and slowly shook his head. "I only did what was necessary. I had to save you and your husband. And I had to save my Special One. This was a major risk, but all would have been lost otherwise."

"All *is* lost!" cried Dorothy. "Look at Earth! We can never go home. We don't even have a home anymore. Utter chaos has broken out all over the planet. Millions of people will probably die because they don't know the first thing about survival. They'll probably commit suicide without their computers, their cell phones, their televisions!"

The Light Being stared at her. "I understand why you are upset. But I am not the cause of Earth's suffering."

Dorothy sobbed and sat down at the card table, where she buried her head in her arms. She released all the frustration, fear and anger that had been building up inside her ever since that morning when the sky had blackened and everything had fallen apart.

When she was finally able to control herself, she looked up and found that the Light Being had left the room. Soon Manley returned and without saying a word he put his arms around her and held her close.

"Oh, Manley," Dorothy sniffed. "I'm afraid I blew up at Elby."

He sighed. "Only a few more hours," he reassured her. "The ship will soon reach Estron, where Elby says Blake is."

"My son..." she sobbed anew. "I *need* my son!" She turned swollen red eyes up at her husband. "I have a terrible feeling, Manley. I have a terrible feeling that it's going to be too late for Blake."

Emrox had spent the major part of the morning at Mission Central. Soolàn was relieved when his skimmer arrived and he stepped out. She had been pacing by the window, trying to still her wandering, worrisome thoughts. Crystal had experienced another difficult night at the medical facility, and Johanna and Serassan were exhausted. Soolàn had sensed the disturbance and gone over to relieve the parents of their vigil so they could grab some rest. Thankfully, Crystal had settled down and had slept peacefully after Soolàn's arrival. Soolàn had always been gifted with a calming presence that acted almost like a tranquilizer.

"Emrox, you have news," Soolàn picked up as he entered the room at their lodging facility.

"Yes." He was grim. "I'd love a cup of your Mupani tea right now."

"I will get some." She started away.

Emrox stopped her. "Wait. First I will reveal the news. It is as we feared. The planet Terra has shifted."

Soolàn drew in her breath.

"There was doubt at first as to its authenticity," Emrox continued. "Dark forces had played a part in manipulating the effect of the Photon Belt. But the tables have turned, as Johanna is so fond of saying. They were hit with the real thing and now those ones who would have taken control of the planet are its victims as well."

"Oh my," sighed Soolàn. "And what about the evacuation plans?"

"It began days ago," Emrox disclosed. "Federation ships have been picking up those Terrans who have proved they are worthy and are giving them refuge on certain mother ships. Most have gone to the *New Jerusalem*, which is nearby. It is well equipped to handle the influx of humans."

Soolàn felt the need to sit down, and Emrox did the same. "So... what has Estron's High Council to offer?"

"I negotiated with them on the Terran problem," Emrox replied. "They have always been reluctant to assist Terra because of the failure of the Earth-Star mission nineteen years ago."

"Don't they regret the methods they used?" Soolàn challenged. "Naturally the Terrans reacted with violence. They had been abducted. Ask Johanna what it was like."

Emrox smiled slightly. "Actually, it is because of Johanna and Serassan that the High Council has agreed to permit colonization on Karos."

Soolàn's blue eyes brightened. "That is welcome news!"

"Of course, Estron cannot host Terrans," Emrox added. "But Karos is well-suited for several thousand of them. Estron has finally agreed to build homes and support a nurturing social structure for them."

"This is a miracle!" Soolàn laughed. "Oh, we must go and tell Johanna and Serassan at once."

"I agree," said Emrox. "But we must also be cautious. It may be too much of a shock when Johanna hears about her home planet."

"You are right," added Soolàn.

Emrox stood up and went to the window. "I could use that cup of Mupani tea now."

Soolàn smiled. "I'll fix myself a cup as well. And then we will leave to spread the news."

41

Recognition

"The planet we have landed on has a different oxygen make-up than Earth's," the Light Being informed Dorothy and Manley as they stood waiting to follow him off the cruiser. "Before we go anywhere, we will all need injections."

Kelly held onto her mother's hand and seemed as excited as her parents to see this new alien world that lay just steps away.

"How long are these injections good for?" asked Manley.

"One full day," said the Light Being. "Some are given to last only a few hours, while others may last several days. It all depends on the dosage."

A Pleiadian crew member smiled at the foursome as they approached the cruiser's exit ramp. Gently she administered each of the injections. Since there was not even a sting, only slight pressure against the skin of her upper arm, Kelly giggled when she received her shot.

"We will be flying in a hovercraft to the City of Domes," the Light Being explained as the doors parted and they followed him outside. Before them was an open field with no grass or trees, but some kind of yellow vegetation grew in rows of ochre-colored dirt. Rock formations of various colors reminded Dorothy and Manley of sand dunes back on their world. A slight wind tousled Dorothy's and Kelly's hair.

"We're not even in an air terminal," commented Manley.

"Ordinarily we would have landed in a more populated spot," said the Light Being. "But I felt it would be better to have the cruiser drop us off here where we are less likely to attract attention from the Estronian people." He was quick to explain. "Although they are not hostile toward other species of humanoids, they have grown a little skeptical toward your race."

"Why is that?" Dorothy wanted to know.

"It goes back several years," the Light Being replied.

"Elby, how do you know so much?" asked Manley.

The Light Being was silent a moment, then said, "That is not really important. We must reach Blake."

A flying disk approached them and settled on the edge of the field nearby. Kelly laughed and clapped her hands when she saw it.

"Come, let's board the skimmer," said the Light Being. "It will take us to our destination."

They stepped onto the narrow ramp and entered the circular structure where a being of medium height, dressed in a dark blue tunic, turned to watch them. He had grayish-white skin and a large bulbous head with wide slanted eyes almost the color of his uniform. Dorothy stifled her surprise and held Kelly closer to her as the pilot signaled for them to take seats. Then the being said something in gibberish. The Light Being answered him in the same language and in the next moment the saucer lifted and zipped away.

Crystal's heart was heavy. She sat at the bedside of the teenage Terran boy, watching him and always hoping that again he would stir. She knew her parents were growing impatient with her. She just couldn't convince them of how much she needed to stay and keep her vigil.

For days she had tumbled the thoughts around in her head, savoring all the times He had been in contact with her. She vividly recalled that first night when His light had appeared in her house as a golden sphere. She hadn't realized at the time that it was actually Him, although she had recognized that the ball of light had come from space and was connected with her.

Then, on board the *Harmony*, held captive in her small cabin, she had sensed His presence again. She heard His voice, promising her that He would come... and He had. She would never forget how He had lit up the bridge on Thorden's ship, and how He had risked His life to save hers.

No one understood. The Estronian therapist least of all. Yet Crystal knew females on Estron were not sympathetic toward love-sick teenage girls. The therapist had listened, but Crystal could tell the subject of love was something the alien woman found uncomfortable discussing.

"When one has such feelings, one must fight to overcome them," had been the therapist's advice to Crystal. "Of course, I do realize you are half Terran, and it's probably only natural that you would be attracted to another... Terran."

But Crystal had argued that the boy's origins had nothing to do with her feelings for him. It was *Him*.

"*Who* are you referring to?" the Estronian therapist had demanded.

"My... my dream man," Crystal had finally admitted. "I've met him in my dreams. I know him from... before."

"Do not speak to anyone of this," the therapist had cautioned. "We must concentrate on getting you well. Are you sure you did not receive a blow to your head during your molestation?"

Anger filled Crystal the more she thought about her so-called therapy and the frustration she felt. She feared that if she said anything to her parents, they would find it as ridiculous as the professionals. She definitely did not want to create any more conflict in her life. Yet she couldn't put the boy out of her mind. It was just too strong a feeling.

Soolàn and Emrox had arrived at the medical facility several minutes ago and had talked Johanna and Serassan into going to the lounge with them.

"Probably they are discussing their whacko granddaughter," Crystal murmured to the unconscious patient. "They're trying to decide what to do about me... and I'll just die if they make me leave here. I've got to stay, at least until you wake up."

Crystal sat in silence a few more minutes, thinking, and then she began to hum. It was the tune of the song she had sung on opening night at the Galactic Arts Center on Karos. No one was around to hear, so she began to sing clearly and sweetly the beautiful words to *Rainbow Love*.

About halfway through the song, the boy in the bed began to make a noise from his throat and his head moved from side to side. Crystal's heart began to beat faster. Convinced that the music had stimulated some kind of response in him, she continued, after a short pause, singing to him softly and fervently.

A commotion in the corridor just outside the room caused Crystal to look toward the doorway. She halted her song abruptly, stunned to find a strange human man and woman peering in at her. They appeared to be Terrans, and with them was a small child, only there was something unique about the little girl's face.

"Don't stop singing," the man called to her as he stepped into the room. "Your singing is beautiful." He had spoken in her mother's tongue.

Suddenly the woman with him lunged toward the bed and cried out, "Blake! Manley, it's Blake!" The woman burst into tears.

Crystal leaped up and watched as the man and their little girl crowded the bedside. "Who... who are you people?" she asked in English. She backed away as they leaned over the boy. The woman sobbed hysterically.

Suddenly Plipquum rushed into the room. "What has happened?" she cried out.

The man and woman looked up in surprise. It was obvious to Crystal that they did not understand the Estronian language.

"What do you want?" Crystal asked them in English.

"This is our son," the man explained. The expression on his face was grim. "His name is Blake."

Crystal gasped. "Blake?"

"Yes. Tell us what is wrong with him."

Crystal turned to Plipquum and immediately translated.

"I must go and find Johanna and Serassan," Plipquum replied. "Do you know where they went?"

Crystal quickly explained about her grandparents' arrival. "I believe you'll find them in the lounge," she added. Turning her attention back to the bed scene, she reached a hand out and touched the woman's quaking shoulders. "The one you call Blake has been in a coma for many days. But I think he is going to come out of it... soon, I hope."

"What is *your* name, young lady?" asked the man, whose eyes were kind and reminded Crystal of her mother.

"I'm... Crystal," she said. "B-but... I'm confused. Aren't you from... Terra?"

"Yes." The man smiled. "And you don't resemble a person native to this planet. Where do you call home?"

"I am half Estronian," she revealed. "B-but... how did you get here from... *who* brought you here?"

"I did." The booming male voice filled the room as the Light

Being stood in the doorway.

When Crystal's gaze fell on the slightly older version of the boy lying on the bed, she drew back in alarm. Then she glanced from the unconscious form lying there to the towering figure whose eyes seemed to peer into her very soul. She went completely speechless.

"Elby, come in," called the man by the bed. "Blake is in here."

As he stepped inside the room, the Light Being's gaze continued to settle on Crystal, whose heart pounded. Her head swam. She truly believed she was caught in some wild and confusing dream. "Who... who are... *you*?" she finally managed to utter.

While the others were fussing over the patient in the bed, the man in the doorway said softly, "You know who I am, Crystal."

Again her throat felt so dry, she could barely speak. "I... I... I don't... under...st-stand."

"We only have a few minutes at the most," the stranger told her in an urgent voice. "He will be waking up soon." He indicated Blake's prostrate form.

Crystal walked over to the bed, where young Blake was beginning to stir in his sleep state. It sounded like he was moaning.

"Manley, he's coming around," the boy's mother cried.

"I hope you're right."

"Crystal..."

She turned to the man in the doorway.

"Give me these few moments," he pleaded. "Let's go out in the hall where we can talk."

Why did his voice suddenly appear so strained? There was a desperate quality to the way he looked at her that compelled her to leave Blake and his family and follow this stranger out of the room. As soon as she caught up with him, the Light Being reached out his hand and led Crystal down the hall. His steps faltered a bit as they ducked into a small storage room.

"Please... close the door," he instructed her.

Suddenly Crystal grew afraid. What did he want? "Really, I don't think this is such a good idea..."

"Close... the... door..." His breathing was unsteady. "Please..."

Without a word Crystal did as he asked, then stared at him. "All right," she said. "I'm waiting. What have you got to say?" Her heart continued to pound, but now from fear. "I heard him call you a name... Elby was it?"

"He calls me that... L.B.," the man struggled to say, "it stands for Light... Being..."

"You're a Light Being?" asked Crystal.

The man nodded, bracing himself against the wall.

"But who are you, and why do you look like... like Bl-Blake?"

"Your... cousin," the Light Being blurted out.

"You're my... *cousin*?" she croaked.

"No." He paused, then told her, "Blake... Blake Dobbs is your cousin. Blake... *Dobbs!*"

Crystal shuddered. "What are you saying?" She turned to the door to go out, but he put a restraining hand on her arm. She spun around. "I'll ask only one more time. *Who are you*?" Tears welled up in Crystal's eyes.

"I look like... Blake," he said. "But I am... who I am... known to you from the beginning. Crystal, I've traveled light-years over time and space to find you. We were... together... in the... beginning."

"The beginning? What are you talking about?" She started to sob. "The beginning of what? Tell me!"

He struggled to control his failing body. "The beginning of time, Crystal. You and I... we are... *twin souls*." He reached for her. "Here, let me show you," he said and drew her close to him.

In the flash of his revelation, Crystal was struck with a vision in her mind's eye. She saw the two of them as one. He was the missing part of her that made the two of them complete. Suddenly, her heart glowed with such ecstasy, she could hardly breathe. In her recognition, it was as if everything she had ever known, in this life and in the others, was surging through her brain. She clung to him as if holding on for dear life itself. The ride they were on lasted only a few seconds, yet the impact of its glory overwhelmed them both. Never had she felt anything like it. And there were no words to tell him how happy she was in that enchanted fraction of a moment that she knew would and already had altered her from that moment on.

Suddenly a blissful peace settled over Crystal. She was floating, oblivious to all, and time no longer had any meaning. Her only care was the hope that this could last forever. And then, quite suddenly, she was back in her body, sprawled on the floor of the storage room, and the Light Being lay beside her, out cold.

"Crystal?" She heard a feminine voice calling her name. "Crystal, are you in there?" It was her mother.

Finally able to rouse herself, Crystal propped herself up and called out, "Mother? I'm in here."

The door opened and Crystal saw Johanna's alarmed face standing over her. "What are you doing... oh my God!"

The next thing she knew, Serassan and Emrox had arrived and were picking her up off the floor. She leaned against her father's strong arm and heard Emrox call out for assistance. "There's an injured young man in here," her grandfather shouted.

Crystal felt groggy as her parents helped her to her room. She was aware of a commotion and thought she heard Plipquum tell someone, "I'm afraid it's too late for that one."

B lake awoke and thought he heard his little sister chattering. "Hey, Kelly Belly," he murmured, "what are you doing in my room?" Everything was blurry, but he made out three heads leaning close to him.

"Blake?" It was his mother's voice.

"Mom?" He blinked several times in order to clear his vision. "Dad? Where's Dad?"

"I'm here, son," said Manley.

"Oh Blake, thank God." Dorothy squeezed his hand. "How are you feeling?"

"Kind of dull," he said, but his vision was starting to clear up.

"We thought we'd lost you," said Manley. His voice was broken with emotion.

"Wow, Dad, I must have had some kind of nightmare. We were..." Suddenly his gaze focused on the tall grayish-white being at the foot of his bed, dressed in a white one-piece uniform. His eyes widened in surprise.

"Space people!" Kelly cried out in delight. "Blake, look!" She laughed. "Now we can play."

Dorothy spoke softly to Manley, who then took hold of Kelly's hand and headed for the door. "I'll be back in a minute," he promised his son.

"Okay, Dad." Blake tried to prop himself up. The being at the foot of his bed tried to stop him. She mumbled something in gibberish.

"That is Plipquum," Dorothy told Blake. She smiled. "She's your doctor. I think she wants you just to take it easy. You've been in a coma for a week now."

"A coma?" Blake settled back down. "What?" His lips felt suddenly dry. "Is there some water?"

Dorothy handed her son a small cask of a drink. He sipped at it urgently, only able to suck up a small amount at a time. It tasted just like sweet water from a natural spring, and without that nasty chlorine aftertaste he was used to on Earth.

His father returned to the room. "Do you remember anything?" Manley ventured.

Blake gazed around at the small room with its stark white walls and instrument panels. It resembled some kind of ICU. "I was on a ship," he related. "I was with my friend Blue Jay." Suddenly his expression darkened. His chest heaved a sob as he recalled the violent scene on board the *Harmony* just before the alien pilot struck him.

A woman with dark hair gathered in a ponytail entered the room. Her gentle brown eyes — not unlike his father's — were bright and doe-like as she cautiously approached them. "How is he doing?" she asked.

Dorothy looked up and smiled, and Manley extended his hand and drew the smaller woman up against him. "Blake," he said, "there is someone I'd like you to meet. This is..."

"Aunt Jo," Blake blurted out. "Yes, I know."

"You do?" Johanna's eyes widened in surprise and then her smile lit up her pretty face, creasing the slight wrinkles at her gently graying temples.

"I saw your picture," Blake explained, recalling the holographic photo Kapri had shown him on board the mother ship. That seemed like such a long time ago.

Manley laughed, still holding his sister close to him. "Your aunt had no idea she had a nephew."

"Or a niece," added Johanna with a glance out in the hallway. "Soolàn is minding her. What a delightful little girl, Manley." She peered lovingly at Blake. "And you, Blake, are a remarkably brave young man."

"Are we on Karos?" asked Blake.

"No, this is the planet Estron," Dorothy told him.

"But I thought I was on my way to Karos, to meet Aunt Jo and her alien husband and... and... my c-cousin..." He lurched forward, causing Plipquum to spring to his side in alarm. "My cousin, Crystal! Is she all right?"

"She is right here," a male voice called out. A tall man with dark wavy hair and deep blue eyes stood in the doorway. A second later the blond-headed Crystal emerged. She hesitated a moment as her equally blue eyes rested on Blake. Then she smiled at him and stepped forward.

"Hello, Blake," she said.

"You're safe!" he exclaimed with relief.

"Thanks to you," Crystal returned.

"We've been waiting for you to wake up," the man in the doorway said. He stepped into the now crowded room. "I am Serassan."

"My uncle," affirmed Blake. "Yes, I know. I was traveling on the *Resilience* to meet you. I found out that you were living on Karos and that I had a cousin."

"You knew we were cousins?" Crystal asked in surprise.

"Well, yes," said Blake. "I figured it out when I saw you on the *Harmony*."

"I didn't know," she said sadly, "and I'm so very sorry about your friend."

Blake looked around at all the faces. "Hey, where is Blue Jay?"

At once Crystal grew alarmed. "You mean, you don't remember?"

"Remember what?"

"Thorden... he..." Crystal sobbed suddenly and turned around to bury her face in her father's shoulder.

Blake felt a rush of horror and met his mother's concerned face. "Blue Jay's... dead?"

"I'm sorry, Blake," Johanna told him softly. A tear formed in her right eye. "Crystal told us what happened. Apparently your friend intercepted laser fire that Thorden intended for Crystal."

"No!" Blake shouted in anger, then fell back against his pillow and bawled like a baby. The anguish he felt at this horrible injustice seized him and he couldn't help but release the tears that burned his eyelids and dry cheeks.

Dorothy cradled his head as the others silently turned away to exchange sympathetic looks. Blake finally exhausted his first wave of grief to sit up in bed and collect his wits.

"Blake, I am to blame," Crystal said.

"No, you're not," he denied. "Don't you ever say that." He sniffed. "As for Blue Jay..." He sighed. "Blue Jay was a terrific friend. I'm going to miss him."

After a moment of silence, Blake looked up and said, "I want to know all that happened after I passed out on the ship."

Crystal began to fill them all in.

Blake interrupted as she finished. "Wait a minute," he said. "I don't remember everything. But I do know one thing. There was someone else there."

Dorothy and Manley looked at each other and then at Johanna and Serassan, who were equally puzzled by Blake's statement. "What do you mean?" asked Dorothy.

"I mean, there was someone who came onto the ship and kind of... took over for me." He blinked as he gazed from one to the other, wondering how he was going to explain this. "He was... a friend of mine... from space."

Crystal's face lit up. "It was Him."

"I don't understand," said Manley. "Just who are you talking about, son?"

"Dad, you won't believe this," said Blake, "but I have this E.T. friend that I met the last night in our house in DeKalb. He's the one who rescued me and Kelly that night. I mean... that *morning*... when it got dark and I got knocked out and the choppers started coming."

"He took you to the mother ship," Dorothy blurted out. "Yes, he came to me and told me you were safe."

"Who?" asked Johanna.

"Elby?" Manley scratched his chin.

"Yes, his name was L.B.," Blake replied. "My E.T. friend was a Light Being. I called him L.B. for short. He... he had to obtain a physical body in a hurry so that he could return to Earth and rescue you and Mom. So I... so I let him clone me."

"Of course, it all makes sense now," said Serassan. "It is all making sense." His eyes focused on his daughter, who continued to stare at Blake in wonder.

"Where is he now?" Blake wanted to know. "I mean, he obviously succeeded at rescuing you. Did he bring you here to this planet?"

"Yes," Dorothy answered. "He did rescue us. It was quite something." She then went on to tell the others how the Light Being had flown his shuttlecraft into the concentration camp just as Ernestine Glenn had issued execution orders, and how the paralyzing beam had struck the misguided feminist leader and then disabled the weapons and melted the gates so all the women could be freed.

"And then he took us to the mother ship," Manley added.

"Where we picked up Kelly," Dorothy put in.

"And then he escorted us to Estron," Manley finished. "He was able to arrange for a cruiser to take us here on short notice."

"So, where is L.B. now?" Blake grinned. "I want to thank him."

Crystal leaned forward and spoke softly to Blake. "He left when you returned."

"Left? Left where?" Blake thought it was all a joke until he saw their somber faces.

"Elby's body gave out," Manley said.

"What?"

"He's... dead," Dorothy pronounced.

"The life force that was keeping him alive came from his connection to you," Serassan explained. "You see, the cloning was performed on the *New Jerusalem* in a hurry so that he could complete his mission. It meant problems for him. Anytime a clone is grown in a short period of time, you can expect serious complications."

Crystal broke down and covered her face in embarrassment. Johanna reached out and drew the girl's head to her breast.

"Because he was drawing the life force from you, Blake, there was danger that you could die. You were at great risk."

"While I was on Thorden's ship, he must have projected himself out of his body... into mine," Blake guessed.

"It took enormous willpower and energy for him to do such a thing," commented Serassan. "He could have expired from that one effort alone."

"But he managed to draw on my energy and finish his task

on Earth," Blake said.

"Putting you at great risk!" cried Johanna.

Blake felt a heaviness in his heart because his friend was gone. "I know L.B. would never have let me die to save himself."

"I wonder where we all would be right now if he hadn't helped us," Dorothy sniffed.

Crystal's crying spell eased and she wiped her eyes.

"Why did he come to help us, anyway?" asked Manley.

"Dad, I think there's one person who can answer that," said Blake. He reached over and touched his cousin's arm. "Crystal?"

The girl looked up at him, her face stained with fresh tears. She brushed the back of her hand against her nose. "What?" she mumbled.

"I know why L.B. contacted me. It was so that he could find *you.*"

The girl blinked, but said nothing.

"Is this true, Crystal?" asked Serassan.

Slowly Crystal nodded her head, then swallowed. "He is the reason I wanted to forsake my singing career and go into space," she explained. "I felt him near me... on several occasions. I needed to find him again."

"Wait, I don't get it," said Manley.

"I do." Johanna smiled and looked lovingly at Serassan.

"The Light Being had discovered his Special One," Serassan surmised. "Am I right, Crystal?"

"Yes," the girl whispered. "My... twin soul."

"And somehow he must have made the connection with our family," Dorothy commented. "Somehow he knew."

Blake chuckled. "He wanted me to teach him how to approach a girl."

"You mean he's a Light Being and he didn't know?" taunted Manley.

"Dad, he didn't have a body, remember!"

Suddenly Crystal burst out laughing. Blake laughed, and then everyone started laughing. But a moment later Crystal's face collapsed again and she turned and ran out of the room.

"Crystal!" Johanna started after her daughter.

Serassan reached out and stopped her. "No, let her go," he advised. "She is overwhelmed."

"This has been an overwhelming experience for us all," said Dorothy.

"Mom," said Blake, propping himself up higher on the bed. "Tell me what happened to you and Dad."

"You mean..."

"After the Photon Belt thingee."

Manley looked around the room. "Better grab some chairs," he said to Johanna and Serassan. "This is going to take a while."

Plipquum, satisfied at last that Blake was holding his own, smiled and signaled her departure so that the family group could carry on without her.

Half an hour later everyone had been filled in on Dorothy's tale of the concentration camp and Manley's escape from the helicopters, ending with the fantastic arrival of L.B.'s shuttle.

"What is happening to Earth now?" asked Blake.

Johanna sighed. "Emrox says Earth has shifted."

"Yes, the Federation is evacuating some of the inhabitants," said Serassan. "They are taking them to the mother ships for re-orientation."

"Can we... can we ever go home?" Blake wanted to know.

Dorothy patted his hand. "It's not the same place you remember, Blake."

"That's for sure," said Manley.

Blake was silent a moment, then said, "So where will we go?"

Manley and Dorothy exchanged looks across the bed.

"I mean, obviously Colorado is out of the question," added Blake.

Johanna smiled and said, "You can make your home on Karos... with us."

Serassan clasped Johanna's hand and smiled. "The High Council on Estron has agreed to assist any Terran refugees who wish to settle on Karos or any of the other outlying planets," he explained. "We have Emrox to thank for his diplomatic gesture in convincing the Council."

"Karos?" Dorothy blinked. "What's it like?"

Manley grinned. "It doesn't matter. It's a new beginning for us all."

"Blake will be an asset to the new Galactic Performing Arts Center," said Johanna.

"More will be arriving in the weeks ahead," Serassan explained. "But everyone will be welcome on Karos."

Blake suddenly felt sleepy, exhausted from all the talk and emotion. Dorothy suggested they let him get some rest and soon everyone shuffled out of the room. An android glided in to check Blake's vital signs and see to his comfort. It had been one crazy day, that's for sure, and Blake easily slipped off to sleep as strains of Crystal's *Rainbow Love* drifted through his brain.

42

Reunion

A month had passed. Crystal stood on the hill above the Terran colony and gazed at the River of Determination as it flowed down the hillside and meandered through a woods toward the little village of stone dwellings. Several new homes were constructed and many more were in the process of being raised as ships continued to bring in humans who had been evacuated from Terra.

The summer wind blew a strand of blond hair across her face and she brushed it aside, thinking how wonderful it was to have more people settling on Karos, including so many younger people. She and Blake had become immediate friends and he was developing his music skills, much to everyone's enjoyment. Her little cousin, Kelly, was a happy child, though simple, and she blended in as if she had always belonged on a planet where people accepted others just as they are.

Crystal recalled how her mother had cried out with delight when a woman showed up on their doorstep a few days ago. The moment the two had set eyes on each other, they had hugged each other and cried. The other woman had been a little younger than her mother and had spoken in a foreign tongue. But then she had managed to tell Johanna in broken English, "I learn to speak like you... *ponnee-maiyu*?"

"Radya Bjelkova!" Johanna had shouted, and the two fell into each other's arms again, laughing.

"I leave *Meer*," the woman cried. "No goo-d. No goo-d no more."

Crystal had then been introduced to Radinka, the ballerina from Russia, who had known her mother nineteen years before, when they had flown across the galaxy after both being abducted.

"Only Radya returned to Earth," Johanna explained to her astonished daughter as the three of them sat drinking tea a little later in the stone cottage.

"I shoo-d have stayed," Radya said, shaking her head.

"Well, you will stay now, won't you?" asked Johanna. "You have heard of our new performing arts center, no doubt."

"*Da*! I hear of gr-r-reat perfor-r-r-mances," Radya declared, rolling her R's. "But... I too old now to dance."

"Nonsense!" Johanna protested. "Radya, you can start the new ballet on Karos."

"I teach? Perhaps." The Russian woman grinned. "I teach... the young ones."

Crystal sat down on the ground and began pulling grass up as her thoughts returned once again to the present and her personal loneliness. Even though there were lots of new friends now, and much more excitement in her life, she missed Him. The Light Being's encounter had left a deep impression on her, and a great sadness tormented her.

"I can't believe you're gone," she moaned, staring at the ground. "You came all that way to find me, only to... disappear." Tears began to form once again as she buried her face in her hands. "I can't bear it... I just can't bear it," she sobbed.

"I'm not gone," a voice spoke behind her.

Crystal gasped in surprise and looked behind her. A golden sphere of light hung in the air just over her left shoulder. But she had distinctly heard His voice.

"I'm right here, Crystal," He said. "I'm a Light Being. I cannot die."

She didn't know what to say, she was so startled.

"There is one thing you must understand," He spoke. "And that is that there is nothing such as death."

"But..." She found her voice. "But what about... Blue Jay? Didn't he... die?"

"The one who was Blake's friend is very much alive," He said to her. "Only you can no longer see him, hear him or touch him. He is grateful that he was able to prevent you from harm."

"But... but..." Crystal stared right into the golden light particles that swirled and sparkled within the globe suspended in the air. "I want to be *with* you," she pleaded. A tear tumbled down her left cheek. "Maybe... maybe if I had been the one to d..."

"No, Crystal." His voice was firm. "You were meant to go on as you started. Your life is important to many. How do you think your parents would have felt if they had lost you?"

Crystal knew how devastated Johanna and Serassan would have been had she been the one to lose her life on board the *Harmony*.

"There are many things that you will do in the years ahead," the Light Being spoke through the glowing orb.

"And... what about you?" she asked.

"I will be nearby," He promised.

"Will I be able to... see you again? I mean, in a body?"

He didn't answer right away. Then the voice said gently, "You are a part of me. You always have been and you always will be. For eons I have drifted... unwilling to incarnate... and now I must remain a Light Being. But I will be close to you from now on, Crystal. All you need to do is think of me and you will feel the love glowing within your heart."

In that very instant He touched her soul, and Crystal was bathed in a caressing light energy that tingled through her entire being. The most beautiful wave of ecstasy came over her.

"Yes," she breathed as a smile spread across her face. "Oh, yes..." It felt like when you sit beside a warm flame on a winter's night, or when someone softly runs their fingers through your hair just as you are drifting off to sleep. It was pure bliss.

"I am with you." The light energy began to fade. "Don't... forget..."

Crystal watched as the sphere withdrew and slowly floated upward. She gazed up at the blue summer sky with its wispy white clouds as the golden ball of light shriveled to the size of a marble, and then a pinpoint, and then she could see it no more.

"I... won't. I won't... forget," she breathed.

Below her, she heard the laughter of children. A smile remained on her face as she watched four Terran children approaching. In a field of wildflowers beside the river, the youngsters, newly arrived on Karos, scampered among the grasses and lifted their arms to embrace the wind and the beauty of a new world.

The Author

Ann Carol Ulrich was born in Madison, Wisconsin in 1952, the daughter of Marvin and Marion Schumacher. She grew up in Monona with three brothers and two sisters, and in 1975 graduated from Michigan State University with a degree in English with a creative writing emphasis.

In the late '70s she, her husband and toddler son moved to Aspen, Colorado. Now the mother of three grown sons, she resides near Paonia, Colorado, with her second husband, Ethan Miller, and their animals, including a dog, Ranger, an elderly cat named Mu, three mules and a flock of chickens. She also works for the bi-weekly environmental newspaper, *High Country News*.

Space interested her since childhood. Later in life she became involved with UFO Contact Center International and became an associate director of that organization, to help contactees and to educate others about the presence of extraterrestrials and the vessels in which they fly. She began publishing a monthly UFO/metaphysical newsletter, *The Star Beacon*, in 1987.

In 1988 her first novel in the space series, *Intimate Abduction*, was published, followed in 1994 by its sequel, *Return To Terra*. *The Light Being* completes the space trilogy. She enjoys playing piano, dabbling in art, and helping others publish their books.